The Mystery

UNIVERSITY PRESS OF FLORIDA

Florida A&M University, Tallahassee
Florida Atlantic University, Boca Raton
Florida Gulf Coast University, Ft. Myers
Florida International University, Miami
Florida State University, Tallahassee
New College of Florida, Sarasota
University of Central Florida, Orlando
University of Florida, Gainesville
University of North Florida, Jacksonville
University of South Florida, Tampa
University of West Florida, Pensacola

The Mystery

H.D.,
edited by
Jane Augustine

University Press of Florida
Gainesville / Tallahassee / Tampa / Boca Raton
Pensacola / Orlando / Miami / Jacksonville / Ft. Myers / Sarasota

Copyright 2009 for the note on the edition, note on the dedication, acknowledgments, list of abbreviations, introduction, editor's notes, and works cited by Jane Augustine.
Printed in the United States of America on acid-free paper. All rights reserved

First cloth printing, 2009
First paperback printing, 2010

Library of Congress Cataloging-in-Publication Data
H. D. (Hilda Doolittle), 1886–1961.
The mystery/H.D.; edited by Jane Augustine.
p. cm.
Includes bibliographical references and index.
ISBN 978-0-8130-3404-1 (acid-free paper); ISBN 978-0-8130-3552-9 (pbk.)
1. Moravians—Fiction. 2. Spiritual life—Fiction. I. Augustine, Jane. II. Title.
PS3507.O726M97 2009
813.'529—dc22   2009020365

The primary text of *The Mystery* by H.D.(Hilda Doolittle) from previously unpublished material, copyright 2009 by the Schaffner Family Foundation and used by permission of New Directions Publishing Corporation, agents. Reprinted by permission of New Directions Publishing Corporation.

Excerpts in this edition from previously unpublished material by H.D. housed in the H.D. Papers courtesy of the Yale Collection of American Literature, Beinecke Rare Book and Manuscript Library: "Majic Ring" (excerpts). Copyright 2009 by the Schaffner Family Foundation, used by permission of New Directions Publishing Corporation. Reprinted by permission of New Directions Publishing Corporation.

Excerpts from "H.D. by *Delia Alton*" ["Notes on Recent Writing"] by H.D. (Hilda Doolittle), copyright 1987 by Perdita Schaffner, used by permission of New Directions Publishing Corporation. Reprinted by permission of New Directions Publishing Corporation.

Chapters 3 and 14 through 19 of *The Mystery* appeared in *Images of H.D./from "The Mystery,"* a memoir by Eric W. White incorporating letters from H.D. beginning in 1932. Published by Enitharmon Press, London, in 1976 in an edition of 350 copies, with an additional 50 copies numbered and signed by Eric W. White. Copyright 1975 by Norman Holmes Pearson.

The University Press of Florida is the scholarly publishing agency for the State University System of Florida, comprising Florida A&M University, Florida Atlantic University, Florida Gulf Coast University, Florida International University, Florida State University, New College of Florida, University of Central Florida, University of Florida, University of North Florida, University of South Florida, and University of West Florida.

University Press of Florida
15 Northwest 15th Street
Gainesville, FL 32611–2079
http://www.upf.com

This Revelation

of

The Mystery

through fact and fantasy

is inscribed

to

Rachel.

Contents

A Note on the Edition ix
A Note on H.D.'s Dedication "to Rachel" xiii
Acknowledgments xv
List of Abbreviations xix
Introduction xxiii

The Mystery by H.D.

I	1
II	4
III	8
IV	11
V	16
VI	21
VII	25
VIII	28

Part II

IX	37
X	43
XI	47
XII	51
XIII	56
XIV	62
XV	66
XVI	70
XVII	74
XVIII	79
XIX	83

Illustrations: Eighteenth Century Origins of *The Mystery* 87

Editor's Notes
[Part I]

I	101
II	107
III	114
IV	120
V	125
VI	129
VII	132
VIII	135

Part II

IX	148
X	155
XI	159
XII	163
XIII	167
XIV	177
XV	188
XVI	195
XVII	198
XVIII	207
XIX	210

Works Cited and Consulted 219
Index 231

A Note on the Edition

The text of *The Mystery* presented here is taken from a photocopy of the third and last typescript. It was proofread by H.D., as is shown by the corrections in her handwriting, although the errors are few. This typescript is in the H.D. Papers in the Yale Collection of American Literature at the Beinecke Rare Book and Manuscript Library in New Haven, Connecticut, where it was conveyed after H.D.'s death in 1961 by Norman Holmes Pearson, professor of English at Yale, and H.D.'s literary executor until his death in 1978. Correspondence between H.D. and Pearson, also among the H.D. Papers, verifies that she sent him sections of the manuscript in installments. Letters from him written in 1951 on January 15, May 4, June 13, June 23, August 16, and August 29 acknowledge receipt of the pages.

The first two typescripts are also at the Beinecke, as are the four original handwritten notebooks that H.D. gave to her typist for transcription. The typing was done by Ethel Christian of the Strand in London. The first typescript was typed with blue ribbon and was bound into a notebook about 8½" by 11". The manuscript notebooks are about 7" by 8½" with dark blue covers and black spines. The title page of the first, with chapters one through eight, reads:

Lugano
June 12 '48
The Mystery
by
Delia Alton

"Delia Alton" is her name for herself in her authorial manifestation as a psychically "gifted" medium, a self-conception that arose from her involvement in spiritualist séances beginning in November 1941. This sense of "gifted" identity developed during her writing of *The Gift* (1942–44), which she attributes to her Moravian church background, a sense that continues with *The Mystery*. "Delia Alton" became the signature for works she believed had come to her because of her "gift," *The Sword Went Out to Sea* (1946–47), its forerunner in psychic experience, *Majic Ring* (1943–44), and "H.D. by *Delia Alton*" (1949–50), her "notes on recent writing" composed and sent to Pearson at the same time as she began to write *The Mystery*.

The second notebook, containing chapters nine through eleven, has a title page reading: "June 12, 1951, Lugano—comte de Saint-Germain." The third notebook's cover reads: "II The Mystery" [Part II]. The fourth notebook's title page reads: "Chapters 1–8 Lugano June 12, 1949," a dating discrepant with notebook #1, and "Chapters 9–19 Lugano, Switzerland, June 12, 1951."

The title page of the third typescript on the upper left side reads:

H.D. Aldington
Villa Verena
Küsnacht
bei Zürich

and slightly lower on the right, after a break indicated by asterisks:

***

THE
MYSTERY

by
DELIA
ALTON

Here "Delia Alton" is firmly struck out by a single stroke and next to it in large handwritten letters *H D* with no periods, unmistakably in the poet's handwriting. My introduction discusses the reasons for her final abandonment of this pseudonym.

Before H.D. sent out the handwritten first version to be typed, she did not heavily revise it. Only a few passages are crossed out and rewritten. Some of these revisions are illuminating and help confirm my reading of the passage involved. In the re-setting of her typescript, no changes in wording have been made. Her idiosyncratic use of commas and British spellings, for example, *saviour* for *savior*, have been retained, except for the anglicized version, Caliostro, of the name Cagliostro. The Italian form has been restored. The American em dash has been substituted for the British form of the dash, space-hyphen-space, consistently typed in the original. In this decision I differ from Cynthia Hogue and Julie Vandivere in their excellent edition of *The Sword Went Out to Sea* (University Press of Florida, 2007), in which they retain the British dash (*S*, x). I felt that here the dashes do not reflect H.D.'s poetics but simply the standards of the British professional typist; em dashes also are easier to read.

No word in the typescript was so illegible that I had to guess at it. The only editing done, therefore, was the correction of a few spelling errors. In chapter 14, the word "vénitienne" was spelled "Venètienne." The most troublesome misspelling, because most frequent, was the name of Casanova de Seingalt, which H.D. continually wrote as "Seignalt." The Faust scholar Eliza M. Butler, with whom H.D. became friendly after reading her novel *Silver Wings* and her study *The Fortunes of Faust* (both 1952) and to whom she sent *The Mystery* because of its Faust references, pointed out this misspelling to H.D. in a letter dated 4.XI.52, but H.D. did not go back and correct. It should be noted that she created a section title page designating part 2 before chapter 9 but did not make a similar section title page for part 1.

Also at the Beinecke are H.D.'s "Zinzendorf Notes" on which the novel is partly based. She wrote these by hand in a slender blue notebook, rather like the old-fashioned examination "blue book," about 8½" by 7" in size with ruled paper inside. Its title page reads: "Lausanne/ winter 1951/ Templars/ Crusaders/ Castles and Zinzendorf notes—(Templar masonry—notes for *Mystery*—Part II—)." A few other notes on smaller unbound sheets are also filed with the "Zinzendorf Notes." The late Louis Silverstein enriched my research by showing me the file of original eighteenth-century letters handwritten by Moravians and given to H.D. by her life companion, the novelist Bryher (Annie Winifred Ellerman) in the early 1940s, including the one by Count Zinzendorf alluded to in chapter 8.

A Note on H.D.'s Dedication "to Rachel"

Just as H.D. was finishing *The Mystery* in 1951, she wrote Norman Holmes Pearson on November 20 to ask for his help in finding a publisher for a friend of hers, Rachel Farrand Taylor, who, H.D. said, had "a stupendous work on the French Renaissance, about 1,000,000 words I believe. (Holy smoke!) . . . I did have to laugh and how I understand her. 'There but for the grace of God go I.'" H.D. had earlier told Pearson, in her letter of June 17, 1951, that she would make her "dear Prague story" into a "proper-sized old-time Gone With the Wind production," so perhaps she dedicated *The Mystery* to Rachel Taylor out of gratitude for having brought her own book to completion in only 140 manuscript pages.

When Perdita Schaffner was asked if she knew anything about this dedication "to Rachel," she said, "Biblical?" Since *The Mystery* invites a medieval allegorical reading, and the Old Testament women, Leah and Rachel, respectively represent the active and the contemplative life, one remembers that, at the foot of the Virgin's throne in the Celestial Rose of Dante's Paradise, sits Beatrice, Divine Love, and next to her Rachel (*Par.* 32.8). It would befit the novel and H.D.'s temperament if she had felt in her inscription to Rachel her own contemplation of the heart of the Rose.

Acknowledgments

I want to thank everyone who helped to make this edition of *The Mystery* possible: first of all, to the late Perdita Schaffner, H.D.'s daughter (1919–2002), her children Valentine, Elizabeth, and Timothy Schaffner, the owners of H.D.'s estate, and New Directions Publishing Corporation, their agents, Declan Spring particularly, for permission to publish *The Mystery*. For permissions to reproduce the art in this volume, I thank the Moravian Archives, Herrnhut, Germany; the Moravian Archives at Bethlehem, Pennsylvania; and the National Portrait Gallery, London.

Perdita Schaffner was always kind and appreciative of my efforts, but importantly so in the beginning stage of my research. She answered many questions, allowed me to photocopy *The Mystery*, to cite passages from H.D.'s other prose and poetry, and to use the Bryher Library at her home in East Hampton, New York, where, at one crisis point a pivotal book appeared without which this edition would have foundered. I am grateful to Patricia Willis, curator of the Yale Collection of American Literature at the Beinecke Rare Book and Manuscript Library, Yale University, for granting the original permission to prepare *The Mystery* for publication, and for her long supportive friendship. I am grateful as well to members of the staff at the Beinecke, David Schoonover, Robert Babcock, Steven Jones, and especially the late Louis H. Silverstein, cataloger of H.D. materials at the Beinecke and her chronologer, for their consistent and courteous help. I thank the Beinecke Library for the H.D. Fellowship in American Literature in 1995 that enriched this manuscript by letting me further explore the links between *The Mystery* and *The Gift*; Arnold Leo, Perdita Schaffner's estate manager and supervisor of the Bryher Library in East Hampton, New York; Virginia Smyers Buxton, who cataloged the books in the Bryher Library; the staff of the University of California at Berkeley and of the library at Berkeley Theological

School, Berkeley, California, especially its librarian Mark Liebenow, who in 1986 identified himself as "just about the only Moravian west of Ohio" and helped get me started.

I am grateful to the many Moravians who have helped from the beginning, especially the late Reverend Henry Williams, former head librarian at Reeves Library, Moravian College, Bethlehem, Pennsylvania, an authority on Moravian hymns, Bethlehem history, and church doctrine, for his generosity in supplying research aid and information on complex issues in Moravianism, anecdotal stories, a visit to H.D.'s grave in Nisky Hill cemetery, and the gift of his tickets to the Moravian Candlelight Christmas Eve in 1988. I am grateful also to J. Thomas Minor, retired head librarian, Reeves Library, Moravian College, Bethlehem, Pennsylvania; the Reverend Vernon Nelson, retired director of the Moravian Archives, Bethlehem; Albert Frank, Moravian music authority recently retired from the Archives at Bethlehem; Susan Dreydoppel and Ann Weisel of the Moravian Historical Society in Bethlehem; Charlene Donchez Mower, Moravian Museum, Bethlehem; Dr. Paul Peucker, present head of the Moravian Archives at Bethlehem; Lanie Graf, assistant archivist there, and Barbara Reeb, assistant archivist at the Moravian Archives in Herrnhut, Germany, with special appreciation for their help in obtaining reproductions of the portraits of Moravian historical figures that illustrate this volume.

I thank the following historians and librarians: A. S. Bell, Head Librarian of the London Library; Alice S. Creighton, Head of Special Collections, Nimitz Library, United States Naval Academy, Annapolis; Monica Crystal, secretary of collections at the Pennsylvania Historical Society, Philadelphia; Rosemarie Zagarri, Professor of American History, George Mason University; Sherri Williams, University of California at San Marcos; the staff of the Genealogy Room, New York Public Library; Alexa Pearce, Jerry Hevery, Kara Whatley and Jessica Alverson, Bobst Library, New York University; Margot Karp, Josephine McSweeney and Joseph M. Cahn, former staff, Pratt Institute Library, Brooklyn, New York; Felicia Bonaparte, Jane Marcus, Charles Molesworth, and the late Alfred Kazin of the City University of New York; the late Professor Emeritus William Blitzstein of the Department of Astronomy and Astrophysics at the University of Pennsylvania; Professor Blitzstein's daughter, Sybil Csigi, former secretary in that department and retired secretary in the department of Classics and Ancient History, for access to their extensive archival material on Charles Doolittle, H.D., and the Flower

Observatory; Charlotte Terrill of West Custer County Library, Westcliffe, Colorado, for interlibrary loan assistance; Frank Allen, Pennsylvania journalist; and Sarah Melhado White, French medievalist, translator, and poet for advice on sources and translation of passages in French.

Since *The Mystery* is the continuation, in another literary form, of *The Gift by H.D.: The Complete Text* (1998), I repeat my thanks, as acknowledged there, for the collaborative base of scholars who did prior work on *The Gift*. For help specifically leading to *The Mystery* I am grateful to Diana Collecott, Diane diPrima, Rachel Blau DuPlessis, Eileen Gregory, Joanna Griffin, the late Barbara Guest, Cynthia Hogue, Donna Hollenberg, the late Frances Jaffer, Adalaide Morris, Alicia Ostriker, Julie Vandivere, Anne Waldman, Emily Mitchell Wallace, and Sherri Williams. The pioneering work of Susan Stanford Friedman, especially on H.D.'s psychoanalysis and her practices of divination, provided important theoretical guidance. Others who helped with this book are Matthew Bailey of the National Portrait Gallery, London; Susan Barell of Dover Publications, Inc.; Fr. William J. Faherty, S.J., of Saint Louis University; Janet Halton of the Moravian Archives, London; Elizabeth Herbert, poet; Heather Hernandez of *www.imagists.org*; Sr. Gabriel Mary Hoare, S.L., of Webster College, Saint Louis, Missouri; Sylvie Schvan of Bernard Grasset Publishers, Paris; Susan Zucker, archivist; David Zucker, poet; my daughter and son-in-law in Paris, Marguerite Morley and Jean-Michel Grèzes, for hospitality and inquiries at the Bibliothèque Nationale and elsewhere; my youngest son, Patrick Morley; my brother, Rolf Augustine, now retired as cataloger in the McHenry Library at the University of California at Santa Cruz; and for technical assistance with reproductions Claudia Carlson and Michael Steinhofer, book designers, and Santo Mollica of The Sources Unlimited, New York City. Extra thanks to Candace Watt.

I thank the editors at the University Press of Florida for their long connection with and strong belief in H.D.'s work. Special thanks go to Amy Gorelick for continuing friendly patience as the book evolved, to diligent copyeditor Beth McDonald, and to Jacqueline Kinghorn Brown, project editor also of *The Gift by H.D.: The Complete Text*, whose prior experience with Moravian materials has greatly helped *The Mystery* to be unveiled.

Finally, very special warm thanks to my husband, Michael Heller, poet and critic, for unending support and assistance of all kinds. My contribution to this edition is dedicated to the memory of my mother, Marguerite St. Clair Augustine Radloff (1897–1987).

Abbreviations

AF   *Analyzing Freud: The Letters of H.D., Bryher and Their Circle*, ed. Susan Stanford Friedman. New York: New Directions, 2002.

AGS   August Gottlieb Spangenberg. *The Life of Nicholas Lewis Count Zinzendorf.* Translation with abridgment by Samuel Jackson. Introduction by the Rev. P. La Trobe. London: Holdsworth, 1838.

Ann.Ind. *Annotated Index to the Cantos of Ezra Pound: Cantos I–LXXXIV*, eds. John Hamilton Edwards and William W. Vasse. Berkeley: University of California Press, 1957; reprint 1971.

BHP   *Between History and Poetry: The Letters of H.D. and Norman Holmes Pearson*, ed. Donna Krolik Hollenberg. Iowa City: University of Iowa Press, 1997.

C   *The Cantos of Ezra Pound.* New York: New Directions, 1970.

CN   Henry Rimius. *A Candid Narrative of the Rise & Progress of the Herrnhuetters* ... London, 1754.

Co.Enc. *Columbia Encyclopedia.* 5th edition. New York: Columbia University Press, 1975; revised 1993.

CP   H.D. *Collected Poems 1912–1944*, ed. Louis L. Martz. New York: New Directions, 1983.

Doc.Hist. *The Documentary History of the State of New York*, ed., E. B. O'Callaghan. Vol. 3: 613–23. Albany: Weed, Parsons and Company, 1850.

Doré   *The Doré Bible Illustrations*, ed. Millicent Rose. New York: Dover Publications, Inc., 1974.

DW   Johann Wolfgang von Goethe. *Dichtung und Wahrheit.* Translated by R. O. Moon under the title *Autobiography*. Washington D.C.: Public Affairs Press, 1949.

EB	*Encyclopedia Britannica*. 10th Edition [1902] and 14th Edition [1957; 1971].
Enc.Occ.	*Encyclopedia of Occultism*, ed. Lewis Spence. New York: Strathmore Press, 1959.
Enc.Rel.Eth.	*Encyclopedia of Religion and Ethics*. Ed. James Hastings. New York: Scribners, 1924–26.
Enc.Sym.	*The Continuum Encyclopedia of Symbols*. Ed. Udo Becker. Translation by Lance W. Garmer. German edition, *Lexikon der Symbole*, 1992. New York: Continuum, 1994.
F.Crit.	*Faust: A Tragedy by Goethe*. A Norton Critical Edition, ed. C. Hamlin. New York: Norton, 1976.
G	*The Gift by H.D.: The Complete Text*, ed. and intro. Jane Augustine. Gainesville: University Press of Florida, 1998.
HB	Joseph Mortimer Levering. *A History of Bethlehem, Pennsylvania 1742–1892*. Bethlehem, Pa.: Times Publishing Co., 1903.
"H.D."	"H.D. by *Delia Alton*." Ed. Adalaide Morris, *Iowa Review* 16, no. 3 (1986): 174–221.
HE	H.D. *Helen in Egypt*. New York: New Directions, 1974.
HLV	*Brief Memoir of Count Henry the LV Reuss-Köstritz*. London: Moravian Archives, 1846.
HM	Éliphas Lévi. *The History of Magic*. London: Rider, 1913.
HMC	Joseph Edmund Hutton. *History of the Moravian Church*. London: Moravian Publication Office, 1909.
HMM	Joseph Edmund Hutton. *History of the Moravian Missions*. London: Moravian Publication Office, 1923.
KU	Harriette Augusta Curtiss and F. Homer Curtiss, M.D. *The Key to the Universe*. Washington D.C.: Curtiss Philosophic Book Co., 1938.
LCSG	Marie-Raymonde Delorme. *Le comte de Saint-Germain: Ses témoins at sa légende*. Paris: Grasset, 1973.
LOA-EP.	Ezra Pound. *Poems and Translations*. Selected with a chronology and notes by Richard Sieburth. New York: Library of America, 2003.
LTDZ	Edmund de Schweinitz. *Life and Times of David Zeisberger*. Philadelphia: J. P. Lippincott, 1870.
MA	Harriette Augusta Curtiss and F. Homer Curtiss, M.D. *The Message of Aquaria*. Washington D.C.: Curtiss Publishing Company, 1932.

MH	Francis Wolle. *A Moravian Heritage*. Boulder, Co.: Empire Reproduction and Printing Co., 1972.
MR	H.D. *Majic Ring*. Ed. and intro. Demetres Tryphonopoulos. Gainesville: University Press of Florida, 2009.
"Myth"	Susan Stanford Friedman. "Mythology, Psychoanalysis and the Occult in the Late Poetry of H.D." Unpublished dissertation. Madison: University of Wisconsin, 1973.
NDG	New Directions edition of *The Gift*. Abridged by Griselda Ohanessian. Intro. Perdita Schaffner. New York: New Directions, 1982.
NDG-V	British edition of *NDG*. Intro. Diana Collecott. London: Virago, 1984.
NHP	Norman Holmes Pearson. [H.D.'s literary executor.]
NTV	H.D. *Notes on Thought and Vision*. San Francisco: City Lights Books, 1982.
PD	*The Portable Dante*. Ed. and intro. Paolo Milano. New York: Viking, 1947.
PR	Susan Stanford Friedman. *Psyche Reborn: The Emergence of H.D.* Bloomington: Indiana University Press, 1981.
PW	Susan Stanford Friedman. *Penelope's Web: Gender and Modernity, H.D.'s Fiction*. New York: Cambridge University Press, 1990.
S	H.D. *The Sword Went Out to Sea (Synthesis of a Dream, by Delia Alton*. Ed. Cynthia Hogue and Julie Vandivere. Gainesville: University Press of Florida, 2007.
SN	H.D. "Séance Notes." Ts. Beinecke Library, Yale University, New Haven, Conn.
Sp.Ex.	*Spiritual Exercises of Saint Ignatius of Loyola*. Translation from the Spanish with commentary by W.H. Longridge. London: Scott, 1922.
SR	Ezra Pound. *The Spirit of Romance*. Introduction by Richard Sieburth. New York: New Directions, 2005.
T	H.D. *Trilogy*. Intro. Norman Holmes Pearson. New York: New Directions, 1973. [Also in *CP*.]
TA	H.D. *Tribute to the Angels*. Book 2 in *Trilogy*. New York: New Directions, 1973. [Also in *CP*.]
TF	H.D. *Tribute to Freud*. New Directions, 1984.
TOP	*Prague*. A Time Out guidebook, 2006.
Trans.	*Translations*, ed. and trans. Ezra Pound. New York: New Directions, 1963.

WDNF   H.D. *The Walls Do Not Fall.* Book 2 in *Trilogy*. New York: New Directions, 1973. [Also in *CP*.]

WDUD   *Webster's Deluxe Unabridged Dictionary*, second edition. New York: Simon and Schuster, 1979.

ZN   H.D. "Zinzendorf Notes." Ms., Beinecke Library, Yale University, New Haven, Conn. [H.D. numbered some pages but not all consecutively. Citations list her page number first, then in brackets the number consecutive from the first page.]

Introduction

The Mystery by H.D. (Hilda Doolittle, 1886–1961), which has been called her "Moravian" novel, is a stylistically inventive historical fiction drawing on materials she used in her memoir, *The Gift by H.D.: The Complete Text*. It further develops the themes originating in H.D.'s notes to *The Gift* on her Moravian church background, which she believed had endowed her with supernormal visionary spiritual and creative powers. *The Mystery* is presented here in a format similar to that of *The Gift*, with my introduction followed by the main text of the novel and explanatory endnotes keyed to names and phrases in that text.

At first sight, *The Mystery* is certainly mysterious. Terse and elliptical, its first chapter opens without exposition into a modernist third-person stream-of-consciousness narrative dense with historical references that, much as in a Poundian canto, require annotation and the introductory information supplied here. The setting is Prague, in and around Saint Vitus's Cathedral and its inner chapel of Saint Wenceslas. The time is late December 1788 on the brink of the French revolution. The consciousness introduced in its opening chapter belongs to H.D.'s redaction of a historical figure, an eighteenth-century reputed magician and alchemist, Count Louis Saint-Germain. This novel in its condensation and oblique approach resembles her imagist poetry more than the lengthy word-associative prose of her immediately preceding novels, signaling its importance as a transitional work in both form and content. It crosses genres in its elevation of eighteenth-century legend into a myth of history steeped in American revolutionary consciousness and the commitment to establish a new religious ideal. It is like the tip of an iceberg; the bulk of H.D.'s knowledge that went into it is hidden, subsumed under her mythic revisionism. My introduction, as with my introduction to *The Gift*, and the extensive endnotes supplied here, are intended to open up this complex text to make it more comprehensible and enjoyable as well as to reveal the range of H.D.'s sources and a view of her intellectual path that has not been presented before. *The Mystery* and H.D.'s readings that went into it pave the way for *Helen in Egypt*, her woman-centered re-working of Homeric epic that parallels and challenges those of her modernist peers, Ezra Pound's *Cantos* and James Joyce's *Ulysses*.

The Mystery, like *The Gift*, is rooted in the childhood life and wartime experience of the author. Hilda Doolitle was born in Bethlehem, Pennsylvania, into a family that, on her mother's side, belonged to the Unitas Fratrum, United Brethren, the Old Church of Bohemia, popularly called the "Moravian" church. Helen Wolle, her mother, was descended from eighteenth-century German missionaries, who, under the leadership of Nicholas Louis Count Zinzendorf (1700–1760), came in a group in 1742 to settle the newly founded community of Bethlehem as a base for spreading the Christian gospel among the Native Americans. They appreciated the religious freedom they found in a sparsely populated America, having suffered from persecution and sectarian wars in Europe, and were determined to live at peace with their neighbors, much like the Quakers around them.

H.D.'s interest in her Moravian church background and its peacemaking history greatly intensified during World War II when, in early December 1941, at her first private spiritualist séance with the medium Arthur Bhaduri, she believed that her dead mother appeared and spoke to her, calling her "sister" (*S*, 7–8). Hilda had been called "sister" as the only girl among brothers and cousins, but "Sister" was also the common form of address among Moravian women. This moment fused psychoanalysis, Christianity, spiritualism, and creative inspiration in H.D.'s mind. It convinced her that she had a psychic "gift," inseparable from her poetic gift, an inheritance that she believed came from her mother's Moravian ancestors and the mystic Count Zinzendorf. This belief guaranteed to her the authenticity of her "gift" and of the spirit-messages telling her that she should use it to help bring peace. Writing became her war effort. Within a few weeks of this séance, she went to work on *The Gift*, begun in 1940 as "a series of family portraits," and finished it with her historical notes to it in 1944 as World War II ended ("H.D.," 188, 203; *G*, 254, 257).

The Gift is H.D.'s first writing directly influenced by spiritualism; *The Mystery* is her last. Bracketed by these is a series of works, some of them her best known, that reveal the ramifications of her sense of "giftedness": *Trilogy*, composed almost simultaneously with *The Gift*; *Majic Ring*, whose first part is made up of her letters to Lord Dowding after she heard him lecture on spiritualism in October 1943 and left unfinished in 1944; "Writing on the Wall," the first section of *Tribute to Freud* written in 1944 and published serially in 1945–46; *The Sword Went Out to Sea*, written in 1946–47 reflecting her nervous breakdown of February 1946 that followed Dowding's rejection of her spirit-messages; *The White Rose and the Red* in 1948; and, finally, *The Mystery*, written between 1949 and 1951.

Now that these works are all in print, we can fully trace the evolution of H.D.'s creative processes and the multiple intertextual effects of her belief in her "gift." Two themes are interwoven throughout: her desire to bring about "world-unity without war," as she phrases a Zinzendorfian idea in *The Mystery*, and her project, begun long before spiritualism, to assert symbolically the union of feminine and masculine in the godhead by rewriting patriarchal theology.

The anti-war and feminist themes unite in the imaginative precursor to *The Mystery*, the visionary final scene in chapter 7 of *The Gift*. Here the Moravian baroness, Anna von Pahlen, exchanges names with the wife of the Delaware chief Paxnous in a ceremony emblematic of the harmony between races and nations that H.D. hoped would come after the war. She associates Anna von Pahlen with *Trilogy*'s dream-Lady, the beneficent mother-goddess who is "mère, mater, Maia, Mary" and also "Anna, Hannah or Grace"(*T*, ix–x, 71; *G*, 13, 223), with *The Mystery*'s central character, Elizabeth de Watteville, historically Zinzendorf's granddaughter. Through Elizabeth, H.D. invokes his radical view of the Holy Spirit as female, a "mother" and the "Comforter"(*G*, 9–10; Fogleman, 76–77). The plot of the novel gradually unfolds to reveal Elizabeth as an incarnation of the feminine Holy Spirit. In this way she represents all Moravian women and thus the spiritual union of H.D. and her mother that prefigures the Helen of *Helen in Egypt*, begun shortly after H.D. finished *The Mystery*.

In "H.D. by *Delia Alton*," the letter-essay and self-critique composed at much the same time as *The Mystery*, the dual authors, "Delia," the poet's mediumistic alter ego, and H.D., her literary self, mirror aspects of *The Mystery*'s "twinned" central characters, Elizabeth and Henry Dohna, who were historically first cousins, both grandchildren of Zinzendorf. H.D.'s mythic mind-set creates them as Isis and Osiris and focuses on Isis's search for the scattered limbs of Osiris, a dominant leitmotif in her work from its beginnings. Her quest for the union of goddess and god is expressed principally through her women characters, who are "individually seeking, as one woman, fragments of the Eternal Lover" ("H.D.," 181). At the same time the woman quester is seeking "not so much the fragments of Osiris, as of his sister, twin or double, the drowned or submerged Isis" ("H.D.," 182). In *The Mystery* H.D. is remembering, metaphorically re-attaching the limbs of a wounded self who is evolving into a higher spirit, an initiate ascending toward the divine. It is her means of recovery from breakdown by the re-assertion of her "gift" impugned by Dowding's pronouncement that she was deceived by "beings of a lower order" (*S*, 32).

At the same time that H.D. identifies with Isis in the Elizabeth figure, she identifies with Osiris as well, in the twin brother Henry Dohna, who has the poet's signature initials "H.D." Osiris also appears in the lover, Louis Saint-Germain, who has seen Elizabeth in Saint Vitus's Cathedral and, unawares, has fallen in love with her. He, like the medieval knight-troubadour of Provence, remnant of De Rougemont's lost "Church of Love," is a quester. Here the Grail quest of medieval Arthurian legend is grafted onto Egpytian myth. Osiris in H.D.'s vision is embarked on the same quest as Isis. He too seeks an ideal lover who is the bearer and exemplar of a higher spirituality and with whom he wishes to be wholly united. Adalaide Morris in her introduction to "H.D. by *Delia Alton*" explains:

> The search for the "Eternal Lover" is the visionary quest for an idea or an ideal, a messenger or visitor from another realm of consciousness, another field of vision or of knowledge. (177)

H.D. emphasizes a male spiritual seeker in this novel out of a need, it seems, to investigate and restore the mythic father-figure as the mother-figure had been restored in *Trilogy*'s dream-Lady. That reconstructed father, with parallels to Freud, is Count Zinzendorf, who actually was the "founder of a new religion," the aspiration that Freud attributed to H.D. (*TF*, 37). He is also in a metaphorical sense the father of Bethlehem. By symbolic literary action she must also bring masculine patriarchal authority into herself to complete her recovery from Dowding's rejection. She could not deny his spiritual authority any more than she could deny the authority of her own experience. She knew she had had "visitations"; a notable example is the "supernormal" apparition of the Man on the Boat in 1920. Whose claim to authentic psychic powers was to be believed?

In view of this dilemma her choice of Louis Saint-Germain as a central character in *The Mystery* is relevant. The issue of true and false claims to magical and psychic powers is passionately discussed by Éliphas Lévi in his *History of Magic* (1913), the volume from which she took much information, almost verbatim, to shape her character. The historical Saint-Germain, who frequented the court of King Louis XVI and Queen Marie Antoinette, was called "Der Wundermann" and "The Deathless;" he was said to possess a secret Elixir of Life. Legends multiplied concerning his magical powers, immortality, and capacity to appear in two places at once and caused nineteenth-century theosophists to make him one of their Twelve Ascended Masters (Godwin, 198–99).

In *The Mystery* H.D. places Saint-Germain in a crisis of mental and physical breakdown similar to her own, in which he must release himself from two kinds of false religious practice: the charlatanism of Cagliostro and the institutional politics of Cardinal de Rohan, both historical personages that H.D. re-designed to fit into her religiously syncretic and mythic vision of history. Saint-Germain experiences an uncertainty of spiritual direction like that felt by H.D., which is resolved through his encounters with the Moravians Henry Dohna and Elizabeth. They act as annunciators of the "visitation," from a higher spiritual realm, of Zinzendorf himself. Whether or not the apparition of Zinzendorf is a dream or a wine-induced hallucination, he is "real" to Saint-Germain, as from 1941 the spirits who appeared in séance were real to H.D. The Moravian leader is real to him as he addresses Zinzendorf's spiritual presence throughout the last chapter of the novel.

Zinzendorf is there from its beginning as well. H.D. meditates on the historical fact that the revival of the Unitas Fratrum took place because the young Saxon nobleman met Christian David, the leader of the persecuted Moravians, "at the house of the Master of the Horse" in Schweinitz, an estate in Saxony near Herrnhut. The legend arose that Zinzendorf was seen at Schweinitz when he was also seen in Dresden, as the historical Saint-Germain was said to have been seen in two places at once, and as H.D. believed that the Man on the Boat in *Majic Ring* had been simultaneously on deck with her and asleep below in his cabin. These legends of bi-location inspired the novel's plot centered on the "Visitor". H.D. says:

It is a mystery not uncommon to folk and fairytales, the mystery of the appearance of a stranger or a near-stranger at a time and in a place where he could not possibly have been. "It could happen at any time, but unless you were aware of its happening, it wasn't the Visitor." . . . So St. Germain, in his role of Brother Antonius muses in the great Cathedral. ("H.D.," 202)

Zinzendorf's mystical character is attested to by stories of his power, his escape from venomous snakes, and his acceptance by the Native Americans as one sent by "Manito," the Great Spirit. The spiritual light of these stories plays over the Bethlehem of H.D.'s memory (*G*, 24, 246–47). In *The Gift* she does not think of herself as merely remembering her childhood but "actually returns to that world" ("H.D.," 192). Her characters are "reincarnations." She feels in "intimate communion or communication" with persons in the past, as, during the wartime period, she believed that her medium's "gift" had enabled dead R.A.F. pilots to speak to her ("H.D.," 195). She wrote *The White Rose and the Red* in 1948 out of a sense of devotion to the legend of William Morris and the circle of Dante Gabriel Rossetti, spiritualist practitioners, that aroused in her a sense of similarities to her own life: "Something of my . . . first urge toward expression in art finds a parallel in the life of Rossetti and Elizabeth Siddall" ("H.D.," 194).

She had been drawn to Siddall because of the similarity of her name to H.D.'s Moravian grandmother's name: Elizabeth Seidel ("H.D.," 202). For her, names are logos, word made flesh. Thus they are vehicles for "reincarnations" or for the "sense of continuity," which H.D. says "renewed my faith at the end of the war-years"("H.D.," 195). The name Elizabeth creates a conduit for another "reincarnation." As H.D. was coming to the end of writing Elizabeth Siddall's story, she began "to live or to 'see' another story," set in the eighteenth century and "fulfilling a latent ambition" to make use of the notes she had made while writing *The Gift*:

> I had become very devoted to the Zinzendorf legend and suddenly one of his grand-daughters, another Elizabeth, steps as it were, out of history to take the place of the (as yet) vaguely questing Elizabeth Siddall. . . . I have a title for the new story. It is called *The Mystery*. ("H.D.," 200)

Thus H.D. blended her artist self with her Moravian grandmother, Mamalie, and, in an imagined scene in chapter 5 of *The Gift*, "The Secret," has the grandmother tell the child Hilda about something the early Moravian church once had but later lost. It was "a special Spirit that some of the Crusaders worshipped," which was part of a *plan*, a word that, when used by Zinzendorf, "didn't mean just *plan* or even company, but referred to some secret society or organization" (*G*, 155). Bethlehem, Pennsylvania, was part of it, since it was "one of a number of Moravian settlements, having to do with a mysterious *Plan* of 'peace on earth'" ("H.D.," 188). In the third chapter of *The Mystery*, Henry Dohna, at Elizabeth's instigation, is reading old documents and recalls a conversation with Goethe in which the German poet said that Zinzendorf had described to him his *Plan* "to form a World State of the Lord's Watch" as "non-political." H.D. is foreshadowing her vision of the *Plan*'s revival and its evolution into a universal "Church of Love" that obviates all sectarian divisions between nations, races, and religions ("H.D.," 202).

The Mystery then, which H.D. calls "my last romance," is basically a love story. It begins in Saint-Germain's consciousness as he remembers meeting Elizabeth coming out of Saint Vitus's Cathedral. He intuits her spiritual power because the cathedral's heavy doors swing open the wrong way for her. She is plainly an "initiate," although unconscious of it. At the time of the revolutionary upheaval about to happen in France, Elizabeth and Henry are in Prague to do what H.D. herself was doing: to go through old books and papers to find out more about what the church had lost, that is, Zinzendorf's secret *Plan* that would bring worldwide peace.

Saint-Germain's first name, Louis, is also one of Zinzendorf's names, indicating a spiritual linkage of which the French count is at first unaware. But he is made aware that he is heading in the wrong direction spiritually when he undergoes a "supernormal" experience in which the Cathedral "veers round," its left side appearing as its right side, much like H.D.'s mystical meeting with the Man on the Boat, which she told to Freud and elaborated on in part 2 of *Majic Ring* (*TF*, 156–58) This reversal comes after Louis, disguised as a monk named Brother Antonius, has witnessed a magical extinction of candles in the cathedral, although there was no wind. He associates this magic with Elizabeth, since the cathedral door reversed itself for her. He intuits that a supernatural Visitor is near, bringing a message. "The Cathedral is the Dream," says H.D., linking this sacred space with her psychoanalytic conception of unconscious mind and eternal spirit as coterminous, equally accessible to initiates of both sexes but in particularly close connection with Zinzendorf's female Holy Spirit ("H.D.," 204).

The veering-round of the Cathedral is the beginning of grave illness for Louis, a symbolic replica of H.D.'s nervous breakdown. Henry visits the sick man, who feels that in his visitor he has found a brother; Elizabeth then visits Louis as "Sister Elizabeth" in her Moravian sister's cap, whose later replica she had seen her grandmother wear (*G*, 136). In his semidelirium he sees her as Our Lady, much the same multilayered image as the dream-Lady, Isis/Mary/Mother of *Tribute to the Angels*. During her several visits to the invalid she tells him stories of Bethlehem, which emphasize the American Indians' recognition of Zinzendorf as a highly developed spiritual being. For instance, the warrior chiefs of the Six Nations gave him a belt of wampum as a token of peace for use as a safe-conduct through their territories (*G*, 237). She treats Saint-Germain's fever with medicinal herbs, Native American remedies taught to Moravian women, who also used them when Bethlehem became a hospital for General Washington's wounded after the battle of Brandywine in the American Revolution.

What H.D. is "devoted" to in the "Zinzendorf legend" is his ecumenism, large-mindedness, and respect for nonwhite races. His mysticism, generous vision, and "heart religion" opposed the petty sectarianism of the eighteenth century. He wanted the Old Church of Bohemia, the pre-Reformation church unseparated from the Church of Rome, to bridge and heal the schism between Protestantism and Catholicism. H.D. joined this vision. She saw the Moravian church as propagating a universal eternal spirituality transcending human divisions—competing sects, warring nations, the personal opposition of male and female.

In the final chapter of the novel, Louis finds himself in a conversation with the supernatural manifestation of Zinzendorf, who materializes immediately after the departure of Elizabeth and Henry. He realizes that his mission is to return to his true knight's identity and commitment to self-sacrifice. He will go back to France as chevalier, keeping a troubadour's faith with his Queen by leading the Swiss Guard in defense of the royal palace. He will die there, because, as history records, and H.D. knew, the revolutionaries slaughtered the guardsmen, whose honor forebade them to give up their posts even after the king and queen had left the palace. It is this loyalty to a transcendent love, in which the erotic and the spiritual are inseparable and pure, that H.D. admires, even venerates. It is the courtly lover's fealty to the lady, the queen of the castle, his *midons* or madonna, who embodies the chivalric ideal to which *The Mystery*, as a romance, pays tribute.

Until H.D. wrote *The Mystery*, the failure of love to be ideal has been a more prominent theme in her prose. Her plots persistently involved an Isis-Osiris couple in painful love-triangles with a third person, a pattern resembling her husband Richard Aldington's early betrayal of her in his affair with Dorothy Yorke. H.D.'s mythicizing of these triangles in fictional form had seemed to constitute a therapy; here it is also a redemption. In her reading for *The Mystery*, she found a love-triangle that is part of the Zinzendorf legend. The Count as a young man had fallen in love with his cousin, Theodora de Castell, but, discovering that his best friend, Henry Count Reuss, was also in love with her, renounced his engagement plans. Henry married Theodora and Zinzendorf married Henry's sister, Erdmuth Dorothea von Reuss. The story is retold in chapter 2 by Elizabeth, who expresses her sense of affinity with Theodora, Zinzendorf's first love, but also with the woman he married, Erdmuth. The passage referring to Elizabeth's grandmother reinforces the child Hilda's connection to Mamalie in *The Gift*, and adumbrates the mythically blended Moravian mother/daughter/dream-Lady figure of Thetis, Achilles' "sea-mother," in *Helen in Egypt*.

Saint-Germain's farewell speech to the "presence" of Zinzendorf proclaims a spiritual union as well as the ultimate significance of Moravian doctrine as H.D. saw it, the "gross and scandalous mysticism" for which Zinzendorf was attacked in the eighteenth century (*G*, 259, 268). He addresses Zinzendorf:

> I would only say that your Mysticism is naturally repulsive to men, who would at all costs elevate the Father above all, and above all, above the Mother. Your poem to that effect—I will not quote it—was enough to burn you at the stake, like that John Huss whom they bound, outside by the cathedral.

The poem referred to and its purportedly heretical content comes from Zinzendorf's 1896th hymn, lines of which H.D. copied into her "Zinzendorf Notes": "God, thou mother of the whole church, eternal wife of God the Father." It reiterates Zinzendorf's unorthodox Trinity in which the Holy Spirit is feminine, a "Mother", the "Comforter" promised by the risen Christ, and it links the last scene of *The Gift* with the last scene of *The Mystery* (*G*, 10–11).

This view of divine love as incorporating both feminine and masculine and its parallel in the Isis-Osiris union of Egyptian myth allowed H.D. to understand her own incorporation of both the mother and the father. Thus in the novel she accomplishes her spiritual goals of this period. She has banished self-doubt and ended her "romantic thralldom" to Dowding. The literary act frees her from dominance by male spiritual authority but lets her accept insights from her male mentors. She regards her astronomer father, her Moravian scientist grandfather, and Freud as palimpsestic "reincarnations" associated with Zinzendorf, with Bethlehem, and with a legend of "a new way of life, a Brotherhood, dedicated to peace and universal understanding" ("H.D.," 189).

In October 1951 after sending the completed text of *The Mystery* to Norman Holmes Pearson, she wrote him: "I wanted you to tell me if you feel it is finished? I do. And FINIS too, to a whole processus or lifetime of experience." It is her final recovery from a spiritualist hangover. Dowding has been symbolically disposed of, made into her lover and vassal and delivered into the next stage of his initiation, no longer a presence troubling her mind. She has completely assimilated her Moravian heritage and does not need to be further preoccupied with establishing its gift to her. Now in possession of spiritual autonomy, she is free to begin her recuperation of archetypal western woman in *Helen in Egypt*: "She herself is the writing."

The Mystery
by
H.D.

I

The name was de Watteville.

It was a mistake to step aside and lift the curtain for her, it was a greater mistake to stoop under the leather fold when he realized in the cold, that she could not open the out-door. The door was usually left open but someone must have closed it from outside, because of the snow. She would dart out. Stephanus had watched her from outside.

The snow had already drifted inside, before they shut the door, or it had blown in under the door, afterwards. Himself, he had a little trouble drawing the half-door inward. He noticed the circle it marked in the fine drift, on the inner pavement. Her scarf caught in the wind. It was howling from the river, into the narrow passage of the Street of the Alchemists.

It was a mistake that he bowed slightly.

In return, her curtsey might have been a belated genuflection. She did not genuflect but inclined her head before the altar. She did not touch the Holy Water. She was to be found, deep in abstraction or meditation, for the most part, in the chapel of Saint Wenceslas.

It was a mistake to wait and watch her blown like a wraith, down the Alchemists' Lane. Stephanus could be depended upon to report that her servant was waiting as usual, in the porch of the *Grape Cluster*. Now, not only might Stephanus reprove his Superior, but the lackey by the *Grape* might note the incident.

The lackey was a Schweinitz. They had found that out. At least, there was some connection with the house of the Master of the Horse in Schweinitz. This information, however, had yet to be translated.

Was Schweinitz, *Schwein*, hog, pig? Or *Schweiss*, sweat? Or *Schweitz*, Swiss? Was it one or all of these things? Her name was French, but he believed it to be of French-Swiss extraction. It was perhaps some indication. This Schweinitz looked and acted like one of the Royal Guard before the palace. It might be permitted to presume that the Queen had granted congé for a short space, to one of her waiting-ladies, or sent her on some secret errand. One might reason that one of the Swiss guard should never be far absent. "It is not reasonable reasoning," thought Brother Antonius. He recalled the rigour and rule of the *Exercitia*. But he was, as it were, roaming at large and even his thoughts were his own, for the time being. He repeated, nevertheless, Saint Ignatius' formal vow of dedication before he prepared to rehearse in his mind, the day's events, preliminary to the withdrawal. "But I must not withdraw to mystic vision," he thought. It was necessary to remind himself that he was, at the moment, a not important lay-brother. He had forgotten, and for the first time, the part that he was playing. "There is no excuse," thought Brother Antonius. He denied himself the pleasure of his usual *Exercitia* in the Chapel.

"The floor-stones are uncommon hard," he thought, though wrapt in meditation, he had not thought of the cold. "England," he thought, "France, Venice, Spain, Naples—the last two fairly recently and within a year of one another." Then Clement XIV had suppressed the Society of Jesus.

The Holy See however, was to be kept informed, through their last secret stronghold in Prague, of the activities of the *franc-maçon*. If the information could be delivered in time, it might serve to reclaim the lost Foundation. It was no mere rumor, his Superior had informed him, that the new nuncio was ready to discuss the re-establishment of the Society, at the next election.

Loyola! War had conditioned him and the wound received at Pampeluna had been the instrument of Grace. It was war, the creation of a military order, spiritually to uphold the Church, as in the old days, the Praetorian Guard had sustained the Emperors in Rome—that was Loyola's object. But the consecration of a Paul III could be annulled by a later Clement. As the crow flies, thought Brother Antonius, the Praetorian endured three hundred years; it protected yet controlled its Emperors, from Augustus to Constantine. Loyola's Praetorian had suffered its first defeat in England, only fifty years after its foundation. That was to be expected from the daughter of the traitor and renegade, Henry VIII. But fifteen years later, there was the more vital blow, the suppression of the Order in France. Was that English machinations—and whose? Certain of the Queen's gentlemen had been conspicuous in Paris, before Bartholomew.

Brother Antonius knelt before the altar containing the relique of Ludmilla, the martyred grandmother of Saint Wenceslas. It was not his custom however, at this hour, to leave by the main entrance. He had been wont to return to his rooms (Antonius' rooms) by the side-door behind the altar. Stephanus would wonder what had kept him. He was on duty in the study that overlooked the court-yard, until the return of the scholarly lay-brother whose work lay, for the most part, in the cloister. Antonius would have preferred a choir of the younger children, but his Superior's wish was that he should insinuate into his lessons on the counter-reformation hints as to the earlier value of Jesuit activities. Antonius felt he could have been more helpful with the youngest, always remembering Saint Ignatius Loyola's precept, "give me your child until he is seven and you can have him afterwards."

He saw her, nun-like. She was a child in serenity. What Convent had she attended? Why was she in Prague? The rooms she occupied below the old Tower were still the property of the House of Köstriz. Polish, Bohemian, Prussian? Frederick had consolidated the Protestant Principalities. She was, more likely, Austrian.

Viduae et Virgines. Was she a widow or had she never married? He crossed himself with a faint apology to Saint Ludmilla. His thoughts had not been with her.

II

"But you are the only one who cares," said Elizabeth.

"You would not think so, if you heard grandpappa on the Dohna legend."

"I have heard your grandpappa on the Dohna legend," said Elizabeth. "I have as great a reverence as he has for the Dohna legend. But to your grandfather and your father even, it has come to an end. We have not eloped. We are not even lovers. But no two could be nearer than you and I, Henri. Why did we come to Prague? It is no insult to the memory of the late Hans Christian Alexander von Schweinitz, my husband. We are still, as in your other grandpappa's day, one family and a legend. I do not speak of the Dohna legend, but of that of your mother, my mother and our Aunt Elizabeth. But mamma and Aunt Elizabeth, Benigna and Elizabeth von Zinzendorf, repeated the same pattern when they married John and Frederick de Watteville. At least, your mother, my Aunt Agnes, the middle one, showed curiosity and a desire to explore outside the Lord's Hedgerows when she married Maurice, Count Dohna, your father."

"You have forgotten Justine, your own sister."

"Justine was the least original of them all. I have yet to find out why her Henry is Count Reuss 55, when the famous Ignatius, nephew of the Countess, was Count Reuss 28. Is it worth the reckoning? But I contradict myself, for my intention has been from the beginning, to inform the old pattern with new life. To become impatient with the Reuss threads, is no good beginning, when the first and most important is grandmamma's contribution to the pattern. We are not likely to forget that the Countess von Zinzendorf, Erdmuth Dorothea of Reuss, was related to Podiebrad, King of Bohemia."

Anna Dorothy Elizabeth de Watteville von Schweinitz was resting on the divan. There was the crackle of the wood-fire and the mellow flame of candles in branched candelabra. There was the silver coffee-set and the Sèvres cups on the small table at her elbow.

"You pour, Henri, if you want more coffee," she said. "Coffee was a ritual with them, do you remember? With us, it is more in the French fashion. It is fortunate that Justine's in-laws still hold the old writ for the Prague property. Back and forth as ambassadors—I suppose there is trouble in Vienna again, though I didn't inquire too closely. The only thing that really mattered was the Tower, and Dorothea told Justine they wouldn't want it till after the New Year. The two servants, she assured Justine, were diplomatically instructed and could be relied on not to gossip. Justine told Nicholas you were writing a book and wanted fresh material on the Old Church. Not that you are likely to get it in Bohemia."

She didn't know if her cousin, Henry Lewis, the only son of Maurice, Count Dohna, were listening.

That is the best thing about Henri, she thought. I can think out loud or I can talk without thinking or I can go on talking to myself and it's the same as if I were talking to him. Henri is there. He will tell the story. I don't mean grandpappa's three hundred voyages—or the three hundred voyages taken in his name. I don't mean the *Sixteen Discourses* and the other momentous works of the illustrious Count Zinzendorf, Bishop of the Ancient Moravian Church. I don't mean the Theocracy or the Hierarchy or whatever it came to be called by his detractors. I don't mean Ludovicus Moraviensis. "Who do they think you are, at the *Grape Cluster*?" said Elizabeth de Watteville.

"I don't know in the least how it happened, but they connect me with the Master of the Horse in Schweinitz."

"But Henri, that sounds familiar."

"Mine host addresses me as Schweinitz."

"Surely, Maria and Jacob here, have not been talking?"

"Of that, I am quite certain."

"Justine forwards our letters, re-addressed to Nicholas, with ambassadorial discretion. But I suppose it would be inhuman not to expect the post-diligence to carry gossip. They still think you are my servant?"

"Rightly."

"It's all right in winter. We could not disproportion you in summer, with Jacobus. But if anything (though Maria re-sewed the buttons) the great-coat would hint of the House of Köstriz."

"They know you stay here—suspect you belong—"

"Well, I do, if my sister Justine's marriage to her Henry—"

"—the 55th Count Reuss, you must remember."

"But I made a mistake again," said Elizabeth de Watteville. "The wind caught my scarf. I felt entangled in it. I couldn't open the door."

"You were outside?"

"No, I mean, I was inside and couldn't open the door."

"It's usually left open."

"That's what I mean. I was running those few steps—no—I mean I wanted to run. He lifted the leather curtain."

Henry was looking at the fire.

"You don't ask me who lifted the leather curtain?"

He did not answer.

"What are you thinking, Henri?"

"I must know why they connected me with the house of the Master of the Horse."

"You mean because grandpappa is reputed to have met Christian David first in Schweinitz—"

"The story began in Schweinitz. We came here on a pious mission, but more (as you say of the Sèvres-set on the table) in the French fashion—"

"That's what I mean, Henri. I hadn't noticed him before and then I felt it had happened somewhere. He lifted the curtain. He unfastened the door. He knew my hands were frozen. As you say the door is usually left open. He couldn't move it. It was frozen or the old hinges had grown stiff. It jerked suddenly and swung in. There was snow on the pavement. The wind snatched at dear god-mamma's old lace. I was somewhere else. Perhaps it was Theodora of Castell—I mean, it was a Castell heirloom. I always wear the lace in the Cathedral. He bowed and I curtseyed to him."

"He waited at the door," said Henry. "His servant or his server saw him waiting."

"I don't know about that. I had never been so—so sharpened in the wind. I mean, I had never felt the wind so sharpen itself against me. Was I the whetstone? You had Jacobus waiting below the steps, with the sleigh."

"Maria insisted on his coming for you."

"I would have driven on forever but I remembered Justine at the last saying we must be considerate. They had taken the coach-horses with them. These were the saddle-horses that we had had on our excursions. I hadn't thought to ask how many there were. We got home."

"It was only this afternoon, this early evening. You make it seem as if it had all happened a long time ago."

"It happened two hours ago. It happened two hundred years ago. It gave me a clue. Why should I curtsey to him? What I mean is, I try to imagine how Elizabeth of Bohemia might have felt in the Cathedral. I don't mean that I thought I was the Winter Queen. I might have been her daughter, Elizabeth of Bohemia, Abbess of Herford."

"And I Prince Rupert?"

"I don't know. I was making mistakes. Surely, you don't curtsey to a lay-brother?"

"I don't know why not."

"But we are not in the Lord's Watch. I mean *they* wouldn't curtsey to him."

"Depending on who they are, and how do you know he is a lay-brother?"

"He doesn't officiate at the Mass. I think he teaches. There is a school in the cloister and I've seen him ordering them, I mean getting their line in order when they file out."

"And he sees you?"

"I don't think he ever saw me—only this evening, when he lifted the leather curtain. Only when the wind would have taken dear god-mamma's scarf—"

"Only when you blew or flew down the Lane of the Alchemists. The place is seething with overtones. A mere lay-brother wouldn't have bowed at the sight of Theodora de Castell's old lace."

III

"The Tower, House of Köstriz, Prague. Faustus—scene of legend. Dr Faustus, the magician. Albertus Magnus. Dr John Dee and his confederates in Prague. Philosopher's Stone, Elixir of Life, symbolical? Alchemists."

Henry Dohna studied the entry. Was this the way to approach the *Unitas Fratrum* and the re-establishment of the suppressed Church of Bohemia? "Christel, Z, in London." There was much there that had not been recorded. He had given up search in the official records and Spangenberg's ponderous biography. There was more actually to be found in the broadsheets and pamphlets of his grandfather's detractors and the innocent pastoral defamations of Andrew Frey who had gone back to Pennsylvania, after crossing with the returned members of the first Sea Congregation. It was Andrew Frey who had given life and character to a portrait, otherwise presented in austere reflection. Henry Dohna had found no other reference to Christian Renatus, the young Count, as Christel.

He was too near, possibly. It needed someone from outside, intelligent and informed, to phrase the question. He had been surprised at his own answers. Christian David was a convert from Rome. My grandfather met him at the house of the Master of the Horse in Schweinitz. Those were simple answers to simple questions.

"Is it true that you have people in almost all parts of the world whom you can easily bring together?"

"It was true in my grandfather's day."

"The *Plan* was to form a World State of the Lord's Watch?"

"Not political."

"I may have access to your records?"

"The library of the Foundation is open to visitors."

"And the *Arcana*—the Secret Records?"

Henry Dohna had not considered Secret Records, until Wolfgang Goethe spoke of *Arcana* to him.

"Of *Arcana*, I know nothing."

If there were secret records or so-called *Arcana*, he had immediately reasoned, they would not be open to visitors, and if he knew of them, he would not be expected to reveal them to a casual stranger. But Goethe had come again, bringing his mistress with him.

It was usual to accommodate the more colourful visitors outside the community, as formerly at Herrnhaag, the Lord's Hedge, rather than at Herrnhut, the Lord's Watch. But Wolfgang Goethe was a poet of distinction. Henry Dohna's Aunt Benigna had herself selected for them, one of the re-modelled dwellings of the original settlement, the one known actually as the First House. It was kept in readiness and was said to contain beams shaped from the first tree, felled by Christian David when, a refugee from Bohemia, he had found sanctuary at Bertholdsdorf, his grandfather's estate in Saxony.

The House was a short distance from the village. It came to be known as the House in the Wood. It was here that the first meetings were held. "They foresaw that God would kindle a light in this place that would enlighten the whole world," read Henry Dohna, as he turned over a page.

In the margin of the next entry, he had indicated a query. "Pennsylv. Serm. or Serm. at Zeist?" The entry was, "It is a house which shall be in being, or perhaps will scarce be finished, when the Saviour comes; he shall lodge and walk about in it; the chandeliers in it shall be lighted for Him."

It was characteristic of his grandfather to recall an eighteenth-century elegance as appropriate to the Saviour. That is, to an eighteenth-century Saviour. Even as it was in character to announce on Christmas Eve, in their First House in America, that the town that should grow from that one log cabin, with its cattle-stall adjoining, should be called Bethlehem. So John Martin Mack recorded—he had written it down somewhere.

Henry Dohna leafed over the pages. He could not find the entry. *Not Jerusalem. Rather Bethlehem.* It was one of Gregor's metres that his grandfather was singing. Gregor—Gregor. He had assembled the notes from his rough copy, after they came here. It would have been better to have re-copied them, in alphabetical or at least, calendar sequence. Castell. She was talking of Castell, before he left her.

It was like that. Reuss, brother of Erdmuth Dorothea (their own grandmother) and his close friend (their grandfather) were both in love with Theodora de Castell. Whether Theodora openly preferred Reuss (it was as Elizabeth had said, confusing, as he too, was Henry) or the young Count managed to efface himself in his friend's interest, Henry Dohna had no way of knowing. At least, asking himself the question, kept the door open to some sort of answer. "The Dowager Countess was an aunt of Z." Why had he thought it necessary to indicate in that way, that Theodora and Zinzendorf were cousins?

In any case, Henry marries Theodora de Castell, and Nicholas Lewis, Count and Lord of Zinzendorf marries Henry's sister, their own grandmother, Erdmuth Dorothea.

Was it all very simple? Or were the threads inexorably tangled? Was inexorable the word he wanted? There was something inevitable about it, simple yet requiring an astute attention, like following the intricate pattern of a set dance. Not a romp as Andrew Frey envisaged those formal Birthdays. He must find that, somewhere.

"Thurnstein and the Vale of Wachovia. Move to Saxony. Austrian estates forfeited by father or grandfather of Z, after thirty years war." He didn't want that. His thoughts were not ordered. He would really do no good, muddling the sequence, and the fire was going. She had left him early. The evening was dedicated to their work together, but tonight she had been numb and exhausted, though she protested that she had found more answers in the Chapel of Saint Wenceslas. He must not let her go there tomorrow, in this cold.

He would find Andrew and then to bed—ah—"Festivals, Merriments, Celebrations of Birthdays, Impious Doctrine and Fantastical Practices."

IV

"It blew shut."

"You told me that, earlier in the evening. But you have yet to explain how it blew shut. The door is on iron-hinges and rusty, I should imagine. You must examine them in the morning. I should stop fussing with the perruque, Stephanus. I do not intend to wear it."

"Orders was, you was to retain your gentleman appearance, as for dinner."

"I don't want any dinner. Or if you insist, the half of the Château Saint Germain that was left from last night. Unless you've swallowed it."

"I should suggest, on such an evening and as it might be, an occasion, that we open a fresh bottle."

"What is the occasion, Stephen? My making four mistakes in the Cathedral? Or my foregoing the *Exercitia*? I was also under the impression, by the altar of Saint Ludmilla, that I would be late in returning, though if my mind had been functioning in the usual groove, I should have realized, by denying myself the proof of the *Exercitia*, I should be, by that, the earlier. You did not expect me. You were not on duty by the study window."

"The window got rimed over with cold, and the lady had already gone by."

"So you had a backstair's chat with the Embassy valet?"

"The stairs is, so to speak, common property. I thought with the cold and his party being delayed, was opportunity—"

"Does he approve of our Château Saint Germain?"

"—and discussion as to what his gentleman was wearing might do for display, in a modest manner—"

"So you showed him the Order of the Garter, the Golden Fleece and the Star?"

"You must have your joke, sir. Nothing is absolute and certain, one must take precaution, especial when the thing seems perfect. Like that door blown shut—one couldn't have foreseen it. The Pedagogy is under the impression you belong to the Confraternity. The Fratres consider you as consultant to the Castle Library. The Castle, such as snoops round our corner, don't think you're worth the noticing. There was always some odd fish housed in the Row. It's really the Castle's business and well thought out, I should hazard. Our apartment from the front, looks like it belongs to the Embassy wing, but it's off of Petty Place lopsided, but the whole town's lopsided. Not the style, he says, he's used to for Ambassadors, but he conceded it's convenient-like and near the Castle."

"Did you show him the moated grange, the underground entrance and the Hide?"

"If this is the Hide, in the manner of speaking, yes. Or is the study or what you might call the vestry, where you kick off your sandals, the Hide?"

Saint-Germain did not answer.

"They're both in their ways, perfect, only a locked door between, and me in a habit over me breeks, at the study window or at most, prowling a few feet in the alley, that side, but locks has been known to be picked."

"They would find nothing very conclusive in Brother Antonius' study, a few volumes from the library and the old texts."

"If a door bangs shut unexpected, a door might, by the same logic, bang open. That's why I asked the valet what he thought was behind the cupboard, suspicious, I said, I thought our wall was. Told him, I went around to see what was back of it, said it seemed part of the Cloister, a monk had it, though being almost in Alchemist's Row. What's that? he said. I said, in the old days, they controlled their experimenters, what they called alchemists, they was working for base metal, I mean, getting gold from it, so they kept them in that Row. Superstition. What was back of their wall? Said he thought it was a by-path between them and the cottages, he'd ask cook. You can never be too careful, I warned him, in a place like this. My gentleman was away, hours at a stretch—well, I hinted it would be worth my place to indicate what business he was up to, but though we lived hole-and-corner, you might say, in the crook of Petty Place, all but elbowed out by their ramshackle Embassy, yet it was—convenient. It was him who had just remarked, it was convenient for the Castle. I was glad to hear his Ambassador would be in residence, I said, and sorry he was snowed up, things was safer when there was residence, not that the Castle didn't adequately protect their, as you might say, outside visitors and the Count was especially advised by *his* people, to maintain a strict incognito—do you like the flavour? I said. What's this? he said. I heard of a

Saint-Germain, he said. Do you mean that about a gentleman, I said, being met years after by his pal, a lad of eighty, and this Saint-Germain being still the same age he was, when they were cadets together? He hadn't heard all the story, not with its sequel about the Saint-Germain in Venice."

"Venice came first, if I am not mistaken," said Saint-Germain.

"I told him there was confusion in the story, the Mystery of Saint-Germain," said Stephanus.

"There was no mystery. A lackey feared to contradict Royalty who mistook me for my uncle."

"It was your great-uncle. But they'd believe anything at Versailles. They want to be hoodwinked. Saint-Germain had nothing against him, I told the valet, they put it on him, the Elixir he had discovered to keep himself young. Get a thing like that started and there's no escaping. Asked him if he had heard of the Cardinal. Was there gossip in Vienna (he made out they were coming from Vienna or going on from here, I couldn't make out which), she being Austrian. I could have got more from him but there was that suspicion from the cupboard. Rats, I said, the rats here is something awful, and fortunate the clock struck and I said, Lord, is it that late—my master—But he was off before the clock finished striking."

She being Austrian. Was that the link or one of the links missing? "I forgot to tell you, Stephen, that I thought the lady might be Austrian." He used Stephanus as a check, not only on his actions but on his thoughts as well. "The name is French, but there is that connection with the House of Köstriz."

"I should suggest, sir," said his servant, "that having broke the charm or the sequence of hours and minutes, that you better let go for the time being, this pro and con and weighing. Be yourself here or yourself, if you like, in the Cathedral, but don't let the weight of the responsibilities put on Brother Anton, spoil Saint-Germain. I mean, the lady was the means of your forgetting. What I suggest is, you forget for the time being, the Cardinal, that rogue Balsamo, the Office, the Masons, as they call themselves, the undermining (as of by rats) by their fraternities, the past that was and English history. It will be small things and little people that will decide the issues."

It was Stephanus' way of talking but there was a ring about it or a rhythm that suggested a fortune-teller on the fair-grounds or before his juggler's table, at the bridge-head. "I reminded myself," said Saint-Germain, "that I felt in Versailles, the cause was the reason for it. Cardinal de Rohan has a vote at the elections, moreover as a man of the world and an astute Churchman, he realized the *franc-maçon* had nothing to check-mate them, since Clement had suppressed the Society of Jesus. Rohan's supposed passion for Marie might hold the State together. But I could not see how such a passion was consistent."

"You mean, this lady being Austrian, reminded you of the Queen?"

"She reminded me that such a Queen might be, and that perhaps de Rohan's imagination could see further than my reasoning. Being Austrian, I do not know why she does not genuflect before the altar."

He was fussy was his master, but elegant. He was lopsided. Anybody could deduce that the lady was a heretic. How could two doors bang shut simultaneous, and nobody outside? It was the Mystery of Saint-Germain that worried him.

"Inquiring at the post, legitimate-like as to when our bag was to go out to Paris, I ascertained that the lady at the Tower travelled ordinary. That seemed odd. They was from Upper Lusatia, just across the border in Saxony. Maybe, on a visit there, she don't seem rightly Saxon. Her man, being Schweinitz, is more in character. The Köstriz house is some old connection. Part of it's shut up. She has the Tower and use of the saddle-horses, her man rides with her. Köstriz or whatever his name is, and his lady is in Vienna."

"Did your valet tell you?"

"We got round to the Tower, somehow, talking of old landmarks. You can always find your way out, if you get caught in the old town, I told him, if you re-direct to the Tower. It's conspicuous. Fortunate you're slender, sir, and can clothe proper under the sackcloth. Orders was, you must remember, you was not to over-do it. Being anyhow, a lay-brother and of no consequence, being pedagogy, no one is like to notice. If you get chilblains, you'll hobble to the Castle, unlike a gentleman. Whatever was to happen, you was not to lose your gentlemanly bearing. That was my orders. Yours may seem, at times, to run contrary. But that's your business. They was double-doors; did I remark, sir, that they slammed shut, simultaneous?"

Give him time to think it over, thought Stephanus. Make time for him. "I'll do up the fire, sir, then half of that cold fowl and I got country-butter again from the second booth to the left, past the gateway, the one I was telling you of, she's convenient and I tell her just in passing-like, my gentleman needs a snack and it was her first suggested my purchase of the fowl, new cooked. It wasn't from the postillion I first heard, they travelled by the common stage-coach. The market didn't get it from the wife nor yet the husband, the two left in charge there at the Tower; old family servants don't talk. The man is called Jacob. Being on the other side, just across the frontier, I should suggest, sir, that the family is political. I mean exiled." Can't bring in religion, thought Stephanus, might put him off, he's got to get his mind working ordinary. Not that I don't hold with Saints, gives a fair excuse for holidays. But that *Exercitia* takes him right off, in a trance-like. "You get in the old brocade dressing-gown," said Stephanus, "and I'll let you off the perruque."

V

Stephanus had insisted on the boots. He had from the first, he assured Antonius, satisfied himself. It was the Poor Brothers of the original Order and the reformed Grey Friars who went barefoot or in sandals. Antonius presumably knew this, as well as the various peculiarities of White and Black Friars. "There is no harm in the boots, fortunate the robe is long and the sleeves ample."

Brother Antonius insisted on knotting his own rope.

"Reckon, not all the young gentlemen will be let struggle through these drifts," said Stephanus. "If the place is blocked up, come back. I'll keep the fire going. I'll wait a bit, before I bolt the communication, in case you return." But Brother Antonius did not return, and after a suitable interval, Stephen muffled in his great-coat, made his way out through Petty Place, or *La Petite Place de la Chatelaine*, toward the steps to the lower city.

His master, blinded by snow and smothered in his hood, encountered another Friar. They were borne as by a tide-wave, toward the main door. Presumably it was the main door. It did not give, when aided by the wind, the two pushed against it. An impersonal presence, hooded and snowed over, his companion might be anybody. Suppose—

Antonius' supposition was dispelled by a fresh swirl of snow and a gruff assurance, issuing from the cowl, like the voice of one of the mastiffs of the Blessed Saint Bernard of Menthon. "Can't budge it, we'd best make for Benedict."

They managed to find shelter in the porch or portal of Saint Benedict on the Walls. "You was making for the Cloister, I should know that, you being punctual, but they ought to have warned you. Some young scamps came early, the foot-prints is blown over or I could have showed you. It's an old trick. They come before the Poor Brothers have shovelled the way through, then announce to their mates throughout, that it's blocked up. You must speak severe, they'll not dare keep away, both afternoon and morning." The school-porter pushed open the door.

"I advise you to get your breath. You can do your Paters in the Cathedral, while resting.

"Where am I," thought Antonius, "this is the side-chapel of Saint Benedict, but it's turned around."

It had happened before, but usually in his own bed. On two or three occasions, it had happened on a crowded thoroughfare. He could walk, forcing himself past familiar landmarks, but it was like walking backward. There was no particular ecstasy, exaltation or grace connected with the experiences, nor their opposite. He did not look upon them as warnings nor premonitions. He was facing the wrong way. Sometimes, waking with the wall on the wrong side of the bed, he would try to hold the sensation, hoping to analyse or explain it. He could say, he was dizzy with the wind, but he did not associate this state of mind with mere physical exhaustion. The distant altar would veer round in time, if he sat quietly.

The porter had ushered him through Benedict into the main Cathedral. The *Exercitia* must not be attempted until the mind was clear of associations. He could ask the porter why he had struggled to push in a door that he must have known swung outward. But did the main doors swing outward?

In time, when the Cathedral righted itself, he would walk the distance that he had already traversed outside in the snow. It was not much more than a stone's throw from the side-door that opened into Alchemists' Lane, to Antonius' own study. But Stephanus had said that the door or doors swung shut, "they slammed shut simultaneous" was his exact expression. If the doors had swung from within, Stephanus would not have noticed anything out of the way, one of the Cathedral attendants might have closed them. According to Stephanus, the doors had shut from outside.

But Antonius remembered how the half-door had swung inward. He had noted the circle marked in the fine drift, on the inner pavement.

It wasn't an ordinary swing-door, for it had clamped shut. Yet it opened inward, though with difficulty. He had never questioned the opening or the shutting of a house-door or Cathedral. He would have examined it and been spared the struggle the long way round, but he had noted from his study-window, that the Alchemists' Lane was swept almost clean of the snow that was banked, half its own height, against the door to the left of the High Altar, as he faced it.

The left of the High Altar? It was still the left of the High Altar? In his mind, his right hand rested on a sword-hilt. It was his way of distinguishing right from left hand, in these moments.

The Chapel of Saint Wenceslas, beyond Benedict, was on his right, as he sat there.

"Funny, him not on his knees," thought the porter. "No harm passing a word with him. It was candles, that last argument with sacristan. No acolyte would dare to blow out the candles, sacristan insisted. I wasn't accusing no acolyte, I told him, but you can't blame it on the wind, neither. If they're half burnt down, he said, you leave them and re-light them in the morning."

As if he didn't know that but he didn't want to be reproved, a school-porter was properly pedagogy. But Brother Anton was in orders, at least it was so whispered. He was putting in time with pedagogy. Sacristy hadn't so good as said so, but his manner with Brother Anton was official. Brother Anton was no ordinary Brother, not that his boots was so out of the way to notice, and pedagogy had special dispensation from the Abbot. Never knew who was superior, the Cathedral or the Castle. Saint Wenceslas was properly speaking, the Castle's chapel, but they had prelates officiating from time to time, in the Castle itself, a special private chapel, set with old glass, but none of them went in there. No one he ever heard of. Unless perhaps, Brother Anton, having affairs with the Abbot with those old books.

The porter approached Antonius. "Would it be taking liberties, do you think, sacristy not having come back yet, to put a taper to the lamp before Our Lady, and re-light what's left to Wenceslas?"

Wenceslas? It had happened before that an ordinary person in ordinary setting—No, this was the school-porter. Anyway, it had never happened, as far as he was aware, in a Cathedral. It could happen at any time, with anybody, but unless you were aware of its happening, it wasn't the Visitor. It was never a vision. Checking over it and back, maybe many years back, as with the first Saint-Germain in Venice, there was never a false step, never an inopportune moment, never an appearance that was exaggerated. It was only some small thing that related the incident to the Mystery, and that not remembered till long after, too late to verify. That is, if you wanted to verify it. You didn't, as a rule, want to verify the Mystery. If it was not true, it was better not to know it.

The first Saint-Germain was taken for himself and started the Mystery. That is, as far as the Mystery of Saint-Germain was concerned. It was left to him to explain it, which on occasion he would do, citing the Versailles story. In Venice, it was not himself, he countered lightly, but his nephew. It was, he considered, supreme tact, on the part of the Visitor. He did not trespass. He would leave the Saints their undisputed portion.

"There was confusion in the story," Stephanus had said, last night. Was it only last night? He had lived back through the story.

Had he nodded to the porter? What had he asked him? If he could light some candles? With an effort, Antonius turned his head toward the left, toward Ludmilla. He had knelt there after . . .

He had explained to Stephanus how his thoughts as well as his actions had been inconsistent. "It will be small things and little people will decide the issue," Stephanus had said. The formula for preparation before the *Exercitia* demanded an examination, not only of the past day's events but also of those small things, careless demeanour, forgetfulness. He had yesterday, for the first time in many months, renounced the *Exercitia*. He had, as Stephanus phrased it, broken the charm or the sequence of his hours and minutes. He could not, according to the rule, return to the *Exercitia*, until he had fully explained to himself the cause of his lapse. It was a long time ago that the porter had spoken to him. He had gone far but he was returning.

"Shall I light first and come back and fetch you?" said the porter. He considered the lay-brother. "But perhaps, on second thoughts, if it's convenient to you, you'll come with me, it will make it right with sacristan and you might explain the candles. It's a Mystery."

Mystery? Was the school-porter following the trail of his own thoughts? It was that way, sometimes, with Stephanus. But Stephen, his familiar, had spent years with him and was, in fact, a valuable asset to the Office. He had spoken to the porter briefly, on some half-dozen occasions, outside the usual greeting. The Visitor could manifest as anybody, he had just rehearsed his absolute conclusion. Then, why should this not be the Visitor? Antonius forced himself to face the Mystery. Was every man equally the Mystery?

"Staring like he was seeing something," thought the porter. "Didn't absolute give me permission to light the taper." He said, "I had that argument with sacristan. Perhaps you could inform me." It was the voice, it was the timbre of the voice, it wasn't the Visitor. The case or the cause would lose its poignancy if it merged too freely, and Antonius reminded himself, the Visitor never, at the moment of his visit, revealed himself completely. It was after the door shut on him that the question arose and with it, that singular lightness, assurance and benediction. "Was I perhaps taking liberties?" asked the porter.

He stood with his raw-hide sandals strapped over the lengths of sacking. There was always that talk of boots and sandals and how a lay-brother should walk. "Or shouldn't, being pedagogy and on special duty with Abbot with those old books," as Stephen had admonished him, when he first shuffled across the court-yard. He had left the matter of bearing and deportment to Stephen, who said after some discreet gossip in the nieghborhood, that his master best be natural, he was pedagogy and half-way to the Castle. No, the Visitor would never wear raw-hide sandals strapped over uneven strips of sacking. But immediately, Antonius reminded himself of Our Lord's Visit.

"It's not in my province," said the porter, "in the manner of speaking. I could tell sacristy you was doing your Paters in the chapel. He wouldn't ask who done it, you being official with the Abbot, and sacristy having that respect for learning." Still he stood like an image at a gateway, holding a light.

From an infinite distance, Antonius heard his own voice. "There are regulations, we know—but the Poor Brothers—"

"—have Saint Francis," said the porter. What did he mean by that? Did he mean Saint Francis would reward them and the thought of Francis? Antonius could not think of Francis. What did he want, standing with the sacking bulging under the straps of the old sandals? What was it that he wanted? For the first time, Antonius doubted his vocation. He could not go on with books, with infinite subtleties, with court and papal intrigues.

VI

The Cathedral had veered round and Antonius with it. He had yet to catch the moment of transition. It always happened this way. He had tried in his own room, to prolong the sensation, in order to understand it, but he had no control over it. It was baffling but not always unpleasant. No doubt, others had had the same experience, but he had never spoken of it. He followed the porter along the side-aisle to the chapel.

Suppose the door were fastened. He remembered having examined the door for the scenes of the Saint wrought on it. But from which side? Was he in the chapel or outside? It was important to remember. The chapel-door was open. Was the door always open? He would examine it to see if it opened both ways, and if it was caught or clamped back. The Cathedral itself did not seem darker, though grown in proportion. Far off, the lamp before Our Lady, glowed like a red coal.

The taper itself as the porter held it in the door-frame, seemed brighter against the darkness.

There were no windows. It was a jewel-box or rather a box, set with its own jewels, uncut jasper, onyx? Antonius had not yet assessed the treasure of Saint Wenceslas.

It seemed warmer here than outside. Incense still hung in the small room. It was not unduly small, but compared with the distance and lofty proportion of the great Cathedral, they were in person, awaiting private audience, in an ante-chamber. The taper seemed to steady itself, as if they had come out of the wind.

"Would you think," said the porter, "they could blow out? There's not a breath of wind in this place." He moved the length of the low-set reliquary. "It's not a proper altar, not like the High, or yet Benedict or Ludmilla. Could I set the taper to the candles?" The candles were set in formation, on the wrought-iron frame that stood on the floor. "Shaped like candelabra, I always think, not like the other candle-stands in the Cathedral."

The porter thought, funny, he doesn't give permission nor not give it. I always wanted to light a whole sconce of candles, but I never was in the Palace and here, a few pence for Our Lady was all I could rightly offer.

The porter said, "I've lighted a penny-dip to Our Lady on occasion, but I never had a taper for a whole row. I always thought, if I had one wish and wished it sudden, it would be to light a row of candles."

He thought, what is the matter with the Brother, if he is a brother, lay or otherwise, though we're not supposed to question, even in our thought, authority. Never got close to a Cardinal, nor even the abbot, but if I was to imagine what one might be—

"What is it that you wanted to ask me?" said Antonius.

"It's what I was saying," said the porter. "We were this side, sacristan and me, he was waiting to lock up, though there's always one door open, according to the old rule. Sacristan remarked on your going by the main door. We went over to Ludmilla, when you left it. The lights from Wenceslas shone out, like it was Candlemas itself. Then, they went out."

There were more stones than Antonius thought possible. He had thought the blue margin was marble. It was lapis.

Staring at the wall, thought the porter. He turned his head. "That's Charles," he said. "You don't notice only sometimes, when he catches fire from the candles." He held the taper steady. "The stone was his, before he wore the iron-crown. It came to Wenceslas because of Christmas." Antonius recalled the legend of Charlemagne's investiture at Rome on Christmas day—800? He believed Wenceslas came later. It was one of his duties to revise or compare the old chronicles. He only saw the surface of an uneven dark stone. So it was an uncut ruby. He was not really looking at the stones. "Who blew out the candles?" he said.

The porter said, "For the sake of argument, when we was catching our breath, I suggested some acolytes. I knew as well as sacristy, the acolytes had gone off and anyway, they wouldn't dare go in there. He said, while we were making our way to Benedict, where he had left his lantern, the wind did it. I waited outside Wenceslas."

"You found everything in order?" Antonius heard himself speaking as if to one of the older school-boys.

"Wenceslas is always in order," said the porter, "but if anything, it was more than usual ordered."

Antonius turned and paced the length of the stone floor. He thought, this must be part of the original foundation. He remembered last night's talk with Stephanus, of causeways and underground entrances. The thought was irreverent. He could not bear to watch the porter light the candles. The wind must have got into his eyes. He brushed his sleeve across them. He turned round. The porter was still waiting.

Was this the reason for his coming to Prague? The others faded—the Queen, de Rohan, that rogue Balsamo, first announced to him by a palace lackey, "by your leave, sir, the Count Alessandro Di Cagliostro." He had swallowed his pride, as had de Rohan who allowed his name and prestige to be involved in a sordid scandal. Saint-Germain had not been involved in the affair of the stolen diamonds, but worse, Balsamo had created the impression at Versailles that he was a companion, an occultist and magician, one of his own sort, and working with him. No man of the world would credit Cardinal de Rohan with so crude a gesture, as the open presentation of a diamond necklace to his mistress, and that lady, the Queen of France. Saint-Germain had not the satisfaction of knowing that his equals would repudiate his association with the so-called Cagliostro.

Was it then, a sort of spiritual pride, his assumption that the Visitor was stamped with the hallmarks of nobility? It had been so, at least, in his case, though the distinction was so subtle, it might seem to escape the outer, though never the inner vision. But the Visit was never a vision; he had always reasoned, as the porter had just now, "if anything, it was more than usual ordered."

Was everything so ordered, that he, Antoine-Louis, Chevalier of France and Count of Saint-Germain, should be sent here precisely to give permission to this—he discarded the phrase *poor hind*, but his mind had touched it. Who was he to give permission?

Antonius said to the school-porter, "Who am I to give you permission to light the candles?"

The porter lowered the taper. He had been holding it like a flambeau. "I did ask you," he muttered.

"And who am I that you should ask me?" The words rang with authority. The porter misunderstood them.

"You having affairs with the Abbot, sorting over the old parchments—" said the porter.

"What right does that give me?" said Antonius.

"The right of learning," said the porter, "that sacristan has such respect for, he wouldn't question."

"Question what and who?" said Antonius.

"The candles being lighted. It's supposed to be respectful to re-light if for some reason, which don't often happen, they goes out."

"But we don't yet know why they went out," said Antonius.

He did know why they went out. *I always thought if I had one wish and wished it sudden, it would be to light a row of candles.*

It was no Mystery. It was ordered, it could be explained exactly. It was part of a Plan, so subtly presented, yet so clearly that you could not miss its meaning.

"Who offered the candles," said Antonius, "do you know that?"

"Most likely the lady who was always in the chapel. Not that we discuss the boxes, but sacristan thought it proper, seeing thieves might have been in, to count the candle-money. There was her usual gold-piece."

So she was part of the Plan.

"Why are you waiting?" said Antonius.

"I thought it being Advent and Wenceslas being Christmas, you might—"

Was he handing the taper to him? No, in God's name—

"You witnessed the Mystery," said Antonius, "Our Lady and Saint Wenceslas chose you to light the candles."

Still he stood there.

"Light the candles," said Antonius. He sank to his knees.

VII

"Nobody must disturb him," said the porter.

"Did he so order?" said sacristan. "I was told special by the messenger, that the Abbot required him in the library. There's no school afternoon nor morning. He'd best go down the way messenger came up, the steps are open below Benedict and the snow blown off the fortress. You're pedagogy, you inform him."

Sacristan hugged his elbows under his long sleeves. Cold as a vault, he thought, I never felt it colder. He asked, "Is he in one of those Meditations? He might freeze to death, in there in Wenceslas."

"It isn't so cold," said the porter, "with the candles."

"He lit the candles, left there?"

"I handed the taper to him—being only the frame, he ordered me to do it."

"Did you mention how thieves might have been in or someone blew out the candles?"

"I told him you and me, over by Ludmilla, saw them go out. No one could blow out all that row, in one breath."

"I said it was the wind," said sacristan.

"The taper burned straight, so did the candles. There's no wind there in Wenceslas."

"Last night, the Alley door blew shut. I noticed on my rounds, after you left. I never knew it to blow shut. It's the one door left open, according to the old foundation Law, but why the Founder, or whoever it was, made it that door, I don't know. It's a haunt of thieves and cut-throats, is that Alley."

"Why did they lodge him there, then?"

"He's not properly, the Alley. That end belongs rightly, to the outer cloister. Alchemists, they called them."

"Your front door was locked, we couldn't get in, but Benedict was open, so I knew you had been. I looked about, because of last night, then went out, thinking to warn him the school-entrance was blocked. We were fair blown into Benedict, fortunate it was open. Aren't you unlocking the front?"

"That's left to my discretion, when it's drifted. Without disturbing his devotion, I could give him a hint." Sacristan was an adept in these matters. He slipped into the sanctuary before the porter realized his intention. Antonius opened his eyes.

It was as he had expected. It had happened before. It was usually an attendant or a server at the altar, on some trivial business, who recalled him. It was the drawing of a curtain, the subdued shuffling of sandals, the opening of a poor-box, the placing in the tray of the fresh candles.

The attendant passed before the reliquary, paused on the far side, glanced at the empty candle-tray, returned, faced the relique, genuflected and went out.

The candles were still burning. He would watch them go out. They were almost level with the holders. But no, they would never go out. "And forgive us our sins as we forgive those who have wronged us," said Antonius. Fresh jewels were lighted, as he stared above the level low row of candles. He would be caught back. He rose to his feet, crossed himself and left the chapel. The porter was waiting for him.

"A messenger, sacristy just told me, from the Castle asks special for you. The steps is open below Benedict, and the snow's blown off the fortress. There's no school."

Antonius turned automatically. He must get out at once, and let the wind and snow recall him. "Walks soldier-like," thought the porter, "wished he had spoke a word to me, after all that that happened. I'll wait till sacristy comes back from looking at that side-door, might ask him—" But Antonius had turned round.

His coming seemed more measured than his going. Antonius spoke as if with difficulty, "The—the school—"

"It's shut for the day, it was sacristy that said that the Abbot asked you special—"

"You will keep up the school-fire as usual," said Antonius, "and thank you."

What had happened? The porter watched Antonius walk soldier-like a second time, to Benedict. "He bowed to me," said the porter. He spoke the words under his breath, yet he spoke them, as if the speaking of them gave them reality. No one must ever know that. As a matter of fact, no one would believe you if you told them.

Would anyone believe about the candles? At least, sacristy would discuss the matter, not the Mystery proper but the lady and why she didn't genuflect and why she didn't leave her gold-piece for Anthony's Bread, sometimes, but always in the candle-box though she didn't always have the candles. There was much to be talked over. He turned his head, there was a shadow like a velvet curtain over the door of Wenceslas. The candles had gone out.

"It must be banked with snow, outside. He went off?" said sacristan.

"He went just before the candles," said the porter.

"I'll clear the stand and put fresh candles in the tray later. What are you waiting for?" said sacristan.

"Can't seem like I could move. Had we best see if the wicks are smoking?" said the porter.

"You leave all that be," said sacristan. "You'll freeze if you stand there. I couldn't be more cold, not in a vault, I couldn't."

The porter was recalled, even as Antonius had been. He said, "He ordered the school-fire to be kept up. We can sit there all day."

VIII

"We can make up for last night," said Elizabeth, "unless we go out."

"We can't expect saddle-horses to plough through these drifts."

"I didn't mean the sleigh. What fun it would be to ride through the woods—could we?"

"Of course not. And we can't stay here forever and until I get permission from the library—"

"You think you'll get it?"

"Jacobus says he thinks so. They were never on unfriendly terms, the Tower and the Castle. It was only our heresy."

"I'll never understand it," said Elizabeth. "The Protestant Court at Dresden managed a case against poor grandpappa, because he said *Aves*, or they said he said them, and worshipped Angels. I've written it down somewhere."

"Don't begin looking out your notes. It's hopeless. We've got to present the story from another angle. We've had the worthies and their long-winded records, and the Missions with their formal reports. But I feel there's something in between the scandals of the pamphleteers and the conventional tributes of the Missions and the Brethren. I feel there's something lost, that our grandfather once had. I felt it suddenly, when Goethe asked to see the *arcana*, and actually I had never thought of secret records. Elizabeth, I must tell you—I seem to have reserved my confession for today. I might have told you sooner. You remember the legend of our grandfather writing letters to his Friend, the Saviour? I asked my mother about it, and your mother, my Aunt Benigna. Their answers did not satisfy me. They were speaking to a child."

"I stopped asking too," said Elizabeth de Watteville. "It was how we came together, children, finding there was something that they wouldn't tell us. And when we were older, there were rational, reasoned answers and that was, if possible, still worse."

"The records weren't really dusty. It was the meticulous order and arrangement of them that depressed me. I think Bishop Spangenberg must have done them. Then, I began unfastening the old tapes wrapped round the letters, and refastening them. I don't know why. I think I felt sorry and ashamed to realize how the things had lain there, beautifully arranged in the old library, in boxes and boxed shelves, out of the dust. But there was a feeling that no one had touched them for years.

"I do not mean the family's private letters. I knew Christian Renatus' letters, especially those written from London just before his death, almost by heart—and Benigna's from Philadelphia and from Bethlehem. I had read of course, as you had, studied and tried to annotate the various editions of the Zinzendorf sermons and poems, with the few hymns of Christian Renatus and his mother. I knew I would be lost if I started sorting out the letters, but I went on unfastening and refastening the faded blue strips of tape or ribbon binding. It seemed all I could do.

"There was a card, attached to each bundle, with the date and name and place.

"There was no date or name on the last bundle that I picked up, but these words, *destroy when read*."

Elizabeth held up her tapestry. "Do you like my Saint Hubertus?" she said.

"You know I like it," said Henry Dohna, "you aren't listening."

"Dear Anna Charity started it," said Elizabeth, "our second grandmamma."

"But this is serious."

"So is my tapestry."

"I thought I'd leave the letters where Goethe would find them."

"Did you leave them?"

"Of course not. They're upstairs in my portfolio. If we read them, we must destroy them. Shall we read them?"

"No," said Elizabeth de Watteville.

"Do you think someone else read them or started to read them—or did the last discoverer shun the responsibility altogether, as we seem likely to do?"

"You think grandpappa wrote them?"

"The three words are unmistakably the writing of the *Ordinarius Fratrum*, our *Ancien Évêque des Frères*."

"But why did you think that Goethe should have the letters?"

"If it had not been for his asking of *Arcana* I should not have troubled to go through the boxes. The printed records are full of curious incidents, but we were brought up in that atmosphere and listened to endless tales of travel and adventure. It was all, in a sense, new to Goethe and he saw it differently. He asked me why it was so particularly stated that our grandfather became acquainted with Christian David at the house of the Master of the Horse in Schweinitz, when the story of Christian David's flight from Moravia across the border is so well known. Our grandfather was in Dresden, at the time. But he returned soon after and helped establish the community. You remember how Pastor Rothe prevailed on the steward to allow the refugees to remain on the estate. The Countess Gersdorf (our grandfather's grandmother) was in charge then. Our grandfather was only twenty-two at the time."

"Why not just write the story?"

"It is not easy to write the story and there are the ponderous records, besides all the old letters and bundles of legal documents. I don't think I should even have thought of writing it, if it had not been for Goethe. He's been working on his Faust since he was twenty."

"What's Faust got to do with the *Ordinarius*?"

"That's what I began to ask myself. I opened my new note-book with the question."

"It's a literary subject—or was there really a real Faust?"

"There's Dr Faustus, the magician. I think he's a legend like the Student of Prague. You remember, they both sold their souls."

"The student sold his shadow, I think."

"It's the same story, but in some way that I can't explain exactly, it's as if Zinzendorf, our excellent *Ordinarius*, had sold his soul, but bargained in some way (and I don't know what I'm saying) with our Saviour."

"Can you bargain with God?"

"I should think so. The incidents are too extravagant, the boat just not sinking because our grandfather calmly informed the Captain that he would speak to his Friend about it, those incredible encounters with the Indians. Why did the so-called Six Nations make a pact with him and give him that bead-belt? That time in Russia, when the prison-doors were opened—it's fantastic."

"You must not worry, Henri. Read the letters if you want to."

How did she know he was worried? He looked round the room. He had beaten his way past the Cathedral, this morning, and the Fortress, in order to get his bearings. Of course, Jacob could escort him to the Castle, if the letter were forthcoming, but he had wanted first to find his way there alone. It was the letter. If they refused him permission to look over their archives, he and Elizabeth could go home. Had he been wrong to bring her?

"It was an exhausting journey. You should have rested afterwards, but you said you wanted to explore the country with me. When Maria told me this morning that she wasn't letting you get up for lunch, I wondered if I had been inconsiderate."

Elizabeth laid aside her sewing. "I am very happy," she said.

"Don't put down your threads, Elizabeth. They are such lovely colours. I found peace with the de Wattevilles, at the Lord's Watch, last summer. I went there to rest."

"You are over-conscientious, Henri. Your father and your grandfather were so ambitious for you."

"I don't think that I have disappointed them, but affairs of the world and state are not my whole life. I wanted to carry on a little of our grandfather's tradition. He was a diplomat of the highest order, but I don't think any of the community at Herrnhut made me feel secure. I mean, there wasn't one of them to whom I could say, there is danger."

"There is danger." She did not ask the question, she simply repeated his words.

"There was something missing. Not that the de Wattevilles, your father and our uncle Frederick aren't astute and conscientious. They are that. But there is a certain *worldliness* (that may seem a strange word to use in this connection) missing.

"Our grandfather was a man of the world. He was in the world and out of it, at the same time. I do not doubt the sincerity of the present Bishops. They just lack something. I felt it suddenly, when Goethe began to question me. They don't ask questions. The Mystery must be re-stated."

"Was it ever really stated?"

"It was implicit in their attitude, their obedience. They obeyed something. They are reputed to have drawn lots, on various occasions, then they dropped all that, I imagine soon after our grandfather's death. As I say, I can't find out anything. I mean, I can't find out *why* they did it."

"There's piety and conscience—"

"You know we are speaking of something else, Elizabeth."

She knew that.

Elizabeth de Watteville said, "I feel I have found it, the answer, the Mystery, when I light the candles in the chapel of Saint Wenceslas."

"You light candles? My dear Elizabeth—"
"Shouldn't I?"
"I don't think so."
"Well, I do it when there's no one about. I don't think anybody notices."
"What about the fellow who opened the door?"

The wind was howling from the river into the narrow passage of the Street of the Alchemists.

"It happened then," said Elizabeth de Watteville.

It had happened before. It had not happened often.

"I know that you are worried, Henri. We were all worried at Herrnhut. You are right about papa and Uncle Frederick. They do not seem to care about the state of the world. The Lord's Watch will maintain them. But their hearts are broken."

She was thinking of Bethlehem.

"It is a question of loyalties. They did not wish to pronounce judgment on the American Revolution. It was the Crown of England that first sanctioned the renewed Brotherhood, the *Jednota* or the *Unitas*. There could be no political criticism of Bethlehem, though certain aspersions were cast on them in the beginning, for so-called Tory sympathies. But the town was concerned with other matters. General Washington made it his headquarters, as you know, and the young Marquis de Lafayette was nursed there. In fact the whole town and its resources were turned over. 'The whole town is still a hospital,' mamma wrote on her last trip, four years ago. Now, that war is over and there remain, they write us, only certain formalities. They expect that General Washington will be the first president of the new Republic.

"But you know all this, Henri. I review it to give myself a sense of direction or of definition. You see, Henri, I can be serious. I do not want to be too serious.

"But I have written it down here."

The loose folder was lying on the table, at her elbow.

"It is a tapestry. At least, we have all the threads even if the picture is not yet clear. It is like Anna Charity's gift to me. I mean, Anna Nitschmann von Zinzendorf's." She picked up the folder.

"Do not read your notes, Elizabeth. Tell me what you remember."

"I don't remember—only Comenius, because of his portrait in the library, with his robe and cross. I don't know his date but I can find it."

"No, I only want you to remember." He took the folder from her.

"I remember his grandson, Jablonsky, received the episcopate of the lost Church from him—the Church within the Church, as our grandfather called it. Jablonsky conferred it on David Nitschmann. I do remember 1722, the year they crossed the frontier from Bohemia and found shelter at Berthelsdorf. David Nitschmann was one of Christian David's party. I do remember 1700, the year grandpappa was born.

"I suppose he was really born the last year of the old century, but at any rate, he brought in the seven or the seventeen.

"They thought so much would come of their eighteenth century, and now, as the sands run low, we are defeated.

"No, not defeated, but in some way deflected from the Plan, the mysterious Plan of a *Jednota*, a unity, a world-unity without war.

"They had been broken in Europe, partitioned and reformed by the religious wars of the seventeenth century, Comenius' century—the Thirty Years War.

"The war began in Bohemia, but where, when and why, I don't know. If you hand back my folder to me, I will give you the dates."

"I have told you that I do not want the dates, Elizabeth. I want something that is timeless. Do you remember last night, talking of Theodora of Castell? I mean, do you remember, when you spoke of the wind catching her lace-scarf? You said, 'it happened two hours ago, it happened two hundred years ago. It gave me a clue.'"

"I felt I was Theodora. That was the clue, partly. If you love people, you live back into their lives. I told you I was remembering the Winter Queen, in the Cathedral. I couldn't enter into her soul, but I could understand her daughter, Elizabeth of Bohemia, Abbess of Herford. I did question, just for a moment, my right to the candles. Then, I said I was lighting them for Elizabeth of Bohemia. Well, we have the family records. We are related to Bohemia."

"George Podiebrad became king of Bohemia, in 1458."

"I thought you said no dates, Henri. The important thing was that he protected Gregory, Archbishop of the old Bohemian party and established him, and the brethren from Prague, on his estates in north-east Bohemia. I mean, the important thing to us is that our grandfather repeated the same pattern, when he welcomed Christian David, David Nitschmann and the little band of refugees, in 1722, at Berthelsdorf.

"I suppose that's what I mean when I say we have all the threads—you and

I together. We have established the facts but there is an emotional clue that is more important. When you get that, you have everything.

"The emotions remain the same, though the dates differ.

"That is what I meant by my clue.

"That is why I try not to worry about Bethlehem, their little City of God.

"David Nitschmann was the official founder, though grandpappa stood sponsor and named it.

"You remember?"

"I was looking over those notes last night."

"Through Father Nitschmann, the foundation inherited the *Jednota*, by way of Jablonsky, Comenius' own grandson. We are step-grandchildren of Anna Charity, Father Nitschmann's daughter, the second Countess von Zinzendorf. Are we step-grandchildren of the foundation?"

"But I don't understand exactly what you mean, when you say you felt you were Theodora?"

"It's something different. It has to do with Bohemia. We are real grandchildren in that instance. Through our own grandmother, the threads run back. It was a long time ago. I mean, I felt in the Cathedral, that Theodora must have loved our grandfather. That is why I said, I felt like Theodora."

Had she said this or only thought it? Henry Dohna was gazing into the fire.

What had she said? She had been thinking out loud. What had she been thinking?

She rolled up her tapestry and unrolled it, again, waiting for Henry Dohna to look up.

Part II

IX

"You take your avocation too seriously," said Cardinal de Rohan. "Why should you go back?"

"It is a question of expediency. The Row is full of faces. The *Grape Cluster* alone could disseminate a rumour that might be the undoing of poor Brother Anton. There is the Cathedral as well. Anton is proverbially punctual."

"But you said there was no school."

"Then, where was Anton? He was sent for, presumably, by the Abbot. Those hours are watched, too. Sacristan had directed him, by way of the school-porter to the steps of Benedict. That was some time ago. I cannot say that I was surprised to see you, but in spite of your information, your logic, your—your offer, I must stay here."

"I have told you it is useless. The affair is already ordered. If you scorn the Hat, there is still the Chair—"

"I am out of practice. My excellent Stephanus has exceeded his orders as to 'gentlemanly bearing,' as he calls it, when I am the Embassy side of the Row. But my brain, except for occasional bouts with the Abbot over medieval Latin, has lost cunning. I mean, wit, repartee, the rapier-point, *au fil de l'epée*, Versailles."

"It is you who turn ironic. And there is another vista. My dear Antoine-Louis and my respected Louis-Antoine, it was never *disproved* that the father of the child—"

"You are drunk, de Rohan—"

"—born at Lentmeritz in Bohemia—"

"Village gossips and small parishes—"

"We have the records. And if we hadn't, we could easily procure them. You are the nearest Louis to the last Louis—"

"There is the Dauphin—"

"Poor child, do not tempt me to indecency, Louis, there is still France."

"And the King—"

"He was never, as you know, mentally or biologically intended—"

"There is—"

"Do not argue about 'Toinette. You remember, that was my province and my problem."

"I said, I was not surprised to see you, when I was ushered into the apartment this morning. Was it only this morning? I was not surprised to see you because at that moment, nothing could surprise me. I had had weighty argument with Stephanus, last night. Was it only last night? I slept little. Blinded by snow and in a half-dream, I felt finally, in the chapel of Saint Wenceslas, I had the answer. The answer, that is, that Antonius, *frater et praeceptor*, was sent here to discover—to decipher. I mean, the alignment or the *media* that was to join the two together. I speak now of the Organisation, as we planned it. Was it your idea or did it originate with the Holy Father? Not this one. It went back to 1118—am I right? There were nine of them, Geoffrey de Saint-Omer and Hugh de Payens were instrumental in the secret alliance with Constantinople—the Greek church. Forgive me for simplicity. You, my Superior, know all the transmutations. Our circle, if I may so call it, did finally justify our Leader Loyola's precept, 'the end justifies the means.' Cardinal de Rohan did not scorn the somewhat undignified role assigned to him by the Fraternity. Nor did the Count of Saint-Germain. We worked together. How we accomplished it is to me still a wonder. Initiated into the highest degree of Knights of Asia, Royal Priests and so on, we attained further—honours. The symbolic bridge of the Knight of the East or Sword was constructed. And we crossed it."

"I told you, your work here is finished."

"How can that be, if as you inform me, Rome has ordered its prelates and more valuable adherents out of Paris?"

"We rehearsed all that this morning, before the interruption by the Abbot and his exemplary servants. The meal was excellent, the wine could not be improved on—it was tactful to leave the flagons on the table. Does he always refer to your outer habit as a great-coat?"

"I cannot remember. It is not always taken from me. No doubt, it is as Stephen remarks to me frequently, 'fortunate that you can dress proper under the sackcloth.'"

"The sackcloth is no longer necessary. A messenger can inform Stephen to collect your belongings. You will lodge here. That is, in the event of this storm continuing. Do you not see the lemon-groves of Tuscany, further, the first almond-flower of the Campagnia? Louis, my dear son, I will permit a slight detour. You shall stop in Venice."

"I do not think that Venice calls me. My experience there was too—ephemeral. I say ephemeral because I have no word or phrase to support my feeling. Did I tell you of it? I must have told Stephanus, or he listened to delirium, while I raved in a fever. I do not know how the fever took me. I only know that in Venice I was seen where I was not. Now, I have said it clearly. And why do I say it to you now, who have never before been able to find words for it? I say it because, as you just remarked, the Abbot's service or the servants left nothing to the imagination—the wine was excellent. I confess that I was hungry. But though Stephen keeps me supplied with delicacies from the market, my peculiar status forbids too much festivity. The Count maintains, he informs the quarter, a strict incognito. The Count, that is, of Saint-Germain."

"This Bohemia," de Rohan cherished his goblet, then turned it slowly, seeming to watch reflections from the embers, "I repeat, leaves nothing to the imagination."

"That is what I discovered," said Saint-Germain. "But I must go back. I must plot a curve—the door swung inward. Did I tell you, snow had drifted on the pavement?"

"I have never known you to lose your head, Louis, even at our most flagrant Palace orgies."

"This Bohemia is more potent than the Chateau Saint-Germain that Stephen insisted on bringing with us. Besides, your story of a coming Revolution has unnerved me. How can it be prevented?"

"It can not be prevented. Our excellent Balsamo, Acharat or Cagliostro, had instructions from Medina. Althotas arranged everything. And by the way, you attained the final—honours. Who is Althotas?"

"My Preceptor, my Superior, Cardinal de Rohan knows as much of the inner—teaching, as I do."

"I know what you have told me. The records are in order. There is only the final checking-up to be done, then my formal presentation at the Vatican. The list, the findings, the description of the—well, Sanctum, the various branches of the *franc-maçons*, the expressed (if secret) intention will be sufficient, I have been formally promised, to re-instate the Jesuits. Loyola had intended this from the beginning. It was only a question of suppressing the lower orders, of finally re-forming on the Praetorian level, the suppressed, authentic Order of the Templars."

"Was it ever actually proved that after disbanding the Order in 1312, Clement V perished miserably?"

"It is the tradition that he and Philip the Fair both died mysteriously. Perhaps history disproves this. Another Clement, XIV if I am not mistaken, suppressed the Jesuits—1773, am I right?"

"Fifteen years ago. It is not a long time to wait."

"After the Revolution, the Society will be re-established."

"After the Revolution—"

"Yes, Louis, I am not as easy in this arm-chair as you might imagine. I must get the list to Rome immediately. Our contribution would lose its value if the storm broke before our information accurately foretold its coming."

"But you say Rome has ordered its prelates to leave Paris?"

"The inner Office had received a personal messenger from Cardinal de Rohan. But the actual papers must be presented for the coming prosecutions. The Abbot's clerk left ink and paper on the desk, behind your shoulder. I recommend a brief interlude. We shall reward ourselves with our Bohemia, after Paris. Ah—he renewed the flagon. I thought ours was the last one. We need no tedious interruption. And this wine-glass and the platter, left there on the table—where did the fruit come from? Rome could not have served us better. Is your brain yet unfrozen? You were right to keep the practice of the *Exercitia*, but from what you told me this morning, I fear you have overdone it. You yourself are frozen. I am not speaking of the weather."

"On the contrary, I am flaming with Bohemia."

"The ruby glass—the red wine—"

"I am not fit to check the list. This transition is too sudden. De Rohan, believe me, I will serve France."

It was fortunate, or perhaps unfortunate, that at this moment, a lackey entered to replenish the fire.

•

"Well, then, the storm still rages," said de Rohan. "Fatigue overtakes me. Perhaps it is as well that I stay here to-night. And what do you know of the Ambassador you say lodges in your Row?"

"I am surprised to learn that he got through. But Stephen had reported from conversation with a valet that they were on the way. That was last night. And our apartment is not technically the Row. There is a fine distinction. The

Row, so-called, is the old alchemists' headquarters. Anton's study, though adjoining, is part of the original cloister. I wish I could show it to you. It is well thought out, though Stephen constantly reminds me that 'you can never be too careful.'"

"I would keep you here, Louis. This room is like a red rose."

"I would swoon into it, if I stayed longer. Let me recall the valet. He will help you to bed."

"Louis, my mind, thanks to my own past habit and the *Exercitia*, runs a dart through me. We must do the list first."

"Your mind may be a drawn sword, my own wanders."

"You were our example, always."

"'You can never be too careful,' Stephen warned me. But I was careless. It was a mistake to step aside and lift the curtain for her."

"Louis," said de Rohan, ignoring this last statement, "your Stephen may be right. Balsamo has accomplices in every quarter. He is a Sicilian." The Cardinal was fumbling with his satchel. "These are the points, trimmed as we last used them." He laid a cluster of goose-quills on the table. "This is not Loyola speaking. The delay is dangerous. They will know that I left Paris. Your Ambassador may have fresh news. It is you who have confused me."

"My own state of mind has been abnormal since I left Paris. I could, I did completely shut out the problem. Can one live in two hermetically sealed compartments? I succeeded. But you recall the question—was it honourable? It was not honest. I confess I felt no personal degradation. Curiosity held me and the thought that, always, I was serving the Fraternity. I cannot give the pass-words that you asked of me this morning. I have forgotten them. I must go back. I thought I was absolved from further contact with the—the magus, when I came here to Prague. It was blackness, unutterable and damnable."

"The end justifies—"

De Rohan was examining the papers in his satchel. "You can at least sign the original inditement. But I forgot this."

He laid a letter by the goose-quills on the table.

"It has been opened," said de Rohan, "the Abbot discussed it with me, while I was waiting for you. A certain Henry—Count, I gather—Dohna wishes access to the records."

It seemed a strange moment for so trivial a business. Why did the Cardinal forget the letter, and why did he remember it? It was de Rohan, it seemed now to Antonius, who was marking time. He seemed confident enough this morning. It was the way he said of Balsamo, he is a Sicilian. It is true the oaths they took at Acharat's so-called initiations, were extravagant to a degree and blasphemous. But they had each other to confide in, and their own security and absolution. If they believed in Loyola and the Order, if they were working to re-establish Loyola's suppressed Society of Jesus, then the broken vows were nothing. Were they nothing?

De Rohan was exhausted. He had no doubt, spent himself even before leaving Paris. For a moment, he had hinted at a truce. There was a letter. It had already been opened. For some reason, the Abbot was asking him to assist a visitor, perhaps on the old scripts that the usual clerks could not decipher. But why should the Abbot discuss the matter with de Rohan? Perhaps this Dohna—

Antonius unfolded the letter. "The Tower, House of Köstriz," he read.

X

Antonius laid the open letter on the table, unread, "If the Ambassador (the only one in our quarter) came from Paris, why did Stephen tell me that the valet told him they were from Vienna or were going to Vienna?"

"No doubt the valet had instructions," said de Rohan.

"If, as you say, this letter is from a certain Count Dohna, why did Stephen tell me the present resident of The Tower is a certain lady—a—a de Watteville?"

"If you read the letter you will perhaps find the answer."

"Why—again—I am speaking to myself, as in preliminary to the *Exercitia*—did the Abbot discuss with Cardinal de Rohan, the contents of a letter, presumably from a stranger, and in the face of astounding revelation, world-shattering news that the Cardinal had already broken to him in his capacity of ecclesiastical *liaison*-officer with the Castle? Or was the letter read first?"

"The Abbot is a diplomat and my host. He realised my anxiety. He may have produced the letter and discussed it in order to ease the tension. In any case, the letter is for you."

Count Dohna. The Tower, House of Köstriz. *Viduae et Virgines*. Was she a widow or had she never married?

If he read the letter, he would know this, or he would not know this. Was Count Dohna—he did not wait to ask himself preliminary questions—her husband?

He could have delayed this question that he put to himself. He could have waited. His mind was trained to watch, to wait, to assemble particulars, to match like a trained worker in mosaic, the various fragments. It was not like him to force a question, to deal himself a stab—almost, you might say, a stab in the dark and mortal. Antonius and Saint-Germain were on more subtle terms with one another, as he himself had phrased it, *au fil de l'epée*.

"I have been trying out a question. I thought you might give the answer. Something that would say *yes*, or something that would say *no*. When I said, 'Did I tell you snow had drifted on the pavement?,' you countered or riposted with the remark that I had lost my head, or that you had never known me to lose my head, even at our most flagrant Palace orgies. When I went on with it, 'It was a mistake to step aside and lift the curtain for her,' you ignored this altogether. It is a Lady. I have followed her—thoughts almost, in the Chapel of Saint Wenceslas, I have never spoken to her. The name is de Watteville. She is apparently related to Köstriz or the House of Köstriz. She is staying at the Tower."

"There is a lady staying at The Tower, the Abbot told me, a cousin or a sister of Count Dohna."

"A lackey is always in attendance. He waits for her, after her devotions, at the *Grape Cluster*. They call him Schweinitz."

"That may be. His mistress is a Countess von Schweinitz."

"His mistress—"

"The lady that we speak of. They imagine, for some reason, that their identities are unknown. An innocent escapade, I should imagine."

"Köstriz or as Stephen says 'whatever his name is,' is in Vienna."

"Your Ambassador is not going to Vienna. He will return to England."

"Is this prophecy?"

"It is what the Abbot told me."

"He knows everything?"

"Our choice of Prague as our last stronghold, has been fully justified."

"Von Schweinitz—"

"She is a widow."

"Why must you tell me this? Stephanus—"

"Louis, you are still the impressionable youth, I first knew, straight from your life of errantry in the forest. We fostered that, as well as the Venetian legend. We waited. You have not failed us. A mythical Prince, Chevalier, at last to save France."

"The legend has been degraded, the source poisoned by Cagliostro and the association of Saint-Germain with the company of Saint-Jakin. The legends contradict one another."

"You are safe with us, Louis. Saint-Jakin and the rest will be forgotten. Rome will be ready with acclamation. By the way, why don't you read your letter?"

"Why do you say that it is my letter?"

"Apparently, it is addressed," de Rohan leaned forward and turned over the folded square of paper, "to the Keeper of the Archives. You are, technically, assistant to the Abbot. Shall I read this:

Most esteemed etcetera, etcetera,

I would deem it a great favour if your secretary would assist me in certain researches. I have reason to believe that there is material, unpublished and so far unprocurable, concerning the early affiliation of my grandfather, the late Count Zinzendorf, with a certain Father de la Tour. There was also a connection at one time, with the Oratory of the Premonstrants. The names Simon d'Albizi and Father Anthony Dionysius have also been recorded.

Yours etcetera, etcetera."

De Rohan laid down the letter.

"I know nothing of this Zinzendorf," said Antonius.

"His properties in Austria were confiscated because of Protestant affiliations. The Saxon court at Dresden later denounced him for Catholic sympathy. The Abbot knew La Tour in Paris. The young Count was marked, as you are marked, for leadership. But after preliminary and, I need hardly add, secret trial with the Dominicans, it was decreed that Zinzendorf's work was other than La Tour wished and as the young Count had anticipated. He was to return to Saxony, inspire an awakening in Protestant Germany. He spent his life and fortune re-establishing or trying to re-establish a branch of the suppressed Church of Bohemia. He called it the Church within the Church. He inspired many but with his death, the Lord's Watch, as he called it, lost touch with the Hierarchy. Actually, the Count was, at one time, exiled from Saxony because of supposed affiliation with Rome."

"The Abbot thinks this Dohna wishes to renew his grandfather's *lié* with—with Rome?"

"Not Rome in the sense that the Saxon Court understood it, when they denounced his grandfather. But the Rome perhaps, of Father d'Albizi, the Dominican Adept."

"I seem out of touch with all this."

"I am considerably older than you are, Louis, and the Abbot is the *philosoph inconnu* of our Society. The inner teaching is handed down orally, as you know."

The wind was howling from the river into the narrow passage of the Street of the Alchemists.

"There is a word that I am trying to remember," said Antonius, "an awkward word—meaning that even the oral teaching to the privileged and the secret cherishing of the legend is not sufficient. It is a word that means *you must act out* the legend for yourself."

———

XI

It was not probable. It was not possible. His right hand rested on a sword-hilt.

Stephanus had said last night (was it only last night?), "locks has been known to be picked."

Was it snow reflected on the ceiling? Was it memory of tricks and diabolic phosphorescence?

He had denied himself the consolation of resting in the Cathedral, but had beaten his way back, in the early twilight.

He should have left the Castle earlier, but Cardinal de Rohan was urgent and insistent. He read aloud the process of inditement. But at the last, Saint-Germain had refused his signature. He had wanted confirmation, if you will, confession. His Superior was qualified to receive it. Could it be possible, the Cardinal laughingly reproached him, that your valet has gifts that I lack? It was Stephanus who said, "If a door bangs shut unexpected, a door might, by the same logic, bang open." He would see Stephanus immediately, he had assured de Rohan, and inquire of the returned Ambassador. It was de Rohan who had first suggested that the Ambassador might have fresh news from Paris. Where was Stephanus? It was unreasonable to expect him to wait at the window, when he must have known that his master had been summoned by the Abbot . . . being "half way to the Castle" . . .

"Brother, said Cagliostro.

It was a small room but he could turn around in it. The dusk would not reveal his habit. In fact, the Castle servant had discreetly slipped the white rope into the wide fold of the skirt-pocket, presumably prompted by the Abbot's reference to his great-coat. The fine, stinging snow had blown off his garments. "It was the first house, they told me," said Cagliostro, "Alchemists' Row. But I didn't expect the luck to find you."

There was the chair on which Cagliostro had been sitting, and the bench. The bench was usually pushed against the side-wall but it had been pulled out. Saint-Germain replaced the bench and bundled his habit under it. "That door leads somewhere," said Cagliostro, "but there was no response to my knocking. I tried both. The signals have been changed somewhat, but perhaps the brothers here don't yet know of it." He turned his chair, with his back to the small window. "There's no way down," he said, "as far as I could find out, in the floor-boarding. I don't understand it. I did have forty-winks. I was exhausted. I don't rightly know how long I've been here. The grooms are not fratres proper, but I had the luck in Paris to save the Ambassador a favorite filly. I was always good with horses. Get in with the stables and you're in right. I was taken on, as extra rider, because of the storm. They would have turned back or rested but I was persuasive and confided in first outrider who got it through to coachman, that there was trouble brewing. No doubt, his Ambassador had had a hint to leave and leave quick. They never tell us nothing, said outrider. I had a pal, I said, related distant to one of the Guard. Very distant, I said. They're Swiss, he said, I always wondered. And now, we're on the subject," said Cagliostro, "I may tell you, they refuse to obey what they call inferiors. They was to be disbanded."

Said Saint-Germain, "I must return to Paris."

"Brother, I'm awake now," said Cagliostro, "you are official. I'm surprised to see you. How did you get word, before Medina actually declared it? You've been gone some time. I always said you were a dark horse, but I never thought they'd send you word first."

"I had heard nothing," said Saint-Germain.

"The thing starts official," said Cagliostro, "when the Guard leaves the Palace."

"The Guard will not leave the Palace," said Saint-Germain.

"That appears plain," said Cagliostro. "In that sense, I see what you aim at, when you say you must go back. They will only take it from you, Chevalier, as they call you simply, as if there wasn't plenty of Chevaliers in Paris. They have some key or clue? I always thought you might be doubling on our circle, but we all do that. Couldn't you get it through, your code-word? You can certainly dismiss them, without yourself facing danger and by now, death. It won't be so bad. We had brother-doctors working on it. It's a new device, efficient and reliable. The Guillotine, they call it."

(What was it de Rohan had said, when he waited for an answer? Something that would say *yes*, or something that would say *no*. "I have never known you to lose your head . . .)

"I have heard discussion of it," said Saint-Germain. "Can not this Revolution be prevented?"

He had asked Cardinal de Rohan the same question. "It can not be prevented," the Cardinal had answered. But "how can it be prevented?" said Cagliostro.

"I had thought," said Saint-Germain, "when serving the Fraternity, that the idea was one of an ideal Brotherhood."

"You have served others," said Cagliostro, "not that we hold that against you."

"My influence in the Palace, such as it was," said Saint-Germain, "was to serve as a bridge between us."

"There was no crossing that bridge," said Cagliostro. "Mind, brother, I had it, straight from Althotas, you were not against us. But official records was got out or being ready to be posted on the lanterns. But the Cardinal was too quick. I was hiding in the stables, so heard only after he had gone. I couldn't follow, so thought best to lie low and the grooms was sympathetic. Even, brother, I could, with my persuasion, find a place for you among them. As soon as things calm down, the Ambassador is off again to England."

It was around him, blackness unutterable. The small room seemed to shrink to one of the infernal dungeons they had used at initiations. He had been standing defensively before the locked door. How could he get through? But why should he get through? *Acroamatique*, it came to him suddenly, the awkward word he had been trying to remember. This was descriptive of a method or a canon. Superficially, he had translated it, *you must act out the legend for yourself*.

"You don't look properly yourself, brother," said Cagliostro.

What was he doing with his hands? There was nothing wrong. He was seated on the wooden bench, now, his hands were clasped on his knees. He was not tearing, tearing at infernal metal. Chained standing? Chained kneeling? Had it ever happened? He had kept it out of consciousness with the sheet of steel or silver metal that the *Exercitia* renewed daily for him, hourly sometimes. He could not remember his boyhood. He was a waif, a legend. Had the so-called initiation begun, even in early childhood? There was that legend—a mother in the forests. He was seven. But later, he was told the mother and forest alike were a symbol. Of what?

"It's being without your perruque; though I'd seen you without, it was in moments of exaltation."

"Exaltation?"

"Lucidity, you know, brother. Not often and only with the inner few, together."

"I have been at the Castle," said Saint-Germain, "almost all day, perhaps the elaborate food and wine have overcome me."

"You lived proper at the Palace," said Cagliostro.

Saint-Germain remembered something. What was it he remembered?

"I have been here in an official capacity," said Saint-Germain, "going over records at the Castle. It was thought better that I appear as a—a clerk. This is my outer study. I have rooms beyond. The communicating door is usually bolted, from the other side, in case of—"

"The out-door wasn't so easy, but I had time and clouded in the snow-drifts—"

If a clock struck, if a voice spoke, if a watchman passed the window with a lantern—"Stephanus," he shouted suddenly, beating on the locked door. He remembered it, he remembered it, *I was immured in the dungeons of the Castle of Ruel.*

The bolt was immediately slipped back. "I heard voices," said Stephanus, "I supposed you was talking confidential."

XII

"No," said Saint-Germain, "I have been telling you all evening. I wined heavily at the Castle."

"That was some hours back," said Stephanus, "almost a half-day, it being well after midnight."

Saint-Germain laid a letter on the table. "Through it all," he said, "I clung to one thing. The Cardinal handed me this letter, from the Abbot. It has nothing to do with anything that I can make out. If you will read it—"

He could survive for—something. He could not steel himself as a Captain of Loyola, nor could he accept messages, no matter how "lucid," to use Cagliostro's word, they may have appeared at the time of the experience. He had never inquired as to what he had said at those infernal meetings, when drugged or hypnotized, he had consciously allowed himself to be used as a voice or a servant of Althotas. Only this evening, Cagliostro told him, it was brotherhood he spoke of. But brotherhood? The Cardinal, according to Cagliostro, had already prepared the public declaration. *À la lanterne*. It was an old catch-word. He could only pray silently (waiting while Stephanus solemnly applied himself to this difficult task of reading) to—"Our Lady and Saint Wenceslas chose you to light the candles." When had he said that? He was "lucid" at that moment, if he ever had been, but the message, the miracle, the manifestation had depended neither on the measured invocation of the *Knights of the East*, nor the controlled Spartan physical alertness of the *Sword*, nor had it revealed itself in a dionysiac de-materialization, through agents that he had referred to, this very afternoon, in conference with the Cardinal, as diabolical. He was sent to Prague, he himself, chosen by the Knights, as best fitted to mediate, should occasion arise, between—Medina and the Pope, to put it crudely. It was tangled and subtle, it was East and West, it was the Devil and God. But who was Devil, who was God, in the midst of this betrayal? The inditement which, thank—thank Our Lady, he had not signed, would serve to re-instate the Jesuits.

"Can't you decipher it, Stephanus, it's clearly written."

He was flattering Stephanus. He could pick out a word here or there; he could not really read the letter.

"My mind is not rightly on it. I'm thinking how taken aback I was, when I heard that tapping. Knew from of old, it was *maçonnerie*. But not as you had informed me. The second try was nearer. My word, I wondered what rat had found our hide-out. Danger, says I, and reminded myself how I had told you, locks was known to be picked. I waited a proper interval and panting to get hold of the valet, what with the trouble of that coach in Petty Place, though I had a word here and there, helping unload—and gracious thanks too, to jingle in my pocket, what with all his worry, from his Excellency. But Lord, only enough Paris news to whet my appetite. I'll pop in to build up the fire, I says to the pleasant fellow on the box, and I'll be back to help drag in the luggage. But Lord, I says, what rat has found our hide-out? It was *maçonnerie*; I says to myself, better watch the rat-hole, this side, but I was overcome, I couldn't bear it. It was dusk then, and blowing proper, so I slipped out. He was in there. Would he stay there? Fidgeting to get the Embassy gossip, my whole soul fighting—will he get out? I was sorry, sir, you had to take the shock of it. My word, and you treating him like a gentleman."

"It was far, far more than I had anticipated," said Saint-Germain, "and I had met him at the Palace."

"Wolfed up tomorrow's dinner. You ate nothing. You could do with what I had intended as a snack for myself, after the Embassy. It's cold bacon, though you usually don't touch it, it's sliced thin. I saved the loaf too, of your preference. They must have had something on the way here, but he was like a hound for hunger."

"He had been hiding for some days. No doubt, the tension had unnerved him. Sometimes—" It was there, he must fight it off, the memory. "Sometimes people can't eat after a great shock. He found out that he was safe here."

"Do I understand you rightly? Thought we was holding him, and discretion what you hinted of (about him, better for his own sake, to keep away from the brethren) was so we would know he was hiding in the stables. I had slipped out, at the hint you gave me—"

"I trust—"

"Oh, I made it all out, how he had helped my old grandmother with his balsam-oil."

"What, Stephanus, did you tell them?"

"Only, we was all sheer knocked over by the news—made out, it had come direct from my master who had had it from the Castle. Nothing they didn't know, but friendly-like—his Excellency surely, he wasn't leaving, what with all the ports watched? But they don't half believe it, nor do I, like children telling each other horrors to see who can scare most. Why did you keep him talking?"

"Frankly, there is a new set of signs and code-words. It is essential that I know them."

"I shouldn't have sat here talking," said Stephanus, "*égalité*. There's no harm your having your own Château, you look worse than I ever seen you. You mark my words, I said to the valet, confidential, it will all blow over. My master, I said, would be paying his respects at the first opportunity. His Excellency must be fair exhausted. I'll give my mind to that letter, once I see you sipping the hot broth I'll fetch you." Stephanus pushed back his chair.

He was fussy was his master but elegant. For all his book-learning, you could see right through him, sometimes. He was going back to Paris.

•

"Poison," said de Rohan. He did not ask the question. He made a legal statement. But "he ate nothing," said Stephanus, "not a mouthful, till after he'd gone. Had a proper time, getting him to swallow his broth, crumbling his bread and paying no attention. Then, he went off, like that time in Venice. Raved proper. Said, would I report immediately to the Castle. Said, would I inform his Eminence how things was. Said, best consult your Eminence about Rome. You can go with him, he says. I told you he was proper raving. Said, could your Eminence not take me, he would arrange with his Excellency, next door, who is off to England. Said things I couldn't follow, but I got him to bed. Balsamo's in the stables."

"Will he stay there?"

"I told him a proper story about the Castle—my own invention but truth in it. Best not to alarm the Abbot, my master says. But the Cardinal must be informed. The Guard here, I said friendly to Balsamo, early this morning, after I left my master sleeping, is aware of these activities. Wouldn't have known the fraters had a hide-out, if he hadn't blundered into the study, thinking it was the Row proper. Somewhere in the Row's their hide-out. He says, special, tell the Cardinal."

"It would be only human of you to escort me to him. I could wait and take him with me."

"That's where he was most emphatic. He said, for all concerned, it would be best, you was off quick. You could almost start, your Eminence, toward evening. He would rest quieter, once you were gone. He has his own plans; as far as expedient, we will keep you informed."

We will keep you informed! Cardinal de Rohan started slightly, then he remembered that this fellow was an asset to the Office. But there was more in this than Stephanus had related. What was this madness? He had known Louis as eminently sane, true, he had confided to him that the sessions with Cagliostro's so-called initiates, had, in the end, unnerved and unbalanced him. Or he feared they would do. He had made a clear enough statement of the proceedings—or had he hidden something? He had refused to give the pass-words or the code-words yesterday. He had not forgotten them. Louis, Louis-Antoine! Cardinal de Rohan had compromised in Paris, had put off further probing, had sent him to Prague.

"How long have you been here?" (How long altogether had Stephanus been with Louis?) "My good fellow, will you summon a servant—a tankard of ale?"

"I must thank your Eminence. The Embassy valet said he would keep an eye on my master. But I must get back."

He was standing, as if at attention. He was stiff-necked. What did he know that Louis had kept hidden? There had been many rumours. But they had flattered themselves that, on the whole, they had kept the secret, secluded the child, waited. This was the moment for apotheosis. Prince Ragoczy of Transylvania had been one of Louis' patrons or legendary fathers. There had been others. He himself had been the last to be entrusted with the secret—and he loved Louis.

"It would be dangerous, sir, for you and all concerned," said Stephanus, "to come near the Row."

The fellow was stiff-necked, a shade impudent and sensitive.

"You will take my—my greeting to him."

"I'm sorry, sir, it's this way. He said, too, he supposed the Abbot would inform the former Brother to take over the school. What he himself said was, it was far more than he had anticipated. He asked me to read a letter."

Stephanus took soldierly steps forward and laid the letter on the table.

"We discussed this yesterday," said de Rohan.

"So he told me. He said, it had nothing to do with anything he could make out. We were about to discuss the matter when he went off. Perhaps, you would advise me."

"You have read it?"

"I glanced it over but as I told him, my mind wasn't on it."

"It is a question of a certain—a certain Count Zinzendorf." De Rohan picked up the letter.

"Could you perhaps, sir, read it to me. My mind—" (*Égalité*, he hated the word, but—suppose the Cardinal refused to read the letter?) "Raved proper about a castle of Ruel. About Brethren of Asia and the Order of Saint Joachim. Spoke like it was yesterday of Venice. It was there I was recommended to his service, counting roughly, it's almost twenty years that I've been with him. I was in Embassy, but only as under supervision, learning—learning manners."

The Cardinal waited, as if he were pondering the matter. He did not look up. Perhaps more would be forthcoming.

"The Tower, House of Köstriz," he read.

XIII

Égalité, thought Stephanus. But this was something different. Couldn't refuse to sit down, what with the way she said it. But the chair though low and wide, he offered, was covered with that *point* work Lamotte showed him in the Palace. One of the sewing-girls, she was, but Balsamo made her "Countess." It was her they put the blame on, for the diamond necklace. A pretty girl, pert and friendly and helpful to him in his capacity. Knew every door and stairway. He must ask Balsamo what he intended for the Queen and Lamotte. They had both been useful to him. "I—I was visiting the stables, before I came here," said Stephanus. "I don't feel proper to sit in that chair." But "Jacob took your great-coat?" asked the gentleman. "And Maria," said the lady, "I'm sure brushed you with that switch-broom. I always begged, when I came in from riding, that she spare me. I'm sure she didn't spare you." "I brushed him proper," said the friendly wife, as she stood in the door. Didn't seem that she thought it strange, if he sat down with them. She set the coffee, and those same cups, Lamotte showed him, on the table. "Might be the Palace," he thought. Maybe, he said it aloud. He found he was seated in one of those very *point* chairs. He must have sat down.

"Perhaps, your—your butler didn't give the message right." Why had he been shown in here?

"Jacob knew of my anxiety. I have been waiting for a letter from the Castle."

She said, "You best drink your coffee, before you begin talking." She said, "My cousin is writing a book on the old Church of Bohemia." What had knocked him silly was, so that he didn't know if or if not he had said out loud that it might be the Palace, was—the gentleman was the fellow that waited, like it might be her servant, in a great-coat that was proper livery.

Might have borrowed it from that Jacob—but why? And his name wasn't

Schweinitz as the *Grape* informed him, but Dohna and Count Dohna, the Cardinal had told him. The Cardinal might have informed him further, but perhaps he thought it equal to what he had told him about his master. Why must he be Schweinitz, when it was the lady who was Countess von Schweinitz, so Count Dohna introduced her formal. The lady was, by right, de Watteville, or so she travelled. By the common-coach. He couldn't deal with all this in a moment. The point was, it was the lady he had watched go by the house so often, the one it was was the means of his forgetting.

That is, Saint-Germain forgetting that he was Brother Anton. It had been too much, the double load he carried, and now the shock of it all being no use. Saint-Germain and Brother Anton got mixed up with one another. It was brain-fever but he talked mostly some foreign language, Italian sometimes. Anyhow, the valet wasn't likely to make mischief, and they was off soon, that is if Balsamo could guarantee protection. They must depend on Balsamo. He could only hint it to the valet. He got some information from him, on his own account, just now, back from the Cardinal, finding his master asleep. If he could keep him here and himself go to Paris—

"Confidential," said Stephanus, "this may not be the message you was wanting." He set down his cup.

"The library or the Castle refuses me admittance?"

"No—no, sir. But what I mean to say is, it's round-about. The—the Abbot who has care of the old records is receptive. That is, as I make out, there is interest in what I was told was the Count, your grandfather. What I mean is, we are not properly, the Castle. My master and I are lodged in Petty Place, by the Embassy, but it was the Abbot chose him as fitting to show you around. But what I mean to say is, he was sudden stricken and couldn't write the letter, inviting you to the archives. He put the matter in my hands. I was to give the message. But last night, he was taken with this fever. I wouldn't know now what to say, except his compliments."

The lady said, "My cousin could call upon him when he is able to see visitors."

"It's more than that, milady. You must forgive indiscretion. I have watched you often go past the house."

"I don't remember this—this Petty Place, you speak of."

"It's rightly *La Petite Place de la Chatelaine*. That's made confusion for us. I mean, confidential, my master had the Row door, as well. It's opposite the Cathedral. It was his duty with the Abbot, to read over old books. That makes him what the letter is addressed to, so the—the Abbot told me—Keeper of the Archives. I don't know what Archives is, proper. But it's what you, sir, seemingly were after. It's something to do with your grandfather and this book you're writing? Perhaps I should not ask it. If it weren't for my master being taken—"

The lady said, "My mother had much experience in nursing. We all—we all were practised. I could myself—"

"It's his mind, milady."

"Delirium, my mother was deeply skilled in potions. Some secret remedies were given her. I must be frank now. We belong to a sect of—of—" How explain the *Unitas*? "I am not a Catholic, but like my grandfather—"

"It was explained in the letter," said Stephanus.

"I wrote chiefly," said Count Dohna to his cousin, "on the Albizi incident, about which you and I were curious, and Father Anthony Dionysius."

It was all confusing, they were heretics, as he first thought. Is that why they came—incognito? The same as Saint-Germain but different.

"You will forgive, sir, but I recognized you. The *Grape* told me you was Schweinitz. The postilion of the old-coach said milady was de Watteville. You will think it strange my making these inquiries—but my master—"

The lady said, "My mother is Baroness de Watteville. My mother in the *Unitas*, is Sister Benigna."

There was the silver coffee-set and the Sèvres cups on the small table at her elbow.

There was the crackle of the wood-fire—she had said all this, they had spoken of this together, she and Henri, seriously endeavouring, while he waited for the answer to his letter, to assemble the chief facts of the history of the *Unitas*. Was it yesterday that they spoke of Bethlehem? The story had begun with a King of Bohemia, at least their personal inheritance of the story. But Henri had gone on to Doctor Faustus and it all seemed unbelievable, the legend and their family. At least the legend seemed to have ended with their mothers, who would not tell them of it. What had happened? "Lilie," she remembered how she had confided in her Aunt Elizabeth, "all in good time."

"I might remark," said Stephanus, almost under his breath, as though fearing to break the silence, "with permission of milady—"

Milady. How quaint it sounded. Her eyes met the serious, deep-set eyes that seemed to question her, across the table. "What is it—sir?" She was not mocking. It's some sort of Brotherhood, thought Stephanus, that works proper. Or Sisterhood of nurses.

"You may have seen my master."

She could not for a moment, overcome a strange sensation. It had happened before. She knew what he would say and prayed, for a moment, that he would not say it. She was the child Lilie, Sister Benigna's daughter, and they had spoken much to her, in her mother's absence, of the miracle and mystery of Benigna and the Indians. They did not call them savages. As a girl of sixteen, on her first visit. . . she, Lilie, had lived through an agony of fire and torture which Benigna, alone with her father and the chiefs of the Six Nations, had not remotely dreamt of. Brother Johannes, they called her grandfather. They were all, after Benigna's first visit to Bethlehem, received formally into the family or Brotherhood of the Six Nations, and the Six Nations into the *Unitas*. This was a mystery and wonder and it seemed to her, forgotten. She was Benigna's daughter.

"A priest in the Cathedral?"

The wind was howling from the river into the narrow passage of the Street of the Alchemists.

The deep eyes held hers. He looked more like a gypsy than a gentleman's courier. A gentleman's courier? It was a priest she spoke of, a lay-brother she had called him. He would not have a courier. He was working in the Castle, with the Abbot on old texts. She was caught in the narrow passage, her hands frozen to the unyielding metal of the great door. He had lifted the leather curtain. He bowed and she curtsied to him. How do you know he is a lay-brother, Henri had half-mocked her. She had not seen him officiating at the Mass, she told him. The place is seething with overtones, said Henri. There were gypsies like that, taken in at Herrnhaag, the Lord's Hedge, before formal protest was made and the settlement abandoned. No—Sister Charity had said, they must not tell your fortune. What was it but telling fortunes, when they opened the Bible at random, eyes shut, a finger or a quill poised for the text? There were the old lots, cast for marriages. She had spoken of that too, with Henri. What did they have? What had been taken from them? Why had it been taken? Surely, not from any lack of piety and devotion. Last night, Henri had laid the letters on the table. I unfastened them, he said. They are addressed to Theodora de Castell. They are for you.

Someone must read the letters. Would—would this priest do?

How cold it was. But she sensed the flame and heard the fall of an ash-stick on the stone-hearth. Was it still snowing?

Her hands moved automatically. There were courtesies. There were traditions, the more sternly maintained because they were all one family. "Henri—our guest—" she said. There were three cups on the table. Why should she remember it now, the little game that she and Justine treasured so long? Perhaps, in her whole life, there was only one deception or one major one—there was, Henri had suggested, perhaps this latest—lighting the candles for Saint Wenceslas. It followed, at any rate, the pattern of her grandfather, and the *Ave* accusation. Does Justine remember? she thought. And what became of the little square box and the cards they spread out, as if against Sister Charity's expressed command. But Sister Charity had not been told of this and she and Justine had not understood what the Bohemians said, any way. They were gypsies but the Council denounced them as Bohemians, and the Lord's Hedge, as a scandal. They had given her the cards with some sort of blessing. There were three cups on the table. She and Justine had played this fortune-game with names, with people, with the clock striking—bells were cups, they said. How many candles had she lighted? There was a time when she would have counted them, matching them with the wands for the seven stars, if there were seven. She was happy again.

"I shouldn't stay," said the gypsy-courier.

"Oh—if you can—if only for a few moments. I would know about your master, his life, his family—"

"He's—he's—well, dedicated. I suppose, I'm his main family."

She had forgotten that he was a priest, but her hands did not falter. There was something about the candles. No, it wasn't yesterday. It was the day before yesterday. *It happened two hours ago, it happened two hundred years ago*, she had said to Henri. It was happening now.

With us, it is more in the French fashion, she had said to Henri, recalling the ritual, as she had called their formal vespers. That was after she came back, that last time, day before yesterday, from the Cathedral. She had lighted the candles, with a special prayer for—for completion, for fulfilment? She did not know what—for Henri and the book he was writing, for an answer to the Mystery. He had lifted the curtain. It was a Castell heirloom, god-mamma's old lace. She had inherited—the letters? They were under her pillow last night, now in the cedar-box where she kept the lace-scarf and a few treasures. It was an old box—yes, she had kept the fortune in it, the cards they called fortune-cards. It had a key then, lost long since. It came back to her, it was her inheritance. She would meet and confer with the Kings of Bohemia—that is, with the tribes of gypsies. Yes, she remembered, like Benigna with the Six Nations, Lilie would hold the tribes together, wanderers, sometimes with tents. She would bring the gypsies into the *Unitas*, as Benigna had brought the Indians. But the gypsies were denounced and the Lord's Hedge, as a scandal, and the Indians were scattered now and made a formal visit to Bethlehem in their canoes, her mother had said the last time she was there, almost a farewell visit. At least, so it seemed, Benigna told them, as Good Peter, Cornplanter, Half-town, Big-tree and La Fayette's young Oneida, Pierre Jaquette drew their canoes back into the shallows, and with a hundred others, faded like shadows, down the Lehigh river. They were shadows. Benigna's heart was broken. There was a time when there were more Indians in the town than white people. White people? It was they who were the shadows. There was something ghostly about *white people*. They called them the Bethlehem Indians.

Why did Lilie take and shake her, as she looked at the gypsy-courier?

It was the Mystery.

"Milady must forgive an indiscretion. It is only proper and polite, after what might seem like prying into your incognito—"

"It was a slight matter," said Count Dohna, "we wanted to see things—naturally and simply. Connections of my cousin's sister hold this property. It would have meant a certain amount of—of visiting, if we had come, as from the family. We wanted moreover, to find out for ourselves, what it was in Prague—"

"It's the Cathedral," said the lady.

"He's not properly a priest," said Stephanus, "it seemed better too, for him to see things clear, if he took—like it was—" How explain it?

"He had the Row door, for his study. A serious scholar, is my master. He taught in the school, too. He left his—his habit in the study. It's the Count of Saint-Germain presents his compliments."

XIV

Morte villana,
di pietà nemica,
di dolor madre antica,
giudizio incontrastabile gravoso . . .

he could go no further.

No, he must not be tempted to send Stephen to the Abbot for the books. Only what was already long-steeped in the deep vat of his being, would match the strands or threads of his busy weaving. It was not a man's work, it was nature or God, it was infinite, tenuous, remote, drawn from his very belly. The strings had freed themselves but he could not remain here, in this rapture, this coma, this half-world, this entire world of bliss. So a child must feel, finding its mother waiting, when it starts upright, rigid, from a nightmare. He need not think about it. He need never write it. His debt would be paid, when he returned to Paris.

His debt would not be paid, if he died here. Nor would his debt be paid . . . it was the feast of the Assumption. She was crossing a bridge. It was Venice, where he met her, knowing how comment had mistaken her for Monna Vanna. That is, she was Primavera and if she was Cavalcanti's mistress, then it was quite clear how their bitter quarrel brought about Guido's banishment, some said his death from fever, contracted during that exile from Florence, under the young Ghibelline's jurisdiction. It did not last long. He himself fled to Verona. But there was time there. Under the burning shadows . . . of the arches . . . it was Primavera who was Beatrice. Guido's deception broke her—Mandetta? It was written in the sonnets. She did not die, the blessed Primavera. She went into a convent. No one had ever known that. The pages fluttered to the floor . . . the old fever took him. It must have been . . . de Rohan? Who was his actual father? It was the same story of betrayal, banishment, but in his case it was prison. He had challenged Leopold Ragoczy, as Dante challenged Cavalcanti.

He must have been speaking Polish to the valet. Stephanus returned soon after. Leopold was gathering them together, conspiring against the Austrian Empire. This was the Guelf and Ghibelline of his later reconstruction. Dante with the *tàvola, tavolàto, tavolètta* (he remembered how he had pondered these words) *tavolière* had precise indications. There could be reconciliation. Mandetta? Was she a symbol merely, as they had reasoned that Beatrice was Divine Philosophy? There need be no Guelf, no Ghibelline, no schism, no chasm, no *crevasse* between them. It was perfect, a formula that fitted history. History? He could not recall the lines but someone (*Morte?* Cavalcanti?) turned, as to slay the *spìriti*. Not him only, not the blessing, not the embodiment of Amor—her name he said was Amor—not Monna Vanna or Johanna, Giovanna, a screen, a veil—he remembered how he had pondered that *velo*, veil and *vela*, sail. But was Johanna a screen for Beatrice or Beatrice a screen or a veil for Johanna, Primavera?

It caught in the wind and the snow captured her. It was a mistake to wait and watch her blown like a wraith down the Alchemists' Lane.

Leopold was his brother; he had then thought that Prince Ragoczy was actually his father. He had not thought it possible that the two worlds could manifest, separately, to the same person. He had not himself known, that last time, what the tablets or the *tavolàto* had intended, but Leopold was possessed with fury. The very words that Dante used, he found later, actually expressed Leopold's obvious madness. He had abused not him, Louis, but the messages or the messengers, he had raged at those very *spìriti*, in the same voice and manner with which Dante described *Morte villana*, that *Morte* that he himself identified as Dante's friend and familiar, an older brother and young father, soldier, man-of-the-world, statesman, scholar, poet, courtier, the invincible Cavalcanti.

It was only years afterwards, that he solved the riddle, the *rubrica*, as Dante called it. It was fear that had seized Leopold. Of what? He remembered but only—only—When had it all happened? *I was immured in the dungeons of the Castle of Ruel.* But that was perhaps a test, he had argued, for he could not lose Leopold. Even when he found that Leopold was associated with the *Comes Cabalicus* and the doctrine of a forbidden Gnosis. It was not the *tavolàto* that had revealed this to him.

Perhaps, he had argued afterwards, it was preliminary to some initiation—but he had been rescued. Perhaps, he had argued afterwards, it was a test, a trial, a proof, *épreuve* of strength, of mental power, endurance, valiance. How had he been rescued? His mind had broken before that happened, and he found himself in the retinue of Prince Karl of Hesse, on the way to Venice.

If he had time, he could reconstruct the entire story. But that would make a memoir of it, not a dream, a fantasy. The papers had fluttered to the floor and afterwards, Stephanus told him, the good Lucia had confessed to him, she burnt them. She had taken them for magic, the broken script, the parallels and circles, he had been tracing, as from the *Paradiso*. The signs of those same planets. Magic was rife in Venice and he had been known to have attended de Seingalt's water-carnivals and festivals. It was Prince Karl who urged him on to that incomparable *fête vénitienne*. Had he really seen her? Casanova de Seingalt was a nobleman, a roué and a gentleman. But he thought of Balsamo.

How long had the Embassy been empty? He had trusted Stephanus, who in any case, had apparently taken things into his own hands. They would take Balsamo to England; it was only whispered among the grooms, that gentleman's agreement. There would be no Revolution. That was the price of his departure. That is, there would be no Revolution, until the Guard left the Palace and the Guard would not leave the Palace.

It was a question of time and he had cheated time. The Fates were those spinning sisters. You only saw the fine web of the texture, when the wings were free. It was a web that folded round her, worn as in Venice, that—*mantilla*. No, that was not the word he wanted. Was de Seingalt, Spanish? There was the enchantment of strings, brushed by Melusine, across the water. He had not been freed by those syrens of Casanova. The wound inflicted by Leopold had been too—poignant? deadly? poisonous? There was no word for that wound. But he had stood between the messages and the bitter repudiation of them. He had stood by the Messenger. Afterwards, there was a sinister or celestial rumour that he himself had had converse with de Seingalt, while Stephanus was witness, before God, that he lay that night on the eve of the Assumption, helpless and weak, in the dark, watching the reflections of the flickering lanterns, across the slats of the drawn blinds, as they passed in the *calle* outside, on the way to the Piazza. It was always carnival. De Seingalt was a roué but a gentleman. He might have been seeing double—he was seeing double. They told me you had the fever, he said afterwards, how did you find your way to the *Miracoli*? His jests were intimate and witty. Was it a laughing matter? He decided afterwards, it was the Visitor. But that was long afterwards. "If anything, it was more than usual ordered," the porter had said of the Chapel of Saint Wenceslas, after the Miracle.

But there had been other manifestations, not often; he had recalled them in the Cathedral, *there was never a false step, never an inopportune moment, never an appearance that was exaggerated.* If the Visitor had chosen him as a—a screen, to use Dante's word, or a veil, as he preferred to call it, He could, it was obvious, use anyone. The Visitor, he had reasoned in the Cathedral and not for the first time, could manifest as anybody. Prince Karl, a Master of the *Ancienne Chevalerie*, had received him, without preliminary trial, into one of the highest circles of the Knights. There was gossip of the Jesuits, at that time in Venice, and threat of the suppression of the Order. He had followed the matter closely and finally undertaken the strict rule of initiation. He had orders to go to Paris, disciplined yet ready for wildest emergency, as de Rohan has expressed it, "most flagrant Palace orgies." And this was no trial to him, he was seeking Leopold. That is, when the time came for a candidate to investigate Cagliostro's orgies, he was chosen. It was clearly demonstrated, it was Euclid and the Church Fathers, it was the role of humility, it was the service of the Order, it was scientific and reasoned investigation, it was research, it was inquiry, it was seasoned summary of a disease, professional diagnosis, he would risk his life as the Fathers in the Indies, it was martyrdom, it was penance toward absolution, it was the pledge of obedience, the pledge of silence, the pledge of secrecy, it was again Service—it was the Inquisition, it was damnable.

But he had paid his debt to Cardinal de Rohan and he had paid his debt to Cagliostro.

XV

"I do not know," she said, and as if she were speaking to a child, "I told you yesterday."

"It is the names, I tried to remember and write them," he said, "but Stephanus took away my quill and paper."

"But it is difficult to write the names. One can only say them."

"Say them."

"Susquehanna, Lenni-Lenape, Z'higochgoharo."

"There was another," he said, "you did not tell me the whole story."

"I cannot—I cannot," she said, "it broke my mother's heart to lose them—"

"They are not lost," he said. He did not know of the intensity of her emotions, as she sat there, Sister Elizabeth, in her white cap and the fine linen folded at her wrists.

"There were many other—names, I mean," she said. "Tganniatarechev."

"Tgan—?"

"It means, between-two-seas, the name they gave to Christopher Pyrlaeus, the musician, who wrote the lists of words of the Mohawk and Mochican dialects. Some pages, copied from the manuscript, are in the library at home," she said.

"Herrnhut," he said.

"The Lord's Watch. My father and my uncle took down many of my grandfather's poems. He is still reputed to be one of the greatest extempore poets that Germany has ever had. But they could not record the music, they said. So Pyrlaeus is said to have explained the Indian language—or languages, there were many."

"There *were* many?"

"It all seems in the past and far away. Pyrlaeus was one of the early settlement. It is only fifty years, not quite fifty years, since the community was established, but in that time, there have been incredible, intolerable transformations." She did not want to talk of this nor recall the heart ache.

"Perhaps my mother thought of them, lived with them, before I was born. I seem to know too much about them, more even than my mother, of whose early visit to the settlement, I have spoken."

"The Six Nations," he said.

"My uncle Frederick, a scholar and something of a classicist, compared them to the Spartans in Greece. They were warriors, held together by political interests and affiliations. They were Iroquois," she explained, "Mohawks, Oneidas, Onondagas, Cayugas, Senecas, Tuscaroras. But I told you yesterday."

"It was those names, I was trying to remember."

"The Athenians, as Uncle Frederick called them, had no confederacy. So the separate tribes dwindled and even then, when Christopher Pyrlaeus began his record of them, some had almost vanished—many had already vanished, I suppose. He said their voices stressed the words, like music. It was music, he said."

"It is music," said Saint-Germain.

"So I seem to feel it. But apart from the usual service and the choir, I was not considered gifted. There were so many accomplished musicians in the community."

"But the Athenians?"

"Ah, that is difficult. There was God, the Great Spirit. There was good and evil, Manito."

"Manito?" he questioned.

"They were Algonquin, the Athenians; the tribes had lost touch with one another. Though scattered and defenceless, they were the high-priests of tradition. *Who is manito?* it was questioned in one of the recorded chants of their mysteries. *He,* is the reply, *who walketh with a serpent, walking on the ground, he is manito.*"

Who was speaking? Where was he? Who was this speaking to him? I am feeling so much better, he thought. Was it the powders she had left, with special directions to Stephanus? There was all-heal implicit in the names of the simples—this, from Herrnhut, this from Bethlehem. He must not touch the Indian remedies, she said, if he feared them or had a superstition of them. They were powdered bark and dried berries. Her mother had witnessed the simple, secret preparation of the formula. It was not witchcraft.

He had smiled for the first time, to hear Our Lady speak of witchcraft, to see Our Lady, wrapped in her fur-mantle, with that same immaculate veil under the half drawn-back fur-hood. She was not a vision. Our Lady and Saint Wenceslas chose you to light the candles. The words she spoke were invocations—of what? Surely, not the powers of darkness—*Manito*? He was God and Devil. But between God and Devil, stood Our Lady. She did not die, the blessed Primavera, she went into a Convent. He was the only one who knew this. What Convent had she attended, he had thought when he first saw her. What Covenant had her grandfather made with God?

Cardinal de Rohan had spoke of himself and Zinzendorf as alike marked for leadership. But according to the story as Dohna had been telling it, the Plan, as he called it, the *Jednota* or *Unitas*, assembled at Herrnhut with its stations or missions in odd corners of the whole world, had lost something. Saint-Germain seemed to know what it was, explaining as best he could, his reading of the matter. Zinzendorf was a Protestant Jesuit.

It was even so rumoured, she had told him, when speaking of—of—

"I have forgotten the name—Pine Plains, you translated it," he said.

She said, "Schekomeko. It was north of Bethlehem, in what is now New York State," she told him. "My grandfather visited there with Benigna. It was the fur-traders. Christian Henry had founded their farm-community. If they had corn, they did not need—"

She hesitated, for it was the crime of a whole nation.

"You need not speak of it," he said, "that degradation. The Jesuit fathers had the same problems, after the *conquistadores*. And the white man's other contribution—"

"Christian Henry brought his whole community to Bethlehem. They were driven out. There was a special law passed in New York, against vagrant preachers, Jesuits, and Moravians—Jesuits in disguise, they called them."

"Moravians?"

"Bohemians, really. It was Christian Henry, they called Z'higochgoharo. I don't know what it means. The Indians far outnumbered the settlers in Bethlehem, so they built a village for them, below the town, on the Menakessi river. Friedenshuetten," she said. But they were being driven, remorselessly through the snow. "Many died on the way."

"From—Pine Plains?"

"Schekomeko," she said, "and a few years after, there was small-pox. They were Mohigans at Schekomeko, one of the lost tribes. Their last chief was buried at Bethlehem. Chingachgook," she said. "They called him John Wasamapah. I don't know why."

"Was there any—any reason that you know of, for calling your grandfather Johannes?"

"That is the sort of question that Henri—my cousin and I ask each other, for they never told us of the things that really seemed to matter."

There was Monna Vanna, Giovanna or Johanna. They were Johannites, but how explain this to her?

"There was a legend," he said, "a heresy, if you will, that Our Lord had transmitted to his favourite Disciple—"

"My grandfather was known as the Disciple," she said.

"He would know," said Saint-Germain, "that Our Lord was not dead. I am not speaking of the transfiguration or the transmutation, or the ascension, the communion, nor even of the Paraclete, the Holy Spirit. Yet, I am speaking of the Holy Spirit. You will forgive me, if my mind seems to wander. I think I can read your *rubrica*, as Dante called it, Countess von—"

"My friend, I am Sister Elizabeth, when I call upon you," she said.

"You were Monna Vanna when I saw you first, wrapt in meditation, in the Chapel of Saint Wenceslas. She was a screen, a veil; Johanna, Primavera was a screen, a veil for Beatrice. She could appear where she was not. I saw her, on a bridge in Venice."

He felt she had sat with the dead and dying, Sister Elizabeth, for she gave no sign that she thought he was demented.

"They can not tell you your grandfather's secrets," he said, "for I do not think they know them."

XVI

"I cannot tell you," he said, "but you ask the sort of questions that Goethe asked me; those questions startled me and inspired me to ask more. But my questions have not been answered. That is, the questions that would give the reason for our visit here. Your special question—?"

"I was wondering through what exact channel of tradition, it was inevitable—inevitable, I say, that the *Little Strength*—you say sailing from Rotterdam?"

"The company assembled from Herrnhaag and Marienborn, met the Herrnhut group at Rotterdam. From there, Captain Garrison carried them to Cowes, where members of the English colony joined them. That is history, family history and recorded. But what is inevitable, to use your word, about the *Little Strength*?"

"The ensign you say she carried. True, the seal is episcopal. But I felt as you told me of it, that your grandfather had some personal, heraldic claim."

"I don't know. There again, is an interesting theory. It might have survived from the Ehrenhold tradition. They were one of the twelve chief reigning Austrian houses. From Ehrenhold to my grandfather, there were twenty-two generations. But surely, I fatigue you with family history?"

"It is more than family history. It is history. You say, the original *Jednota* was established by the Greek church?"

"In the ninth century, by Cyril and Methodius of Constantinople."

"Then, the lamb *passant* with the cross or the cross and banner, is the Templar's or the Crusader's emblem?"

"I am out of my depth. Your theories fascinate and bewilder me a little."

"You must forgive my pedantry. I was in charge of a certain—certain branch of theological or if you will, mystical investigation. I myself am gaining insight into my own bewilderment. *Vicit Agnus noster*, you say the seal read. *In hoc signo vinces*. It is the same seal."

"But my cousin will reproach me, when I go back. I have tired you."

"No," said Saint-Germain, "but why do I think of England?"

"Because I am thinking of England," said Henry Dohna.

"We have been speaking of England," said Saint-Germain, "and the *Little Strength*."

"Myself, it recalled a carol or poem that Christian Renatus—I told you of him—sent from London. They had Lindsay House on the Chelsea river, or on the Thames at Chelsea. He must have watched the sails passing the window, as he lay there, those last days. *I saw three ships a-sailing* is the first line of the carol. A Christmas carol."

"It is nearing Christmas," said Saint-Germain.

"My cousin especially wants to spend it with you."

"Stephanus has followed her instructions and you see me, almost myself again."

Saint-Germain was propped upright in a low arm-chair. He wore the rose-brocade dressing-gown, which he remembered (as he lifted his arm to pull the bell-cord, to his right as he sat there) was part of the decor, the decoration, the costume, the beginning of it, that evening when he came back after his first meeting with her. This was that Saint-Germain. Myself again? Almost myself again? He had re-assembled that self, during his enforced retirement. There was nothing he could do. The Abbot had sent special messages, after Cardinal de Rohan's departure for Rome, but Stephanus had tactfully spared his master. There were only two visitors. Visitors?

"The Château for Count Dohna," said Saint-Germain to Stephanus.

"The Château? I do not follow," said Henry Dohna.

"Stephanus understands," said Saint-Germain, and almost immediately Stephanus had returned with glasses and decanter. "I expected this, sir," he said, "so I had the Château ready."

"It's our Château Saint-Germain," said Saint-Germain. "You cannot refuse France. I shall soon be leaving."

"You should not go. We have so much to say to one another. And you told me that you would help me with the book. We have assembled the historical facts, rather we have sifted the old matter and saved only what we felt was true gold. There is, as I told you, a veritable mountain of legal documents and letters. And, by the way, I have a commission for you. May it prove a blessing on your journey, if you must go. But why go? You yourself say that this threat of trouble, of which in fact, we ourselves, before we came here, heard strange rumours, is now over. You yourself say there will be no—"

He did not wish to speak that word, associating it as he did, with America and Elizabeth's distress. Nicholas de Reuss had written diplomatically, at great length, from Vienna, reviewing the situation and forecasting grave disaster. It was even argued that the American war was the match that would light the tinder.

"My cousin, de Reuss, in Vienna, writes me," said Henry Dohna, "that the crisis is past."

This will break Elizabeth's heart, he thought. Does he know she loves him?

"I had spoken to the—the Abbot," said Saint-Germain, "of the contents of your letter, the last time I was at the Castle. He had known Father de la Tour, in Paris. The Abbot is a very old man. He had heard of the—the *lié* between your grandfather and the Premonstrants. It was his opinion that your grandfather was ready to join the Dominican Order. How old was he at the time?"

"About twenty, I think," said Henry Dohna. "We have a portrait of him at that period, *en chevalier*, I mean, in perruque and court dress."

"Do you know what altered his obvious calling or intention?"

"He returned from Paris, on a formal visit to Castell. There was some sort of crisis. He was ill there. Actually, he had fallen deeply in love with Theodora de Castell, his youngest cousin."

"Your grandmother?"

"No, he married the sister of his dearest friend, his alter ego, Henry de Reuss. De Reuss married Theodora de Castell."

"I should have thought this disappointment would have sent him back to Paris, at least, to Father d'Albizi of whom you speak in your letter."

"I don't know, here is the Mystery." Henry Dohna reached for the portfolio which contained the notes they had been discussing. "This is the commission of which I just spoke to you. I found these letters, when I was searching the archives at Herrnhut, after Goethe spoke to me of secret records or of *Arcana*. I have a feeling that whatever secret records there were, were carefully destroyed and traces of the Mystery. I found my own clues obliquely. For instance, Bishop Spangenberg in his official biography of my grandfather, speaks of Christian Renatus' return, as it were, to grace, before his death in London. He was entangled, as the good Bishop says, with the extravagances which prevailed at some of the Moravian stations. We know of the scandal of Herrnhaag and our grandfather's exile from Saxony. As I say, there was no use trying to find the answer to the Mystery, in the veritable mountain of reports, records, legal documents and endless, tabulated bundles of old letters. But while going through the shelves and boxes, I found these." Henry Dohna laid the letters on the table. "My grandfather's script is inclined to be cramped, rather than expansive, as one would expect. He wrote closely, as a rule, on both sides of the paper. There is no date. The simple direction, destroy when read, is Zinzendorf's. I have not read the letters. They are addressed to Theodora de Castell."

"You wish me to read the letters?"

"My cousin sent them to you."

"My youth's dear book," said Saint-Germain.

"My youth's—"

"It is Dante's description of the *Vita Nuova*, the poem or prose-poem he wrote to—to Beatrice, on which he later built the whole structure, the *Plan* of the Commedia. You speak of Wolfgang von Goethe and the manuscript chapters that he lent you, of his book. Do you think his Faustus can compare with the Commedia?"

"I don't know," said Henry Dohna. "But I myself compared Faustus with my grandfather. I don't know why. I did not think of Dante. I have only a superficial knowledge of his work and only in translation. But the letters?"

"I do not think I can destroy them," said Saint-Germain. "His youth's dear book—it is a poem to Beatrice."

XVII

He seemed to know the whole story. He seemed to know what was in the letters. He had pretended to be sleeping, when Stephanus came in to make up the fire. The decanter and goblets were still on the table. Dohna was aware of the present danger. He had invited him, after the New Year, to the Lord's Watch. The New Year?

There were still some days left, more than a week left. He could burn out like a flambeau, he could flame out and be finished. But the *Plan* compelled him, a mysterious plan of world-unity without war. So Zinzendorf had seen it, but it was formula already registered, already put in practice. He had thought in the Cathedral, *it was no Mystery. It was ordered, it could be explained exactly. It was part of a Plan, so subtly presented, yet so clearly that you could not miss its meaning.* That was the candles that had gone out, in the Chapel of Saint Wenceslas. They were her candles. "There was her usual gold piece," the porter had said.

He had gone on, through the tempest, through the lower causeway. He had not been surprised to see de Rohan, for his mind was functioning in another dimension. "It will be small things and little people therefore that will decide the issue," Stephanus had said, that evening, when he returned, after that first greeting. It was not de Rohan who had so decided. "And forgive us our sins as we forgive those who have wronged us," he had prayed as he watched the reflection of the level low row of candles, in the jewels beyond the altar. He had been lighted from within by that reflection, like "Charles," as the porter called the heart-shaped ruby. He had not known, his mind had not realized redemption, though his heart had touched it. "And forgive us our sins as we forgive those who have wronged us." It was only afterwards that he remembered Leopold.

It was the shock of finding Balsamo, wild-eyed and shivering in the study. No doubt, it was an equal check to Balsamo to find him. Dohna had told him that Goethe, in his search for material for his Doctor Faustus, had visited a certain master of the black arts in Sicily. "You may have heard of him," Dohna had said, "he was at one time, in Paris. Cagliostro." Yes, there had been rumours of occult practices, he had countered, but was it necessary for Wolfgang von Goethe to encounter this—this magician, in order to portray the temptation or the fate of Faustus? Why had he connected the Faustus legend with his grandfather? "I was trying to explain it to my cousin," Dohna had said. "I felt that our grandfather's experience was the same—in contradiction. That is, that he had sold his soul or his shadow, as some legends tell it, but for saving—to his Saviour, to save others. He had originally gathered a very small group about him. *Candace* souls, he called them, but had later been inspired to extend his teaching. Perhaps that was a mistake, Dohna had continued, "at least, I mean, from my own point of view." He explained the early division of the already persecuted Church of Bohemia. There were Hussites, followers of the martyr, John Huss, and *Calixthenes*, the original scholars and aristocrats. Not unlike, though vastly different, from the Cromwellians or Puritans in England, and the artists—Royalists in art and drama, who succeeded Shakespeare, rather than the actual Catholic faction.

Calixthenes?

Dohna had explained it; they claimed to be the actual inheritors of the original *Jednota*. They were the cup-bearers or the upholders of the old Communion.

Communication?

Saint-Germain could not go into all that. They were Johannites; he had tried to explain yesterday to—to—

The name was de Watteville.

He had sold his shadow, he had bartered his soul, equally to God and Devil.

He could see the hieroglyphs, like light and shadow on the wall before him, though his eyes were half-closed. His eyes were closed really, but he saw the flickering of the lanterns, through the slats of the Venetian blinds, as they passed down the *calle* to the Piazza, that eve of the Assumption. It was that evening or at mid-night, that de Seingalt had spoken with him. Had Wolfgang von Goethe experienced the—the Visitor? Why had he questioned Dohna so closely on the matter of Zinzendorf, meeting Christian David at the house of the Master of the Horse in Schweinitz? That Goethe should so question, puzzled Dohna. Was the poet seeking, as he had apparently sought in Sicily, material for his epic? And why should he speak of *Arcana*? It was Dohna's question. Goethe seeking material, seizing on a legend had opened the door to Dohna's inquiry and ambition. Could he assemble the material, the inner reading? He, Saint-Germain was prepared to do this, would do this, but time was lacking. He could at least, indicate as clearly as possible, the sources of the legend, and Dohna could follow, with—with Elizabeth to help him. Count Zinzendorf was apparently in Dresden, when he made his pact with Christian David, the convert from Rome, at the house of the Master of the Horse in Schweinitz.

It was a play or an epic. It was already written. The players followed on, from other players. It was a small round, but it contained the universe. He had challenged Leopold Ragoczy as Dante challenged Cavalcanti. The Visitor had manifested to Christian David, as the young Count, though it would only be Zinzendorf himself who would know this. The Visitor had manifested to de Seingalt as Saint-Germain, but only Saint-Germain would solve the Mystery and that, long afterwards. It was written and easy to understand, but only by those who had had experience of it. Was that a more astute definition of the canon or the method, described as *acroamatique*? He had tried to recall the word, while the Cardinal spoke of the inner teaching. He had only remembered it, as Balsamo finished speaking . . . "the grooms were sympathetic. Even, brother, I could with my persuasion, find a place for you among them."

Balsamo was on his way to England, perhaps would soon be there. The Cardinal had by this time, presented his credentials to the Vatican. It was the old story. He had spoken of that first circle to the Cardinal. Hugh de Payens had not intended primarily, to serve the Patriarchs of Constantinople, by the secret alliance of the Templars with the Greek Church. That secret clothed or veiled another secret, the alliance within the alliance, with Theoclet, the Eastern Adept, who claimed to have inherited the Secret Doctrine, by uninterrupted transmission from Saint John. No doubt, the doctrine had been degraded and the Church had punished the apostates. But there was still the legend of an undefiled transmission. It had been their purpose to re-establish the Templars, within the Order of the Jesuits. But treason and betrayal was no corner-stone for that foundation. Almost, Balsamo recalled him—but he could go no further than he already had gone. Dante with his numbers, his circles, his revelation of Love, was Johannite and Gnostic. But it was only after he had reached the lowest depth of the Inferno that he retraced his path toward Paradise. There was treachery inherent in the return process. How did he get back—it was acrobatic (was that *acroamatique*?) He reversed dogma, he escaped from Tartarus, by standing on his head.

Was it possible that these Greeks, Cyril and Methodius of Constantinople, of whom Dohna had spoken, here and only an hour ago, had transmitted the Doctrine, unpolluted, to the Bohemians? Was it possible that the Doctrine had been received here and cherished, some centuries before Hugh de Payens received it from Theoclet? Was it possible that Theoclet's doctrine was already polluted, or should he say diluted with the dark magian power? Or was Theoclet, as they claimed for each new Master, living the Christ in his own person? Was the Doctrine degraded by the Templars, or the Templars by the Doctrine?

It was not a question of *Candace* souls, but a question of power and expansion with de Payens. And what exactly did *Candace* signify? It suggested superficially and yet inevitably, *lilium candidum*, the *Ave coeleste Lilium* of Saint Francis. It was said, a holy frenzy had inflamed his followers. So it seemed, from Dohna's first outline of the story, that Zinzendorf's disciples had scattered, like seeds burst from a weighted seed-pod, over the whole earth. They had assembled the Tibetan dictionary, even before the Jesuits got there. But though no doubt, they were now faithful guardians of the original stations or missions, the flame, the fantasy or the fanaticism had gone. They were as Dohna astutely reasoned, like the Cromwellians or Puritans in England. No flame of that red-rose or of that fire-lily! They were no more *Calixthenes*, nor even perhaps had ever heard of them, the worthy brethren. Was not Christian Renatus nearer their reality, encouraging or perhaps inspiring those extravagances which prevailed at the stations, so frowned upon by the good Bishop, Dohna quoted? It was Saint John who bore the cup, Saint John inseparable companion of Our Lady. What did she know of this, Our Lady, embarrassed by a lapse, "how foolish you must think me. As a child, they called me Lilie."

He saw her, as with the young Count—Renatus? But she was the next generation. Christian Renatus had inherited that red-rose of Bohemia, revealed some three centuries before Hugh de Payens claimed Messiahship for the Templars. Hugh de Payens' history was recorded and the descent of the

Military Masons, through the twenty-two Grand Masters of the Temple, before 1312 and the suppression of the Order. There were the names of those fortresses in Syria and Phoenicia and nearer to Jerusalem, Montgizard, Ibelin, Blanche Garde, Beth Gibelin, Ascalon, Darum, Montreal, Ile de Graye. What castles had the true Crusaders or the inheritors of the lost Grail?

Castell—her name was Theodora de Castell, so Dohna told him.

XVIII

It was white wine, the Saint-Germain. He was surprised that Stephanus left him, after beating up his pillows and re-arranging another chair with more blankets, for him to rest in. He did not want to break the continuity. There were two goblets on the table. Stephanus had left more candles on the small table at his elbow, after placing the single lighted one by the decanter and the glasses. No, he did not want his quill and paper. It seemed almost as if Stephanus were following directions, as if she had instructed him after her last visit, we must humour him, now he is convalescent. He could hear the low voice with the at times, quaintly stressed old-world French way of speaking. He forgot so easily, for all of Herrnhut, Marienborn and their talk of Herrnhaag and Friedenshuetten, that she was German-speaking. De Watteville? But her father was French, probably exiled Huguenot from Switzerland. Her father? It was her grandfather that had brought her to Prague, that had brought them together, through Henry Dohna's letter. He had lost his father when Leopold Ragoczy turned on him, revealing bastardy.

He had regained his father in Prince Karl and in de Rohan. Though Prince Karl had hinted of his origin, he had not told him of it. It was de Rohan who revealed it to him, and the fantastic theory that a little quibbling and a pontifical blessing from Rome would prove him the legitimate heir to the French throne. There was another Louis, half-imbecile and impotent, in the direct line—his brother? There was a child whom no one considered seriously, as the Dauphin of France.

There was a legend of knight-errantry, Prince Karl had told him, and a mother in the forest. He was seven. Was this symbolism, he had asked himself, after the Cardinal's reference to the story. "We fostered that, as well as the Venetian legend," the Cardinal had said. He remembered this, when, seated on the wooden bench, he had faced Cagliostro in the small room. He must remember to tell Stephanus that he had bundled his habit under the bench, but no doubt Stephanus had already found it and hung it on its usual peg beside the locked door. Was the door locked? It was there, to his left, as he lay, propped upright as he had been, when Dohna was talking to him. What had they left unsaid? There was nothing, really. "You cannot refuse France," he had said to Dohna, and the decanter was almost empty when he left. He turned his eyes to catch reflection of the candle, in the glass bowl, but the decanter was not empty. Stephanus must have replenished it, while he was preparing for bed; this bed, actually, with its nest of pillows, was more comfortable than the narrow cot upstairs in his own room. He had not thought—where have the cushions come from? Had Stephanus been plundering the House of Köstriz or had Jacobus, of whom he had spoken been sent around with them?

It was impossible, he could not have forgotten. "Give me your child until he is seven," had become a favourite Jesuit axiom. He had thought often of it, but himself (the child) he had banished from memory. Only the shock of de Rohan's treachery, or rather with the shock of connecting Balsamo with Leopold, did it reveal itself, but screened symbolically. It was neither de Rohan nor Leopold who was responsible for the first blow. Was it a King of France who had deserted and then re-called his mother? He was seven and the then Dauphin was already perhaps unpleasing to his father. Prince Ragoczy of Transylvania was entrusted with the secret and the welfare of Antoine-Louis—Saint-Germain, as they called him. It was an hereditary title, the Prince had told him, the second son had his holdings in France. He could not have forgotten. Her fur-hood fell back from the lace-scarf, bound over her hair, as she stooped to kiss him.

She had told him that the scarf was inherited from her godmother, Theodora de Castell, she said, as she unfastened the clasp of her cloak and drew the lace from under the fur-hood. It reminded him of something, he had said, but he was certain that she thought he was delirious, as she had answered, "Sir, I will leave it with you, for your memories." No, he had not touched her. He had not flung himself against the soft fur, he had not been enfolded in the fall of the white veil, he had not clutched, like a small animal, at the fragrant pelt whose very substance he was. He had propped himself up on an elbow, such power and strength had suddenly renewed him, and he had smiled for the first time, to hear Our Lady speak of witchcraft.

It was a slow renewal. The memory had not come like a flash of lightning, nor reviewed his whole life in a single series of pictures that moved instantaneously before the mind, as the legends say has been reported by some, saved at the last breath, from drowning. Was that too, symbolical? The pictures had returned, but inward pictures, not startling, not visionary. He was waiting with Stephanus but it was not Stephanus. It had happened before. She had gone off, this other said, before, alone in the sleigh, and there was nothing to it. "Nought to it," he said. That was not Stephanus speaking. Hadn't she always come back? He was tearing at a great door, a heavy knob, almost too high to reach, and past it, he was struggling with a giant-bolt but it slipped finally with a clatter and the door swung back. He stood in the snow that had drifted in the hall-way, the wind was howling from the river. There were no marks in the snow. Had he ever had a mother?

". . . the foot-prints is blown over or I could have showed you," the school-porter had said, when they finally found shelter in Saint Benedict on the Walls.

The Cathedral had turned round, but that had happened before, though usually in his own bed, waking at night. The scene had veered around, *acroamatique*, was he standing on his head? Perhaps, after his abstinence, it was the Saint-Germain, but he drew the decanter toward him. He had found his brother in the astute, aristocratic Dohna. My Aunt Agnes met Henri's father, my Uncle Maurice, she had said, at an assembly at *San Souci*. Frederick had instituted a little France, within his empire. He had entertained Count Zinzendorf and had admired his writings. One or the other must have told him of it. They were inseparable in his imagination. He had found his brother in the only son of Maurice, Count Dohna, but he had not found his sister in the daughter of Baron John de Watteville. The names were so important. They seemed more allied to France than to Germany. The Order of the Temple had not deeply touched the Teutonic Knights, but these two, in their sympathy and outlook, seemed to accept both factions, even as their grandfather had imagined a world-unity.

Father d'Albizi? He wished he knew more about him, could have given Dohna further details of the Dominican connection. When he returned to Paris—but he would have other problems. Perhaps, as the Cardinal put it, the more important adherents of the Church would leave. But he did not see the heroic Daughters of Saint Genevieve or the simple Friars of Francis leaving Paris.

His right hand rested on a sword-hilt. It was his way of distinguishing right from left hand, in these moments. If he had not deliberately, for purposes of policy, followed the left-hand path, he would never have found her. And this was not Jesuitical defence nor argument. He would not have bound himself to Althotas, he would not have sworn loyalty to Acharat. The vows could not be broken. It was the Cardinal who was Judas. He was standing on his head now. He had been elected, instructed to bring the two together. But "there was no crossing that bridge," Cagliostro had said.

He would not touch the veil that she held toward him. He watched her re-arrange the scarf. He saw her face as in a mirror. They were *Candace* souls. There was another of their company. No, she did not return to Versailles, nor did she die, the blessed Primavera. She was going away. She spoke between the candles, Our Lady of the Snow, Louis, you will serve France.

XIX

He would be sleeping in the hall, Stephanus. He would know when the fire died down, but Saint-Germain did not think that Stephanus would disturb him. "So, you married the nun Charity?" He spoke to the presence opposite whose goblet he re-filled when his own was empty. "He never knew me to lose my head," he explained, "so we will go on with our Saint-Germain. Yes, the family was waiting to receive me—it is like you to ask about the family—the lesser and greater Saint-Germains, the King's cousins. It was natural for the senile Saint-Étienne to mistake me for my uncle or my great-uncle, as Stephanus had insisted. So the legend started—or the legend renewed another legend. I could explain away the fatuous Elixir. I could explain to Versailles, when the Venetian legend found its way there, that I was mistaken for a nephew. But I could not explain to myself how I appeared to de Seingalt, Giovanni Jacopo Casanova de Seingalt. Another Giovanni. It was by the bridge, before Mary of Miracles, that we talked together. What I wanted to ask de Seingalt, and never did ask, was: what was I wearing? An odd irrelevance, you may consider. I never dared ask de Seingalt nor inquire further.

"Nor did you inquire how Christian David found you (in riding-cloak? in court dress?) at the house of the Master of the Horse, in Schweinitz?

"It can be explained with lines and parallels and reflecting mirrors.

"He was a Shadow of God—when and how did you discover it?—Who was again a Reflection.

"It was exactly indicated to Saint John. How has it escaped the orthodox? You remember, if all the things done by Our Lord were recorded, *I suppose that even the world itself could not contain the books that should be written.* But there is a freshness and simplicity that would escape even those books . . . *sur la berge, fleurit un rosier, à l'unique rose épanouis que butine un immense papillon.* There were twelve children. I did not even wonder nor ask if she had children. She told over their names like the beads in a rosary. There was Christian Frederick, there was Theodora Caritas, there was Anna Theresa, there was Christian Louis, there was Salome—I can not remember the others, all children. I know Benigna, Agnes, Elizabeth and Christian Renatus grew up, though Renatus died in London. They were all important to me, for my nephews and nieces—cousins, really—were a later importation. Or I was later grafted to that *La France* rose which—but we must not speak about it. The wings were not freed by those syrens. There had been that earlier enchantment of strings, brushed by Melusine, across the water. But the wound inflected by Leopold was not healed and *La France* and Melusine were, alike, temporary opiates. No doubt, you loved your Countess and revered her. There were twelve children. They seemed stars around her head, like an image of Our Lady, as she told them. Your children, but she claimed them. Were your wings freed by Theodora de Castell, before you married Erdmuth Dorothea de Reuss?

"It is written somewhere, among the many heresies that it was my—my duty to decipher, that it is experienced once in fifty years, that is, once in a lifetime.

"You have written it in these letters? My friend, you cannot refuse France. He never knew me to lose my head, so we will re-fill our glasses. And you talked to the chairs, she told me—another child in Our Lady's rosary—because your father died (Nicholas, she called you then) and your mother married a Prussian field-marshal, when you were four.

"You were accused of gross and scandalous mysticism, so Dohna told me.

•

"You are no devil, Louis, so to tempt me. The Guard could be disbanded? No, Louis, it is not possible. France would never be the same, if the Guard were so disbanded. Look—I sacrifice the Guard for a dream, a legend that has already vanished? You say, Louis, that France is no more, but the lilies can not be—disbanded. You can not dismiss the lilies. You say, they are good fellows, let them go home. And Stephanus, why should he go back there? Ah my friend, how neatly you play into our hands—Stephanus? There is Lamotte, a sewing-girl she was, as he reminded me but recently, it was Cagliostro made her 'Countess.' What plan had Balsamo for Lamotte and the Queen, he asked me. I had no answer but he knew the answer.

"You know the answer—there is Lamotte and the Queen.

"They could be smuggled out of Paris? Not now, my dear Louis, later perhaps, with our help and the new pass words.

"France would never be the same, if we let Lamotte and the Queen perish. But enough of tragedy. There will be a fine flourish and I feel a giant. I will pay my respects to the Castle. Stephanus brought all my trappings. We will borrow the Castle's coach-and-four or sleigh-and-four. We will be driven to the Tower in fine style, to make our adieux. You see, that little rumour has blown over. We return, summoned by the Palace, *en chevalier*, to re-inaugurate and re-dedicate the Guard, as is customary New Year's Eve. So we will see the New Year in, and even at Versailles, *the chandeliers shall be lighted for Him*. You see how I remember? Dohna was reading to me from a Pennsylvania sermon or a sermon at Zeist.

"My friend, the *Little Strength*? He saw three ships a-sailing. He lay dying in Lindsay House in London, on the Thames. Christian Renatus sent them this Christmas carol, Dohna told me, and later he explained the myth, legend or Mystery. They were Joseph of Arimathaea's ships—but why three? To honour the Trinity, you will tell me. It was One Ship or Three-in-One-Ship, wasn't it? Or it was three journeys of one Ship? They took the Grail to England. The *Little Strength* renewed that Mystery with your Lamb *passant* and then to America. America? But it was not America, it was Transylvania, I mean Pennsylvania and it was Bethlehem. But they brought the Grail back, so she told me, or so she seemed to tell me, when the Bethlehem Indians left Friedenshuetten.

"Let there be no more argument, my dear Louis—to you, Nicholas Louis, Count and Lord of Zinzendorf and Pottendorf; Lord of the Baronies of Freydeck, Schoeneck, Thurnstein and the Vale of Wachovia; Lord of the Manor of Upper, Middle and Lower Berthelsdorf—(you see how I remember, that is the *Exercitia* that laid its iron-rule upon me)—and Hereditary Warden of the Chase to his Imperial Roman Majesty, in the Duchy of Austria, below the Ems.

"Also the Dresden Socrates.

"But we have no time for Socratic argument. This is the last candle. No, save the half-goblet, for the decanter is quite empty. I would only say that your Mysticism is naturally repulsive to men, who would at all costs elevate the Father above all, and above all, above the Mother. Your poem to that effect—I will not quote it—was enough to burn you at the stake, like that John Huss whom they bound, outside here by the Cathedral. Your heresy goes deeper than his, but you are an older soul, my Dresden Socrates, and the Dominicans had a part in your instruction. You worshipped the Wounds of Our Lord—the Wound *in excelsis* in Our Lord's side, as the *rosa mystica*. This, my friend, is gross and scandalous mysticism, as the Protestant Court decided. But Louis, your proscribed *Aves* reached heaven.

"They heard you and they sent Our Lady to us. No, I will not read the letters. I will take them to her with the Star five-pointed, the fingers of a hand, the nails or the Wounds of God.

"But with happiness—almost intolerable exaltation.

"And—*à bientôt*, Nicholas."

Eighteenth-Century Origins of The Mystery

Count Louis Saint-Germain (1696?–1784)

This "only known portrait of the Count of Saint-Germain" was painted circa 1756 by Pietro Antonio Rotari (1707–62) at the request of the Marquise D'Urfé, a wealthy Parisian occultist. Stories of Saint-Germain's "deathlessness" began circulating at this time, and he was called "the most mysterious man in Paris."

Louis René Édouard Cardinal de Rohan (1734–1803)

This portrait was published in 1786 in his *Requête au Parlement*, his petition to the Parliament of Paris as he defended himself in his trial on charges of theft in "the affair of the necklace." The scandal fueled popular unrest and helped to bring on the French Revolution. Artist unknown.

Alessandro, Count Cagliostro, born Giuseppe Balsamo (1743–95)

Detail from "A Masonic Anecdote" by James Gillray (1751–1815).
This cartoon illustrates Cagliostro's style and ridicules his claims to possess magical healing powers acquired through secret Masonic rites. Hand-colored etching published November 21, 1786. National Portrait Gallery, London, England.

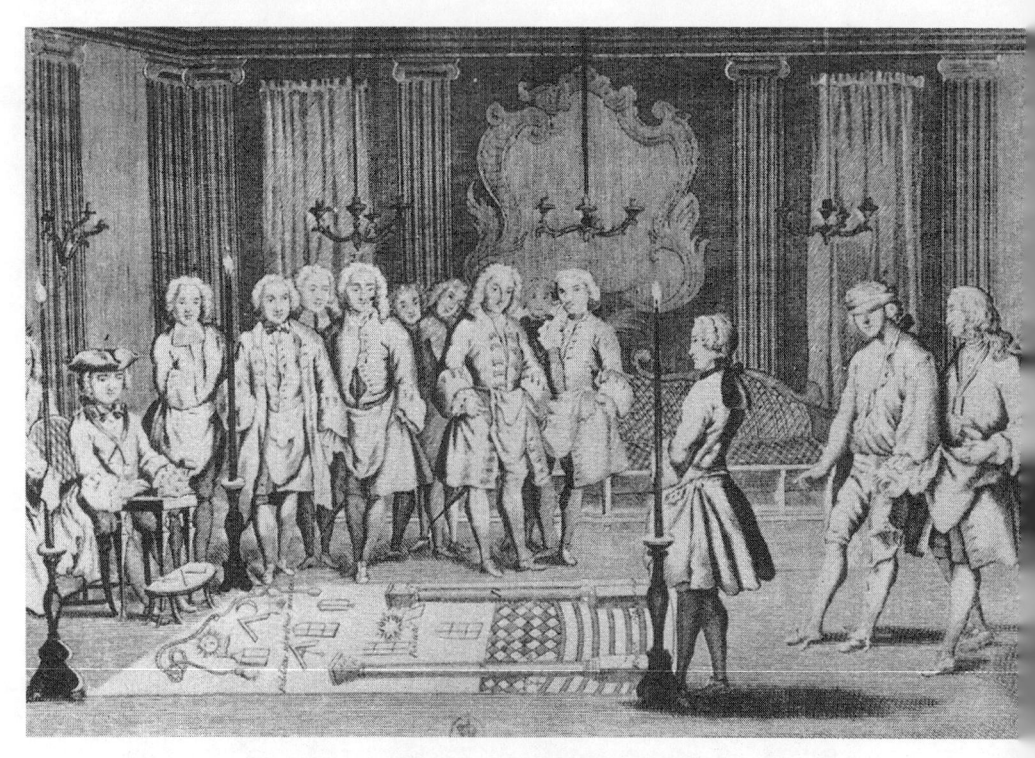

Initiation into a Masonic Lodge in the eighteenth century

The pillars of the Temple of Solomon, symbolically laid out before the terrified initiate, were named Jachin ("standing") and Boaz ("strength") by King Solomon (1 Kings 7.21). The letters *J* and *B* are faintly visible on the pillars. Artist and date unknown.

Nicholas Louis Count von Zinzendorf (1700–1760)

The count wears courtroom attire as aulic councillor, that is, a judge, at Dresden, his position in 1722 when the first refugee Moravians arrived on his estate. Oil on canvas by Elias Gottlob Hausman (1695–1774), undated, probably circa 1725. GS 031, Moravian Archives, Herrnhut, Germany.

Erdmuth Dorothea von Zinzendorf (1700–1756)

Count Zinzendorf's first wife, née von Reuss; married him in 1721; managed his estates and church finances after he was banished from Saxony in 1732; bore twelve children. Oil on canvas, artist and date unknown. GS 035, Moravian Archives, Herrnhut, Germany

Sophie Theodora Countess von Reuss (1703–77)

Née von Castell, first cousin of Zinzendorf; married his close friend, Henry von Reuss in 1721, the same year that Zinzendorf married Henry's sister, Erdmuth. Oil on canvas by Antoinette Sophie Emilia Damnitz, undated. GS 081, Moravian Archives, Herrnhut, Germany.

Benigna Henriette Justine Countess von Watteville (1725–89).

First child and oldest daughter of Erdmuth and Nicholas von Zinzendorf; married John von Watteville in 1746; mother of Elisabeth (1754–1813), fictionalized here as Elizabeth de Watteville. Oil on canvas by John Valentine Haidt (1700–1780), undated. GS 053, Moravian Archives, Herrnhut.

Christian David (1676–1758)

Known as "the carpenter from Moravia" and intensely religious, he felt deep compulsion to save the Old Church of Bohemia; met Zinzendorf "at the house of the master of the horse in Schweinitz" and brought the first refugees to the Count's estate in Saxony in 1722. GS357, Moravian Archives, Herrnhut, Germany.

David "Father" Nitschmann (1676–1758)

One of the "Five Pillars of the Moravian Church," the five men who worked to reestablish the Unitas Fratrum at Herrnhut; pioneering missionary in Pennsylvania 1740–44; great-uncle of Anna Nitschmann. Oil on canvas by John Valentine Haidt, undated. PC 027, Moravian Archives, Bethlehem, Pennsylvania.

Anna Caritas Nitschmann (1715–60)

The most respected and powerful woman leader among eighteenth-century Moravians; preached extensively and counselled many women privately; wrote hymns. A close coworker with Zinzendorf, she became his second wife in 1757. Oil on canvas by John Valentine Haidt, undated. GS 067, Moravian Archives, Herrnhut, Germany.

Count Zinzendorf as Teacher of the Peoples of the World

Zinzendorf taught a mystically inspired "heart-religion" that his followers carried to nations and races ignored by other churches. The earliest converts were Africans. He called them "Candace-souls," after Philip's conversion of the Ethiopian Queen Candace's eunuch (Acts 8.26–40.) Oil on canvas, John Valentine Haidt, before 1750. GS 583, Moravian Archives, Herrnhut, Germany.

The First Fruits

The early Moravian converts who died in the 1740s, among them West Indians, Native Americans, and Inuits, are depicted here gathered around the throne of Christ in heaven. *These were redeemed from among men, being the first fruits unto God and the Lamb* (Rev. 14.4). Oil on canvas, John Valentine Haidt, circa 1760. PC 19, Moravian Archives, Bethlehem, Pa.

The Crowned Virgin: A Vision of John

Detail from a Gustave Doré engraving illustrating Revelation 12.1: *And there appeared a great wonder in heaven; a woman clothed with the sun, and the moon under her feet, and upon her head a crown of twelve stars.* Published 1875 in Germany. From Gustave Doré, *The Doré Bible Illustrations*, Dover Publications, Inc., New York. Reprinted through permission of the publisher.

Editor's Notes

These notes are keyed to italicized phrases from the novel.

Chapter I, pp. 1–3

The name was de Watteville. The reader is plunged immediately into the consciousness of a central character identified in the next sentence as male by the pronoun "he." He has just learned the family name of the mysterious woman for whom he opened the cathedral door earlier in the day. Since he calls this gesture "a mistake," he is plainly disturbed by her. Her full name is Elizabeth de Watteville. She is a fictionalized version of the historical granddaughter, Elisabeth von Watteville, of Nicholas Louis (or Lewis; Ger: Nikolaus Ludwig) Count von Zinzendorf. She was born April 25, 1754, to his daughter, Benigna, who was married in 1746 to Johann von Watteville, the adopted son of a close friend of Count Zinzendorf. The novel is set in Prague within and near Saint Vitus's Cathedral in December 1788 as the French Revolution is about to break out. Prague is the capital of old Bohemia, a name often understood as applying to the whole region including the provinces of Bohemia, Moravia, and Czech Silesia that make up the present-day Czech Republic. In the period of this novel, Bohemia was a Hapsburg crown land and Roman Catholicism the established religion (*Co.Enc.*, 321).

Stephanus is the name of the narrator's servant.

The river Vltava (German: Moldau) makes a huge curve through Prague and is visible from Hradčany hill where Saint Vitus's Cathedral stands above the city as the principal monument within Prague Castle, also called Hradčany Castle, a large fortified complex of buildings created by ancient Bohemian kings. The cathedral was founded by the king-saint Wenceslas (Czech: Václav) in 925–29 when he built the Rotunda of Saint Vitus, "the first stone edifice in Bohemia" on a site sacred since ancient pre-Christian times (*Praha*, 1958). Svatovit, the Slavic god of fertility, was worshipped there, which "gives a clue as to why the cathedral was dedicated to his near namesake Saint Vitus (Czech: svatý Vit)," a fourth-century Sicilian martyr (*TOP*, 76). "He is one of the Fourteen Holy Helpers, a collective cult of saints that originated in the 14th-century Rhineland, and believed to intercede effectively against various diseases" (*Co.Enc.*, 2901). Because his feast day was celebrated by dancing, he became the saint invoked to aid sufferers from epilepsy and Sydenham's chorea, called "Saint Vitus's Dance" since its symptoms are involuntary muscle movements. H.D. very likely knew the healing legend of Saint Vitus.

Street of the Alchemists. H.D. always uses this translation of the name for the street that in German was called *Alchimistengässchen*, the name she would have seen in 1931 for the little lane also called *Goldenes Gässchen* and now called Golden Lane (Czech: Zlatá ulick). There "tiny cottages cling to Prague Castle's northern walls," dwarf buildings that had been thrown up by poor people left homeless after the Great Fire of 1541 destroyed most of the city (Wechsberg, 57; *TOP*, 81). The legend influencing H.D. here says that "in the time of Rudolf II [1552–1612] alchemists were housed" in Golden Lane and his "goldsmiths and goldbeaters plied their craft here" (Michalitschke, 147; *Praha*, 1958). The old double name associating gold with alchemy and magic apparently arose from Rudolf II's interest in both. In 1584 the Englishman Edward Kelly (or Kelley) was appointed "court alchemist" by Rudolf, who had been convinced that Kelly possessed the philosopher's stone and could produce gold by transmutation. In 1585 Kelly bought a house in Prague where "Prince Wenceslas Opavský had already installed an alchemist's laboratory," no. 502–40 Charles Square, which later became known as the "Faust House," as it was said that the "Czech Doctor Faustus" lived there (Wechsberg, 57). Although not near the Street of the Alchemists, this house and its story account for an association of Prague with Faust that plays a role in this novel.

H.D. wrote to Norman Holmes Pearson on August 20, 1951, from Lugano where she composed the second half of *The Mystery*. "I was in Prague once, en route to Vienna and was much impressed with it, the Street of the Alchemists, the Chapel of Saint Wenceslas and the rest." She had been in psychoanalytic sessions in Berlin with Dr. Hanns Sachs from November 27 until shortly before Christmas in 1931. Sachs suggested that she come to Vienna for the holidays, as he would be spending them there, and travel by way of Prague. She was in Prague December 19 to 21 and wrote: "Prague bitter cold, but a wonderful experience" (*AN*, 23). Sachs later recommended that she go to Freud to continue psychoanalysis.

St. Wenceslas Chapel. Judged the most beautiful of the twenty-one chapels in Saint Vitus's Cathedral and "a crowning work of Czech Gothic," it was built in 1345 and has walls "encrusted with Bohemian semi-precious stones . . . 1,345 polished amethysts, agates and jaspers, with gilded mortar as a bond" and decorated with scenes of Christ's Passion and of Saint Wenceslas's life (Svoboda, 70). Saint Wenceslas is buried under the chapel, which was erected on the site of the old rotunda and now lies inside the cathedral, whose construction began in 1344 under Charles IV (1316–78) with Matthew of Arras, using Narbonne Cathedral as model (Svoboda, 70; *TOP*, 76–77).

his Superior. This term, capitalized, hints at the as yet unrevealed religious identity of the narrator, who is the "Superior" of Stephanus. He is thinking that his servant will reprove him for watching the woman, which would be improper behavior for a monk.

de Schweinitz is the name of a major lineage in American Moravian history. Hans Christian Alexander von Schweinitz was appointed Bethlehem's first official community administrator in 1770. He and Elisabeth von Watteville were married in 1779 in Bethlehem. They had seven children. The oldest, Ludwig, changed the name from the German form to the French "de Schweinitz." Ludwig had three sons, all eventually prominent in the Moravian Church. Emil, a bishop; Robert, a pastor; and Edmund, a bishop, theologian, and historian. Their descendants were the "real de Schweinitz children" with whom H.D. went to school, as she wrote to NHP on April 16, 1951.

The house of the Master of the Horse in Schweinitz. Zinzendorf first met Christian David (1692–1751), leader of the refugees from the old church of Bohemia, the *Unitas Fratrum* or Bohemian Brethren, in 1722, says A.G. Spangenberg, Zinzendorf's friend and biographer (AGS, 39). H.C.A. von Schweinitz was born on family estates at Nieder Leuba in Upper Lusatia [Ober Lausitz], which is presumably the place named "Schweinitz" in this reference.

the Royal Guard. Because the narrator feels that there are French-Swiss associations to the name de Watteville, he is reminded of the Swiss Guard, the "Royal Guard" assigned to protect the French royal family, in this period King Louis XVI and Queen Marie Antoinette. There is a hint here of the novel's time frame, in that the French revolution that began in early 1789 brought about the abolition of the monarchy, and therefore there was no Swiss Guard in France after it. The phrase "Swiss Guard" that comes two sentences later clarifies the reference.

the Queen is Marie Antoinette.

congé, the French word for "vacation" or "holiday," enhances the narrator's conjecture that because of her aristocratic name and appearance the woman might be a lady-in-waiting to the queen of France.

one of the Swiss Guard. The narrator reasons that if the woman named de Watteville is close to royalty, the man with her, Schweinitz, must be a member of the Swiss Guard assigned to protect her. The revolutionaries massacred the Swiss Guard in 1789 after they refused to abandon Louis XVI's palace, even though he and his family had already left it. This historical fact is central to the novel's plot and theme.

Brother Antonius. This first use of Antonius's name and title tells the reader the narrator's identity and the church setting.

Exercitia is short for *Exercitia Spiritualia S.P. Ignatii de Loyola,* the *Spiritual Exercises* composed by Saint Ignatius of Loyola (1491–1556), Spanish nobleman and then soldier who was converted to the religious life in 1521 while recovering from a battle wound in Pamplona in northern Spain. Jesuits are expected to perform the *Exercitia* daily.

formal vow of dedication. No vow appears with that title in the *Spiritual Exercises*. Probably the reference is to a well-known prayer of dedication composed by Saint Ignatius:

> Take, Lord, all my liberty. Receive my memory, my understanding and my whole will. Whatever I have and possess thou has given to me; to thee I restore it wholly, and to thy will I utterly surrender it for thy direction. Give me the love of thee only, with thy grace, and I am rich enough; nor ask I anything beside. (Sp.Ex., 20)

Possibly, however, another popular prayer of Saint Ignatius is being referred to.

> Teach us, good Lord, to serve Thee as Thou deservest.
> To give and not count the cost;
> To fight and not heed the wounds;
> To toil and not to seek for rest;
> To labour and not ask for any reward
> Save that of knowing that we do Thy Will.

Withdrawal. Part of the *Exercitia* is self-examination by the method Saint Ignatius calls "the particular survey," done several times a day by the retreatant. "toward the end of the morning . . . he makes his first survey of the day. . . . he exacts of himself acknowledgement of each moral failure regarding the particular sin or fault . . . reviewing each portion of the day . . . up to the present moment" (Delmage, 17). Saint Ignatius advised those "occupied with public affairs" to use this method, adding. "In this way Father Antonius Possevinus made the Exercises when he was secretary of the Society" (*Sp.Ex.*, 20). This passage possibly suggested to H.D. the name Antonius for her character. "The withdrawal" can be seen as a reflection of Saint Ignatius's idea that earthly things were meant to aid man to save his soul and he should "withdraw himself" when they hinder him (*Sp.Ex.*, 29).

a not important lay–brother . . . forgotten the role. These lines reveal that Antonius is in disguise; he is only "at the moment" playing the role of a poor lay-brother. His Jesuit thoughts of the *Exercitia* have been intended as a clue that he is a member of the suppressed order. The theme of Jesuit discipline is linked to Count Zinzendorf as the novel progresses.

Wrapt. This old form of "wrapped" is a deliberate archaism. Both "wrapt" and "wrapped" with "in" mean "deeply absorbed in," but here there is a punning connotation of "rapt," as in a rapture or trance.

England, France, Venice, Spain, Naples. Antonius is naming to himself the places into which Freemasonry moved swiftly after a Grand Masonic lodge was established in England in 1717. Then came one in France in 1725 and others in Spain and Italy. Freemasons are Protestants, and he is a Jesuit particularly involved in opposing Protestantism. The cold stones on which he is kneeling reminded him of Freemasonry, which originated in the medieval stone-masons' guild.

Clement XIV. The pope preceding the then current pope Pius VI, pope from 1775 to 1779, had been jealous of Jesuit power and in 1773 suppressed the Society of Jesus, although they could have helped him combat the spread of Protestant Masonry. The *franc-maçon*, the French Freemasons, posed particular danger as they were said to be instigating a revolution against the Crown of France.

their last secret stronghold in Prague. "Their" in this sentence refers to the remnant of loyal Jesuits, not to the Holy See or to the *franc-maçon*. Antonius is thinking that, as a Jesuit, he will work to supply the pope with information on the Freemasons. His usefulness might move the pope to reinstate the Society of Jesus. Loyola was apparently influenced by Freemasonry when he established degrees of initiation for the Jesuits "like those of the Freemasons" (*Enc.Rel.Eth.*, vii, 500–505).

Pampeluna is a variant of the name of Pamplona, the capital of Navarre in northern Spain bordering on the Pyrenées. At times in its history it has been part of France.

The Praetorian Guard. Augustus Caesar, first Roman emperor (63 BC-AD 14) created the Praetorian Guard as an imperial bodyguard. The *cohortes praetoria* consisted of nine cohorts of 1,000 men each, some of whom were always with the emperor. The only body of troops in the city of Rome, they became an elite possessing decisive political power, as when they made Claudius emperor in AD 41. They lasted until the division of the empire after Constantine (d. 337). H.D. is stressing similarities between the Christian and non-Christian organizations.

Paul III, pope in 1540, formally established in that year the *Compañia Jesus Christus* (Company of Jesus) created by Ignatius with six friends, including Francis Xavier, circa 1531. He translated its Spanish name into Latin as *Societas Jesu*, the Society of Jesus.

Defeat . . . only fifty years after. In 1581, approximately fifty years after the founding of the Society of Jesus, the English Jesuit, Edmund Campion, was executed as a traitor under the penal laws, evidently the "defeat" referred to. Campion, Robert Persons, and other English refugee Jesuits had returned secretly from Douai and Louvain to England to support Catholics there. While they themselves were nonpolitical, the Romanist revival they stimulated in the 1580s led to attempts on Queen Elizabeth's life by those who hoped to restore a Catholic monarchy. Her response was to execute Jesuits and other purported instigators (*EB* [1957], 4: 685).

daughter of the traitor and renegade Henry VIII. Antonius is vilifying Queen Elizabeth I of England, who reigned from 1558 to 1603 and continued her father's anti–Roman Catholic policies (*EB* [1957], 4: 685).

Fifteen years later. The Jesuit failure in England gives a fairly precise date for the suppression in France alluded to here. In 1594 Henry IV, who had made a political conversion to Catholicism in 1593, was attacked by a man named Jean Chastel, who nicked the King with a knife-blade. "In order to deflect blame from themselves, outspoken critics of Henry's cause threw blame on the Jesuits. The king confiscated their college, Clermont, in Paris and had several executed. Later, in gratitude for the work of a Jesuit cardinal, Toletus, in having him reconciled to the church, Henry gave the college back. Any suppression was temporary" (W. Faherty, S.J., Saint Louis University Department of History, letter to the editor, October 29, 1987).

Bartholomew refers to the Saint Bartholomew's Day Massacre of Huguenots that took place on August 24, 1572, instigated by King Charles IX under the influence of his mother, Catherine de Medicis, who was jealous of the increasing power of Admiral de Coligny, a Huguenot adviser to the King. Since many Huguenot nobles were expected to come to Paris on that day for the wedding of Catherine's daughter, Marguerite de Valois, to the Huguenot Henry of Navarre, later King Henry IV, a mass slaughter was arranged and carried out. Murders of Huguenots continued throughout France until October, with a conservative estimate of over 2,000 slain. Antonius speculates that Queen Elizabeth's agents made contact with Henry before his wedding and so were able later to persuade him that Jesuits were responsible for Chastel's assassination attempt. By seeing to it that blame was cast on the Jesuits, Elizabeth could feel justified in her continued persecutions of them.

Ludmilla, called Saint Ludmilla (Czech: Ludmila), was born c. 860. She married Borivoy, Duke of Bohemia, its ruler, and became a Christian with him after he was baptized by Saint Methodius. Their son Ratislav married a Slav princess, Drahomira, who bore a son, Wenceslas, in 907. Ludmila arranged to take charge of his upbringing so that he would be a Christian. When Ratislav, who ruled Bohemia after 915, was killed in battle, Drahomira became regent, pursuing anti-Christian policies favored by the semipagan nobility. Ludmila urged Wenceslas, by then about twenty-two years old, to assume leadership. To block her plan, two nobles went to Ludmila's castle at Tetin and strangled her on September 16, 921. She was hailed as a martyr and heroine of Bohemia. Although her "relique" is mentioned here, her body actually lies in Saint George's Basilica, near Saint Vitus Cathedral in the Prague Castle complex. Wenceslas became king but was murdered in 929 by his younger brother, "the notorious Boleslav the Cruel." Immediately venerated as a martyr, Wenceslas became and remains the patron saint of Bohemia (*TOP*, 79; Thurston III, 570. 663–64).

He was on duty. Not Antonius but Stephanus, the servant, is on duty as watchman. The pronoun reference might be misleading.

The scholarly lay-brother. Antonius is describing himself in his disguise as a Franciscan monk and scholar, assistant to the abbot of the cloister in Prague Castle. His prior meditations show that his inner life belongs to the Jesuits. When H.D. visited the Prague Castle complex in 1932, she probably had been shown the Capuchin cloister, the oldest foundation of that order in Bohemia (*Praha*, 66).

"Give me your child until he is seven . . . " This statement is popularly attributed to Saint Ignatius, but it was not made by him, according to Jesuit authorities. Jesuits did not teach in elementary schools in Ignatius's lifetime nor operate in situations with small children (W. Faherty, letter to the editor, October 29, 1987). This idea appears to come from anti-Catholic sources.

The *House of Köstriz*. This name, also spelled Köstritz, refers to both the lands and the noble lineage of the Reuss family. Spangenberg says that Elisabeth de Watteville's younger sister, Maria Justine, married "Henry the 55th Count Reuss of the House of Köstritz" (AGS, xxxi). The list of Zinzendorf's descendents and a memoir confirm that Count Henry LV was born "at the family seat at Köstritz, near Gera" in Thuringia 45 miles SSW of Leipzig (*HLV*, 5). Gera had been the property of the Reuss family since the twelfth century. Justine apparently married a distant cousin, since her grandmother, Zinzendorf's wife, Erdmuth Dorothea, was also a Reuss, and therefore a member of the house of Köstriz. Erdmuth was a descendent of George of Podiebrad (or Podebrad), King of Bohemia from 1458 to 1471, the only native and non-Catholic king of Bohemia (*HB*, 7; *USE*, 934). Through this known descendence H.D. imagines that the house of Köstriz might hold property in Prague Castle, having obtained it earlier, since it was Emperor Sigismund (1368–1437) who gave the family "the dignity of the Counts of Reuss" (*HLV*, 5). I have been unable to find any documentary verification of such ownership at any time.

Polish, Bohemian, Prussian. Antonius is questioning which one of the nationalities might be Elizabeth de Watteville's.

Frederick had consolidated the Protestant Principalities. Frederick the Great (1712–86), king of Prussia, by military brilliance and diplomacy, greatly expanded his kingdom by acquiring Silesia in 1745 and part of Poland in 1772. His efforts checked Catholic Austria and so consolidated the Protestant principalities (*EB* [1957], 9: 716–19). Antonius's disjointed train of thought results from his suspicion that, since the mysterious woman did not genuflect, she is Protestant. If so, she is in danger, having come into Catholic territory.

more likely, Austrian. Despite the religious contradiction, H.D. makes Antonius guess that the woman is Austrian because, although he does not yet know that she is Zinzendorf's granddaughter, H.D. knows that the Zinzendorf family originally came from Austria (AGS, v).

Viduae et Virgines. This Latin phrase translates as "widows and virgins," categories of women likely to became nuns. In H.D.'s handwritten first draft, she wrote the English words but crossed them out and wrote in the Latin, the language of the church appropriate to Antonius. She underlined the phrase. It echoes descriptions of virtuous women on monuments and in saints' legends. Although the narrator sees the mysterious woman as nun-like, he is very interested in her marital status.

Chapter II, pp. 4–7

Elizabeth. The use of this feminine first name shows that she is the woman surnamed de Watteville observed by Antonius. The setting is her apartment in what H.D. calls the "Old Tower." Prague Castle has several towers, none by this exact name, but probably H.D. has in mind the largest, the Mihulka or Powder Tower, built in the fifteenth century. Legend says that here Rudolf II's alchemists worked to distill the Elixir of Life and transmute base metals into gold (*TOP*, 79). This tower stands north of Saint Vitus's Cathedral off of Vikářská Lane, which lies to the west of Golden Lane.

the Dohna legend. The speaker is Henry Dohna, whom Antonius thought was a "lackey" named Schweinitz. He is also taken from a historical figure, Heinrich Dohna, whose name H.D. saw in A. G. Spangenberg's *Life of Nicholas Lewis Count Zinzendorf*. He was Elisabeth's first cousin, another grandchild of Count Zinzendorf; he never married. The allusion here, however, is to Henry's Dohna grandfather, Christoph, who was commanding general of the Prussian army in East Prussia during the Seven Years War. His "legend" is presumably a military one.

Hans Christian Alexander von Schweinitz. The historical Elisabeth outlived her husband, as here, but he died in 1802 and she in 1813, dates not fitting this novel's scheme.

the other grandpappa. Count Zinzendorf is "other" in relation to the Dohna and de Watteville grandfathers.

mamma. Elisabeth's mother is Benigna Henriette Justine von Zinzendorf (b. December 28, 1725), Count Zinzendorf's oldest child and first daughter, one of the four of his twelve children who survived to adulthood. In 1746 at Zeist she married Baron John von Watteville (b. October 18, 1718). His true name was John Michael Langguth, and his father was a Lutheran pastor, but he was adopted by Zinzendorf's lifelong friend, Baron Frederick von Watteville, and thus obtained the title "Freiherr von Wattewille." The Germanic spelling of this name has given way to the French style in most of the translated documents.

de Watteville. Frederick Rudolph von Watteville, biological son of Frederick Baron von Watteville, was born in Montmirail, Switzerland, in 1738, which made him legally the brother of John von Watteville. Elisabeth von Zinzendorf, Benigna's younger sister (b. April 25, 1740), married Frederick Rudolf in 1768.

Aunt Agnes. Maria Agnes von Zinzendorf was born November 6, 1735, and is therefore the middle sister between Benigna and Justine. H.D. also had an Aunt Agnes, her mother's half-sister, the daughter of Elizabeth Weiss Seidel Wolle ("Mamalie") and her first husband, Christian Seidel. In *The Gift*'s chapter 5, "The Secret," H.D. invents the scene in which her grandmother, Mamalie, in mediumistic trance calls child Hilda Agnes or Aggie (*G*, 150–51, 178–79, 304 refs.).

the Lord's Hedgerows translates the German word Herrnhaag, the name of the Moravian community near Frankfort-am-Main, founded in 1736 after Zinzendorf was banished from Saxony in 1732 and shortly before he was ordained as bishop of the Moravian Church on May 20, 1737. H.D. calls it *the Lord's Hedge* in chapter 13. See notes to that chapter.

your father. Agnes married Maurice German: Moritz Wilhelm) Count von Dohna (b. December 2, 1737) in 1767 in Fulneck, England, a Moravian settlement. Their son, Henry Lewis German: Heinrich Ludwig), was born October 22, 1772. Moritz von Dohna died in 1777.

Count Reuss 55. Elisabeth's sister Marie Justine von Watteville (b. November 18, 1762) married Henry Count Reuss 55 [LV] who was born December 1, 1768 at Köstriz. Since her grandmother, wife of Count Zinzendorf, was a Reuss, as becomes clear in the next paragraph, Justine's husband is also some sort of cousin, though perhaps distant. By marrying a relative Justine has repeated the pattern and is therefore "the least original of them all." H.D.'s "Zinzendorf Notes" record the numbers of these von Reusses (ZN, 1, 2 [11, 13]). "A curious custom prevailed in the house of Reuss. The male members of both branches of the family all bore the name of Henry (Heinrich), the individuals being distinguished by numbers" (*EB* [1957], 19: 238; H. Williams, letter to the editor October 24, 1987).

the famous Ignatius. Since this Ignatius Reuss is identified as "nephew of the Countess" and is also called "Count Reuss 28," he must be the same as "Count Henry XXVIII Reuss" mentioned by Spangenberg as one of Zinzendorf's closest companions and present at his deathbed, hence "famous" among Moravians (AGS, 501; *G*, 248). He would seem to be the son of Count Henry Reuss XXIX and brother of Erdmuth (ZN, 12, 13; *HB*, 271). In daily life other names must have been used to distinguish the Henrys, brothers and cousins, from one another. Ignatius is an example.

the Countess is Erdmuth, Count Zinzendorf's wife. H.D. in her "Zinzendorf Notes" observes that Spangenberg always refers to Zinzendorf as "The Count," implying that, despite Zinzendorf's use of many names—he was "Brother Johanan" or "Brother Ludwig" in America—Spangenberg, his best friend and most reliable supporter, never forgot rank (ZN, 8).

grandmamma. Elizabeth gives this affectionate name to Erdmuth.

Podiebrad, King of Bohemia. Also known as George of Podiebrad (1420–71), he was crowned King of Bohemia in 1458, making it a Protestant country and himself a hero of Bohemian nationalism. The nationalists had been challenging the rulers of the Holy Roman Empire ever since the martyrdom of Jan Hus in 1415 and the Hussite wars from 1416 to 1436. Hus's followers became known as the "Bohemian Brethren," a designation for members of the Unitas Fratrum.

Coffee was a ritual. The serving of coffee and buns constitutes the "lovefeast," a Moravian ritual that was begun soon after the founding of Herrnhut in 1722. It consisted of a simple serving of rye bread and water and the recitation of a prayer as an ending to the small evening meetings in the first settlers' houses (*HMC*, 220). The lovefeast later evolved into a more elaborate meal. It was not the equivalent of the communion service. In H.D.'s childhood lovefeasts were "held on Sunday afternoons for special groups at various times of the year," her cousin Francis Wolle wrote. He described the Children's Love Feast which H.D. went to as well, as it was grownup and exciting:

> Here was a whole religious service dedicated solely to us, and we had our big mugs of coffee and buns just like everyone else. . . . and we felt a special glow of pride that we, too, were regarded as individuals, not merely kids, and that we belonged to the Moravian Church. (MH, 19)

It seems to have been a formative experience for H.D. as well as for her cousin.

trouble in Vienna. Since the Reuss family is Austrian but with property in Bohemia, they can mediate as ambassadors from Prague to Vienna, the seat of the Holy Roman Empress Maria Theresa. The "trouble" is linked to the incipient French Revolution. Queen Marie Antoinette of France, Maria Theresa's daughter, at this time sent ambassadors to ask Austria's aid in support of her husband, the king.

Dorothea is Justine's mother-in law, Dorothea von Reuss, the mother of Justine's husband, Henry von Reuss.

Nicholas is the father of Justine's husband, who is also Henry Count Reuss LV. He should not be confused with Nicholas Count Zinzendorf. H.D. is deliberately emphasizing these duplicated names as psychic linkage, just as her own grandmother's name, Elizabeth, connects her with Elisabeth de Watteville.

the Old Church. The Unitas Fratrum was founded by the Bohemian saints Cyril (827–69) and Methodius (825–85), called the "apostles to the Slavs," who christianized the Danube region. Born in Thessalonika and probably Grecized Slavs, they translated the Scriptures into the language later called Old Church Slavonic and invented the Cyrillic alphabet for the purpose (*Co.Enc.*, 705).

Not that you are likely to get it in Bohemia. The Roman Catholic rulers had suppressed the Old Church, and therefore information on it would be quite difficult to find in Prague.

three hundred voyages. Historically, Zinzendorf and his followers made about three hundred missionary voyages, some to wild and remote places. They went to Greenland, Tibet, South Africa, the Caribbean, and the United States, where they founded towns in the Carolinas, especially in the Winston-Salem area, and in Pennsylvania. Foremost among these were Nazareth and Bethlehem.

Sixteen Discourses. Two editions of Zinzendorf's collected sermons begin with the words *Sixteen Discourses*, one published in 1740 and one in 1751 (Sessler, 250).

Bishop of the Ancient Moravian Church. This title was given to Zinzendorf when he and his followers were ousted from the official Lutheran church. Because the Church of Bohemia was descended from the Greek Orthodox Church, its bishops and clergy are in the apostolic succession, that is, their ordinations are said to have come down from Jesus' apostles. With the consecration of David Nitschmann (1695–1772) as its first bishop in 1735, the Renewed Church of the Unitas Fratrum was created. The apostolic succession was important to H.D. in its guarantee of true Christianity. It meant there was no separation between the Unitas Fratrum and the Roman Catholic Church.

his detractors. Zinzendorf's detractors, mostly Protestant clergymen, issued a number of publications in the 1750s, after the excessive "enthusiasm" and abuses of the "Sifting Time" or "Time of Sifting" (German: Sichtungszeit) became known. H.D. owned and read several of these diatribes, two of which especially impressed her. Both were published in 1753: *The True and Authentic Account of Andrew Frey*, an autobiographical account by a former Moravian who had lived in the Herrnhaag community at Marienborn in the 1740s (Weinlick, 214) and Henry Rimius's *A Candid Narrative of the Rise & Progress of the Herrnhuters*. . . . H.D. wrote in her "Zinzendorf Notes" the term "Theocracy" from Rimius (ZN, 36), who used it as a derogation. She also owned a copy of *Moravians Compared and Detected* by George Lavington, the Bishop of Exeter, who denounced Zinzendorf for preaching doctrine identical to that of the heretical Gnostics, but no notes on it appear in ZN. Spangenberg, as Zinzendorf's friend and official biographer, omits details and deals in generalities when discussing this period. Levering explains it more fully. The term Sifting Time, or Time of Sifting, refers to the years from, roughly, 1745 to 1750 as a time when, as Spangenberg reticently said, "Satan almost prevailed." The Count had left his young son, Christian Renatus, in charge at Marienborn, and the job was more than the youth could handle. After a repentant Zinzendorf corrected the excesses, which were both doctrinal and behavioral, he invented the term Sifting Time, based on Luke 22.31, and used it in a recuperative effort to suppress scandal and to show that the Moravians had "cleaned house" (*G*, 20–21; *HB*, 186).

Ludovicus Moraviensis. Rimius took as evidence of Zinzendorf's lust for power and prestige this use of the episcopal title in the Roman Catholic manner. Rimius wrote that "according to the custom of bishops, he made use of his Christian name and that of his see, *viz., Ludovicus Moraviensis*," Latin for "Lewis of Moravia." Zinzendorf did use his various family names at different times, occasionally signing himself "Ludovicus Ecclesiae Moravo-Slavicae Episcopus," Latin for "Lewis, Bishop of the Moravian-Slavic Church" (Weinlick, 137). Elizabeth has been thinking silently at this point but as if speaking to Dohna. Her next words are spoken aloud, asking him who they think he is at the inn.

the Grape Cluster. H.D. has invented a name for an inn near the Tower, and *Mine host* refers to its proprietor, who has mistaken Henry Dohna for Elizabeth's husband, even though they have different names.

Maria and Jacob name the characters who are the servants of Justine and her in-laws, in whose home in the Tower Elizabeth and Henry are staying incognito.

letters re-addressed to Nicholas. Justine apparently aids the concealment of the true identities of Elizabeth and Henry by receiving, in Vienna, letters addressed to them and re-forwarding these back to Prague in envelopes with the name of Nicholas von Reuss, Justine's father-in-law, on the outer envelope. This concealment hints that they are aware of being in danger since they are Protestants now within the boundaries of the Holy Roman Empire.

Jacobus. This Latinate version of the name Jacob accords with H.D.'s religious theme. Elizabeth is saying that in summer Henry would be uncomfortably hot disguised as a servant in a great-coat like Jacob's, but in winter he can wear his own coat with the buttons changed so the heraldic motif on them would not give away his true identity as a nobleman.

suspect you belong—. This broken-off sentence should end with "to the house of Köstriz" or "to the Reuss family," which also means being German and therefore belonging to the Protestant faction in Bohemia, a suspect position even for nobility.

if Justine's marriage . . . . This sentence should end "makes her a member of the House of Köstriz." Justine and her husband, being ambassadors and nobility, can live in Prague, even though they are both foreigners and Protestants.

couldn't open the door. As a suspect person concealing her identity, Elizabeth made a "mistake" in attracting the friar's attention as she tried to open the mysteriously closed church door. Church doors are supposed to be open always, never locked against anyone who wants to come in at any hour for prayer or worship.

Christian David (1690–1752), a farmer and carpenter, was born Roman Catholic in Senftleben (Czech: Zenklava), Moravia. Through Bible reading and questioning, he had, like Zinzendorf, developed "heart-religion"—a very personal mystical experience of God's love. In 1722, searching for religious liberty, he led the first group of Bohemian Brethren, the Neisser brothers and their families, to Zinzendorf's estate in Saxony. He had met Zinzendorf through John Andrew Rothe, private tutor to Baron de Schweinitz of Leube (Rechcigl, 2).

Theodora of Castell (1703–77) was historically a first cousin of Zinzendorf; at one point he had wanted to marry her. H.D. here constructs her as the "dear god-mamma," Elizabeth's godmother who gave her the old lace. I could not find evidence that Theodora was historically the godmother of Elisabeth von Watteville.

the coach-horses took Justine and Nicholas to Vienna. Only the saddle horses are left, not large or strong enough to pull a sleigh through the snow.

Elizabeth of Bohemia (1596–1662), daughter of James I of England, married Frederick V, elector palatine of the Rhine in 1613. He was elected King of Bohemia in 1619 by the Protestant diet after they refused to accept the Catholic Ferdinand II as king (Langton, 49). Frederick's Protestant army was badly defeated by Ferdinand and combined forces of the Catholic League under Maximilian I of Bavaria in the Battle of White Mountain (German: Weissenberg) that took place between November 8 and

18, 1620 (Co.Enc. 2733; Rechcigl, 2). Frederick was stripped of his lands. Because he ruled Bohemia only one winter, 1619–20, he was called "the Winter King" and his wife "the Winter Queen" (*Co.Enc.*, 857).

her daughter.... Eldest daughter of the Winter King and Queen, this Elizabeth of Bohemia (1618–80) is described as "a philosophical princess and a pupil of Descartes." She became abbess, with princely rank and a seat in the imperial diet, of the Benedictine nunnery of Herford in the Prussian province of Westphalia. In 1670 she invited the Labadists, followers of Jean de la Badie (1610–74), often in trouble for their separatist views, to live at Herford. Labadists' beliefs bear some similarity to the Moravian, and, like the Moravians, they were accused of "enthusiasm" (*EB* [1971], 13: 363; *EB* [1957], 11: 500; 13: 532).

Prince Rupert (1619–82), the third son of the Winter King and Queen, was born in Prague just before Frederick's defeat. After the loss of Bohemia, the family settled in the Netherlands where Rupert grew up. Loyal to his uncle, Charles I of England, he led the Royalist forces against Cromwell during the Civil War. The suggestion is that Henry and Elizabeth, close as brother and sister, are spiritual counterparts or possible "reincarnations" of these royal siblings.

the Lord's Watch. This phrase translates the German Herrnhut, which can also be translated as "The Lord's Protection." It is the name Zinzendorf gave to the Moravian settlers' village because it was located on a hill, Hutberg, "Watch Hill."

they *wouldn't curtsey*. With the emphasis on "*they*," Elizabeth is presupposing that Herrnhutters, descendents of religious refugees driven out of their native land by the Holy Roman Emperor under penalty of death, would not make any gesture of respect to a lay-brother in a Roman Catholic monastic order.

Depending on who they are. Henry questions Elizabeth's assertion because Zinzendorf himself respected as true Christians the members of many denominations, including Roman Catholic leaders such as Cardinal de Noailles and Father D'Albizi, whom Zinzendorf had met in 1719 when studying in Paris. H.D. made notes from *The Life of Nicholas Lewis Count Zinzendorf* (AGS). "Father Anthony Dionysius Simeon D'Albizi. oratory of the Premonstrants" (ZN, 6) and Father D'Albizi—Dominican monk—Z , "I must . . . admire the sincerity" (ZN, 7). Zinzendorf's ecumenicity infuriated his detractors, who accused him of being a Papist, and it gave rise to false rumors during the French and Indian War in America. His broadmindedness and mysticism attracted H.D., however, and became the reasons why she was "very devoted to the Zinzendorf legend" ("H.D.," 200; *G*, 10).

seething with overtones. H.D. had sent the first chapters of *The Mystery* to Pearson in late December 1950, along with "H.D. by *Delia Alton*." He responded on January 15, 1951:

I am delighted by The Mystery, so beautifully written and haunting in its shifting scenes . . . It lifts the leather curtain to silver and sevres. "The place is seething with overtones." This is one of the very best. Your chevalier bows low. (BHP, 101)

Chapter III, pp. 8–10

Prague. Henry, alone in his rooms in the Tower, is reading aloud to himself from his notes on the Bohemian Brethren who began in Prague. Then by free association he thinks of Prague as the practice-site of historical magicians.

Faustus—scene of legend. "Faust's House," at 502/40 Charles Street, Prague, according to nineteenth-century legend, was occupied by the so-called "Czech Doctor Faust," a student, Jan Stastny, whose name in Czech is a translation of the Latin "faustus" (faustus = stastny = happy). The story is that he came from Kutna Hora to study and was attracted by this sixteenth-century house, which was deserted. He moved in and, as he investigated the house, found a thaler in the library. The next day he found a second thaler, the third another, and so on. He gave up studying and took up high living, but soon the thalers would not meet his needs, and so he began to study "the black art," that is, alchemy. While drunk in a tavern one night, he boasted to his friends that he would always "have as much gold as he needed." He left and was never seen alive again. His friends went to look for him at the house, found it wrecked—with blood on the walls and a hole torn in the ceiling—and concluded that the devil had dragged him off (*Praha*, 40–41).

the magician. A historical Doctor Faustus existed, as letters of Johannes Trithemius in 1507, Konrad Mutianus Rufus in 1513, and Philipp Begardi in 1539 testify. Although Begardi praised his medical knowledge, all three regarded him as a charlatan. The legend of his supernatural gifts and pact with the devil began in sermons of Johann Gast, preached in 1543. Manlius reported (c. 1550) that Melancthon had known Faustus as a "disgraceful beast and sewer of many devils" who was born at Kindling and studied magic at Cracow. The 1587 Faustbook of Johannes Spiess and Hogel's *Erfurt Chronicle* record Faustus's magical feats performed in Prague. From Spiess's account came the legends transformed by Marlowe and Goethe (E. Butler, *FF*, 121–30; *EB* [1957], 9: 120–23).

Albertus Magnus (1200–1280), German scholastic philosopher well read in Aristotle, knowledgeable in the natural sciences, and interested in the transmutation of metals, was therefore thought in the Middle Ages to be a magician and alchemist and consequently suspected of being in league with the devil. He lived in Prague in 1263–64.

John Dee (1527–1608). This English scientist, respected by Queen Elizabeth I, became persuaded in middle age by the claims of Edward Kelly (or Kelley, 1555–93) that Kelly could transmute base metal into gold by means of the Philosopher's Stone. Dee went with him as his assistant to Prague in 1583 where Kelly became the court alchemist of Rudolf II, promising the emperor large amounts of gold. The failure to keep this promise eventually forced both Dee and Kelly to leave Prague in disgrace.

Elixir of Life, symbolical?. This question mark after the name of a magic potion and before "Alchemists" suggests that H.D. is wondering whether she should take the view of "transcendental alchemy," in which "gold" means the symbolic gold of the *grand arcanum*, or the secret of reality itself. It was said that this secret when applied would develop the latent potentialities within human beings (Enc.Occ., 11).

Unitas Fratrum is the Latin version of the Czech *Jednota Bratrska*, Unity of the Brethren; the church today calls itself "The Unity." *Jednota* also means "association" or "society." This name was adopted by followers of the reformer Jan Hus, born in Prague circa 1371 and burned at the stake as a heretic after the Council of Constance in 1415. Hussites, seeking more national independence, won important rights through the Compactata of 1436 and forced Emperor Sigismund to accept a democratized constitution for Bohemia. After King Frederick's defeat at White Mountain in 1620, continuing persecution drove the Bohemian Brethren into exile. In 1722, the small group led by Christian David escaped over the border into Protestant Saxony to settle on Count Zinzendorf's estate at Berthelsdorf and establish the community of Herrnhut. After Jablonsky, exiled bishop of the *Unitas*, ordained Zinzendorf bishop in 1737, the whole community became known as the *Unitas Fratrum* or the "Renewed Moravian Church," usually now called simply "the Moravian Church"(*HMC*, 259, 273).

Christel, a diminutive of the name "Christian," was given to Zinzendorf's son, Christian Renatus (1727–52). After a rift between father and son over Christian's purported role in the excesses of the Sifting Time at Marienborn, they were reconciled in London at Christian's deathbed. Only four of Zinzendorf's twelve children lived to adulthood. Christel was the only son. "Christal" is mentioned by Lavington in *Moravians Compared and Detected by the Author of the Enthusiasm of Methodists and Papists Compared* (1755, 62), a book attacking Zinzendorf that H.D. owned and read. J. E. Hutton, in *History of the Moravian Church* (1909), refers to "Christel," but it appears that H.D. did not read this book. The primary source of her historical knowledge is Joseph M. Levering's *A History of Bethlehem, Pennsylvania* (1903). When H.D. refers to "Hutton" in ZN she means his *History of Moravian Missions* (1923).

ponderous biography. August Gottlieb Spangenberg's "official" has over 900 pages in the German edition. H.D. read the shortened English version, *Life of Nicholas Lewis Count Zinzendorf*, translated by Samuel Jackson.

Detractors. H.D. owned, read, and took extensive notes on one of the most widely distributed eighteenth-century denunciations of Zinzendorf, a lengthy and detailed document by Henry Rimius titled *A Candid Narrative of the Rise & Progress of the Herrnhueters, commonly call'd Moravians, or Unitas Fratrum* . . . (London, 1752; Philadelphia, 1753).

Andrew Frey wrote an attack on Zinzendorf titled *The True and Authentic Account of Andrew Frey* (1753). H.D. owned a copy.

the first Sea Congregation. Led by Peter Boehler, this group of fifty-six Moravians sailed from England with Captain Thomas Gladman in the *Catherine*, arriving in America on July 7, 1742, and settling in Bethlehem. Some returned to Europe within a few years, Frey among them, but he came back to America a second time, outraged by the Marienborn excesses in the Sifting Time.

the young Count is Christian Renatus.

someone from outside. The outsider, or non-Moravian church member, is the poet Goethe, who, Henry recalls, had come to Herrnhut and had asked questions that Henry could not fully answer. The historic fact is that Goethe visited the Moravians several times, not at Herrnhut, but at Herrnhaag, near Frankfort, and became so deeply involved in theological discussions that he was expected to join their community. He did not. The reasons for both his attraction and his disaffection are recorded in his autobiography *Dichtung und Wahrheit* (*DW*, 294–95, 561–63).

simple questions. Goethe must have asked something like "Who was the leader of the refugee Bohemian Brethren?" and "Where did he meet Count Zinzendorf?"

easily bring together. Goethe is speaking as Henry remembers him. Goethe's question refers to the worldwide Moravian missions. By 1788 they had established "ecclesiolae"—"little churches" within the larger one—all over Europe, America, the West Indies, Greenland, Surinam and South Africa, and elsewhere. Goethe's mention of the *Plan* echoes Rimius's charge that Zinzendorf had a secret "Plan" to control a worldwide following "as power seems to be what he chiefly aims at" (*CN*, 30).

Foundation here means the Moravian community, but H.D. is deliberately creating a parallel to Antonius's reference in chapter 1 to the Society of Jesus as a foundation. H.D. read Hutton, who makes a connection between the Jesuits and Moravian missions. Jesuit missionaries from Pekin inspired Leibnitz's *Novissima Linica*, the reading of which awakened the missionary spirit in August Hermann Francke (1663–1727), the Pietist leader who was Zinzendorf's mentor at the University of Halle, and Francke communicated it to Zinzendorf (*HMM*, 13–14). H.D. later refers to Zinzendorf as a Protestant Jesuit.

Arcana. Rimius charges that ordinary Herrnhutters were kept in ignorance of the "*Arcana* or secret Counsels of the Leaders." He objected to the Moravians' "Secrecy in respect to their Doctrines" and "Secrecy in their Transactions. They had People in almost all Parts of the World . . . whom they can easily bring together." He thought that this secrecy and mystery meant either, in H.D.'s words, "a diabolical bid for world-dictatorship" or "gross and scandalous . . . Mysticism" (*CN*, 11; *ZN*, 21 [53]; *G*, 268). Goethe studied kabbalists and alchemists, so that for him, as for H.D., the term *Arcana* is positive, associated with secrets of reality (*DW*, 297).

bringing his mistress. Goethe's mistress, Susannah von Klettenberg, the "schöne

Seele" (fair saint) of his novel *Wilhelm Meister*, had originally introduced Goethe to the Moravians.

the Lord's Hedge (or *Hedgerows*) translates Herrnhaag, the name of the Moravian community established in 1735 in two ruined castles, Rotteburg and Marienborn, thirty miles northeast of Frankfort-am-Main in the county of Büdingen. Modeled after Herrnhut, it later included a theological college (*HMC*, 255–59).

Herrnhut. The Lord's Watch (or Protection) is the name for the refugee community that settled on Zinzendorf's estate. John Heitz, the estate's steward, later wrote to Zinzendorf his hopes that this town would "not only itself abide under the Lord's Watch" (German: unter des Herrn Hut) but also that the inhabitants would continue "on the watch for the Lord" (German: auf des Herrn Hut). Christian David had inspired the exiles with a vision of Herrnhut as a "glorious city of God" (Weinlick, 62; *HMC*, 198–99; *CN*, 8).

the First House was built where Heitz, concerned to help the Moravians settle, uttered a prayer for them: "Upon this spot, in Thy name, I will build for them the first house." The building of the first house began on June 17, 1722 (*ZN*, 14). Christian David, after Heitz showed him which trees he might fell, seized his axe, struck it into a tree, and exclaimed: "Yea, the sparrow hath found a house, and the swallow a nest for herself" (*HMC*, 198).

Berthelsdorf, the village nearest Zinzendorf's estate, lay only ten miles from the Bohemian border.

House in the Wood. H.D.'s notes from Rimius on page 7 read: "House in a Wood . . . these people held their first meeting there" (*ZN*, 32). These meetings grew in size and importance into "Congregation Day," a daylong Saturday meeting once a month. By 1732, the community numbered 600 (*ZN*, 34; *HMC*, 220).

God would kindle a light. This remark, much quoted by Moravians, was made by Melchior Schaeffer, a Pietist pastor at Görlitz in Silesia, who befriended Christian David and was in part responsible for Christian David's conversion (Weinlick, 60). Rimius saw this statement as evidence of Zinzendorf's conspiratorial Plan to take over the world. In ZN, H.D. quoted Rimius: "'Tis said, that they foresaw that God would *kindle a Light* in this Place that would enlighten all the Country" (*CN*, 7; *ZN*, 34).

Zeist? . . . lighted for him. H.D. copied in her notes a passage from Rimius's *A Supplement to the Candid Narrative . . .* (1755), xxvii:

> Speaking of a building of theirs [the Moravians], he [Zinzendorf] tells them, "It is a house which shall be in being, or perhaps will scarce be finished, when the Saviour comes; he shall lodge & walk about in it; the chandeliers in it shall be lighted for him." Serm. [sermon] at Zeist, p. 104 (*ZN*, 68)

A passage from a Pennsylvania sermon immediately preceding speaks of Christ's "last coming" as a time when he "himself will bring about & establish his new plan which he promised his disciples" (ZN, 68). Zinzendorf preached many sermons during a synod at Zeist, Holland, in April and May of 1746. His daughter, Benigna, and John de Watteville were married there at that time.

their First House in America was a cabin on Monocacy Creek built in 1740 by David "Father" Nitschmann and the first Moravians in Pennsylvania. These were Nitschmann's grand-niece, Anna Caritas (or Charity) who later became Zinzendorf's second wife; her friend Johanna Molther, and Christian Frohlich, a group which had come north from the Georgia settlement headed by Peter Boehler. The second house, built in 1741, next door to the first, was the Gemein Haus (Common House), now the oldest structure in Bethlehem and containing the Moravian Museum. It stands "to the east of the Church on Church Street. It was used for residences in H.D.'s time. The First House was taken down about 1823. Where it stood is now the parking lot of the Hotel Bethlehem" (H. Williams, letter to the editor, November 30, 1987).

John Martin Mack, an early settler writing in German, provides the principal source from which Levering derived an account of this famous Christmas scene, a story continually re-told in the Bethlehem community. Zinzendorf's party arrived at the as-yet unnamed place on December 21, 1741.

Not Jerusalem. Rather Bethlehem. These words come, slightly altered, from a much loved Moravian hymn that was often sung at Christmas in German in the earliest days and later in English. Its second stanza opens: *Not Jerusalem / Lowly Bethlehem / 'Twas that gave us / Christ to save us.* The story is that, as Zinzendorf was celebrating the Christmas Eve vigil with the little groups of emigrants, they became aware of the cattle barn adjoining the First House under its same roof. The count began to sing this hymn. Then he seized a candle and led the congregation into the barn, still singing. Afterwards, "by general consent the name of the ancient town of David was adopted and the place was called Bethlehem." This hymn is no. 511 in the *Office of Worship and Hymnal* of 1891 that was in use in H.D.'s childhood (Myers, 17; *HB*, 77–79).

one of Gregor's metres. Hymn no. 511 is set to the tune known as "Gregor's 46th metre," *Jesu rufe mich* [Jesus calls me]. Christian Gregor (1723–1801) was leader in music at Herrnhaag in 1748 and at Zeist in 1749 but lived most of his life at Herrnhut. He wrote many hymns. Henry Williams wrote of Gregor that he "brought the chaos of Moravian hymnody (German) under control in his hymnal of 1778. These were hymn texts. He also issued his *Choralebuch* in 1784 in which he arranged the tunes (over 400, I think) by meter and numbered them. . . . [T]he numbering became, to Moravians, the identification (letter to the editor, November 12, 1987). Gregor's metres are plentiful in the 1891 hymn book, of which H.D. owned a copy and from which she would have sung in the required daily morning chapel service at the parochial school, according to her cousin Francis Wolle's memoir, *A Moravian Heritage* (*MH*, 15). Francis Wolle became an Episcopal clergyman late in life.

Castell. Henry is recalling his most recent conversation with Elizabeth, when she had spoken of Theodora de Castell, Zinzendorf's cousin, whom he met when he was twenty years old and had just left the University of Paris. On a visit to his paternal aunt at Castell, her home in Switzerland, he became ill and, during several months of recuperation there, fell in love with the eighteen-year-old Theodora. He asked her to marry him and received an ambiguous acceptance. Then he learned that his closest friend, Henry Count von Reuss, wanted to marry, and—according to the romantic story—broke off the engagement to clear the way for his friend. Henry and Theodora were formally betrothed on March 9, 1721, and Zinzendorf wrote a cantata for the occasion. He married Henry's sister, Erdmuth Dorothea von Reuss on September 7, 1721, at Ebersdorf, the Reuss family estate (*HMC*, 188–89; AGS, 26–27).

no way of knowing. Many interpretations have been made of Zinzendorf's behavior on this occasion. Hutton, basing his remarks on AGS (26), speaks of "a beautiful contest" in which Reuss and Zinzendorf each wanted to give up Theodora to the other (*HMC*, 188). Weinlick cites a more factual account, given fifty years later in a letter to AGS from the widowed Theodora, concerning her reluctance to marry Zinzendorf. She had agreed to an engagement when her mother pressed her not to refuse him outright (AGS, 50).

Dowager Countess is the Countess of Castell, Theodora's mother.

Cousins. Zinzendorf's grandmother, Countess von Gersdorf, expressed reservations about his marrying too close a blood relation (AGS, 25). H.D. is emphasizing the closeness of Elizabeth and Henry as well as setting up parallelism in the romantic triangles.

formal Birthdays. All Moravian communities, not merely Herrnhaag, loved to stage celebrations on important anniversaries, especially on August 13, the day in 1727 when the church received its "spiritual baptism" through a descent of the Holy Spirit experienced in Berthelsdorf chapel by the entire Herrnhut community. From around 1745 to 1750–51 at Herrnhaag and Marienborn especially, in the Sifting Time, celebrations became over-frequent, costly, unbridled, and marked by the extreme imagery expressing Zinzendorf's "Blood and Wounds" theology. Scandals resulted from which the Moravian church's reputation did not fully recover for nearly a hundred years.

Thurnstein . . . Wachovia. Henry is reading random notes on Zinzendorf, which resemble H.D.'s own "Zinzendorf Notes." Zinzendorf used an old family name "Thurnstein" in America when he wanted to de-emphasize his noble status. "Vale of Wachovia" refers to Wachau, Zinzendorf's ancestral Austrian estate, as well as to its namesake, the Wachovia tract, North Carolina, 100,000 acres bought from the Earl of Granville around 1740. The tract is now the city of Winston-Salem, and Wachovia remains the name of a U.S. national bank originally established there.

move to Saxony. Zinzendorf's father, George Louis, was a "premier minister" in the court of the Elector of Saxony at Dresden, where Nicholas was born on May 26, 1700. His father died six weeks later (AGS, vi, 8, 9). His grandfather, not his father, forfeited the Austrian lands. The Reverend Peter La Trobe, in his introduction to AGS, notes: "The grandfather of the Count, Maximilian Erasmus, emigrated from his native land, and settled at Oberberg, near Nuremberg, esteeming the loss of all his estates counterbalanced by the superior liberty of conscience which he thus obtained" (viii) H.D. was deeply impressed by this choice of religious freedom over possession of land and wealth.

thirty years war. A devastating war of religion between Roman Catholics and Protestants in German-speaking lands from 1618 to 1648 came to be called the Thirty Years' War.

Andrew is Henry's brief reference to the book titled *The True and Authentic Account of Andrew Frey* (1753), of which he has a copy in hand, as H.D. herself often did. This title reads in full: "A True and Authentic Account of Andrew Frey; containing the occasion of his coming among the HERRNHUTERS or MORAVIANS, his Observations on *their Conferences, Casting Lots, Marriages, Festivals, Merriments, Celebrations of Birth-Days, Impious Doctrines*, and *Fantastical Practices; Abuse of Charitable Contributions, Linnen Images, Ostentatious Profuseness*, and *Rancour* against any who in the least differ from them; together with the Motive for publishing this Account. *Faithfully translated from the* German." H.D.'s copy is now at the Beinecke. The Moravian archives at Bethlehem also own a copy. In the period of recovery after the Sifting Time, the Moravians did not altogether destroy records of the period nor the works of their attackers.

Chapter IV, pp. 11–15

It blew shut. Stephanus, Antonius's servant, is speaking to his master in the privacy of their living quarters in a building, possibly the Convent of Saint George, near the Street of the Alchemists and Saint Vitus's Cathedral in the Prague castle complex. He is explaining why Antonius had to open the cathedral door for Elizabeth.

Perruque. The use of the elaborately coiffed and often powdered wig worn by eighteenth-century French aristocracy reveals that Brother Antonius, the supposed Franciscan lay-brother who was seen meditating in the Jesuit style in chapter 1, has yet another layer to his identity—that of a "gentleman" who must at times keep up his aristocratic appearance because of "orders" from a source unknown.

Château Saint-Germain. This naming of a vintage wine gives further information on Antonius's true identity, since it links him to a castle and a French wine-growing estate. Later in the chapter he is identified as Louis Comte de Saint-Germain, another figure fictionalized from history. He was said to have been born around 1696 or 1700. His actual birth name was never recorded. He was a reputed alchemist and magician, an associate of Cagliostro (or competitor with him), and was said to possess supernormal powers, including the power to reincarnate. He was called *der Wundermann*, "the man of mystery," and "the deathless" ("imperissable"). This reputation, and the legendary stories that he had been seen in two places at the same time, led H.D. to make him the hero of this novel. (LCSG, 27-39, 92, 95-110)

Embassy valet. In this novel's setting, embassies—ambassadorial parties from other countries—are quartered in buildings adjoining Antonius's rooms. The Prague castle complex today is still the working center of Czech government, and its buildings house offices where ambassadors are received. Antonius teases Stephanus by accusing him of a drinking bout with the valet in order to find out who the valet's "gentleman" is and who they think Antonius is.

Order of the Garter . . . Star. These decorations show that Antonius/Saint-Germain has been knighted, presumably for valor in battle and service to royalty, as in the Middle Ages. The Elizabethan ceremony creating a knight involved the prince's saying "Soys chevalier." Norman Holmes Pearson, in his letters of this period to H.D. called himself her "literary chevalier servante" (*BHP*, 68). She took up the phrase, often addressing him as "chevalier" or simply "C." See final note to chapter 2. The Order of the Garter, the highest order of English knighthood, was established by Edward III, circa 1346. The Order of the Golden Fleece was instituted by Philip the Good, Duke of Burgundy, in 1429, and was also a Spanish and Austrian honor. These two "Prime Orders of Christendom" are associated with the Knights Templars whose history figures in this story. If the "Star" is a conscious allusion to the Star of India, one of the nine orders of English knighthood, it is an anachronism, as that order was created by Queen Victoria in 1861. More likely, H.D. is making a general allusion to the iconography of paintings in which a "knight grand cross" or "knight commander" is shown wearing a star on every medal on his breast or on a wide ribbon over his shoulder or around his neck. The Star of Bethlehem is a Moravian icon and a recurring motif in H.D.'s synthesis of Christianity and eastern magical religions.

The Pedagogy is a metonymy for the teaching branch of the Franciscan order of which Antonius is supposedly a member. Although he is teaching in the cloister school, his fellow teachers sense that, although he is merely in "secular" orders, he somehow has a higher status.

the Confraternity refers to the body of friars, somewhat higher ranking than the teaching friars, who carry on the traditional work of preaching, hearing confessions, and exercising pastoral care outside of the cloister.

Fratres is Latin for "brothers," members of the Confraternity, the friars individually.

The Castle. This metonymy alludes primarily to members of noble families, their attendants and servants, who live in the castle's palaces, of which there are many, for example, Lobkovic, Sternberk, Schwartzenberg among others (TOP, 76–81).

the Row. H.D. uses this term for the tiny cottages set against the castle walls in the Street of the Alchemists. Her apparent invention of this immediate proximity of an embassy wing to Antonius/Saint-Germain's rooms, as well as the suggestion of secret passageways, accords with fortified and intricate architecture of Prague Castle.

Petty Place is the short anglicized version of the full name, given later, of La Petite Place de la Chatelaine. I have been unable to find a street by this name on maps of Prague Castle.

the Hide. Antonius/Saint-Germain mocks Stephanus's taste for intrigue in the style of medieval romance and at the same time reveals that a hidden entrance exists.

the vestry of a church is a room adjacent to the chancel in which clergy put on vestments before conducting services. Here the reference is to the small antechamber where Antonius dons and doffs his disguise, his friar's habit.

Saint-Germain. For the first time in this novel, the true name of its central character is given, and it becomes clear that he and Brother Antonius are the same person. In 1957, six years after this novel was finished, H.D. gave the name "Germain" to Erich Heydt, her German-speaking psychiatrist, in *Sagesse*, book 2 of *Hermetic Definition*, in which she constructs him as a version of the Eternal Lover (*HD*, 8, 9, 14; *PR*, 21). She links "*Germain*" with the word *german*, meaning closely related, as in *cousin-german*, first cousin, and with the homonym *germen*, figuratively a germ or seed. *Germane*, meaning "relevant, pertinent" is an intentional punning association. The English word *german* comes from the Old French *germain*. H.D. believed that linguistic word-connection revealed spiritual connection. In this way she interpreted the fragmentary messages she received in her wartime spiritualist séances. Her novel, written in 1943–44, *Majic Ring* uses this principle extensively.

a monk. Stephanus is reinforcing the disguise but is also letting the valet know obliquely how someone might get from the Embassy quarters to Saint-Germain's lodgings undetected. The suggestion is that Antonius/Saint-Germain is involved in an important political intrigue that includes this newly arrived ambassador.

worth my place. Stephanus is saying that he would lose his job if he gossiped about the business that kept his "gentleman" away for hours—that is, the hours in which Saint-Germain is disguised as Brother Antonius.

the Count. Stephanus is referring to Henry Count Reuss LV, resident of the castle, who was advised not to display his rank but to appear in public in ordinary citizen's dress. It is a hint of the coming "trouble," the French Revolution.

the flavour. Stephanus is telling his master that, by this apparently casual question while pouring the wine, he let the valet see the wine-bottle label and got his reaction to the name Saint-Germain. The valet had heard the name. Stephanus therefore knew that this ambassadorial party had come from France. Then Stephanus tells the valet the various stories about the historical Saint-Germain that had circulated at the French court.

Saint-Germain in Venice. One version of the story that gave rise to his soubriquet, the "Deathless," is given by Andrew Lang, in *Historical Mysteries*. It was reported as a conversation between Saint-Germain and Mme. de Pompadour (1721–64), mistress of King Louis XV, in a memoir published in 1824 by Mme. du Hausset, who was a lady's-maid to Pompadour:

> A man who was as amazing as a witch came often to see Madame de Pompadour. This was the Comte de Saint-Germain, who wished to make people believe that he had lived for several centuries. One day Madame said to him, while at her toilet, . . . "But you do not tell us your age, and you give yourself out as very old. Madame de Gergy, who was wife of the French ambassador at Venice fifty years ago, I think, says that she knew you there, and that you are not changed in the least." "It is true, madame, that I knew Madame de Gergy long ago." "But according to her story you must now be over a century old." "It may be so, but I admit that even more possibly the respected lady is in her dotage" (Lang, 261–62; LCSG, 235).

uncle. . . . great-uncle. Stephanus's correction of his master mildly reflects another legend. Saint-Germain was once telling a noble dinner-party that he conversed with Richard the Lion-Hearted in Palestine (AD 1191). Seeing his listeners' incredulity, he asked his servant, standing behind his chair, if he had not spoken truth. The servant replied that he could not say, adding "You forget, sir, I have only been five hundred years in your service" (Mackay, 236; *LCSG*, 241).

the Elixir. Stephanus says that the present Court of Louis XVI enjoys perpetuating the rumors, begun in Louis XV's time, that Saint-Germain possessed a secret formula, the Elixir of Life that kept him always young. Mme. Pompadour had wanted him to give Louis XV this elixir. Saint-Germain refused, saying, "I should be mad if I gave the King a drug" (Lang, 263; Mackay, 231–32; *LCSG*, 58).

the Cardinal. Louis René Edouard, Cardinal de Rohan (1734–1803), became infamous for having been duped, in 1784, by Jeanne de Lamotte and Cagliostro (a.k.a. Balsamo) in "the affair of the Diamond Necklace," a humiliating scandal that involved Marie Antoinette and caused gossip all over Europe. The episode increased the resentment of Louis XVI that was growing among the Parisian populace and thus contributed to the French Revolution and the king's death. See notes to chapter 13.

she being Austrian. This phrase refers to Queen Marie Antoinette of France. The ambassador traveling from Paris to Vienna is perhaps on an embassy to ask for help from Joseph II, Marie Antoinette's older brother, who became Holy Roman Emperor upon the death of their father, Francis I, in 1765. Maria Theresa had arranged Marie Antoinette's marriage to cement an alliance between Austria and France.

suspicion from the cupboard. Stephanus hears a suspicious sound, which he attributes with deliberate deceptiveness to "rats," but the valet takes off, also believing that someone is hiding in a secret passageway behind the cupboard.

She being Austrian. This repeated phrase connects Elizabeth de Watteville with Marie Antoinette and queenliness. Her appearance in the cathedral was responsible for Antonius's forgetting to pray properly with Ignatius's *Exercitia*.

Balsamo. Giuseppe Balsamo (1743–95), born in a Palermo slum, re-created himself as Count Alessandro Cagliostro and was said to possess great powers as a magician, necromancer, and healer (*LCSG*, 197–98).

the Office is the Holy Office of the Inquisition. The suggestion is that Saint-Germain is involved with its vicious secret investigations and punishments for heresy.

Masons. Cagliostro was a Freemason, having been initiated in London in 1777, after which he never admitted that his name had been Balsamo. Made Grand Master almost immediately after initiation, he went to Europe where he met Freemasons in many cities and was credited with miraculous healings. He developed his own form of Masonry, the "Egyptian Rite," and as its Grand Master, "the Great Copt," introduced its elaborate pageantry to the receptive haute monde of Paris. Cagliostro could gain foothold there because Voltaire and Diderot, among numerous Encyclopedians, were Freemasons. They participated in the Egyptian rites, having "found in the humanitarian and cosmopolitan ideals of Freemasonry—that 'Jesuit Order of the Enlightenment'—the reflection of their own aspirations" (Gervaso, 48–50, 59–60, 64–133; *LCSG* 202).

fraternities alludes to cell-groups of French Freemasons who were credited (or blamed) for having planted the seeds of the Revolution. The word "fraternity" echoes the Revolution's call for "Liberté, Egalité, Fraternité" and ideas of Freemasonry, which "preached liberty, equality, fraternity and tolerance, condemned every kind of authoritarianism . . . and fought against the dogmatism of the Church" (Gervaso, 56). The word also echoes the earlier reference to "Confraternities."

the past that was and English history. Stephanus is urging Saint-Germain to forget about England's establishment of the Protestant religion and its penal laws, enforced by Queen Elizabeth, which blocked Jesuits and Catholics from holding power there.

fortune-teller . . . bridge-head. Saint-Germain visualizes his servant as similar to the Prague fortune-tellers, latter-day magicians, purportedly "gifted," who practiced in the Street of the Alchemists up until World War II. That street leads to the gate of the castle and out to the Charles Bridge over the Vltava river, hence the "bridge-head." In *The Gift* the fortune teller's prediction to her mother assured H.D. of her own psychic "gift." H.D. often told fortunes for her friends by various divinatory methods. See notes to chapter 9 on "the seven or the seventeen."

in Versailles, the cause. . . . the elections. Saint-Germain's cause is the restoration of the Society of Jesus. De Rohan wants to save the monarchy. Saint-Germain offered him Jesuit help to oppose the Freemasons organizing the overthrow of the Crown. As a reward he expected that the Cardinal would vote for a pro-Jesuit pope at the next papal elections.

supposed passion for Marie. De Rohan became enamored of Marie Antoinette through letters forged by Jeanne de Lamotte, which made him believe that the queen was in love with him. The resulting "affair of the Diamond Necklace" led to his disgrace and exile. Saint-Germain views the affair as if no swindle were involved. He sees it as part of a deeper plan to serve a higher cause in much the same way that H.D. saw the scandals of the Moravian Sifting Time.

Being Austrian, I do not know. This dangling construction refers not to Saint-Germain or Marie Antoinette, but to Elizabeth. If she is Austrian and presumably Catholic, he is puzzled that she does not genuflect to the altar.

Upper Lusatia. Zinzendorf's estate in Upper Lusatia (German: Ober Lausitz), a part of Saxony bordering Catholic Moravia, provided a natural site of refuge for the persecuted "Bohemian Brethren" escaping over the mountains.

exiled means religious exile, nearly indistinguishable from political exile in the eighteenth century. Stephanus's remark draws a reverse comparison between the return of these Moravians across the border into Bohemia and the original exodus of Bohemian Brethren in the opposite direction.

trance-like. The state of trance, or super normal experience, disturbs Antonius/Saint-Germain's mind and indicates a struggle between his two identities. It is not always possible to see a difference between the magician's false mysticism and the religious devotee's true ecstasy. The Lady's appearance offers transcendence of this dichotomy. H.D. is obliquely reflecting on her own supernormal visions and the dream-Lady of *Trilogy*.

Chapter V, pp. 16–20

Poor Brothers. Antonius/Saint-Germain in his disguise as a Franciscan friar wears a brown habit. (The Jesuits are priests, not monks, and so wear either priestly garb or ordinary clothes.) The "original Order" of the Franciscans, most widespread of the four great medieval mendicant orders, is the Frairs Minor, founded in 1209 by Saint Francis of Assisi (1181–1226). Mystically inspired, Saint Francis strove to imitate Jesus' actual life, stressing its poverty. His followers were therefore called "Poor Brothers."

Grey Friars are English Franciscans, called so after the color of their habit. In their general reform of 1370, after expansion of the order led to quarrels over ownership of property, they decided on "poor and scanty use" of worldly goods as a compromise between Saint Francis's strict rule and an overly relaxed worldliness. The strict view insisted on bare feet.

White and Black Friars. English Carmelites, of a mendicant order founded in the mid-twelfth century, wore a white mantle over a brown habit. The Dominicans, founded by Saint Dominic in 1215, wore a black mantle worn over a white habit.

young gentlemen refers to the children in the school where Antonius teaches. The heavy snow may keep them home. H.D. herself experienced this snow. She wrote to Pearson on June 17, 1951, from Lausanne:

> I started a new chapter on my dear Prague story, perhaps the excessive heat reminds me of those weeks before your arrival, year before last, when I went into the Prague snow-storm. The book enchants me so much that I shall probably do a few chapters a year . . . and if I live so long, will present my poor long-suffering C with a proper-sized old-time Gone with the Wind production. But it comes with the wind—the swirl of 18c prophecy—you will be surprised "in our next" to see what a two-faced Imago Saint-Germain turns out to be—though you have had hint of it in the perruque picture.

bolt the communication. A secret door connects Saint-Germain's living quarters and the vestry where he changes clothing to become Antonius.

toward the steps to the lower city. The Old Staircase down to the city begins at the end of George Street (Czech: Jirská ulice), which leads off of the square of Saint George's Basilica that stands behind Saint Vitus's Cathedral. Golden Lane opens off of a byway from George Street, and this byway may be what H.D. is calling Petty Place.

Suppose—. This broken-off thought might be completed as "Suppose this stranger is a supernatural being." The dark figure that looms out of the blizzard, face concealed by his cowl pulled up to form a hood, further unsettles Antonius/Saint-Germain's mind. He thinks he might be seeing mystical apparitions, of which perhaps the Lady was the first.

Saint Bernard of Menthon (who died around 1081), founded, or re-founded, the community of Austin (Augustinian) canons whose Alpine hospices kept the huge work-dogs, the Saint Bernards, famed as the rescuers of travelers snow-trapped in the Great Saint Bernard Pass (8,094 ft.) in the Swiss Alps.

Benedict is short for the Chapel of Saint Benedict on the Walls, one of the side chapels of the cathedral. It has its own entrance. As the mysterious cowled friar pushes open the chapel door, Antonius/Saint-Germain recognizes him as the school-porter, whom he saw daily but now sees in a new aspect. A visionary experience or hallucination—he is not sure which—has come over him.

Paters. This colloquial shortened term for prayers comes from "Pater Noster," the Latin for "Our Father," the first words of the Lord's Prayer, the most frequently recited Christian prayer.

but it's turned around. Saint-Germain is seeing the chapel as reversed, like a photograph printed from the back side of a negative. What is actually on the right hand, he perceives as on the left. This reversal of direction, with no other changes in the so-called real world, is the sign of passage into another dimension of reality. Since reversal or dizziness seems to have characterized H.D.'s breakdown of 1946, this scene attempts to recuperate illness as mystical experience. Reversal also characterized the experience of "the Man on the Boat" in 1920, which H.D. describes in *Tribute to Freud* (155–58, 164) and dwells on at length in her roman à clef *Majic Ring* (1943–44). H.D. and Pieter Rodeck, "Mr. Van Eck" in the novel, had begun what she told Freud was "a conventional meeting or voyage-out romance" on the *Borodino* sailing to Greece (*TF*, 164). According to her, on the afternoon of February 9 (H.D. note, *MA*, 33), he and she stood together on the deck and saw land lying to the right when the coast of France had to be on the left. This reversal of reality signified to her that together they had stepped out of time into another dimension and the land they saw was Atlantis. Later, Rodeck could not confirm that he was there, and she conjectured that the experience was "a message from the Being or Spirit who had directed, who had even impersonated" him (*MR*, ts., 144).

sword-hilt. As a knight, Saint-Germain would wear a sword when dressed in full regalia at court. He is using his right hand on his sword hilt as a reality test. The door to Saint Wenceslas's chapel has reversed its location from left to right. He feels that he has been transported into another dimension.

sacristan is the church official who oversees care of the altars and liturgical vessels, which are usually kept in a room adjacent to the altar. In this passage sacristy, by metonymy, refers to him. The parallel metonymy, *pedagogy*, refers to the group of friars who are teachers; they have lower rank than priests but higher than sacristans. The school-porter senses Brother Antonius's higher status, indicated by his wearing boots although the rule is to wear only sandals, and supposes that he is a priest doing special work with "those old books." Since Henry Dohna is also doing research in old records, the hint is that they will meet in the library.

none of them went in. "Them" refers to friars of the lower orders. Only high-ranking clergy would officiate in the aristocrats' private chapel.

the Visitor is H.D.'s expression for a messenger or projection from the Divine who makes a visitation, that is, comes to an initiate to change his or her religious path. The initiate must have psychic sensitivity in order to be aware of the Visitor, who, to the non-initiate, appears to be an ordinary person. The Visitor does not necessarily know that he or she is the instrument of divine intervention. In this scene, the instrument is the humble school-porter. The reversal of the cathedral itself, like the reversal of its door when Saint-Germain opened it for the Lady, suggests that she too is a "Visitor."

some small thing. Examples in this case are the candles mysteriously blown out in the presence of the school-porter and the pattern of the cathedral door opening the wrong direction into the snow when the Lady needed help with it. But these small things reveal the Mystery.

The first Saint-Germain . . . the Versailles story. Antonius/Saint-Germain knows that he is "deathless," having the power to reincarnate, but he must explain the story circulating at Versailles that Mme. de Gergy had seen him fifty years before in Venice. The idea seems to be that Saint-Germain publicly puts out a mistaken-identity explanation, as given earlier to Stephanus, for the Venice apparition. It was, however, neither himself nor his nephew but a Visitor, a spiritual emanation in Saint-Germain's form. H.D. is explaining the reason that he gives to himself as to why he was seen in two places at once.

supreme tact. In this phrase, H.D. is saying that the Visitor does not overuse his supernormal powers. He takes Saint-Germain's form but keeps his inner being intact, so he is still a rational man. He now has more mystical supersensitivity.

their undisputed portion. Even though saints have been graced with especially strong religious insight as a result of "Visitors," they must develop individually and make their contributions to the world without supernatural help. The Visitor cannot do the work that is the saint's "undisputed portion," just as a medium does not know how to interpret the message he delivers.

knelt there after. . . . The completion of this thought is "after he held open the door for the lady [Elizabeth] to leave."

He had gone far. The experience of reversed orientation is an intrusion of eternity, so he lost track of time. It was in fact only a minute or two since the school-porter had spoken to him.

Mystery . . . asset to the Office . . . equally the Mystery. The purport of this passage is that the school-porter and Stephanus can enter Saint-Germain's mind-stream and think his thoughts. Even though lower class and servants, they are his spiritual equals, equally possessed of "the Mystery." Stephanus is therefore his master's full partner and is similarly helping his spiritual growth. These realizations mark the change that is overtaking the French nobleman, making him uncomfortable.

". . . inform me." It was the voice. The school-porter stops speaking and the narrative resumes with Antonius/Saint-Germain's inner thoughts in an impersonal sentence structure similar to the novel's opening sentence.

the Visitor never . . . after the door shut on him. By strict pronoun reference rules in this sentence sequence, "him" should refer to the Visitor, but it refers to Saint-Germain, who is thinking of the Cathedral door when it closed after he had opened it for the Lady, and he felt he had been given a blessing.

Our Lord's Visit. Antonius/Saint-Germain is apparently thinking of Jesus' entire life, his incarnation and appearance on earth as a Visitation, the apparition of a Visitor. It is a theological position close to Docetism or Gnosticism. But he is not thinking philosophically. He is reacting emotionally, not as a Jesuit but as a Franciscan renunciate, taking to heart Jesus' poverty. He looks again at the school-porter's sandaled feet bundled in sacking and must revise his view that the Visitor would have a beautiful or glorious appearance. His class consciousness and his religious assumptions are both shaken. He himself wears boots because he is involved in a status-conscious church hierarchy, and Stephanus, as a status-conscious nobleman's servant, has insisted that his master maintain appearances even in private, so as not to forget his mission or his noble birth. But the deep snow and the porter's crude footwear for the same weather reminds him of the Franciscan commitment to a true spiritual life and their resistance to worldly power and custom.

not in my province. The school–porter is too lowly to be given duty of lighting the candles in the Cathedral, a more sacred place than the school. In the hierarchy the sacristan must light them. The school-porter will not transgress even in a minor matter and so is waiting for permission from Brother Antonius.

image at a gateway. The school-porter, standing with a lighted taper in his hand, appears to Antonius as if he were a holy statue lit by a votive light or a seventeenth-century Spanish painting of a hooded monk holding a candle. As an "image at a gateway," the porter also suggests a guardian of the limen, the threshold or point of transition between the conscious and the unconscious, an entrance to a new level of spiritual growth.

From an infinite distance. Disorientation of space as well as time accompanies Antonius's mystical experience, which is heightened by the presence of the humble friar.

"—have Saint Francis." Antonius is puzzled, wondering whether the Poor Brothers' thinking of Saint Francis would get them a reward, which, in Antonius's mind, would be a "Visit," perhaps from Saint Francis himself. The school-porter is saying that Saint Francis is always with them. They don't need a special visitation from the mystic-saint to bring them in contact with that eternal dimension that feeds the spiritual life.

What did he want. . . . What was it that he wanted?. The first "he" refers to the school-porter, the second to Antonius, or rather to Saint-Germain, because it is the hidden vocation of the Jesuit intriguer, not the purported vocation of the false friar that has suddenly become problematic. The metaphysical question is the conscious parallel of the practical question he just asked himself regarding the porter. What does he want to do as a knight or as a human being? What path does he want to take to be nearer to God? What is the Visitor telling him?

Chapter VI, pp. 21–24

The Cathedral had veered round. Antonius perceives the cathedral as swinging back through 180 degrees to its proper orientation, which also restores his own correct sense of direction.

the chapel toward which Antonius is walking is the Chapel of Saint Wenceslas, whose interior door opens into the main cathedral.

scenes of the Saint. Scenes from the life of Saint Wenceslas decorate the exterior door of the chapel, the door to the street which Antonius had opened for Elizabeth.

the lamp before Our Lady. A votive light perpetually burning in a sconce of deep-red glass usually hangs from the ceiling before the high altar in Roman Catholic churches. In large cathedrals a similar one usually hangs before a nearby Lady chapel dedicated to the Virgin Mary. Usually the high altar's central icon is a cross or crucifix representing Christ, but H.D. gives Christ's mother the central position as she creates a mythic scene to suit her theme of feminine spiritual power.

treasure of Saint Wenceslas. Today no one can meditate within the gem-encrusted walls. The chapel is closed to the public—"too many sweaty bodies were causing the gilded mortar to disintegrate, but you can catch a glint of the treasure trove over the railings" (*TOP*, 77).

awaiting private audience. Antonius sees the chapel as a royal antechamber because the main church is the throne room of Our Lady. The "audience" that he and the porter seem to wait for would then be with the Queen of Heaven or another manifestation of the Virgin Mary, which might be a "visitation" by Elizabeth, since she is associated with the chapel, queenliness, and blessing. The Lady in H.D.'s *Trilogy* is another manifestation with similar associations.

imagine what one might be—. This incomplete thought of the porter's should end. "he would be like Brother Anton." He senses the power of Antonius/Saint-Germain who has gone into a mystical trance induced by the chapel still apparently imbued with Elizabeth's presence.

the old rule. The old rule for both Protestant and Catholic churches is that one door should remain unlocked at all times. In modern times and in large cities, it is not always practical to hold to this rule.

Candlemas itself. Candlemas is an ancient Christian festival, celebrated on February 2, marking the presentation of Christ in the Temple. Also called the Feast of the Purification of the Blessed Virgin Mary (Lat: Candelaria or Festum candelarum sive luminum), it is celebrated by a candlelight procession as a remembrance of the entrance of Christ, the "True Light," into the Church (*Dct.Xn. chap.* 226). The candle is a powerful icon for H.D., evoking her memories of the beautiful Moravian candlelight Christmas Eve service (*G*, 115).

"That's Charles". The porter is following Antonius's gaze at the gems on the walls. The largest of these is called "Charles" because it was said to have belonged to Charlemagne.

the iron-crown. Charlemagne (742–814) was crowned as the first Holy Roman Emperor by Pope Leo III in Rome on Christmas Day, AD 800, with, according to legend, the Iron Crown of Lombardy, "said to contain a nail from the true Cross" (*EB* [1957], 6: 759).

to Wenceslas because of Christmas. H.D. appears to associate Christmas with Wenceslas because of the popular nineteenth-century hymn and Christmas carol "Good King Wenceslas," written by J. M. Neale to a thirteenth-century tune, "*Tempus adest floridum*" (Thurston, 664). I have not been able to find a native Bohemian legend corresponding to the story in the hymn.

Wenceslas came later. King Wenceslas's dates are AD 907 to 929.

the original foundation. Antonius is not walking on the original stones but on the fourteenth-century ones. However, the Romanesque Rotunda built by Saint Wenceslas in 925–29 still remains under the chapel.

a palace lackey. The palace is Versailles; Antonius is having a flashback to his meeting the frauds and court intriguers in France. The historical Saint-Germain and Cagliostro did meet, probably in association with Egyptian Masonry.

he was a companion . . . one of his own sort, and working with him. The pronouns are confusing here. "He" refers to Saint-Germain; "his" and "him" refer to Cagliostro. Saint-Germain is deploring the historical fact that he and Cagliostro, both being occultists and magicians, were sometimes confused with each other as varying legends about them circulated. In H.D.'s construction, Saint-Germain is a true nobleman, although only conjecture exists regarding the historical figure's birth and origins. His beginnings may well have been much like Cagliostro's.

hallmarks of nobility. One of the submerged themes of this novel is the tension between a monarchic system, a remnant of medievalism, with its clear hierarchies and rich symbols, and a democratic system, herald of the modern world, about to arise in the French Revolution that was inspired by the American Revolution. In the real world H.D. is an American with egalitarian ideals based on Protestant learning and individual responsibility for one's salvation, but she is also a romantic who lives in an imaginary world of fairy tales, medieval chivalry, and the idealized troubadour knight who addresses his songs to the distant beloved in religious ecstasy. Several of H.D.'s views informing this novel come from Denis de Rougemont's *Love in the Western World* and are tinged with Ezra Pound's ideas in *The Spirit of Romance*, especially in his essay "Psychology and Troubadours" (*SR*, 87–100.)

Antoine-Louis. Saint-Germain's ironic self-consciousness of his noble titles augments the spiritual contrast between him and the school-porter. His use of his full first name emphasizes the connection between his true and false identities. The narrative language switches to "Antonius" from "Saint-Germain" to show his inner change of allegiance from Jesuit institutional politics to the Franciscan intention to live more truly in emulation of Jesus. This intention coincides with the Pietist ideal that influenced Zinzendorf in childhood. The identity Saint-Germain assumed as a disguise is now his inner reality.

The porter misunderstood. Antonius's tone does not accord with his words' intention, which was to abjure whatever authority has accrued to his false identity.

He did know why. The candles went out so that the pious porter's wish could be granted. Higher spiritual powers are at work, which Antonius attributes to the lady who offered the candles. The hint is that she is always present in spirit because of the perpetually lit candle over Our Lady's shrine.

a Plan is the eternal preexisting Plan to bring heaven on earth. H.D. thought of Zinzendorf as divinely ordained to carry out this plan. He used the word *Plan* often to describe the expanding Moravian communities worldwide, putting a special slant on the German word *Plan*, which normally has the same meaning as the English word. Later in this novel, H.D. expresses the Plan as working toward "world-unity without war." See chapter 8.

Advent is the season in the Christian year that begins on the Sunday nearest November 30 and lasts until Christmas Eve. Roman Catholics and Anglicans traditionally regard it as a period of penitence and fasting with only an undercurrent of joyous anticipation. Now anticipation dominates as a culture-wide phenomenon. Originally Advent was seen as a time of preparation for the feast of Christ's nativity, celebrating the great gift of God to human beings, the arrival of the Saviour on earth. "But during the middle ages, this meaning was extended to include preparation for Christ's second coming, as well as Christ's present coming through grace" (*Co.Enc.*, 23). This medieval understanding makes clear the reason for H.D.'s giving the title "Advent" to the second part of *Tribute to Freud*, which she put together after the war from her 1933 notes made during the psychoanalysis itself. In her postwar postspiritualist view, psychoanalysis heralded the coming of her "gift" of seeing into past lives and of her union with the female Holy Spirit, a Mother and the "Comforter," as expressed in Zinzendorf's unique Trinitarian theology.

You witnessed the Mystery. The capital *M* in Mystery indicates three meanings combined: the porter's lack of explanation for the candles going out; Antonius/Saint-Germain's sense of being in the hands of divine powers; and the suggestion that Elizabeth, the Lady, is able to control natural forces when she is not present. The capitalized "Mystery" suggests that H.D. has other references in mind as well to the Christian Mystery of the Incarnation, of God coming to earth as a human being, from which the medieval "Mystery Plays" got their name, and to the non-Christian Mystery Religions of the Near East centered on a dying and re-arising god. Her effort is to syncretize these associations in a large ecumenical vision that she sees as rooted in her personal Moravian church heritage.

Chapter VII, pp. 25–27

the fortress. Prague Castle began as a border fortress to protect the eastern boundaries of territories settled by the Slav tribe of Czechs who drove out the Boii, probably a Celtic tribe, between the first and fifth centuries CE. The old fort occupied the eastern part of the present complex. The original defenses, earthworks and timber, were replaced about 1135 by solid rag-stone ramparts. A stone palace with guard-towers east and west was built about the same time. The allusion here is apparently to some remnant of these.

those Meditations. Antonius is in a trancelike state, which the sacristan attributes to one of the Meditations prescribed by the *Exercitia*. This state, close to dream, is a conduit to the unconscious for H.D., who unites it with mystical religious experience.

being only the frame. The tall candles are mounted in a metal frame standing on the floor, not on the sacred altar itself, so the porter has an excuse for Antonius's seeming irregularity in ordering him to light the candles.

the Founder. King Wenceslas founded Saint Vitus's Cathedral but did not build the present building. The position of a door would have been decided by the architect, presumably Matthew of Arras. Arras died eight years into the project and Peter Parler completed its design in late German Gothic style (*TOP*, 76). See notes to chapter 1.

that Alley. Wherever alchemists lived would naturally have a bad reputation with Christian clergy, who regard them as heretics, hence criminals as well.

not properly, the Alley. Stephanus says in chapter 4 that Antonius's quarters open off of a little street called Petty Place that adjoins the Street of the Alchemists. Here the servant is indicating that his master has nothing to do with the lowlife and fraudulent magicians associated with that street.

Alchemists, they called them is the porter's tacit correction of the sacristan's "thieves and cut-throats." Overall, H.D. takes a valorized view that emphasizes the connections between pagan magic and alchemy, the root of modern science, and mystical experience within formal Christian religion.

an adept. The sacristan, as upholder of the institutional church, plans to do something to break into Antonius's meditative trance. "Adept" is used ironically here, since in the mystical tradition it means a highly advanced initiate, a spiritual master. "The term was originally used to refer to alchemists who claimed to have found the philosopher's stone or panacea" (*WDUD*, 23). H.D. must have known this derivation of the word.

the sanctuary. The area, considered especially holy, around the altar and behind the rails in Roman Catholic and Anglican churches.

who recalled him. The interruption recalls him in the sense of calling him back to present reality out of the semi-trancelike state, or the "withdrawal into mystic vision" that he had forbidden to himself in the novel's first chapter.

the reliquary. The chapel of Saint Wenceslas "contains a stone tomb monument to the saint . . . encrusted like the walls with Bohemian stones. The facing side of the tomb is covered with glass and contains a 14th-century silver bust of Saint Wenceslas, along with his relics" (Svoboda, 71).

the relique. The relic—H.D. uses the French and archaic English form of the word—is visible through a glass side of the reliquary. The sacristan does busywork intended to disturb Antonius so that he will get up and leave the chapel. Once he is outside, the sacristan can deliver the urgent message from the Abbot.

they would never go out. The suggestion here is that Elizabeth has the power to keep the candles burning even when the wick and wax are gone, just as she had the power to make them go out in order to grant the porter his wish.

"And forgive us our sins . . . those who have wronged us". Antonius sinned by pretending to be what he is not, a humble monk, a pose he thought was justified by his Jesuit mission. His hypocrisy makes him recite the Lord's Prayer for forgiveness. His religious leaders who involved him in the intrigue are presumably those who wronged him.

Fresh jewels were lighted. The candlelight catches facets in the walls' jewels that he had not seen before, a sign that his own "enlightenment" is progressing. The hint is that Elizabeth is present in spirit, real but invisible, and makes the candles burn more brightly.

caught back. He is aware that he could fall into mystical trance if he is not careful.

Walks soldier-like. The Abbot's summons has made Antonius/Saint-Germain revert to his Jesuit role of "soldier of Christ."

Antonius had turned round. This sentence contains a deliberate pun. Antonius has passed the porter and has walked halfway down the aisle toward the door of Saint Benedict's Chapel when he turns around, physically. But that act is the result of his having "turned around" spiritually, equivalent of the Cathedral's "veering around" into its correct orientation. Now he is heading in the right direction. He turned around because his change of heart made him take pity on the shoeless porter in the bitter cold and ask him to keep up the school fire even though there are no students. He is also symbolically appointing the porter to the priestlike office of "keeper of the sacred flame." This scene also suggests a parallel to Bryher's compassionate rescue of the pregnant H.D. in early 1919, ordering that fires be kept burning in her room in the nursing home.

as if the speaking of them gave them reality. In H.D.'s magical and poetic view, speaking the words does bestow reality. The porter's words to himself make the event real. Antonius really did bow to him in a social gesture universally recognized as a mark of deference and respect. In the class system, the one who bows is lower class. The school-porter also has undergone a reversal of sorts.

why she didn't genuflect. Genuflection is a bending of the knees, the right foot forward, head slightly bowed, as a mark of respect to God in the form of the Blessed Sacrament, the consecrated bread of the Eucharist, or Holy Communion service, which is reserved in a tabernacle on the high altar of Roman Catholic and sometimes of Anglican churches. It is regarded as the "Real Presence" of Christ. Parishioners genuflect just before entering a pew from the church's center aisle. High Church Anglicans also genuflect, but other Protestants do not, since they do not have the practice of reserving the consecrated bread on the altar. The puzzle for the porter and the sacristan is why a Protestant would be worshipping in a Catholic church, an unimaginable, even life-threatening act for anyone during the eighteenth-century wars of religion.

Anthony's Bread (or St. Anthony's Bread), is the name given to alms donated for prayers to Saint Anthony of Padua on behalf of the poor. A box for these alms frequently stood by the church door. Saint Anthony (1195–1231), Franciscan friar and eloquent preacher, is known as the Patron of the Poor (Delaney, 63).

a shadow like a velvet curtain. The porter feels that Our Lady is present as a shadow and makes the candles go out again. He could not move, having witnessed a "miracle" that accords with Antonius's bow to him, also a miraculous event. "The Miracle" was at one point the working title of this novel.

Chapter VIII, pp. 28–34

We can make up for last night. The conversation between Elizabeth and Henry had been broken off by her exhaustion the night before. Now, as they sit in the same place, she suggests that they continue their discussion of their motives for coming to Prague.

permission from the library. Henry wants to search library records because he is doing exactly what H.D. herself is doing in this novel, writing a book that investigates the true spirit within the Old Church of Bohemia. Pearson wrote to her on August 29, 1951, answering her hesitations about going on after having written the early chapters, saying that what "you are doing is what you are describing which is the life of this writing. Don't try to go on with it until you feel the pull of the grail again" (*BHP*, 105).

our heresy. Because members of the Unitas Fratrum are Protestants and "heretics," caution must be exercised in allowing them access to old records, even though the von Reusses of the Tower, as landed nobility, have cordial relations with the Catholic aristocracy resident in Prague Castle.

Protestant Court at Dresden. Around 1730, after Herrnhut had grown into a large Pietist-influenced community including not only Moravians but also Lutheran and Reform church members, Lutheran clerics questioned Zinzendorf's orthodoxy in official councils and asked whether he adhered completely to the Augsburg Confession, the official statement of Lutheran doctrine. Reports on Zinzendorf led them to suspect that he might be a secret Papist. They also feared that the Herrnhut refugees might be a secret army ready to help the Holy Roman Emperor invade Saxony. As a result, Zinzendorf was banished in 1732. He turned his properties over to his wife and made Frankfort the home base from which he constantly traveled to visit his worldwide mission stations.

Because he said Aves. The most commonly used Roman Catholic prayer begins in Latin, "Ave Maria," in English "Hail Mary." "Aves" is a synecdoche for "prayers." Rimius testifies to the feeling that Zinzendorf is too congenial to Catholicism, which led to these false charges. He is offended by Zinzendorf's allowing other Protestant denominations to live in groups ("tropes") among the refugees from Moravia. "Why not a Roman Catholic trope?" Rimius asks ironically, since to him it was entirely unthinkable (*CN*, 30). Two centuries later, however, H.D. was thinking it. She fervently admired the ecumenical impulse in Zinzendorf that brought upon him these hostile attacks.

worthies and their long-winded records. The principal "worthy" is the level-headed, efficient Spangenberg, author of the mammoth biography and a leader in the reorganization of the Unitas Fratrum that had to be made after Zinzendorf's death.

formal reports. Moravians kept detailed records of their pioneering foreign missions. These records are a rich resource now stored in Moravian archives. This scene parallels H.D's own research, much of which she did in wartime London while she was writing and polishing *The Gift* (1940–44).

Pamphleteers. H.D. knew best the pamphleteers Rimius, Lavington, and Frey, but there were numerous others of whom she seems to have been aware.

conventional tributes. La Trobe makes a conventional tribute to Zinzendorf in the introduction to the English translation of AGS's *Life*, published in 1838:

> Count Zinzendorf was undoubtedly one of the most extraordinary personages that have appeared in the church of Christ since the period of the Reformation. By the worldly-wise, he has been acknowledged as a man of original genius and extensive acquirements; by evangelical divines, as a sound, though occasionally eccentric theologian; by children of God of every denomination, as a single-minded and faithful servant of Christ, whose witness of the truth as it is in Jesus was blessed to thousands, both within and without the pale of his own communion.(xiv)

Spangenberg tells this charming and much-repeated story about the Count as a little boy:

> [I]n his seventh and eighth years. . . . when he had pen, ink and paper before him, he wrote a little note to his beloved Saviour, told him in it how his heart felt towards him, and threw it out of the window, in the hopes that he would find it. His covenant with the Saviour was, "Be thou mine, dear Saviour, and I will be thine!" and this he often renewed (AGS, 4).

Zinzendorf in his own words described his mystical contact with Jesus:

> I continued to converse with him when I was quite alone, and believed sincerely that he was very near me. (AGS, 4; Stoeffler, 133)

they wouldn't tell us. The "enthusiasm," not to say orgies, and the lurid symbology of the Sifting Time would not have been discussed with young children because of the references to sexuality, but discussion was similarly repressed among adult Moravians in H.D.'s nineteenth-century childhood. The details of this period appear in the notes to chapter 13.

reasoned answers. Parents' attempts to smooth over the Sifting Time with generalities in talking to older children would be "reasoned answers" but would not explain what actually happened then.

Bishop Spangenberg. This decent and careful man, who knew Zinzendorf's mind very well, did much to establish the Moravian habit of keeping complete records and to govern the "Economy," as eighteenth-century Bethlehem was called. He was its chief administrator for much of the period 1745 to 1762.

the old library. The scene in H.D.'s mind may be a transformed library of the Moravian Female Seminary where her grandfather, Francis Wolle (1817–93), whom she called "Papalie," was principal from 1861 to 1881. The seminary is now Moravian College.

Christian Renatus' letters. Zinzendorf's son, Christian Renatus, wrote many letters and diary entries in the last months of his life trying to undo the harm he felt he had done during the Sifting Time. AGS records how, after his son's death, the father's "tears flowed still more freely, on looking over his son's papers when he found what he had noted down of his daily intercourse with the Saviour" (420). H.D. wrote Pearson on December 18, 1950, that she had

> precious letters that Bryher got for me, one from Zinzendorf himself, Christian Renatus' valentine to one of his cousins, some American "brethren" writing—and Br got me some old books, all of which should be housed sometime when/if I depart to the place of the spirits.

The loose papers are now housed in a manuscript file at the Beinecke and the Rimius and Lavington volumes in the library of the Yale Divinity School.

and Benigna's from Philadelphia. One of Benigna's letters contains an interesting sidelight. She founded the first school for girls in North America, on May 4, 1742, in the house that Zinzendorf, under the name of "Brother Ludwig," had rented from John Ashmead in Germantown. She wrote to the European congregations:

> Nun hat mich das Lamm auf einen Posten geführet. Ich habe eine Kinderanstalt von 25 Mägdchen und da habe ich mich willig dazu aufgeopfert. (Now

the Lamb has guided me to a job. I have a kindergarten with 25 little girls and willingly have I sacrificed myself to it.)(Reichel, Memorials, 183).

Zinzendorf sermons and poems. The quantity of Zinzendorf's writing is enormous. The listing alone, *Bibliographisches Handbuch zur Zinzendorf-Forschung* contains 459 pages (Dietrich). H.D. noted in ZN that Zinzendorf had written "periodicals, books, etc. treatises, hymns, tracts" and that he is a "master-singer" with "540 hymns in hymnbooks," some of which Wesley translated. Of hymns "40 by Countess Z., 60 by C. Rn.—died London 1752" (ZN, 7 [4]; AGS, xxviii).

the letters . . . ribbon binding. These letters from Zinzendorf to Theodora de Castell do not exist, as far as Moravian archivists know (V. Nelson, H. Williams personal communications with the editor). A parallel and contrast exists in H.D., who kept all of Lord Dowding's letters to her. They are at the Beinecke and are being incorporated into my dual biographical study, *The Poet and the Airman: H.D. and Lord Dowding in Wartime London.*

her tapestry. H.D. sewed tapestries while living in London with Bryher during the World War II bombings, at the time she was researching and writing *The Gift*. "It was something to do with her hands while talking to people or sitting around," said her daughter, Perdita Schaffner (interview with the editor, November 13, 1987). The tapestry functions here as an "objective correlative." It was made of "threads" as are the "mystery" and the genealogical lineage. Pearson saw "H.D. by *Delia Alton*" similarly. "It is like one of your needlepoints with the scene there in colors, a kind of small tapestry of history. It sets things right, so there can be no doubt" (letter Jan.15, 1951, *BHP*, 101).

my Saint Hubertus. Elizabeth's choice of this saint reflects the medieval motifs that H.D. chose for her tapestries. She gave Pearson one of these, taken from a design in Cluny Museum in Paris; he acknowledges it in his letter of August 2, 1951. Saint Hubert (d. 727), a courtier under Pepin of Heristal (Pepin II), turned to religion after a mystical experience in which he saw a crucifix in the horns of the stag he was hunting (Delaney, 291; *Co.Enc.*, 2015.). Saint Hubert appears in Pound's early poem, "A Villonaud. Ballad of the Gibbet," in his symbolism as patron saint of hunters (*LOA-EP*, 30.16, n1257.

our second grandmamma. Erdmuth died on July 19, 1756. Zinzendorf married Anna Charity [Caritas] Nitschmann on June 27, 1757; thus she became the "second grandmamma." Anna Nitschmann was the daughter of David Nitschmann, the bishop, who was the nephew of David "Father" Nitschmann (1676–1758), both of whom came to Herrnhut from Moravia in 1725 in a later party also led by Christian David. Before he became bishop, David Nitschmann went in 1732–34 with Leonard Dober to Saint Thomas and established a mission among the African slaves on the plantations (AGS, 59–60, 190). At present a majority of Moravian church members worldwide, about 66 percent, are of black African descent as a result of the eighteenth-century missionaries' work (H. Williams, personal communication, December 12, 1987). Anna Nitschmann had been "awakened whilst a child" and in 1730 was made the first female elder at Herrnhut. She also traveled courageously in the wilds of North America and was known as "the Count's first associate in regard to the pastoral labors amongst the sisters" (AGS, 60, 470).

unmistakably the writing. H.D. knew Zinzendorf's authentic handwriting from the letter she owned. "Ordinarius Fratrum" is Latin for "The Brethren's Bishop" or "Ordinary of the Brethren." When Zinzendorf was ordained bishop of the Bohemian Brethren in 1737, he was not giving up his position as a Lutheran minister; he had been ordained in the Lutheran church in 1734 after resigning from government service in 1732. He thought of his Moravian bishop's role as a public necessity in dealing with civil authorities, because the communities of which he was leader had members from several Christian denominations. He also wanted the episcopate of the Old Church of Bohemia to remain unbroken. In July 1741, when he planned to go to Pennsylvania where he wanted to be known simply as a Lutheran minister, he retired from this episcopacy. "He then called himself, so far as his relation specifically to the Moravian Church was concerned, *Ancien Évêque des Frères*—retired senior, or bishop of the Brethren" (*HB*, 91). (Ancien Évêque can also be translated "former bishop.") After 1744 and after his return from America to Europe, he never used the title of a bishop "but used that of *Ordinarius*." His followers sometimes called him "The Disciple." H.D. read these titles in Levering and made a note beside them in her copy.

full of curious incidents. One "curious incident" often told of Zinzendorf is illustrative; H.D. tells it in her notes to *The Gift* (*G*, 70, 73, 245). John Martin Mack recorded that on a journey through Indian territory in 1742, the count was seated in his tent reading papers scattered around him when two puff adders, small venomous snakes, "slipped into the tent, and gliding over the Disciple's thigh, disappeared among his papers" (*G*, 245). Lydia Sigourney published in 1841 a long Victorian Romantic poem, "Zinzendorff," based on this incident to which she attributes the conversions of many North American Indians to Christianity. Historically, it was not this incident but the count's meeting with the chiefs of the Six Nations in Tulpehocken (in Berks County about twenty miles northwest of Reading, Pennsylvania) on August 3, 1742 that established the Moravians' amicable relations with the Indians (*HMM*, 91-2). More details appear in the later note *bead-belt*.

Christian David's flight. Elizabeth is referring to the first trip in 1722, but Christian David made a second trip. One day at Herrnhut in 1725, without a word to anyone, he laid down his carpenter's tools and left for Moravia, although Zinzendorf had warned him of political trouble with the emperor if more refugees crossed the border. David brought back to Herrnhut five Moravians, including the three Nitschmanns, who had the "definite goal of re-establishing the Unitas there" (Rechcigl, 3).

in Dresden. In 1721, having just come of age, Zinzendorf wanted to enter the Lutheran ministry then but succumbed to family pressure to study law and go into goverment service. He accepted appointment as Aulic Councillor, that is, a judge, in Dresden, the capitol of Saxony, and was in that city when the Moravian refugees arrived on his estate, which is about fourteen miles east of the city.

Pastor Rothe. John Andrew Rothe was the pastor of Berthelsdorf parish church in the village about a mile from Zinzendorf's estate. As lord of the manor, the count had the power to give the pastorate to Rothe, whom he chose as an aide in his lifelong project to amend the Lutheran church according to the Pietism of the theologian Phillipp Jakob Spener (1635–1705). "That which first gave rise to the institutions in Upper Lusatia, was Spener's idea of planting little churches in the great church" (Lat: ecclesiolae in ecclesia) (AGS, 41).

the steward. Heitz hesitated to let the refugees stay only because of the count's absence. He sympathized with their search for religious freedom.

The Countess Gersdorf. Henriette Catherine, Countess von Gersdorf, Zinzendorf's maternal grandmother, raised him until he was ten years old on her estate at Great Hennersdorf, not far from Berthelsdorf. She was a close friend of Spener and one of the "very gifted women of her age," intellectually encompassing all of its movements and motivated by "a profound desire to be of help to people" (Stoeffler, 132). She supervised Zinzendorf's properties while he lived in Dresden. When she heard that small children had arrived in the group of refugees from Moravia, she sent them a cow to supply them with milk (Langton, 59).

Our grandfather was only twenty-two. Zinzendorf was born on May 26, 1700, so he inherited his title and the family properties on May 26, 1721, bought Berthelsdorf manor and continued to serve in the government at Dresden but, following his own Christian convictions, spent as much time as possible preaching the gospel.

Goethe. It is historically accurate that the German poet Johann Wolfgang von Goethe (b. 1749) was working on *Faust* in 1788, having begun it around 1769. In 1772 he finished a Faust play, long undiscovered and now referred to as the *Urfaust*. *Faust: Part One* was published in 1808.

Dr Faustus. The life of the "real" George Sabellicus Faust is almost completely smothered in legend. At least one fact is known. On May 10, 1532, the city of Nuremberg denied a safe-conduct to Doctor Faust, "'the great sodomite and necromancer'" (*MM*, 123). He is reported as having engaged in magical practices in the German cities Helmstadt, Munster, and others, from 1507 to 1540.

the Student of Prague is a legend and variant of the "Czech Doctor Faust" story, which is also referred to as "the Doctor Jekyll and Mr. Hyde of German legend" for its similarities to the Robert Louis Stevenson novel.

sold his shadow. H.D. wrote a review-essay in the third number (September 1927) of *Close Up*, Bryher's film magazine, on a Conrad Veidt film titled *The Student of Prague*, in which the hero, Baldwin, sells his image in the mirror to the devil. She writes:

> For by a magnificent trick of sustained camera magic we have Baldwin the famous fencer student selling his shadow, rather his brave reflection to the little obvious Italian magician of the first reel. The little Punchinello obtains it, by a trick; gold poured and poured Danae shower, upon the bare scrubbed table of the student's attic, "for something in his room." The student has lifted his magnificent blade ruefully. . . . It is not that blade that our friend Punchinello's after. He beckons with his obvious buffoon's gesture toward the mirror. Baldwin regards (in its polished surface) the face of Baldwin. (CU, 121)

The story evolves as the now wealthy young man, Faust-like, finds his Gretchen, who is betrothed to another. His Mephisto-like magician-double kills her fiancé, and Baldwin is ruined. The camera follows the look-alikes in and out of mirrors until finally the devil-spectre is framed in the student's attic mirror again. H.D.'s words are:

> He shoots the spectre only to find himself bleeding with the bullet wound. . . . I have lost everything says Baldwin but not one thing. Raising himself on one elbow along the glass, he realises that his death has brought him his fulfillment. More than his lady, more than his steel blade, himself. Baldwin, dying, clasps a broken edge of triangulated glass to his stained breast. Containing his image simply. (CU, 124)

he would speak to his Friend. This incident occurred on Zinzendorf's return voyage to Europe in 1743. Captain Nicholas Garrison of the vessel, the *James*, wrote an account of what happened:

> On the 14th of February, when we were near the Scilly islands, and the wind blew tempestuously from the south, we were in great danger of foundering upon the rocks. . . . The Count . . . comforted me . . . and told me . . . the storm would be over in two hours. But . . . I took it for granted, that this was something which no one could know beforehand. Hence I made myself ready for death, by prayer and supplication. . . . When the two hours . . . were elapsed, he told me to go upon deck. . . . Scarcely had I been there two minutes, when the storm subsided, the wind changed to the south-west, and we were soon out of all danger (AGS, 316).

When Garrison questioned him, Zinzendorf said that he had for twenty years enjoyed "heartfelt intercourse" with the Saviour, and in any dangerous situation would first ask himself if he were to blame for it and if so would beg forgiveness.

My gracious Saviour then gives me to feel, that he has forgiven me, and generally lets me know how the matter will terminate. But if it does not please him to do this, I remain passive. . . . But this time he let me know that the storm would be over in two hours. (AGS, 316–17)

encounters with the Indians. Zinzendorf survived two other close calls after the puff adder incident. He fell off his horse while fording a river and was nearly drowned (Mack, 107). Later the Shawnese, painted red and black and carrying long knives, crowded around his tent threatening to scalp him for having come to steal silver from a mine near the tent site (*HMM*, 93; Wallace, 140).

bead-belt. During a journey to an Indian village in late July, 1742, Zinzendorf was seized with a premonition that he should go at once to see Conrad Weiser, "the well-known mediator and interpreter." He had the impulse "in strong faith . . . knowing neither why nor wherefore," but set out immediately, "accompanied by Peter Böhler, Frederick Martin and his own daughter Benigna" for Weiser's house in Tulpehocken (Weinlick, 175). Arriving on August 3, 1742, he found there the chiefs of the Six Nations of the Iroquois—the Mohawks, Oneidas, Onondagas, Senecas, Tuscaroras, and Cayugas—who were returning from a conference in Philadelphia. He asked their permission to come into Indian country bringing messages from the Great Spirit, with whom he was "specially and intimately acquainted." The chiefs in their formal reply said:

> Brother, you have journey [sic] a long way, from beyond the sea, in order to preach to the white people and the Indians. You did not know that we were here; we had no knowledge of your coming. The Great Spirit has brought us together. Come to our people. You shall be welcome. Take this fathom of wampum. It is a token that our words are true. (Wallace, 134; *HMM*, 91; AGS, 304–5)

A fathom is about six feet, the length of the arms extended. H.D. noted: "*[H]e was handed by the six Kings a fathom of one hundred and eighty-six white beads,*" white, *symbol of peace and good-will*, "*safe Conduct*" (*HMM*, 92; ZN, 20). The emphasis is H.D.'s. Hutton adds that the count gave the fathom to Spangenberg, who, as chief elder at Bethlehem, would need it in Zinzendorf's absence to travel safely and negotiate in Native American territory.

prison doors were opened. Zinzendorf was imprisoned at Riga in Russia in 1744 as a politically suspect person but was treated well and set free rather promptly because the empress wanted to get him out of the country. Spangenberg's account implies nothing supernatural, contrary to what H.D. suggests here (AGS, 335–36).

if the letter were forthcoming. Henry is speaking of a positive response to the letter he sent asking permission to use the castle library.

go home. "Home" is Saxony. H.D. imagines Elizabeth as living at Herrnhut, "the Lord's Watch," and Henry perhaps on an estate nearby. Historically, Dohna's parents lived in England at least for a while.

Grandfather . . . ambitious for you. The Dohna grandfather, not Zinzendorf, is being referred to here. What ambitions the historical Henry Dohna was to fulfill are not known. His occupation is not given in the records, other than what is implied by his title Burggraf.

our grandfather's tradition. Henry now is alluding to Zinzendorf and his church and missionary diplomacy, not his somewhat brief career in Dresden.

the present bishops. Spangenberg and John de Watteville were prominent bishops after Zinzendorf's death, but the Moravian Church "really had to start all over again" at that time, Henry Williams said, because the count had made all the decisions. The bishops were conscientious but not men with their former leader's charismatic fire. Moravian bishops do not have the direct care of a diocese as in Roman Catholic and Anglican churches. The bishop's position is largely honorary and advisory, while elders or synods manage the church's practical affairs (H. Williams, personal communications, September 12, 1986, and December 24, 1987).

reputed to have drawn lots. Zinzendorf originated the Moravian practice of "drawing lots" as a way of addressing important church decisions to the guidance of the Saviour. He used the lot "when the clear letter of Scripture . . . did not afford sufficient light" (AGS, 92). He carried apparatus for the "lot" in his pocket—a little green book with removable pages, each with a verse from the Old Testament written on it. When in doubt, he pulled out a page and followed the biblical instruction. In public meetings, he picked a slip at random from a box. The first twelve elders who presided at Herrnhut were also chosen by this method (AGS, 84). The lot was also used as a source for a spontaneous sermon or talk. The Moravians' enemies deplored the irrationality of this decision-making method. Rimius accused Zinzendorf of using it to control his followers and deprive them of personal choice.

they dropped all that. Elizabeth is wondering why the Moravians abandoned a practice of the "lot" since, in her view, it is based on a central tenet of their faith, that their Saviour was always personally with them. In *The Gift* H.D. envisions Mamalie as revealing "the secret" to the child Hilda. She recalls the last line of Matthew's gospel (Matt. 26.20) when Jesus assures his followers: *Lo, I am with you always, even unto the end of the world* (G, 157). H.D. herself felt this confidence in the divine presence in the form of the feminine Holy Spirit, not separate from Christ (cf. Fogleman, 74–78).

The wind was howling. H.D. italicized this phrase to signal a "fold" or "pleat" in time, in which "different time periods touch, or unfold to reveal a different historical time" (S, xxxiii). In *The Sword Went Out to Sea*, H.D. explains it: "If you understand one fold or pleat, one superimposition, you understand another" (S, 91). Here in

The Mystery, she gives the fold a reincarnational twist. Henry's evocation of Antonius opening the cathedral door propels Elizabeth into "living back" into that moment of contact with the unknown supposed friar. The wind symbolically suggests the Holy Spirit, and its blowing along the Street of the Alchemists suggests magical transformation.

It had happened before. The language of Elizabeth's mystical perception is identical with Antonius's comment on his "reversal." It may also be seen as H.D.'s recuperative view of her nervous breakdown as a religious experience, a trial that purifies the initiate.

you are worried . . . about the state of the world. The worry concerns the upcoming French Revolution and whether it will sweep all Europe into war, just as H.D. worried about war signs she saw in Vienna in 1933 that led into World War II.

thinking of Bethlehem. Elizabeth is thinking specifically of the mission at Gnadenhuetten (German: Gnadenhütten) a few miles from Bethlehem, where on November 24, 1755, eleven Moravians, including women and an infant, were slaughtered by Shawnese incited by the French. It was the tragic nadir of Moravian missionary efforts. In the Seven Years War (1755–63) between England and France, the Native American tribes sided with the French, having reportedly been told by French Catholic priests that Christ had been born at Paris and was crucified by the English. While many of the Moravians were ethnically German, many were English, and the Bethlehem community was still loyal to the English crown at that time, although it was well aware of the revolutionary sentiments building in the American colonies (*HMM*, 99–101).

Jednota *or* Unitas. In 1749, during the high tide of gossip about the Moravians at Herrnhaag, a committee of forty members of the House of Commons investigated the Moravian Church in England and found nothing irregular about the organization itself. Archbishop John Potter, among others, certified that it was "an ancient Protestant episcopal church," the legitimate successor of the Bohemian Brethren" (Weinlick, 197). Parliament then passed and the crown approved this official status and granted members of the Unitas Fratrum exemption from taking oaths, from jury duty, and from military service in the American colonies "under reasonable conditions" (AGS, 389; "H.D.", 188).

Tory sympathies. The vindication of the Moravians and their sanction by the Crown of England enabled them to go to live in the English colonies. They were therefore inclined to be pro-English, or at least their neighbors perceived them as such. When the American Revolution began to build, the Moravians tried not to take sides, feeling their loyalties divided between their new country and their old, but desiring most of all to be nonpolitical, continuing their collective religious vocation. They failed to make their position clear, as the Gnadenhuetten massacre unhappily showed.

General Washington requisitioned Bethlehem as a mass army hospital in December 1776 (*HB*, 451).

Marquis de Lafayette. On September 21, 1777, the "brave and gallant young French nobleman, the Marquis de la Fayette," who had been wounded at Brandywine, was taken to the house of George Frederick Boeckel where he was nursed by Boeckel's wife Barbara and daughter Liesel until October 18. Many "pretty little stories with variations," says Levering, entered local tradition as a result of the Marquis's graciousness (*HB*, 465). H.D. had a romantic attachment to such stories about nobility; they resemble fairy tales in which the aristocratic characters symbolize ideal virtues.

still a hospital. Particularly after the British took Philadelphia in 1777, many wounded were brought to Bethlehem. Moravians vacated their own living quarters to accommodate them, a situation that continued into 1778 and 1779 and did not ease off until the time of the first peace treaty of January 20, 1783 (*HB*, 525–26).

four years ago. Benigna and John von Watteville arrived in Bethlehem on June 2, 1784, where their daughter and son-in-law, Elisabeth and Alexander von Schweinitz were eagerly waiting to greet them. John von Watteville's job was to help the community adjust to the terms of the new government and to upgrade its schools, which had suffered during the war period but were well known for their high quality.

president of the new Republic. Elizabeth's remark aids the dating of this novel. The Constitutional Convention presided over by General George Washington took place from May through August 1787. Ratification proceeded through 1788, during which the question arose as to who would be president of the new Republic. Electors chosen early in 1789 voted unanimously for Washington, who was inaugurated in New York on April 30, 1789. The French Revolution began that year.

only Comenius. Johann Amos Comenius (Czech: Jan Amos Komenský, 1592–1670) was called the "last bishop" of the Moravian Church as it had existed under the Holy Roman Emperors. The Unitas Fratrum, earlier known as "The Brethren of the Law of Christ," began in the branch of Jan Hus's followers called the Calixtines (Lat: calix = cup) because of their insistence on communion in both kinds, that is, with both bread and wine. Persecutions drove Comenius to Poland in 1621, where he worked for educational reform and a universal system including the education of women. Comenius influenced Zinzendorf in an extraordinary way. In 1727, the count found, in a library at Zittau near his grandmother's estate, a copy of Comenius's Latin version of the old Brethren's "Account of Discipline." Greatly moved by this first encounter with Old Church records, Zinzendorf said to the Herrnhut community:

> I could not read the lamentations of old Comenius . . . that the Church of the Brethren had come to an end . . . "Turn Thou us unto Thee, O Lord, and we shall be turned; renew our days as of old" without resolving . . . to help bring about this renewal. (AGS, 81)

He also found that the rules for the ancient community were almost the same as the rules he had just drawn up for the refugees. This connection inspired the exiles with new faith. When the entire community was invited by Pastor Rothe to Berthelsdorf parish church to celebrate Holy Communion together on August 13, 1727, all present felt that they were "one in Christ," touched by the "purifying flame of the Holy Ghost." August 13 is still celebrated as the "birthday" of the renewed Moravian Church whan all members received "spiritual baptism" (*HMC*, 208–9; *Offices*, vi). H.D. spells the name as Commenius, following AGS (81).

his robe and cross. Several portraits of Comenius are hung in prominent places in Bethlehem where H.D. would easily have seen them, but none show him with a cross. The cross was not a symbol used by Moravians, who associated it with Roman Catholicism; they preferred another ancient symbol, the Agnus Dei (H. Williams, letter to the editor, November 12, 1987). Agnus Dei is Latin for "Lamb of God," an epithet for Jesus. H.D. describes it in *The Gift* as the "Lamb with the Banner, the same emblem that the Templars in Europe had used" (*G*, 156, 170). Her long historical note on it (*G*, 264–66) contains the seeds of this novel.

Jablonsky. An important link in the Moravian apostolic succession, Daniel Ernst Jablonsky (or Jablonski, 1660–1741), was born near Danzig, the son of a Moravian minister. He married Comenius's daughter and from 1686 to 1691 was head of the Moravian College at Lissa, Poland, a position his grandfather had held. Ordained bishop by Comenius in 1699, he was court chaplain to the King of Prussia when Zinzendorf asked him to ordain David Nitschmann.

the lost Church. The Old Church was "lost" to Comenius and Jablonsky because they had no hope for their return to Bohemia. H.D. refers to it as "the dispersed or 'lost' Church of Bohemia" in "H.D. by *Delia Alton*" (202) and connects it with the Old Church of Provence in a statement quoted by Pearson in his foreword to *Hermetic Definition*. He had gone with H.D. and Bryher to Bethlehem in September 1956 (Silverstein, pt. 6.20) and recalled the occasion:

> [S]he stood in the aisle of the Central Church, remembering love feasts and the Unitas Fratrum. She was fascinated by Zinzendorf and his re-establishment of "a branch of the dispersed or 'lost' church of Provence, the Church of Love that we touch on in By Avon River." It was not casual when, as we left the church, she signed the Register and added "Baptized Moravian." (HD, v)

This "lost" church of Provence is the Church of the Cathars from which, according to Denis de Rougemont's *Love in the Western World*, the troubadours derived their concept of Love. De Rougemont's book influenced H.D. immensely. She said in a letter to Viola Jordan (July 30, 1941 or 1944, year uncertain). "THAT IS MY BIBLE, if you will" (*PR*, 309; Guest, 329). H.D. notes Zinzendorf's assertion that the Unitas Fratrum descended from the Waldenses, a branch of the Cathars

(*USE*, 9037). It was another claim that offended the arch-Protestant Rimius, who wrote of Zinzendorf:

> He pretends that these Brethren originally were of the Greek Church, and in Process of Time had united with the Waldenses, who derived their Origins from the Latin Church. He bestows the greatest encomiums on their Moravian Church, eclipsed & forgot afterwards, and at length, if Credit may be given him, revived under his Auspices at Herrnhut. He gives her the most pompous titles; as the Church of the Cross, the Church of the Lamb, the Church of the Blood & Wounds, the Theocracy, a People whereunto never was seen the like, they are the Hundred-forty-four Thousand Servants of God mark'd on their Foreheads. (Rev. 14.1).

The emphasis is Rimius's; H.D. also underlined "their Moravian Church" (ZN, 6 [36]; *CN*, 13).

The Church within the Church. Spener's idea of the "little church within the great church" was applied by Zinzendorf to the whole Herrnhut community as well as to the Moravian refugee segment of that community. Thus the community had a subdivision or "trope" (Lat: tropus, Zinzendorf's term) for each denomination—Lutheran, Reformed, and Bohemian Brethren.

conferred it on David Nitschmann. After consulting his colleague in Poland, Bishop Christian Sitkovius, who gave his approval, Jablonsky ordained Nitschmann in Berlin on March 13, 1735 (ZN, 9 [12], quoting AGS).

Christian David's party. H.D.'s narrative does not allow for the historical fact that the emigration from Moravia to Herrnhut took place in several stages (Rechcigl, 3). The factual error does not alter her point.

the seven or the seventeen. H.D. saw numerological significance in 1700, the year of Zinzendorf's birth. She was familiar with numerology and its system of telling fortunes by numbers based on the letters in one's name, although astrology was her preferred system of divination in the 1930s. Her interest in both systems appears in her letter to Eric White of March 6, 1932, which he printed along with the chapters of *The Mystery* she sent him in 1960 because of his interest in Moravian history (White, 21, 27–28). The symbolism of sevens also permeates the Revelation of Saint John the Divine, the biblical book that highly influenced both H.D.'s thought and Zinzendorf's theology of "Blood and Wounds."

world-unity without war is the leitmotif and key theme of this novel. The phrase links the word "unity" with the Moravian church name Unitas and with Zinzendorf's vision of the worldwide Plan.

the Thirty Years War (1618–1648) began when the Bohemians refused to elect the Catholic Ferdinand to the Bohemian throne, and instead chose Frederick, who became the "Winter King" after his defeat at White Mountain, near Prague, in 1620, and Catholic repression of Bohemian national religion began. Religious war in Bohemia, however, can be seen as actually beginning with the martyrdom of Jan Hus in the fifteenth century. Prague, Hus's home, is therefore the place for the questing Elizabeth and Henry to do research to find what that church has lost.

you live back into their lives. "Living back" is both theme and method of this romance, as it combines H.D.'s sense of dream-interpretive skills from psychoanalysis and her sense of "gifted" mediumship from spiritualism. She felt that her "gifts," literary and psychic combined, lifted her out of time. In the act of writing, she was not merely imagining women's past lives but actually re-entering them; in *The Gift* she re-enters the life of her mother, her grandmother, and the pioneer Anna von Pahlen. It is her version of "inspiration by the Muse."

Gregory, Archbishop. Levering describes "the seed of the Brethren's church" as

> a colony under the leadership of Gregory, a nephew of Rokycana . . . located, early in the year 1457, near the village of Kunwald on the domain of Lititz in the north-eastern part of Bohemia, the property of George Podiebrad who the next year became King of Bohemia. (*HB*, 9)

official founder. In H.D.'s family metaphor here, David Nitschmann is "father" of the town, while Zinzendorf, having named it on Christmas Eve, 1741, is its godfather. "Father" perhaps also echoes Roman Catholic usage, since among Moravians the customary form of address would have been "Brother." Zinzendorf was "Brother Ludwig" and Spangenberg "Brother Joseph" (cf. Wallace, 134; Reichel, *Bethlehem Souvenir*).

the foundation inherited the Jednota. H.D. calls Bethlehem a "foundation" as if it were a monastic institution. She has confused Bishop David Nitschmann, whom she just called Father Nitschmann, with his uncle, old "Father" David Nitschmann. Both uncle and nephew came with Anna in the first party of Brethren to arrive in Pennsylvania in late December 1740, a year before the Count and Benigna came. The bishop had a commission to buy land and establish a Moravian community "to become the heart and center of a wide-spread spiritual enterprise" (Hamilton, 86). H.D. seems to have known the facts from Levering (*HB*, 54–55) but has blended the two David Nitschmanns in the service of her tight-knit family analogy that makes Elizabeth and Henry step-grandchildren of the Moravian Church because they are step-grandchildren of Anna Charity Nitschmann.

Chapter IX, pp. 37–42

go back . . . proverbially punctual. The scene is the Abbot's quarters, somewhere in the castle precincts. When summoned, Antonius/Saint-Germain found not the Abbot—the summons was a ruse—but Cardinal de Rohan, in flight from Paris. Now they are speaking together after having dined. De Rohan as architect of the Jesuit intrigue speaks to Saint-Germain as a fellow conspirator, who has the "avocation" of posing as the poor Brother Anton. The pose has become reality, and Antonius/Saint-Germain does not want to go through with his original mission. He makes an excuse to break off the conversation by saying that he must go back to the cathedral to meditate, or suspicions will be aroused. He is stalling for time.

The Hat . . . the Chair. De Rohan has asked Saint-Germain to give up his disguise, leave Prague, and come with him to Rome to present the names of French Freemasons to the Office of the Inquisition. Saint-Germain, whose identity is increasingly that of Antonius, resists, although the cardinal is his superior. High reward will ensue, de Rohan tells him. "It is already ordered," says the prelate, in an echo of the school-porter's words in Saint Wenceslas's chapel. Saint-Germain can be made a cardinal (wear "the Hat") or perhaps become Pope (assume "the Chair" of Peter). In the original manuscript, H.D. handwrote "the Chair" after crossing out "the papacy."

Embassy side of the Row. Saint-Germain must be perceived by visiting ambassadors as a nobleman, hence his servant's insistence on his maintaining the attitudes and attributes of a nobleman: court attire, perruque, and medals. But having been a monk for a while, he is "out of practice" at living in the grand style of the princes of the church. There is some mockery in his tone.

the rapier point, au fil de l'epée. Saint-Germain insists that he is no longer clever enough to keep up at Versailles. His mind is not "on the sword's edge," that is, he no longer has the rapierlike or "cutting" wit expected in Court circles.

never disproved . . . *Lentmeritz in Bohemia.* H.D. took much information on Louis Saint-Germain from *The History of Magic* by Éliphas Lévi, the pen name of Alphonse-Louis Constant (1810–75), who belonged to the Illuminés, a Gnostic syncretic religious movement that integrated Christianity with neo-Platonism and occultism. Lévi wrote that "the Comte de Saint-Germain was born at Lentmeritz in Bohemia at the end of the seventeenth century," a birth account drawn from the legend that the historical Saint-Germain was an illegitimate son of a king of France, presumably King Louis XV (*HM*, 296). De Rohan's broken-off sentence should end. "was the King of France." Lang says that Louis XV "knew, or thought he knew, the secret of Saint-Germain's birth" (*HM*, 263). There is apparently no historical information whatsoever about his birth, and only minimal and conflicting reports about his death.

the last Louis refers to Louis XV, the most recent king before the present one in the novel, Louis XVI.

the Dauphin. The oldest son of Louis XVI and Marie Antoinette, born in 1781, was sickly and retarded, so de Rohan calls him "poor child" and hopes that, for the sake of France, he will be prevented, by some means, from coming to the throne. The child died, presumably of natural causes, in 1789.

And the King—. Saint-Germain is referring to the impediments to his coming to the throne if the rumors of his birth proved true. Louis XVI was a grandson of Louis XV. A son would take precedence, dethroning him.

biologically intended—. De Rohan is prevented from completing his thought in this sentence, which should end "to rule." Louis XVI (1754–93) was reputed to have been born dull-witted. An encyclopedia summarizes his contribution to pre-Revolutionary France:

> He was weak and incapable as king, and not overly intelligent. He preferred to spend his time at hobbies such as hunting and making locks . . . and permitted his wife to influence him unduly. The unpopularity of the queen was a major factor in the outbreak of the Revolution (USE, 5407).

"*There is*—." This sentence should end with the words "the Queen."

'Toinette. De Rohan's rather contemptuous use of the diminutive for Marie Antoinette suggests that he had a love affair with her but he is saying that it was not genuine but policy—"my province"—and part of the larger plan. Antonius had earlier mused on whether de Rohan's passion for the Queen could save the State, that is, the French monarchy, since it has been allied with the Papacy since the days of Charlemagne.

frater et praeceptor is Latin for "brother and teacher," the roles Saint-Germain plays as Antonius. Later Saint-Germain calls de Rohan his "praeceptor."

the media . . . *the Organisation, as we planned it. Media* should be translated as "means," although H.D. also intends wordplay; "media" is the plural of "medium" with its spiritualist associations. In the succeeding passages it becomes clear that "the two" to be joined are the Society of Jesus and a revived order of the Knights Templar.

Holy Father? Not this one. Antonius/Saint-Germain is not talking about the current Pope in the novel's time-scheme, Pius VI, but an earlier one, Pope Paul III, who approved the Jesuit order in 1540.

It went back to 1118. The military order of the Knights Templar was constituted in 1118 during the Crusades. H.D. read Robin Fedden's *Crusader Castles* and took notes: "Fraternities of fighting monks. / Hospital & Temple. / Grand Master of the Temple. / conducted last defence of Acre— / Templars took name from the / temple enclosure in Jerusalem. / constituted as military order 1118" (Fedden, 1957 ed., 71; ZN, 2).

Geoffrey de Saint-Omer. Lévi says in *The History of Magic*:

> In 1118 nine crusading knights, then in the East—among whom were Geoffrey de Saint-Omer and Hugh de Payens—dedicated themselves to religion, placing their vows in the hands of the Patriarch of Constantinople, which had always been hostile, secretly or openly, to that of Rome since the days

of Photius. The avowed object of the Templars was to protect Christians on pilgrimage to holy places; their concealed end was to rebuild the Temple of Solomon. . . . so rebuilt and consecrated to the Catholic worship, the Temple of Solomon would have been in effect the metropolis of the universe. East would prevail over West and the patriarchs of Constantinople would seize the Papacy. (207)

Loyola's precept *'the end justifies the means'*. A present-day history of the Society of Jesus describes the source of this expression:

> Herman Busenbaum, gifted teacher at the University of Cologne, published in 1650 his celebrated An Epitome of Moral Theology. . . . Despite Busenbaum's prestige, a strange myth has enveloped his name. To him, and frequently by association to all Jesuits, has been attributed the doctrine that the end justifies the means, be the means intrinsically good or evil. Quite explicitly, however, Busenbaum excluded the use of bad means. (Bangert, 223)

The point here is that de Rohan and Saint-Germain broke church rules in practicing magic after they deceptively became members of the Egyptian Masonic lodge in Paris dominated by Cagliostro. They thought they had a legitimate end: to get the names of revolutionary French Freemasons, give them to the Inquisition at Rome, and receive as reward the re-establishment of the Society of Jesus.

Fraternity. While "Fraternity" is the Freemasons' term for themselves, here it refers to the secret organization to which both the count and the cardinal belong. In this view whatever happens is predestined by a greater plan dictated from on high. The historical de Rohan believed Cagliostro's claims to magical powers, but the historical Saint-Germain saw Cagliostro as a competing healer and a false dabbler in the occult (Gervaso, 116, 120).

Knights of Asia, Royal Priests are degrees, or prescribed stages, in Egyptian Freemasonry, each with elaborate symbolic initiations that progressively require greater secrecy and commitment.

symbolic bridge of the Knight of the East or Sword. Saint-Germain is saying that he and de Rohan in achieving high degrees in Freemasonry have also achieved genuine spiritual elevation despite their duplicitous aims.

ordered . . . out of Paris. The church had begun to respond to rumors that their property would be seized by the revolutionaries to finance their operation, and wealthy bishops, many of whom were also aristocrats aligned with the monarchy, had been instructed by the pope to leave France.

a great-coat. That Antonius/Saint-Germain wears a great-coat as his disguise links him with Henry Dohna, who also hides his noble rank disguised by the great-coat of the castle servant Jacobus.

Tuscany . . . Campagnia. The cardinal is ordering his subordinate to escape to Italy and, to lure him, evokes the beauties of its landscape, particularly in the Campagnia, the area around Naples. The images are intentionally reminiscent of Goethe's famous lyric, "Kennst du das Land wo die Zitronen blühen," sung by the child Mignon in *Wilhelm Meisters Lehrjahr*. In "Writing on the Wall," H.D. identifies her "soul" with Mignon and translates this poem within a long meditation on Freud that has a number of emotional resonances with this scene (*TF*, 106–11).

Bohemia. For de Rohan this word means the excellent "Bohemian wine" that is intoxicating him, producing a supernormal state of mind, but Saint-Germain applies the word to the whole country and to his mystical experiences associated with Elizabeth.

the door swung inward. . . . Palace orgies. Saint-Germain's digression makes de Rohan think that his companion has gone slightly mad, as he never had before, even during wild parties in the palace of Marie Antoinette at Versailles.

a coming Revolution. For the first time in this novel, the submerged context of the French Revolution has clearly surfaced.

Acharat was the name under which Cagliostro said he had been raised at Medina, Arabia, and had been taught occult magic by Althotas, the mysterious head of Egyptian Masonry (Gervaso, 28–30; Photiades, 197).

Althotas arranged everything. The suggestion here is that Althotas has instigated the revolution in France as part of the larger plan, using Cagliostro as his instrument. This belief in the supreme power of magic seems to override any thought in H.D.'s mind that social forces might be stronger determinants of historical events. To such believers Cagliostro would appear instrumental because of his prognostications. Father Luca Benedetti reported that he witnessed at Rome in September 1789 a séance in which Cagliostro predicted the downfall of Louis XVI:

> The Count [Cagliostro] called a girl into the room and ordered her to look into a glass bottle full of water. The girl, whom he called his pupil, said that she saw a road leading from a great city to another one nearby, crossed by a huge crowd of men and women who ran along shouting . . . "Down with the King!" Cagliostro asked her what place this was. She answered that she could hear the crowd clamouring. "To Versailles!" . . . The magician turned to us and announced. "The pupil has foretold the future. In a short time from now, Louis XVI will be attacked by the populace in his palace in Versailles . . . the monarchy will be overthrown, the Bastille razed to the ground, and freedom will triumph over tyranny." (Gervaso, 205)

Saint-Germain made the same prediction of overthrow in person to Marie Antoinette in 1775, according to the memoirs of Mme. d'Adhémar, a lady-in-waiting to the queen. He said that the end of the monarchy would come after several years of "deceptive calm." The queen did not want to hear this news, but the count persisted. "I am Cassandra, and France is the empire of Priam." Fourteen years later, in 1789, according to this account, the queen received a letter signed "Comte de Saint-Germain," saying "I was Cassandra, and my words struck your ears in vain. . . . today, it is too late." In a private letter to Mme. d'Adhémar, he blamed the "démon Cagliostro" for the "infernal" horror to come (*LCSG*, 212, 213, 217). The only problem with this story is that Saint-Germain was reported to have died in Germany in 1784 (*LCSG*, 190). The report perhaps did not matter much, since the public rumor was well-entrenched that he was "deathless" and therefore could resurrect.

Who is Althotas? De Rohan is trying to get Saint-Germain to admit that he is Althotas. Éliphas Lévi writes: "It is said that Saint-Germain was no other than that mysterious Althotas who was Master of Magic of another adept . . . who took the Kabalistic name of Acharat. The supposition has no foundation" (*HM*, 300). Saint-Germain hedges by saying that de Rohan knows as much as he does.

presentation at the Vatican. Historically, the Inquisition did have spies tracking Cagliostro and reporting his activities, as de Rohan is doing. In 1789, the Holy Office persuaded Cagliostro's wife, Seraphina, to denounce her husband as a heretic Freemason not long after the séance attended by Fr. Benedetti was reported to the Vatican by Cardinal de Bernis, the French ambassador, who was also there. He demanded that the pope act against Cagliostro (Gervaso, 206–7).

Sanctum circuitously names the secret location of Masonic rites. Saint-Germain hesitates to call it a "temple," which would violate his latent Templar's sense that there is only one Temple, that in Jerusalem.

the expressed (if secret) intention of the Freemasons is to overthrow the monarchy and abolish the Catholic religion.

suppressing the lower orders. De Rohan sees the suppression of the Jesuits not as a Vatican political maneuver or a consequence of their activities but as the manifestation of a plan preconceived by Loyola. The suppression is a test that would weed out the less committed Jesuits so that a spiritual elite could emerge that would re-form the authentic Order of the Templars.

Clement V perished miserably. Pope Clement V died in 1314, two years after suppressing the Templars in 1312, an act of subservience to Philip the Fair, King of France, who wanted to appropriate their wealth. Philip also died in 1314.

Perhaps history disproves this. De Rohan is discounting the truth of a superstitious tradition that untimely death comes to popes who suppress the Society of Jesus. The tradition arose from a historical coincidence. In 1773 Clement XIV suppressed the order, evidently to please European monarchs who had demanded withdrawal of Jesuits from their countries, and he died on September 22, 1774, as the result, according to an official statement "of the natural process of a fatal disease," a euphemism for brain tumor, a nonrespectable form of death, since it was associated with mental illness (Barthel, 231).

Fifteen years ago. This figure sets the precise date of this novel as 1788.

After the Revolution. The Jesuits were restored in 1814 by Pius VII, who was pope from 1800 to 1823. He succeeded Pius VI, pope from 1775 to 1799, as successor of Clement XIV.

the list names Freemasons purportedly organizing against the monarch.

the inner Office. The Office of the Inquisition had gotten secret notice from de Rohan, so they already know what is coming and have given warning to French churchmen to leave the country.

our Bohemia, after Paris. De Rohan is saying metonymically that after they write down the names of the Paris revolutionaries, they can go back to drinking Bohemian wine.

the flagon. . . . the fruit. The magical appearance of fruit and replenishment of wine makes this banquet a replica of ones produced, according to legend, by Faust, "with the choicest and rarest foods, fruit out of season and exquisite wines" (*MM*, 139). In Goethe's *Faust*, his hero produces spontaneously flowing wine in Auerbach's cellar. Legend says that the "alchymyst" Albertus Magnus, in the depths of a winter snowstorm produced for his friends a summer garden with flowering trees under which stood a banquet table laden with delicacies (Mackay, 107–8). Saint-Germain's conversion and his refusal to name names seem to contribute to the magic that brings about this feast. It is a contest to see whose magic is the stronger.

ruby glass. Bohemia is famous for the manufacture of the much-valued "Bohemian glass," which has a rich ruby color.

like a red rose. De Rohan is drunk and is looking at the room through his ruby-tinted wine glass. The "red rose" is an objective correlative for Elizabeth, in whose person erotic love and spiritual love co-exist. The suggestion is that her spiritual power has produced the feast as it produced Saint-Germain's conversion.

not Loyola. De Rohan is saying that he does not know the plan and outcome of things as the Jesuit leader did, but, as a non-visionary, he has to finish his mundane task of writing down names to give to the Inquisition so that they will have the revolutionaries killed and the monarchy will continue to rule France.

two hermetically sealed compartments. In "H.D. by *Delia Alton*," "Delia Alton" says of H.D.: "She has her two visions or her two fields of vision. She realizes these in two separate compartments of her mind . . . two streams or realms of knowledge or of consciousness" ("H.D.," 185). They correspond roughly to this world of everyday reality and the "other" world of dream, trance, or séance. Saint-Germain sealed off from his mind his commitment to the Jesuits while with the Freemasons, but now he has forgotten Jesuit affairs and their passwords. He has stepped into the other compartment of his mind. The two, however, do not stay very clearly separated.

the magus. The reference is to Cagliostro. Saint-Germain hesitates to use the adept's name "Acharat," because he thinks Balsamo is a fraud, and yet the name itself has magical power.

It was blackness, unutterable and damnable. "It" refers to the two men's involvement with the "Egyptian Rites," not with the rites themselves. He feels it is evil to betray to the Inquisition those with whom he swore profound oaths of loyalty and secrecy—in short, he no longer feels that the end justifies the means.

the original inditement. De Rohan is willing to excuse Saint-Germain from writing out the names of Freemasons but wants the count's signature on a sheet of formal charges against them. As this is a death warrant, Saint-Germain is trying to find a way not to sign.

Sicilian connotes the Mafia stereotype of a criminal conspirator who takes loyalty very seriously and is famous for extravagant revenge against those who betray him or any member of his "family."

Were they nothing?. It is a matter of no moral consequence, asserts Saint-Germain to himself, if he and de Rohan break the vows they took during the Masonic rites. But then he thinks those vows might not be "nothing." Maybe they have true power and are binding, since perhaps in the world of the spirit, all is one, not divided into compartments or sects. And the false vows had after all brought him to Prague to meet his "mystery" named de Watteville.

a truce. The letter seems delivered by divine intervention and provides a "truce" in this silent struggle between the two men and between false and true religion. Saint-Germain can use it to avoid signing the inditement for the Inquisition.

Chapter X, pp. 43–46

His mistress—. Saint-Germain at first reacts to the word "mistress" in its sexual connotations as "lover" rather than in its intended meaning as "employer of a servant."

Your Ambassador. De Rohan says to Saint-Germain that the newly arrived ambassador from France is "yours," because he is lodged next door to the disguised count and offers him a means of escape in this time of crisis.

Our choice of Prague. The pronoun "our" refers to the underground Templar-Jesuits. The Abbot, who does not appear as a character in the novel, knows their secrets, as he is one of them, although he is Franciscan. His aid and skill led the "Organisation" to choose Prague as the place for their renewal to begin.

"Von Schweinitz. . . . Stephanus—". The completed thought is: "Stephanus told me her name was de Watteville." The new name von Schweinitz makes Saint-Germain think that she is married to the man whom he supposed to be her servant, a highly disturbing thought.

your life of errantry in the forest. This allusion to Saint-Germain's past comes from Lévi, who says: "Saint-Germain never spoke of his father but he mentions having led a life of proscription and errantry in the world of forest, having his mother as companion" (*HM*, 296; *LCSG*, 89).

the source poisoned by Cagliostro. Cagliostro's *Mémoires pour servir à l'histoire du Comte de Cagliostro* state that Saint-Germain was the founder of Freemasonry and in Germany had initiated Cagliostro into its secret rites (*EB* [1957], 4: 530). Much in these *Mémoires* is unverifiable and must be taken as fiction.

company of Saint-Jakin. One legend recounted by Lévi concerning Saint-Germain is that he founded "an association under the title of Saint-Jakin—which has been turned into Saint Joachim." This organization was reported to engage in an initiation in which a candidate for membership in their order was asked to give up his life. The candidate was bled till he swooned but was not killed; then he was awakened as one supposedly resurrected from the dead. Some initiates believed that they had really been resurrected and so thought they would never die. Lévi comments:

> The heads of the society thus had at the service of their concealed projects the most formidable of all instruments, namely madness. . . . The sect of Saint-Jakin was therefore an Order of Gnostics steeped in the illusions of the Magic of Fascination; it drew from Rosicrucians and Templars; and its particular name was one of two names—Jachin and Boaz—engraved on the pillars of Solomon's Temple [1 Kings 7.21]. (*HM*, 299)

In Masonic initiations the pillars represent the extremes of life and death. Saint-Germain is depicted here as wanting to dissociate himself from false and deceptive magic, as did both Lévi and H.D.

Father de La Tour. Zinzendorf met Father de La Tour, who was General of the Society of the Oratory, in Paris in 1719 (AGS, 20).

the Premonstrants. Also called *Premonstratensians*, this order took its name from Premontre, near Aisne, in the diocese of Laon in France, site of their first monastery, founded by Saint Norbert in 1120. Not monks but canons regular, they were preachers and pastors of parishes incorporated within their monasteries. Zinzendorf visited a church of the Premonstrants when he was a student in Paris (AGS, 21).

The names. On page 6 of ZN, among notes from AGS, H.D. wrote the following list:

Father Anthony Dionysius
Simon D'Albizi.
oratory of the Premonstrants.

In composing this chapter, H.D. evidently re-read these notes, which appear to record two names as if of two persons, although in fact they refer to one person only.

According to Spangenberg, Zinzendorf heard, in the church of the Premonstrants, a sermon that led him to go to the oratory of the Premonstrants to meet the preacher, a Dominican monk whose full name is given as Father Anthony Dionysius Simon D'Albizi (AGS, 21).

Protestant affiliations. The wording here is very close to a passage in "H.D. by *Delia Alton*": "Zinzendorf's father was an Austrian, exiled or self-exiled to Saxony, because of his Protestant affiliations" (188). It was actually Zinzendorf's grandfather's lands in Austria that were confiscated, and he resettled in Bavaria, not in Saxony (AGS, vi). See notes to ch.3.

secret trial with the Dominicans. "Trial" does not mean a legal process, but a period of testing communication or ecumenical liaison. The testing failed because the Dominicans were only interested in converting Zinzendorf, not in the ecumenical dialogue he was proposing.

re-establish a branch of the suppressed Church of Bohemia. It must be said that, historically, Zinzendorf wanted to foster "heart-religion" in everyone, of whatever background or denomination. The re-establishment of the Old Church of Bohemia offered him an opportunity to move toward this goal and heal the sectarian divisions within Christianity, but his efforts to avoid creating a separate denomination ultimately failed under the weight of historic pressures (*HB*, 80–86).

lost touch with the Hierarchy. The Moravian Church after Zinzendorf's death in 1760 did not emphasize its hierarchical structure of bishops that linked it back to the ancient Church of Bohemia, but it also did not abandon its episcopacy. It looked forward into missionary fields, especially in the Americas. The connection back to the ancient church, embedded in Bohemian nationalism, seemed a less compelling emphasis, although the center at Herrnhut has been maintained. H.D. seemed to feel that the Hierarchy is eternal, greater than the episcopal succession back to Christ himself, although that succession is important to her as its earthly manifestation.

exiled from Saxony. In 1732 Zinzendorf was ordered into exile and compelled to sell his estates by the Protestant government of Saxony, who wanted to destroy the Herrnhut community. They suspected that the Moravian refugees were not religious seekers but infiltrators employed by the Catholic rulers of Bohemia to instigate a political takeover. This view, and the stories of Zinzendorf's student contacts with Catholic prelates in Paris, led them to conclude that he had Catholic sympathies, which was not true in the narrow or political sense construed by his enemies.

Dominican Adept. H.D.'s choice of the label "adept," a term popular in occultism, to describe Fr. D'Albizi is her clear attempt to blend official Christian religion with nonchurch forms of spirituality, signifying that the "eternal Order" is all-embracing and universal.

older than you. Historically, de Rohan lived from 1734 to 1803 and Saint-Germain from circa 1700 to 1784. But it is not problematic that Saint-Germain "the deathless" should appear as a young man in this romance novel.

the philosoph inconnu *of our Society.* The Abbot is the "unknown philosopher" of an eternal and ecumenical Society of Jesus. The phrase specifically identifies him as a Martinist. Lévi, who was himself a Martinist, wrote:

> The school of unknown philosophers founded by Martines de Pasqually and continued by L. C. de Saint-Martin seems to have incorporated, the last adepts of true initiation. . . . The Martinists were the last Christians in the cohort of illuminés. (*HM*, 305)

Martines de Pasqually (1711–74) recruited among high-degree Freemasons to found *L'Ordre des Chevaliers Maçons Élus-Cohens de l'Univers* (The Order of Mason Knights Elected Priests of the Universe; "cohen" is Hebrew for "priest"). He and his followers believed in "The Divine Glory of Man's Origins." They considered

> Man to be in exile in this earthly existence, deprived of his real powers. Man's main aim must be, therefore, to work at becoming restored to the condition that was his originally.

The work of "reintegration" involved secret techniques in ceremonial magic aimed at achieving that "glorious Divinity." The Élus-Cohen included Louis-Claude de Saint-Martin (1743–1803), who wrote under the name "le philosoph inconnu" and gathered around him a group united by special initiations. Martinist thought, with its links to Illuminism and Rosicrucianism, influenced H.D. through the books of Jean Chaboseau and Robert Ambelain, both of whom were Grand Masters in Martinist orders after World War II, although Chaboseau withdrew from Martinism in 1947. (http//www.orderofthegrail.org/a_short_history_of_martinism.htm, unsigned, 1985, p. 4; website updated February 2008.)

handed down orally. East Asian religion, especially Buddhism, holds that the authentic teachings can only be communicated orally, from a spiritually developed teacher to a student, in contrast to western religion's emphasis on Scripture, the written word of the Bible, as definitive. Hermetic, occult, and Masonic practices in the west similarly follow this tradition. After oral testing by the teacher, the student undergoes initiation to be able to receive higher teachings. This process continues through a number of levels until the student is an "adept" and becomes a teacher.

The wind was howling. Saint-Germain has a moment of "living back" to seeing Elizabeth leave the cathedral. It parallels her flash of "living back" in chapter 8. The rush of wind is also symbolically a descent of the Holy Spirit.

a word that means you must act out *the legend for yourself.* This injunction, spoken by Saint-Germain to himself, mirrors an idea held by the Order of Saint-Joachim or Saint-Jakin, who were successors to the old Rosicrucians but who, according to Lévi,

> had become a mystical sect and had embraced zealously the Templar magical doctrines, as a result of which they regarded themselves as the sole repositories of the secrets intimated by the Gospel according to St. John. They regarded the narrative of that Gospel as an allegorical sequence of rites designed to complete initiation, and they believed that the history of Christ must be realized in the person of each one of the adepts. (*HM*, 298)

Realizing Christian history within oneself is equivalent to "you must act out the legend for yourself," which itself is a precursor, both conceptually and linguistically, of the key phrase in *Helen in Egypt*. "She herself is the writing." In Pallinode 1.3 the epigraph in full reads:

> Helen herself denies an actual intellectual knowledge of the temple-symbols. But she is nearer to them than the instructed scribe; for her, the secret of the stone-writing is repeated in natural or human symbols. She herself is the writing. (*HE*, 22)

Chapter XI, pp. 47–50

not possible. The scene is the unlighted vestry or antechamber adjacent to Antonius's rooms. He has just entered in the dark and feels a presence. Someone is there although the door was locked. Saint-Germain is dizzy with shock and must right himself by putting his hand where a sword-hilt would be, as he had done during his "reversal" experience in the cathedral. Whatever is going on manifests a similar spiritual power that overwhelms him.

diabolic phosphorescence. A faint abnormal light in the room suggests Faustian black magic has produced the presence.

had beaten his way back. The continuing snowstorm meant he had to struggle through the snow to get back to his rooms after he left the Abbot's quarters. The external weather is an objective correlative to the internal spiritual struggle.

confession. Saint-Germain wanted absolution of sin from de Rohan for refusing to sign over to the Inquisition the names of Freemasons—Cagliostro's would be at the top—to whom he had sworn loyalty as a brother, even if the initiations in which he had sworn were blasphemous and demonic.

Brother. Cagliostro's greeting, "Brother," which is traditional among Freemasons, carries an ironic double entendre in view of Saint-Germain's new embrace of his Franciscan friar's disguise. It also echoes the Moravian custom of addressing one another as "Brother" and "Sister."

That door leads somewhere. Cagliostro is indicating the door to Saint-Germain's rooms.

I tried both. He tried knocking with both secret codes, that is, the one official code and the secret one used by the deviant cabal within the Freemasons, but neither of them worked.

the brothers are members of the "Fraternity of Free-masons," as an official document terms them. "Brothers" also echoes "Brethren" of the Unitas Fratrum.

no way down. He looked for a secret tunnel entrance entered through a trapdoor in the floor, as he expected from Masonic conspirators, but he couldn't find one. It is another Faustian overtone.

not fratres proper. Even though the grooms in the diplomat's stable in Paris were not really Freemasons or "brothers," Cagliostro got their help as readily as if they had been.

extra rider, because of the storm. The weight of another rider on the outside of the Ambassador's carriage would keep it from turning over in the snowstorm.

related distant to one of the Guard. Cagliostro explains his fabricated excuse for knowing that they had to leave Paris speedily. He says that he got word from a friend with a distant relative in the Swiss Guard who overheard in the King's palace that there was "trouble brewing."

I always wondered. The groom wonders where the Guardsmen's loyalties lie. Being Swiss rather than French, will they go over to the revolutionaries or stay loyal to the King? Their supposed warning to their friends hinted to the groom that the Guard might defect.

they refuse. Cagliostro is saying that the Swiss Guard will not obey the revolutionaries because they are lower in class than the Guardsmen. In any case, a proper military unit takes orders only from its designated leading officer.

before Medina actually declared it. Cagliostro jealously thinks that Saint-Germain must be very high in Masonry indeed and have great spiritual powers, since he apparently got word about the revolution from Althotas in Medina even before Cagliostro, his favored pupil, got it. This observation supports the suggestion that Saint-Germain is himself Althotas, the source.

The thing is the French Revolution.

The Guard will not leave the Palace. Saint-Germain's declaration makes Cagliostro understand why the chevalier has to go back to Paris: to see that the Guard does not leave the Palace. If they do not leave, Saint-Germain believes that the Revolution will fail, the monarchy will remain and the queen, to whom he has sworn fealty as a courtly lover, will be safe and continue to reign.

key or clue? . . . doubling on our circle. Cagliostro is asking whether Saint-Germain has set up a code with the Swiss Guard to tell them what to do. He now recognizes

Saint-Germain as a double agent since he sides with the Catholic King, not with the revolutionary Protestant Freemasons. The hint is that Cagliostro "doubles" as well when it suits him.

It won't be so bad. The death that the revolutionaries will inflict on the king and queen will not be as painful as it might have been before the "new device."

The Guillotine, they call it. Dr. Guillotin proposed in the French Assembly on December 1, 1789, that all executions should be performed the same way, by decapitation through use of a machine. Previously, death by decapitation, by an executioner's axe, had been a privilege of nobility only. It was also thought desirable to make the process as swift and painless as possible. With Dr. Guillotin's refined machine, executions were felt to be both egalitarian and merciful, and with many people to be executed, the guillotine was a time-saver.

to lose your head. Saint-Germain's thoughts have an ironic double meaning. He wants to keep his head, that is, stay sane, under the pressure of Cagliostro's presence and implicit threat, but his decision also means that he will lose his head, literally, under the blade of the guillotine.

posted on the lanterns. Printed public notices, both official and informal, were hung from the lampposts—"posted" *à la lanterne*—on the street corners of Paris so that everyone could read them. Revolutionary statements so posted had begun to warn of violence.

a place for you. Even though Cagliostro knows that Saint-Germain is a double agent who joined the Freemasons on a false pretext, he is offering him an escape route, like his own, with the ambassador's grooms.

blackness unutterable. Saint-Germain feels the charlatan's presence as overwhelmingly evil, black magic in operation. This temptation to abandon his commitment to true knighthood produces a version of the "dark night of the soul." He is also standing in a small dark room. The objective and subjective conditions coincide.

infernal dungeons. Initiations into the higher degrees of Freemasonry, as with the rites of Saint-Jakin, often involved semitorture as a purification and a test of the initiate's physical and spiritual endurance.

could he get through?... should he. Saint-Germain wants to escape but cannot and realizes that he is being put to a test by supernatural forces.

Acroamatique. This French word is in English *acroamatic*, the same word as *acroatic*, pertaining to deep learning and higher spirituality, a general synonym for "esoteric" but more precisely translated as "self-secret." "Acroamatic" teachings are those given to advanced students who can understand them. To the uninitiated they are incomprehensible. H.D. saw this word in a book she owned by the Martinist Jean Chaboseau, *Le Tarot. essai d'interprétation selon les principes de l'herméticisme* (Paris: Editions Niclaus, 1946). The passage reads:

> La Mission de l'Artiste sera donc de traduire en langue symbolique, selon les canons acroamatiques d'une règle perpétuelle ou par les canons nouveaux qu'il inventera et qu'il appartiendra aux générations futures de dechiffrer, les vérites, et la Vérité, dont il est le fidèle dépositaire. (The Mission of the Artist therefore will be to translate in symbolic language, according to the self-secret canons of an eternal order or by new canons which he will invent that it will belong to future generations to decipher, the truths, and the Truth, of which he is the faithful trustee.) (p. 21, quoted in "Myth," 419, trans. by editor)

This passage clearly expresses H.D.'s sense of a religious vocation to write. She is obligated to use her united poetic and psychic "gifts" to transmit Gnosis, Divine Knowledge, to the world. "Acroamatique" is an encapsulation of "you must get out the legend for yourself." The spiritual seeker does not understand phenomena in an external way but must experience them internally by living through them, an applied notion of "self-secret."

What was he doing with his hands?. Saint-Germain has begun to "act out" his legend by "living back" through a terrifying prior experience of imprisonment, possibly in a past life, since he is the "the deathless one." In any case, the experience is buried in his unconscious. Encountering Cagliostro is an initiation test that makes him feel the physical sensation of chains on his wrists.

sheet of steel. In "Advent," the second section of *Tribute to Freud*, composed by H.D. in December 1948 from her 1933 notebooks containing notes she made during her psychoanalysis, she speaks of using her intellect the way Saint-Germain uses the *Exercitia*, to keep from being overwhelmed by consciousness of painful events. "If I do not let ice-thin window-glass intellect protect my soul or emotion, I let death in" (*TF*, 117).

mother and forest alike were a symbol. Lévi explains the symbolism of Saint-Germain's life of errantry in "the world of forest":

> This was at the age of seven years, which, however, is to be understood symbolically and is that of the initiate when he is advanced to the grade of Master. His mother was the Science of the Adepts, while the forest, in the same kind of language, signifies empires devoid of true civilization and light. (*HM*, 296)

exaltation . . . lucidity. Cagliostro, trying to explain why Saint-Germain does not "look properly" himself, lets him know that he had observed his comrade's mystical transports during Masonic rites in Paris.

at the Palace. Cagliostro does not accept Saint-Germain's excuse for his strange appearance. The chevalier, after all, was used to elaborate food and wine at Versailles as guest of the king and queen.

The out-door wasn't so easy. He explains that he broke in by picking the lock of the outside door while the snowstorm concealed him.

If a clock struck . . . a lantern. If any of these things happens, the mystical spell of "living back" will be broken and its revelation lost. H.D. described to Freud a comparable moment as she was seeing the "writing on the wall" in *Tribute to Freud*:

> I, though seated upright, am in a sense diving, head-down underwater, in another element, and as I seem now so near to getting the answer, I feel that my whole life . . . will be blighted forever if I miss this chance. (53)

Her imagery also echoes the "jellyfish experience" of *Notes on Thought and Vision* (18–20).

the Castle of Ruel. Lévi continues Saint-Germain's story:

> The principles of Saint-Germain were those of the Rosy Cross, and in his own country [purportedly Hungary] he established a society from which he separated subsequently when anarchic doctrines became prevalent in fellowships which incorporated new partisanship of the Gnosis. Hence he was disowned by his brethren, was charged even with treason, and some memorials on illuminism seem to hint that he was immured in the dungeons of the Castle of Ruel. (*HM*, 296)

Saint-Germain, as he feels the chains on his wrists, is re-living this imprisonment, a parallel to a high Masonic initiatory rite as well as to the psychoanalytic experience of uncovering past suffering buried in the unconscious.

Chapter XII, pp. 51–55

"No," said Saint-Germain. This "no" is evidently an answer to a question from Stephanus. "Did Cagliostro do something to you that has made you ill?" Saint-Germain makes a rational excuse, concealing his *acroamatique* experience of "living back" into the time of his having been imprisoned.

Captain of Loyola. "Captains of Loyola," in the military metaphor of Saint Ignatius, carry out under his generalship his ideal of military rigor and Christian conquest of paganism and ignorance. Saint Francis Xavier exemplifies the true "Captain." Saint-Germain feels that he cannot take this military approach with its implicit violence.

nor could he accept messages. H.D. has made her character Saint-Germain, who is a surrogate of Lord Dowding, admit that he had been taken over by "spirits of a lower order," as he said she had been in her séances, and, as he is in part H.D., she is re-aligning herself with the truer spiritual powers of her Moravian ancestry represented by Elizabeth.

a servant of Althotas. The magic rituals took place in Paris, but in Cagliostro's eyes Saint-Germain, having the "gifts" of a medium, was channeling messages from Althotas in Medina. If Saint-Germain is Althotas, of course, no channeling is needed.

brotherhood. Cagliostro thought it was strange of Saint-Germain to speak of "brotherhood" when de Rohan is about to indite his Masonic brothers before the Inquisition. The suggestion is that Antonius/Saint-Germain has in mind the Franciscan friars and the greater brotherhood.

an old catch-word. As the revolution progressed, the old catch-word "*à la lanterne*," became the cry of a lynch mob, meaning "String him up!," that is, execute an "enemy of the people" by hanging him or her from a street lamppost (Fr: la lanterne). Saint-Germain is envisioning first that the declaration will be posted on the lampposts and then the violence will begin in which people will be hanged on them. The thought moves him to pray to "Our Lady," but as he says those two words to himself, the words he had spoken to the school-porter the day before come back into his mind. "Our Lady chose you. . . . "

the message, the miracle . . . Knights of the East. The "miracle" of the candles blown out in the cathedral did not depend upon his achieving high levels in Freemasonry. Lévi notes a link to Saint-Germain's history: "the Order of the Initiated Knights and Brethren of Asia became the Order of St. Joachim around 1786" (*HM*, 296).

dionysiac de-materialization. H.D. crossed out the "a" when her typist wrote "dionysiac," but because "dionysic" is so obscure a form, the more usual spelling is used here. Contemporary records give a flavor of "dionysiac de-materialization" in Cagliostro's rites. In one account of a lodge initiation for ladies, after several midnight hours of questioning and drinking during which the ladies were attended by their lovers in disguise, the "Grand Copt," dressed as a magician in red and gold, floated slowly down from the temple ceiling on a huge gilded ball to address the assembly as the "Genius of Truth." He instructed them to "open your souls to pure tenderness," and then was wafted away, de-materializing into the darkness above. His wife, who presided over the ladies' lodge, added, "Love conquers all, but you must keep the rules" (Gervaso, 126–27). The ceremony created a sensation in Paris.

Demonstrations of Cagliostro's necromancy were equally sensational. On one occasion he invited six men to dinner, including Voltaire, Diderot, and Montesquieu, each of whom was asked to name on the spot a dead person with whom he would like to dine. Cagliostro called their names and the six appeared; the group of thirteen dined until dawn, when the ghosts departed (Gervaso, 128–30).

this betrayal. Multiple betrayals are occurring. The Freemasons are being betrayed by de Rohan; Saint-Germain is reneging on his promises to de Rohan and the Templar-Jesuit knights; and in the background the French people, having been betrayed and deprived by the monarchy, are about to betray the monarchy in turn. Saint-Germain is losing his moral bearings.

maçonnerie. The French word for masonry or stonework, in this context refers to Freemasonry.

that coach. Because of the storm and the piled-up snow, the large carriage of the ambassador, on which Cagliostro was outrider, could not negotiate the small crooked corner of Petty Place and had to be unloaded outside.

his Excellency is the ambassador from the Holy Roman Emperor Joseph II to France who is now on his way back to Vienna to avoid the revolution. Prague is a stopover. He rewarded Stephanus with a sizable tip for his help.

had met him at the Palace. The historical Cagliostro, despite his being the reigning celebrity of Paris in 1784 and 1785, was never received by the king and queen, because he was a friend of de Rohan, who was persona non grata to Marie Antoinette. It was this animosity that led to the "affair of the Diamond Necklace," which comes back into Stephanus's mind in the next chapter.

fight it off, the memory. Saint-Germain does not want to re-live his imprisonment "in the dungeons of the Castle of Ruel."

safe here. Stephanus is startled by the word "safe." He thought that Saint-Germain wanted to keep Cagliostro prisoner, so the servant hid the magician in the stable with the excuse to him that the friars should not see him. Stephanus does not know that his master has had a change of heart and no longer wants to turn Cagliostro over to the Inquisition

"I trust—". This sentence should end "you were discreet."

his balsam-oil. Stephanus had to give the grooms in the stable a reason why he was doing Cagliostro a favor, so he invented a story fitting Cagliostro's claim as a healer whose balsam-oil would cure all ills. See illustration "A Masonic Anecdote."

the ports watched. The ambassador is expected to go to England, so Stephanus has hinted to the embassy servants that it would be dangerous for the ambassador because he will be stopped and apprehended at a port. Stephanus was trying to prevent the ambassador's leaving because Cagliostro would escape with him, again as outrider.

They don't half believe it. The servants are not convinced that the Revolution will come, but it must be serious because their masters are evacuating.

new set of signs and codes. The revolutionary Freemasons regularly change the codes by which they identify one another. Saint-Germain must know these if he is to return to Paris.

égalité. The French word for "equality" here is used by Stephanus disapprovingly to mean "speaking as equals," a violation of the aristocratic rule. He thinks that Saint-Germain must be ill because he spent so much time talking with a social inferior.

The servant offers to bring his master some wine, the Château Saint-Germain from his own estate, as a curative and reminder of his position.

paying his respects. Stephanus told the valet that Saint-Germain would soon pay the ambassador a visit, as protocol requires.

going back to Paris. Saint-Germain's remark about the codes may have been Stephanus's clue to the new decision his master has made, or perhaps the servant has telepathic powers.

"Poison," said de Rohan. The scene has shifted. Stephanus is in the castle suite of de Rohan, who is responding to an implied prior statement by Stephanus that his master became extremely ill and delirious after Cagliostro's arrival. The cardinal supposes that Cagliostro has poisoned Saint-Germain.

he went off, like that time in Venice. "Went off" is Stephanus's way of referring to Saint-Germain's going into trance. The reference to the Venice episode suggests that this illness is a supernormal experience, since there is a word-link with the name of the *Hotel Angleterre et Belle Venise* on Corfu where H.D. saw the "writing on the wall" in 1920.

You can go with him. "You" refers to Stephanus, who is quoting directly Saint-Germain's instructions intended to get Stephanus to safety by traveling with the cardinal to Rome.

could your Eminence not take me. This subjunctive structure might be confusing. The meaning is that if de Rohan could not take Stephanus with him, then Saint-Germain would ask the ambassador, with whom Cagliostro has just arrived, to take his servant along on the next stage of his escape. Saint-Germain wants to save the loyal Stephanus's life by keeping him from coming back to Paris with his master.

The Guard here. This reference to the Swiss Guard is Stephanus's warning to Cagliostro to stay in hiding in case he might be seen by one of the guardsmen. Stephanus is relaying to the cardinal what he said to Cagliostro as a way of letting de Rohan know that he and Saint-Germain have the magician under their control.

Wouldn't have known . . . fraters . . . the Row. The implied subject of this sentence is "we," Stephanus and Saint-Germain, who had not realized until Cagliostro got into Antonius's study by mistake that the Freemasons had a hide-out somewhere in "the Row," the place Cagliostro was originally looking for. Saint-Germain wants Stephanus to tell de Rohan the new fact that there are spies present in Prague Castle. Cagliostro's use of the word "Fraters," the same Latin word as *fratres*, brothers, here refers to the Freemasons, not the brothers or friars resident in the convent. Here, however, the reference to brothers is multilayered; H.D. is indicating an ultimate spiritual union of all religions in accordance with the views of Ambelain and Chaboseau, a Brotherhood of Man.

he had confided. The pronoun references might be hard to sort out here. Saint-Germain confided to de Rohan, not the other way around.

He was standing. These thoughts are de Rohan's as he looks at Stephanus, standing at attention. He observes him as proud and reserved, not in the attitude of a servant, and wonders if he had become his master's full confidant, in possession of secrets concerning which had been kept hidden from de Rohan.

they had flattered themselves. The pronoun "they" is an apparent allusion to a higher level of promonarchy conspirators who have been more in control of Saint-Germain's destiny than he realized.

Prince Ragoczy of Transylvania. Ragoczy, also spelled Rakoczy or Rakoczi (Hung: Rákóczy), is the name of an ancient and noble family of Hungary, of which Transylvania was then a dominant part. Its members are famous for their struggles to obtain religious liberty under the Austrians from the time of Sigismund on (1607). The allusion here is to the legend that Saint-Germain was the son of Francis Leopold Rakoczy (1676–1735), also known as Francis II Rakoczy, prince of Transylvania, who was elected "ruling prince" of Hungary in 1704 after leading the Hungarians in a rebellion against Hapsburg oppression (*Co.Enc.*, 2274; *LCSG*, 85, 270). Lévi also notes this legend (*HM*, 296n).

entrusted with the secret. "The secret," an unquestioned fact in de Rohan's mind, is that Saint-Germain is heir-apparent to the French throne.

the former Brother. Saint-Germain is asking de Rohan to ask the abbot to invite the teaching brother who was formerly head of the school to come back since "Brother Antonius" is leaving.

Égalité. "Equality" is the excuse Stephanus makes to himself for presumptuously asking de Rohan to read the letter to him. The servant dislikes the spirit of egalitarianism of the French Revolution, but since he is illiterate, he has no choice. He has to learn the contents of the letter somehow.

Ruel. . . . Saint Joachim. Saint-Germain has discovered his true identity as an Adept by breaking through to the memory of imprisonment in the dungeons of Ruel. The breakthrough came as the result of his dissociating himself from the false magic practiced by the Society of Saint Joachim or "Saint Jakin." Then, as now, he wanted to move toward a truer spiritual goal. Now he must further dissociate himself from both the gross and the subtle manipulators and move up to a higher level of spirituality. H.D. is re-defining her breakdown as an initiation trial leading to re-birth.

Chapter XIII, pp. 56–61

that point *work.* Stephanus has been ushered into the reception room of Elizabeth's quarters in the Tower where she and Henry had been talking in chapter 2. She invites the servant to sit down. He is looking at the petit point upholstery on the chair and is reminded of the French court.

Lamotte. Jeanne de Saint-Remy de Lamotte (or de la Motte), born in 1756 in

Bar-sur-Aube, in Champagne, was a servant in the royal palace, but documents had shown her to be directly descended from an illegitimate son of Henry II (1519–59) and therefore of the royal house of Valois (Chamier, 12). She lured de Rohan into the "affair of the Diamond Necklace" by posing to him as a friend and confidante of the queen. She is here viewed as Cagliostro's mistress, which she may have been, but there is more historical evidence that she was de Rohan's mistress, at least for a time.

Balsamo made her "Countess". Cagliostro did not give her the name. She herself decided that her ancestry entitled her to call herself "Countess de Valois." When she married a penniless officer, Mark Anthony de Lamotte, he easily became "Count" de Lamotte. In 1871 the newly titled pair moved from the country to Paris to seek their fortunes.

It was her they put the blame on. De Lamotte deserved all the blame she got for the Diamond Necklace affair. The facts in outline are these. Cardinal de Rohan was hated by Marie Antoinette, since he had behaved badly while on diplomatic appointment to the court of Maria Theresa, her mother, Empress of Austria. He very much wanted to be reconciled with the queen, and de Lamotte saw an opportunity. In 1785 she suggested that he write the queen an apology. He did, and de Lamotte brought him a forged letter in reply, opening a clandestine correspondence in which the "queen's" letters grew increasingly warm in tone. The gullible de Rohan believed that the queen was in love with him. De Lamotte then engineered a secret meeting at midnight in the dark woods of the park at Versailles, hiring a girl who resembled Marie Antoinette to meet de Rohan for a moment and hand him a note and a rose.

De Rohan was then ripe for de Lamotte's next proposal that he act as intermediary for the queen in the purchase of an enormously expensive pearl-and-diamond necklace originally made for Louis XV's mistress, Mme. du Barry. De Rohan arranged for installment payments and the necklace was delivered to him. He gave it to Jeanne to deliver to the queen. Jeanne, with her husband and her lover, Villette, immediately cut up the necklace and sold the stones piecemeal. When the fraud was discovered, de Lamotte accused Cagliostro of stealing the necklace with de Rohan's complicity. The two men were tried but acquitted after Villette confessed. Popular sentiment supported them, which annoyed the king, who saw that the episode increased the unpopularity of his Austrian queen. He ordered Cagliostro out of Paris, which began the magician's decline into trial by the Inquisition, prison, madness, and death in Saint Leo fortress in 1795 (Carlyle, *Essays* 5: 131–200; Gervaso, 207; *LCSG*, 199–201).

the friendly wife is Maria, whose husband is Jacob or Jacobus. The two are the Tower servants.

those same cups, Lamotte showed him. Elizabeth is serving coffee in Sèvres cups, as she had done earlier when she and Henry were discussing their reasons for coming to Prague.

Why had he been shown in. Stephanus had expected only to deliver a message to servants at the Tower, not to be brought into the drawing-room personally.

knocked him silly. The "him" of this sentence is Stephanus. The language is intended as slang conveying his lack of education.

proper livery. Stephanus is astonished to see that the "lackey" named Schweinitz is really a "gentleman," though there is no question that this is the same man Stephanus had seen wearing the livery proper to servants.

The Cardinal might. . . . As Stephanus had been taciturn, not volunteering information to the cardinal about Saint-Germain, he surmises that the cardinal paid him back by not discussing the identity of the new Tower residents with him.

Italian sometimes. The historical Saint-Germain is said to have spoken German, English, Italian, French (with a Piedmontese accent), Portuguese, and Spanish. Horace Walpole wrote of him in 1745, when Saint-Germain was in London. "He is called an Italian, a Spaniard, a Pole . . . a priest, a fiddler, a vast nobleman." Another legend of his birth made him son of a Portuguese banker and the Queen of Spain (Lang, 258, 265–67; *LCSG*, 27–28, 83).

to make mischief . . . off soon. Stephanus is thinking that the embassy valet, who is at the moment watching the feverish Saint-Germain, knows it is not in his interests to talk too much about them. In any case, the ambassadorial party will soon go.

some information. From the valet's report, Stephanus understands the extent of the danger, and he wants to take his master's place in going back into a Paris about to explode.

we all were practised. Bethlehem women learned healing methods from the Native Americans. In 1747 a communal garden was laid out, in part of which grew medicinal herbs for the Bethlehem pharmacy. Wild herbs known for healing were collected from among local flora, notably snake root and sassafras berries. The community's physician in its early days, Doctor John Matthew Otto, was directed to compile a pharmacopoeia. Levering says that Dr. Otto did not seem to manifest any disdain when

> certain salves and plasters among "home remedies" prepared by experienced Pennsylvania women, that had become known to members of Bethlehem's Board of Health, were mentioned as desirable items of this repertory. (*HB*, 203)

Moravian women proved skilled nurses of Washington's wounded troops when the General Hospital of the Continental Army was moved to Bethlehem in December of 1776.

The same as Saint-Germain but different. Elizabeth and Henry, like Saint-Germain, have put aside their accoutrements of rank in order to carry out a religious quest. The difference is of course that they are Protestant and his master is Catholic.

she had said all this. The pronoun "she" is a cue to a shift in point of view from Stephanus to Elizabeth. Now the stream of consciousness is hers.

a King of Bohemia is a reference to George of Podiebrad. See notes to chapter 2.

"Lilie". Elizabeth remembers her aunt speaking to her, using the pet name "Lilie," a diminutive for "Elizabeth," but also evoking the "lily," shaped like the "cup," which is the sigil of the Calixtines, forerunners of the renewed Bohemian Brethren, and the chalice of the Holy Grail. The lily and the cup—seidel—appear in *The Gift* as potent personal and Moravian Christian story-symbols related to H.D.'s grandmother, Elizabeth Weiss Seidel Wolle, her names, and H.D.'s dream of the gardener who gives her a lily. See *G*, chapter 5 "The Secret," esp. 101–2, 159, 169, 175–80, 285n149.

"What is it—sir?". When Elizabeth addresses the servant respectfully as "sir," Stephanus thinks of "fraternity" as well as "equality" in the French revolutionary slogan. Her attitude convinces him that the Unitas Fratrum has a true vision of the brotherhood of man, in contrast to the current Fraternity of Freemasons, who call each other "Brother" but whose corrupt Brotherhood does not "work proper."

She knew what he would say. This enigmatic statement seems to be a moment of clairvoyance, "out of time," in which Elizabeth foresees that Stephanus will tell her Antonius's identity because "it had happened before" that a message has come by from the Eternal Lover. In medieval times the troubadour poet, worshipping the queen or lady of the castle as his divine beloved, would send her a love poem. H.D.'s view of reincarnation, based on her "gift" of "living back," is here blended with de Rougemont's view of the Provençal troubadours' love songs as secret religious hymns of devotion to the Virgin Mary.

in her mother's absence. H.D. imagines Elizabeth as a small child growing up at Herrnhut, where in fact she was born, and being left there while her mother, Benigna, went with Zinzendorf on one of many trips to America. While her mother was away, the people caring for her told her the famous story of her mother and grandfather's meeting with the Native American chiefs of the Six Nations at Tulpehocken in 1742.

As a girl of sixteen. Benigna, born in 1725, was sixteen years old when she went to America in 1741 for the first time, accompanying her father on his first visit (AGS, 291).

lived through an agony of fire and torture. The wording of this suffering seems extreme for the emotion of the child separated from her mother. Elizabeth seems to be recalling an "out of time" experience in which she re-lived the Gnadenhuetten massacre of November 26, 1755, as if she were there in spiritual union with the eleven Moravians, including women and children, who were burned to death or scalped by hostile Indians. The child Hilda also re-lives this massacre momentarily in *The*

Gift, as she is drawn into her grandmother's "gift" of vision (179–81; 287n233). The language here also suggests H.D.'s experience of the London blitz that re-invoked her childhood fear of burning to death. The story that created this fear opens chapter 1 of *The Gift*.

Brother Johannes, they called her grandfather. The Native American name for Zinzendorf was, more exactly, *Johanan*, which the Moravians heard as a version of "John," "Johan," or "Johannes" in German, making him "Brother Johannes" as well as "Brother Louis" and "Bruder Ludwig." H.D. links this name with Saint John the disciple, Saint John the author of the gospel, and Saint John the Divine, author of the Book of Revelation and also with the Gnostics' Secret Book of John and the sects that it inspired, and with the medieval Knights of St. John of Jerusalem, contemporary with the Knights Templar (*HB*, 242; Fries, vi).

received formally into the family or Brotherhood of the Six Nations. H.D. is interpreting Zinzendorf's 1742 meeting with the Iroquois chiefs at Tulpehocken as an initiation ceremony at which he was made a member of those tribes, which is not quite accurate but fits the novel's themes. But in describing the Six Nations' presentation of the fathom of white beads, she says in *The Gift*, that as "white is the almost universal symbol of peace and good-will," the bead-belt signified a peace treaty, but, even more, "a pledge or pact, *thy people shall be my people.*" The biblical quotation from Ruth 1.16 heightens the family theme and echoes the women's name-exchange in the last chapter of *The Gift* (*G*, 213, 237, 281nn56–58). See notes to chapter 8.

"A priest in the Cathedral?". Elizabeth is speaking to Stephanus, intuitively identifying his master, although he has not given her any other clues. The memory itself induces her to "live back" into the moment when the disguised friar opened the cathedral door for her. The fact that "the wind was howling" along the Street of the Alchemists made it a magical or out-of-time moment as well as a real in-time event.

like a gypsy. Stephanus's gypsylike appearance makes Elizabeth think of the Native Americans, who are also black-haired and tawny-skinned, and links him to the fortune-teller whom her mother consults in chapter 2 of *The Gift*, as well as to the general iconography of hermeticism. While the gypsies have always been a migratory people, many of them, the tziganes, lived in Transylvania and Hungary. This association resonates with the theory that Saint-Germain was the son of Francis Leopold Rakoczi, prince of Transylvania.

the settlement abandoned. The fact that gypsies lived with the Moravians in the Herrnhaag community in Marienborn castle added to the scandal of the excesses there in the Sifting Time. As a result, the government of the county of Büdingen demanded an oath of allegiance to the secular rulers and a denial of the Moravians' loyalty to their leaders, Zinzendorf especially. Starting in 1750, therefore, Herrnhaag's population of nearly a thousand dispersed, resettling elsewhere. By 1753 the buildings were deserted (*HB*, 106, 188).

Sister Charity. Anna Charity Nitschmann, the Single Sisters' chief elder, was responsible for the spiritual welfare of that group. To handle the sudden influx of refugees at Herrnhut, Zinzendorf had organized them into groups according to sex and marital status called "choirs." "Choir" translates the German word "Chor" meaning "group, organizational unit," not necessarily musical. Each choir, such as the Single Sisters, Single Brethren, and Widows, occupied a communal house, ate meals and prayed together, and shared household responsibilities. After marriage, couples had their own homes, but the husband joined the Married Men's choir and the wife the Married Women's choir, which met together regularly for prayer, a sermon, a love feast, or support and companionship in crisis. Children also had a choir. Each group had its leader, and the council of elders governed the entire community. Because of this system, Bethlehem and Nazareth built larger buildings than in neighboring communities. Communal living ceased after the towns incorporated and the buildings were no longer church property, but a Widows' House in Bethlehem still functions (H. Williams, letter, November 30, 1987; cf. K. Hamilton, *Church Street*, 12, 15).

the old lots, cast for marriages. Casting lots was not an exclusively Moravian custom. It was frequently done by Germans in general, but Zinzendorf made a special sanctified practice of it. Use of the lot for marriages of those serving as ministers and missionaries, Levering says, "arose under an overwrought system devised to carry out lofty ideals of a completely consecrated associate and individual life under Christ the Head; and of complete subjection to Divine guidance" (*HB*, 103). The custom of making decisions and electing officials by lot was institutionalized after Zinzendorf's death, but by 1782 was being modified. The use of the lot for marriages among missionaries had been protested for many years and disappeared after 1818 (*HB*, 103–4; *HMC*, 274; *G*, 23, 162, 285n150).

They are for you. Henry Dohna says that the letters are for Elizabeth because she had earlier thought of herself as Theodora de Castell. The hint is that they are love letters from Zinzendorf and will offer a clue as to "what had been been taken from" the Moravian church.

"Henri—our guest". Elizabeth reflects that all Moravians are one family through maintenance of their traditions, which include kindness to people of all races and classes, like the servant sitting before her, so she is reminding Henry to pour more coffee, as at a "love-feast." Friedman mistakenly says in *Psyche Reborn* that the "love feast" was regarded by Moravians as a "'scandal' best to be forgotten" (183), as if it had been part of the Sifting Time excesses. On the contrary, it was a central and beneficent ritual. Levering says that

> the "love-feast" was a term somewhat freely applied to a wide range of occasions . . . informal gatherings of a few in a social way, fraternal welcomes,

farewells . . . commemorative occasions . . . giving them a more or less religious character. (*HB*, 66)

It is also not true that "many Moravians were burned for witchcraft, but they continued to worship secretly with a cup decorated with an 'S'" (*PR*, 183). These mistakes apparently arose because Friedman misread as historical truth H.D.'s inventions in *The Gift*'s fifth chapter, "The Secret," and overlooked H.D.'s comments in her notes to *The Gift* and "H.D. by *Delia Alton*" in both of which she describes her fictionalizing methods and contrasts her view with her grandmother's actual history (*G*, 232, 257, 259–60, 267; "H.D.," 188, 189). It is also not true that H.D. learned the Blood and Wounds theology through its having been "endlessly imaged in the hymns H.D. sang as a child" (*PR*, 231). H.D. knew nothing of that theology and the Sifting Time until she read Levering, Rimius, and other historical sources during World War II. The Blood and Wounds hymns were not sung by anybody after 1752 when Zinzendorf suppressed the Twelfth Appendix to the Moravian hymnal; historic copies have been preserved. See notes to chapter 2.

candles for Saint Wenceslas. This "latest deception" in lighting candles is that Elizabeth appears to be a Roman Catholic believer while doing it. H.D. engaged in similar ceremonies by using a rosary and performing novenas to Saint Thérèse of Lisieux at least from the mid-1930s (*PR*, 200–201; "Myth," 339–44). This saint, who is called the "Little Flower," said that after her death she would send a "shower of roses," that is, blessings. Her devotees metaphorically call any blessing a "white rose." In *Majic Ring* H.D. describes her prayers to Saint Thérèse, invoking her aid in relation to Lord Dowding: "and I 'told' my Swiss wooden beads in her name and went to sleep." When a letter from him arrives, postmarked Dec. 6, 1943, she calls it a "white-rose" (*MR*, ts. 83).

the "Ave" accusation made by Rimius about Zinzendorf might well bring down on Elizabeth a similar accusation of "catholic sympathy" for her behavior. See notes to chapter 8.

the cards they spread out are presumably tarot cards, the gypsy "fortune-cards."

Bohemians. The governing council of Büdingen in which Marienborn was located, near Frankfort-am-Main, apparently thought that the settlers, being originally from Bohemia, were the same as the gypsies from Hungary and Transylvania.

the Lord's Hedge. The scandals that took place at Herrnhaag, "the Lord's Hedge," in the Sifting Time began in part quite innocently from Zinzendorf's organization of "The Order of the Little Fools." He took its name from Jesus' words in Matthew xi.25: "thou hast hid these things from the wise and prudent, and hast revealed them unto babes." His followers took him too literally. Affectionate diminutives that Germans usually use only with children were applied to nearly everybody and everything as expressions of piety. Zinzendorf was "Papa" and "little Papa." Christ, the Agnus

Dei, Lamb of God, was "Lämlein," little lamb, and "Brother Lambkin." Zinzendorf's theology emphasized Jesus' atoning death on the cross and the symbolism of the side-wound to the exclusion of other aspects of the gospel. His "Litany of the Wounds" expresses the obsession that seized him and the Brethren for a time:

> We stick to the Blood and Wounds Theology. We will preach nothing but Jesus the Crucified. We will look for nothing else in the Bible but the Lamb and his Wounds, and again Wounds, and Blood and Blood. . . . We shall stay forever in the little side-hole, where we are so unspeakably blessed. (*HMC,* 275–76)

H.D. read in Levering an explanation of this emphasis. Zinzendorf wanted to "foster a genial conception of spiritual life over against the austere type of pietism" and to encourage "heart-religion" in place of legalism and perfectionism, but he lost his common sense, especially when he described the morality of sexual relations "in the plainest possible language," that is, rather pornographically, certainly tastelessly, in countless sermons and hymns. He lost his organizational acumen as well and unwisely left his inexperienced young son, Christian Renatus, in charge of Herrnhaag while he himself traveled to visit missions all over the world. During his long absences, his vulnerable followers abandoned discipline and fell further into silliness and misbehavior. "A rage for the spectacular" took over. Interior walls of Marienborn castle were painted with murals depicting Jesus' sufferings. Transparencies depicting his side-wound and other illuminations abounded. Large and expensive parties were given on the birthdays of Zinzendorf, members of his family, and other worthies. For these the castle was ornamented with cut evergreen boughs and thousands of candles. This self-indulgence came about through the Moravians' "fanatical idealizing of the congregation . . . as the special, selected favorites of Jesus." It was a distorted interpretation of the mystical closeness to Jesus the Savior felt by Zinzendorf himself. Money problems followed spiritual and political problems. Zinzendorf found that the only solution was to disband the community. H.D. made a note from AGS: "1750—Moravians retire from Herrnhaag" (ZN, 10 [14]). The text from which Zinzendorf took the name Sifting Time is Luke 22.31–32, containing the words that Jesus spoke to Peter at the last supper:

> Simon, Simon, behold, Satan hath desired to have you, that he may sift you as wheat: but I have prayed for thee, that thy faith fail not: and when thou are converted, strengthen thy brethren. (*HMC,* 274–82; *HB,* 86–89)

bells were cups. In the fortune-telling game they invented as children, Elizabeth and Justine interpreted sounds into shapes. If the clock struck four, it meant the tarot card of the four of cups. Bells were cups because a bell looks like an upside-down cup. Cups, depicted as chalices in the tarot deck designed by Pamela Colman-Smith for the Company of the Golden Dawn with which Yeats was associated, are one of the four major suits of the tarot, equivalent to hearts in the present standard deck of playing cards.

matching them with the wands. The tall slender candles in the cathedral suggest the tarot wands to H.D. Her counting them and matching them with the tarot would syncretize numerology with visual symbology to create a double method of divination, thus double protection against the continually uncertain future. The tarot "wand," equivalent to clubs, was drawn by Colman-Smith as a budding branch, symbol of growth. The magician's traditional "magic wand" is also alluded to here. A relevant passage linking the magic wand and growth occurs in a book that H.D. owned and first read in the late 1930s, written by the Christian theosophists Harriet Augusta and F. Homer Curtiss and titled *The Key to the Universe.* H.D. annotated this passage:

> For when man can hold the 7 stars in his right hand, his girdle will be a visible current of spiritual life-force passing through his heart. (*KU*, 267)

In several of the "Curtiss Books"—H.D. owned the series—the authors do not spell out numbers but use Arabic numerals, since "words are symbols of ideas, but numbers are symbols of divine realities" (*KU*, 18). H.D. is also drawing on a passage in Rev. 1.12–13 in which "the Son of man" appears in a golden candlestick with seven stars in his hand. H.D. often incorporated into her poetry lines from the Book of Revelation, a divinatory and prophetic document. A notable example appears in sec. 3, l.1 in *Tribute to the Angels.*

the seven stars are the Pleiades. In *The Key to the Universe* H.D., a devoted astrologer, marked a passage with a long pencil-stroke in the margin:

> As the Pleiades are connected with the closing of cycles—as their number 7, perfection, indicates—they have to do with the tests which each soul must pass ere it can evolve out of one cycle of spiritual enfoldment into the next.... This power [to progress] is gained by assimilating the sweet influences of love, compassion, faith, intrepidity, action, patience and devotion focused by the Pleiades. (*KU*, 277)

if there were seven. The doubt of the number arises from the astronomically observable fact that one of the Pleiades is always dim and frequently hidden.

the gypsy-courier. Elizabeth is now seeing Stephanus not only as a gypsy associated with the Moravians' transgressive past but also as a "courier" or spiritual "messenger" come to bring her a vital message.

No, it wasn't yesterday. . . . it happened two hundred years ago, *she had said.* H.D.'s emphasis shows that Elizabeth is experiencing a "fold in time." She is aware that her "gift" of "living back" means that, at any moment without warning, she can be swept up into an out-of-time experience, or transported through time. It is H.D.'s version of reincarnation that she sees as operating with particular power in the Moravian church traditions handed down through Moravian women.

for an answer to the Mystery. The pronoun "he" does not refer to "Henri," its nearest preceding noun but to Antonius/Saint-Germain. Thinking of the "mystery" has taken Elizabeth's thoughts back to the unknown man who held open the leather door-curtain of the cathedral for her. The "Mystery" in her mind is expressed as her question (and quest): "what did the Moravian church have that it has now lost and that we are here in Prague to find?" The "answer" given her by events seems to be "to meet this man" who is Stephanus's master. The theme of the Eternal Lover appears.

it was her inheritance. "It" refers both to the batch of letters and to the Moravian history that they represent, the whole Plan of unity that Zinzendorf conceptualized and incorporated into the Unitas. Behind Elizabeth's commitment to this mission lies H.D.'s own desire for "a world-unity without war" that she felt had been planned by Zinzendorf. Her visions and his coalesce, as was signaled in chapter 8.

as Benigna had brought the Indians. Benigna was present at Tulpehocken when her father met with the Native American chieftains, according to Zinzendorf's diary account (Reichel, *Memorials*, 45–61; *HMC*, 91). Another entry in Reichel, however, says that, although she had traveled at first with her father into the wilderness, she was sent back to Bethlehem before the Tulpehocken part of the journey. Levering reports that on this trip Zinzendorf had only two other men with him, Jacob Lischy and William Zander (*HB*, 152).

Good Peter . . . Pierre Jacquette. These names appear in Levering's description of "the last visit to Bethlehem by Indians in any considerable number" on March 9, 1792. H.D.'s account is anachronistic; plainly she relished the descriptive and metaphorical names. Levering records the event:

> Fifty-one chiefs . . . of the Six Nations arrived at Bethlehem en route for Philadelphia, on invitation of Washington. . . . The principal one was the famous Red Jacket. Cornplanter and Big-tree were again of the number. Others were Farmer's Brother, Little Billy, Captain Shanks and La Fayette's young Oneida, Pierre Jacquette, who died at Philadelphia. . . . they were addressed by Bishop Ettwein, who reminded them of . . . the several covenants of friendship made, beginning with that by Count Zinzendorf in 1742. The pupils of the boarding school [for girls] were present and one of them read an address to the Indian visitors. Red Jacket responded in dignified language to the Bishop, and the old man, Good Peter, to the young ladies. (*HB*, 561–62)

This incident is also recounted in Reichel's *Bethlehem Souvenir*, 98.

something ghostly about white people. *They called them the Bethlehem Indians*. This sentence and the one preceding it create a non sequitur. It is not the white people who are called "the Bethlehem Indians" but those Indians who were baptized and lived in or near the community.

Why did Lilie take and shake her. Elizabeth is feeling a physical invasion as if her old child-self, with the child-name Lilie were taking over her body. It is a heightened episode of "living back" into the past, a parallel to Saint-Germain's feeling again the shackles of his imprisonment in Ruel. Since it is the "courier" Stephanus whose eyes on Elizabeth produce this effect, this scene parallels the archangel Gabriel's annunciation to the Virgin Mary of a miraculous birth to come. In the iconography of Renaissance art, a white lily, symbol of purity, is painted next to the kneeling girl as God's messenger speaks to her.

It's the Cathedral. H.D., writing as "Delia Alton," her mediumistic self, looks at her series of stories as

> individually separate, dedicatory Chapels or Chapters. . . . they are Chapter-houses, adjoining some vast Cathedral.
>
> Yes, they are that. The Cathedral is a Dream, the Synthesis of a Dream [subtitle of The Sword Went Out to Sea]. I have already compared the Dream to a Cathedral, in the "Advent" of the Freud "Writing [on the wall]." The Dream is there in the "Writing." ("H.D.," 204)

The passage in "Advent," referring to the Cathedral of Saint Stephen (German: Stephansdom) in Vienna, reads:

> I dream of a Cathedral. I walk through Stephens dom almost daily. . . . It is really the Cathedral that is all-important. Inside the Cathedral we find regeneration or reintegration. This room [Freud's consulting-room] is the Cathedral. . . . The house is home, the house is the Cathedral. He wanted me to feel at home here.
>
> The house in some indescribable way depends on father-mother. At the point of integration or regeneration, there is no conflict over rival loyalties. (*TF,* 145–46)

Chapter XIV, pp. 62–65

Morte villana . . . In English this passage reads.

> Death alway cruel
> Pity's foe in chief,
> Mother who brought forth grief,
> Merciless judgement and without appeal!

These lines open the second sonnet in chapter eight of *La Vita Nuova* (1293) by Dante Alighieri (1265–1321). The translation is by Dante Gabriel Rossetti and appears in *The Portable Dante* (1947), which H.D. owned and read. In *La Vita Nuova* Dante traces his love for Beatrice, which would lead him later to write a poem "more worthy" of her, the *Commedia*, *The Divine Comedy*. He wrote this sonnet on the death of a young woman, "remembering that I had seen her in the company of excellent Beatrice" (*PD*, 555–56).

he could go no further. The narration returns to within Saint-Germain's stream of consciousness. Lying on his bed in his rooms, feverish, as Stephanus had reported to Elizabeth, he is also recalling having read the *Vita Nuova*, in which the motifs of love and death are intermixed, as in Dante's Provençal models later alluded to by de Rougemont. Louis's illness has brought on a quasi-mystical mind-state, but it is also clear that he is in love with Elizabeth, whom he associates with Dante's Beatrice. Both women then appear to him as the embodiment of divine Love.

The strings are the "strands or threads" of Saint-Germain's confusion that entangle him in his conflicting roles and loyalties. They are freed by his decision to return to Paris, although he knows he will die there. The "threads" link back to the symbolism of Elizabeth's tapestry in chapter 8.

His debt would be paid. He thinks he owes something to de Rohan as his father-figure. He will repay the "debt" by going back to Paris to defend de Rohan's aristocratic interests by keeping the Swiss Guard from leaving the royal palace.

the feast of the Assumption. Saint-Germain has gone into a trance and is "living back" to Venice, the site of his mystical "visitation," where he had been seen fifty years earlier. The Feast of the Assumption is celebrated on August 15. On this day, according to Roman Catholic doctrine, the Blessed Virgin Mary did not die, but her body was carried physically, "assumed" into heaven inseparable from her soul. This immediate resurrection and union with God was the reward for her unique purity and perfect goodness. The feast was not instituted until the sixth century. It remains very popular among Catholics and is a holiday in France. Protestants do not celebrate it since it has no basis in Scripture or in the practice of the early church.

She was crossing a bridge. In his trancelike state of "living back," he recalls seeing an unknown woman, reminiscent now of Elizabeth, the sight of whom corresponds to Dante's first sight of Beatrice. The bridge is a muted symbol of connection between this world and the next, between magic and religion and normal and supernormal consciousnesses, a theme that reappears throughout the novel.

Monna Vanna is a kind of pet name, roughly translatable as something like "my Joanie." Vanna is short for Giovanna, the same name as Joan, Joanna, Jane, or Jeanne.

She was Primavera. Cavalcanti alludes to Giovanna as Primavera and plays on his naming her thus in his poem beginning *Fresca rosa novella, piacente Primavera* ("O fresh, new rose, O pleasing Spring") (Musa, 113). Cavalcanti (c. 1250–1300), ten years older than Dante, encouraged him to write the commentary in the *Vita*

Nuova in Italian instead of Latin. Cavalcanti was a Guelph and Dante a Ghibelline in the bloody political oppositions of medieval Florence. Ezra Pound (1885–1972), H.D.'s one-time fiancé and champion of her as *Imagiste* in 1912, translated Cavalcanti beginning around 1910. Pound comments on Dante's sonnet twenty-four, and the prose preceding it, in which Dante weaves "his fancy about Primavera, the first coming Spring, St. John the Forerunner, with Beatrice following Monna Vanna, as in incarnate love" (*Trans.*, 22; LOA-EP, 192). In Pisan Canto LXXVI, Pound sees in a memory-vision women he has known; they appear as "Dryas, Hamadryas ac Heliades," tree-nymphs, and among them she "who was named Spring (It: Primavera)" (*C*, 452). He is not only connecting himself with Dante and Cavalcanti but with H.D., whom he had called "Dryad" from the time he wrote "Hilda's Book" (1905–6). Its last poem opens: "She hath some tree-born spirit of the wood / About her" (*C*, 452; *ET*, 18; LOA-EP, 17). The Pisan Cantos were published in 1948 and read by H.D. that year (*S*, xlvii). There is little doubt that H.D. read all of Pound's work. She would have registered the allusions in Cantos LXXVI and LXXIX, where he addresses her in her aspect of maenad, priestess of Dionysus: "O Lynx, my love, my lovely lynx" and asks her to keep the flame of poetry alive (*C*, 487). The lynx is sacred to Dionysus, the Greek god of wine, fertility, and the ecstasy H.D. sought (*Ann.Ind.*, 52, 132). Her consciousness of Pound is clear when she refers to *Helen in Egypt* as "my Cantos," a doubly relevant reference in this context, since Pound took his title and inspiration from Dante's *Commedia* (*ET*, 32).

Cavalcanti's mistress. In the passage Pound refers to above, in the prose preceding sonnet 24 of the *Vita Nuova* in Rossetti's translation, Dante writes:

> I saw coming toward me a certain lady who was very famous for her beauty, and of whom . . . the first among my friends [the poet Cavalcanti] has long been enamoured. Her name was Joan, but because of her comeliness . . . she was called of many Primavera (Spring), and went by that name among them. Then looking again, I perceived that the most noble Beatrice followed after her. . . . [I]t seemed to me that Love spake again in my heart, saying. "She that came first was called Spring, . . . seeing that as the Spring cometh first in the year so should she come first [prima verrá], when Beatrice was to show herself after the vision of her servant. . . . inasmuch as her name, Joan, is taken from that John, who went before the True Light, saying. 'I am a voice of one crying in the wilderness. Prepare ye the way of the Lord'" [Matt. 3.3]. And also it seemed to me that he added other words, to wit: "He who should inquire delicately touching this matter, could not but call Beatrice by mine own name, which is to say, Love; beholding her so like unto me." (*PD*, 589)

The suggestion is that, to Saint-Germain, Elizabeth is a manifestation of Love in this same way with its Christian overtones.

Their bitter quarrel. The pronoun "their" refers not to Cavalcanti and his mistress but to Dante and Cavalcanti, who quarreled because they belonged to opposing parties.

the young Ghibelline's jurisdiction. Cavalcanti was banished with other "white" Guelphs while Dante, the "young Ghibelline," was one of the six Priors governing Florence between June 15 and August 14, 1300. With them Dante signed the order for his friend's banishment to swampy Maremma, where Guido caught a fever and soon died (*EB* [1957], 7: 38).

It did not last long. "It" refers to the two-month period of Dante's secure place of power in Florentine politics.

fled to Verona. Dante himself was exiled in January 1302 by the "black" Guelphs who were in power opposing both Ghibellines and "white" Guelphs. Dante was falsely charged with barratry and ordered into exile under penalty of death if he returned to Florence. By 1303 he had found refuge in Verona at the house of Bartolommeo della Scala, to whose son, Can Grande, he wrote the famous letter describing the scheme of the *Divine Comedy* and dedicated the *Paradiso*.

Primavera who was Beatrice. Saint-Germain's feverish free associations blend into one idealized and transcendent woman who is Love.

Mandetta. In addition to Giovanna, Cavalcanti is thought to have been in love with a Frenchwoman, Mandetta of Toulouse, or *Tolosa*, as the city is called in Occitans, the language of Languedoc, which is also referred to as Provençal, although it was, and still is, spoken in areas of southern France outside of Provence.

written in the sonnets. Some of Cavalcanti's sonnets and ballate address Mandetta. Pound translated sonnet 12, which begins "The grace of youth in Toulouse ventureth; / She's noble and fair" and ends "Then with sad sighing in the heart he stirs / Feeling his death-wound as that dart doth fall / Which this Tolosan by departure casteth" (*Trans.*, 49; LOA-EP, 202). Ballata 7 reads: "my memories render / Tolosa and the dusk and these things blended. / A lady in a corded bodice, slender / —Mandetta is the name Love's spirits lend her—" (*Trans.*, 113; LOA-EP, 20). Pound holds the view that Giovanna was Cavalcanti's true love and that "Mandetta of Toulouse was an incident" (*Trans.*, 22; LOA-EP, 192).

She did not die. Giovanna was supposed to have died young, but H.D./Saint-Germain envisions her as eternal Love who, as the Virgin Mary, did not die but was directly "assumed" into heaven and united with God, the "miracle" that is celebrated on the feast day he is remembering.

the old fever took him. Saint-Germain realizes that his former mystical experience in Venice was brought on or associated with physical illness. Dante had been ill just before he had a vision of "Primavera" and Beatrice and saw them as a parallel to John the Baptist preceding Christ, "his perceptions being perhaps sharpened by his illness and convalescence"(*PD*, 589; Musa, 21). H.D. sees her "gifts" and her breakdown similarly, as a spiritual collapse and healing on the path to higher enlightenment. She is drawing a parallel between herself and Dante as poets of comprehensive religious vision in which the Divine is embodied in an ideal woman.

Leopold Ragoczy (Hung: Rákóczy, Rakoczi) Incidents in the life of Francis Leopold Rakoczi II (1676–1735), fifth in a line of Magyar kings, suggest why legend connects Saint-Germain with this family. Leopold's father, Francis Leopold I, died the year the child was born. Leopold II's mother, Helen Zrinyi, a fervent Magyar patriot, married in 1682 Imre Thokoly, leader of the Hungarian Protestants and organizer of anti-Hapsburg uprisings. At the age of twelve in 1688, Leopold was imprisoned with his mother by the Austrians but then was torn violently from her and taken to Vienna to be brought up as an Austrian Catholic. He was sent to a Jesuit school at Neuhaus in Bohemia. Rebellious, he continued his studies in Prague and when of age married and settled on his estates. He then began a series of campaigns against Austria. Betrayed during an uprising, he was imprisoned at Wiener-Neustadt but escaped disguised as a dragoon officer. In 1707 he was elected Prince of Transylvania. Final defeat of his hopes sent him into exile at the court of Louis XIV in 1713, where he lived until 1718 when he went to Turkey, his abode until he died in 1735. He had two sons, one of whom the Turks encouraged to think of himself as prince of Transylvania (*EB* [1902], 20: 261, 274). These details suggest how the historical Saint-Germain might be a half-brother or a son of Prince Rakoczi. Lang reports that Saint-Germain lived for a time at the court of the Margrave of Anspach "under the name of Tsarogy," an anagram of Rakoczy or Ragotsky, as it is sometimes spelled.

speaking Polish to the valet. Saint-Germain thinks that in his delirium he spoke Polish to the valet, who watched him while Stephanus went to speak to Elizabeth. Suggestive connections abound here: the historical Saint-Germain spoke Polish (*LCSG*, 27); H.D.'s original Moravian ancestor, Peter Wolle, came from Poland where Comenius had maintained the old Church of Bohemia (*G*, 228, 279n9; see notes to chap. 8); and World War II began when Great Britain declared war after Hitler invaded Poland on September 1, 1939. Saint-Germain in delirium makes a connection to the story of Leopold Rakoczi, who took refuge in Poland after escaping from Wiener-Neustadt. In 1703 he was offered the Polish crown, which he refused, preferring to return to Hungary to lead a peasant revolt called the *kurucz* or "crusader" uprising against Austria and Hapsburg oppression of Magyar nationalism (*EB* [1957], 18: 959). H.D. uses the same words for Leopold's mission—"gathering them together"—that Elizabeth used in the previous chapter when she expressed her intention to gather together the disputing sects within Christianity as her mother and the Moravians had gathered together the Native American tribes. Both "gatherings" are a step toward "world-unity without war."

This was the Guelph and Ghibelline of his later reconstruction. These names are Italian corruptions of the German words "Welf" and "Waiblingen," the names of two opposing parties in twelfth-century Germany. The Welf, party of the Dukes of Saxony and Bavaria, took their name from Welf, an eleventh- century Duke of Bavaria, and the Waiblingen, party of the lords of Hohenstaufen, took theirs from an estate near Castle Waiblingen. Saint-Germain "reconstructs" the Rakoczy-Austrian opposition of his era as a later version of the party oppositions of fourteenth-century Florence. It is also precursor and parallel to the Protestant Freemasons in France, the revolutionaries, in opposition to the French monarchy supported by the Pope.

Tàvola. This Italian word means "table," and the cognate words H.D. associates with it are variations on "table." A *tavolàto* is a little table; *tavolètta* means "small table" and also "tablet"; *tavolière* means "card-table" or "chess board." H.D., in drawing a parallel between her visions and Dante's, is looking for the right word for her small three-legged table that once belonged to William Morris, which she used during World War II for spiritualist séances, first with her medium, Arthur Bhaduri, and Bryher present, later by herself. The table sent her the "out-of-time" vision of the Viking Ship that convinced her of her psychic "gift" and her past-life connection with Lord Dowding (*S*, 10–11). In this novel the Protestant-Catholic oppositions, which H.D. wants to transcend, are reflected in the opposition between H.D. and Dowding. That opposition, she reasons, should not have happened because the séance table proclaimed them Eternal Lovers. The Catholic-Protestant split should not be happening either, because in truth an all-embracing religion unites them. The friendship between Dante and Cavalcanti despite their political opposition also figures in H.D.'s multiple construction of mirrored relationships.

There could be reconciliation. Since "Mandetta?" appears just before this sentence, the idea is that Mandetta and Primavera can be reconciled since both are symbolically Love, as "they," the literary critics and philosophical interpreters of Dante, have declared Beatrice to be. This interpretation creates a continuum between her and the Lady Philosophy of Dante's *Convivio*, the embodiment of "Divine Philosophy," as well as a linkage with Elizabeth.

a formula that fitted history is the phrase that indicates what H.D. is searching for in this novel. If each woman—Beatrice, Primavera, Mandetta, Elizabeth de Watteville—is a symbol of Love, then each living woman joins every other as incarnation of the eternal feminine Divine. All human beings can be so joined, overriding the national and religious factionalism that produces war.

to slay the spìriti. H.D. uses the Italian word for "spirits," whose meaning Pound glosses as "the 'senses,' or the 'intelligence of the senses,' perhaps even the 'moods,' when they are considered as 'spirits of the mind'" (*Trans.*, 18; LOA-EP, 188). She is referring to a passage in chapter 11 of the *Vita Nuova* in which Dante, wholly possessed by Love, Amor, describes waiting for a greeting from Beatrice:

And what time she made ready to salute me, the spirit of Love, destroying all other perceptions, thrust forth the feeble spirits of mine eyes, saying, "Do homage unto your mistress," and putting itself in their place to obey; so that he who would might then have beheld Love. (*PD*, 559)

Johanna. Saint-Germain translates "Giovanna" into its German form, "Johanna," to reinforce the name-link, or "spiritual etymology," with Saint John and the Johannites as well as with Zinzendorf's name "Johannan" and title "Brother Johannes." The underlying hint is that "a world unity without war" would require reconciliation with the defeated Germans.

a screen, a veil—he remembered how he had pondered that velo, veil. In the *Vita Nuova*, Dante describes gazing at Beatrice in church one Sunday when another woman "of pleasant favor," who was seated between them, thought he was looking at her. "It immediately came into my mind that I might make use of this lady as a screen (It: *velo*) to the truth," that is, a "veil" that will conceal his true feelings. He then began paying attention to her so that his friends would not know of his extreme devotion to Beatrice (*PD*, 552).

It caught in the wind. "It" refers to an unspoken noun, *velo*, veil, the word Dante uses in describing his screen-love, which comes into Saint-Germain's mind associated with *vela*, Latin for sail, and reminds him of seeing Elizabeth's white old-lace scarf that "caught in the wind" like a sail as she left the Cathedral the day he held the door for her. The association links Elizabeth to his screen-love, the stand-in for Beatrice, and to Cavalcanti's lovers all as women commanding total love and adoration in the medieval courtly lover's tradition, a tradition that also demands concealment, the high-born Lady being out of reach.

Leopold was his brother. Saint-Germain's drifting thoughts are reconstructing his childhood. Leopold (Francis Leopold II) was his brother because he thought both of them were sons of the Prince Rakoczi, Francis Leopold I, ruler of Transylvania. When Saint-Germain was told that he was the illegitimate son of Louis XV, he realized that the Prince was not his "actual" biological father.

the two worlds that "could manifest, separately, to the same person" are this mortal world and the eternal world beyond death. These worlds both appear to Leopold, whom H.D. is constructing as a "past-life" manifestation of Lord Dowding in this elaborate set of parallels. The method is much the same as in *The Sword Went Out to Sea*.

that last time, what the tablets or the tavolàto had intended. This memory-scene re-creates the circumstances of Dowding's rejection in symbolic parallelism. "That last time" refers to H.D.'s last sessions at the William Morris table when she received the spirit messages that Dowding later rejected. It was a breach in their spiritual twinship, or "brotherhood," as had happened with Dante/Cavalcanti and, in this construction, with the historical Leopold and Saint-Germain.

obvious madness . . . had raged at those very spìriti. H.D. is asserting that the symbolic Dowding believed in the spirits while denying their authenticity, an insane contradiction that made her decide he was obviously "mad."

that Morte. Saint-Germain/H.D. sees Dante as uniting Cavalcanti with death, "Morte," in the same way that he united Beatrice/Giovanna with "Amor." Both love and death are eternal and inseparable forces. Dante's *Commedia*, celebrating Beatrice as the Divine Love that conquers death, is set in the year of the death of Cavalcanti, Dante's "older brother" and forerunner in poetry. In *Helen in Egypt* H.D.'s sound-link *L'Amour/La Mort,* translating from French as "love/death," binds these forces together in a transcendent ending (*HE*, 301).

the rubrica. In English "rubric" is a term used for directions in a prayer book or missal that are traditionally printed in red (Lat: rubeus, ruber = red) to distinguish them from the liturgical text. The allusion is to the famous opening paragraph of Dante's *Vita Nuova*.

> In that part of the book of my memory before the which is little that can be read, there is a rubric, saying, "Here beginneth the New Life." Under such rubric I find written many things; and among them the words which I purpose to copy into this little book. (*PD,* 547)

This is the translation of the Italian that H.D. read, but Dante in his original essay used Latin, the church language, for his rubric *Incipit vita nova* (Musa, 3). His "new life" began when he first saw Beatrice. He was then nine years old (*PD*, xvii, 547).

Comes Cabalicus. Èliphas Lévi says that Saint-Germain was either the natural or an adopted son of a Rosicrucian who called himself *Comes Cabalicus*, the Companion Kabbalist. Since Saint-Germain also was reported to have told Prince Karl of Hesse that he was a son of Prince Rakoczi, H.D. is trying to make these stories tally with each other and with the Louis XV parentage.

épreuve is the French word for "trial" or "test." One of H.D.'s theories about Dowding's rejection of her was that he, knowingly or not, was part of an initiation ceremony that higher powers had ordained for her, as in the initiations in Freemasonry.

His mind had broken. In 1946, after H.D.'s "mind had broken," she could not remember how she was rescued and flown to Switzerland by Bryher, who had to recount it to her in a letter (September 29, 1946; Guest, 278).

Prince Karl of Hesse. The historical Saint-Germain, after having lived at several European courts, finally took up residence in Schleswig-Holstein at the court of Prince Charles (Karl) of Hesse, who was a student and patron of the occult sciences. Saint-Germain is believed to have died in Schleswig sometime between 1780 and

1785, but he was also reported "to have been seen in Paris in 1789" (*EB* [1902], 20: 5; *LCSG*, 179–82, 223).

the good Lucia (It: light) is the symbolically chosen name of their Italian housemaid in Venice in this purported "past life" of the "deathless one."

as from the Paradiso. Saint-Germain had been writing the astrological signs for the planets, evidently casting his horoscope. The first seven of the ten heavens of Dante's Paradise are each governed by a planet: (1) the Moon, (2) Mercury, (3) Venus, (4) the Sun, (5) Mars, (6) Jupiter, (7) Saturn. The position of the planets at the time of one's birth modifies the general qualities of the zodiacal sign. H.D. studied astrology and "continually had horoscopes cast for herself and her friends" ("Myth," 293–338). It should not be forgotten that H.D.'s father was an astronomer.

de Seingalt is better known as Casanova. His full name was Giovanni Jacopo Casanova de Seingalt. This adventurer, born in Venice in 1725, lived all over Europe and assumed many roles, including journalist, alchemist, preacher, police informant, and spy. From 1756 to 1759 he was director of state lotteries in France, made considerable money, and frequented high society. He met Cagliostro in Aix, France, in 1769. From 1774 to 1782 Casanova was a police spy in Venice. His inauthentic *Mémoires authentiques*, which H.D. apparently read, recount the numerous love-affairs with which he credits himself and that have made his name a synonym for "seducer." Casanova and the historical Saint-Germain first met at Tournai in 1763 (*LCSG*, 14, 149).

Fête vénitienne translates as "Venetian festival," but since "lanterne vénitienne" means "Chinese lantern," the image here is of a festival glowing with paper lanterns, a parallel to "chandeliers . . . lighted for him" in Zinzendorf's sermon at Zeist. See notes to chapter 3.

he thought of Balsamo. The similarity in character and nationality between Casanova and Cagliostro – and the fact that the historical Saint-Germain knew both— brings the mind of the character Saint-Germain back to the present and to Balsamo hidden in the stable. He realizes that during his illness, Stephanus has engineered Balsamo's escape with the ambassador leaving for England. Saint-Germain is now freed from the Jesuit pledge to deliver his former magician-colleague to torture and death at the hands of the Inquisition. Now it is up to Saint-Germain to do what he can to prevent the revolution by enacting his newly understood role of chevalier and troubadour.

the Guard would not leave the Palace because Saint-Germain is returning to Paris to take his proper place in command of it. His vision is that of the medieval Knights Templar, military knighthood in the service of a true and pure Christian religion centered in God's divine Love.

he had cheated time is an allusion to Saint-Germain's "deathlessness" and purported ability to reincarnate, but these qualities had not really been his; they belonged to a "Visitor."

those spinning sisters. The Three Fates of Greek mythology, the goddesses of destiny, Clotho, Lachesis, and Atropos respectively spin, weave, and cut the thread of life. The metaphor of life as a fabric woven of many strands suggests H.D.'s consciousness of her style of this novel. Elizabeth's sewing a tapestry fits this theme, as in chapter 8.

when the wings were free. The "fabric of life" is here seen as the web of the cocoon, which is left behind at the body's death when the butterfly, the soul, emerges and frees its wings. The theme permeates *The Walls Do Not Fall*. In H.D.'s writing in the 1940s and after, *Trilogy* and *Majic Ring*, her references to "wings" carry associations with Dowding and the dead R.A.F. boys who had sacrificed their lives in a noble cause. See, for example, *S*, 262–63.

mantilla. Elizabeth's white lace scarf or veil resembles the cocoon's white threads, and the way she wears it reminds him of the woman on the bridge at Venice. She appears nunlike to Saint-Germain, so perhaps the word he searches for is "wimple."

Melusine. French folklore speaks of Melusine as a fairy voice in the fountain of Lusignan in Poitiers. Thus singing and music floating across the water in Venice seemed to Saint-Germain to have an enchanted origin. He also thinks of the song of the sirens who lured Odysseus, so perhaps a momentary sweetheart is implied, an "incident," as Pound said Mandetta had been in the life of Cavalcanti.

the Messenger with a capital *M* in H.D.'s syncretistic thinking associates the angel Gabriel of the Annunciation with the dead R.A.F. pilots who came to her in séance and, further, with the Greek-Egyptian Hermes-Thoth, shape-shifter and message-bearer of the gods, at this time particularly in his form as Hermes Trismegistus, founder of alchemy (*TA*, sec. 1).

flickering lanterns, across the slats. Saint-Germain has the power to be in two places at once but his awareness does not. Rumor says he conversed with de Seingalt while he lay ill at home, seeing the festival lights through the blinds, an image parallel to H.D.'s vision of the "writing on the wall" in Corfu. "I thought, at first, that it was sunlight flickering from the shadows cast from or across the orange trees" (*TF*, 44–45).

calle is the Italian word for street.

the Piazza. The central square of Venice, called the Piazza San Marco, opens before the famed Church of Saint Mark and the Palace of the Doges. It is fabulously beautiful and always swarms with people, fewer at night when soft amber lanterns on its pillars contribute to the effect of enchantment.

It was always carnival. In Roman Catholic countries from medieval times, "carnival" refers to Mardi Gras (Fat Tuesday), the French word for Shrove Tuesday or the day before Ash Wednesday, a last fling of eating, drinking, and pleasure-taking before the Lenten season of fasting and abstinence that occupies the forty days before Easter. Now in great cities such as Rio de Janeiro, Cologne, Nice, and New Orleans, elaborate Mardi Gras festivals begin a week or more before the day itself. The theme here echoes with the Moravians' elaborate celebrations that got out of hand in the Sifting Time.

He might have been seeing double. Saint-Germain is trying to explain to himself how de Seingalt could have seen Saint-Germain "where he was not." De Seingalt is also said to have been "a cabbalist" and involved in the then new and "occult sect of Free-Masons," Egyptian Masonry (Bolitho, 70, 74).

find your way to the Miracoli. H.D. wrote in *End to Torment* of being in Venice with Ezra Pound around 1914. He wanted to show her a church. She says:

> We darted in and out of alleys or calles, across bridges. . . . It was very hot, May, I think. The church was cool, with a balcony of icy mermaids, Santa Maria dei Miracoli. (*ET,* 6)

In section 31 of *Tribute to the Angels,* H.D. sees an aspect of the "Lady"—in this novel linked to Beatrice/Primavera—in "the marble sea-maids in Venice, / who climb the altar-stair / at *Santa Maria dei Miracoli.*" This church's name translates as "Saint Mary of the Miracles."

after the Miracle. In this train of associated thoughts, the sound-link to "Miracoli" makes Saint-Germain think of the candles' going out as a "Miracle" performed by Elizabeth, even though she had already left the Chapel of Saint Wenceslas.

Ancienne Chevalerie is the "old" or "former chivalry" of the Knights Templar, the most perfect manifestation, in H.D.'s view, of medieval knighthood.

the suppression of the Order—the Society of Jesus—by the Pope would mean that from then on, this "eternal order" within it would have to work underground to stem Protestant Freemasonry. Saint-Germain, recovering from illness, sees more clearly now the conflict between the institutional church's demands and those of the universal spiritual powers.

it was Euclid. This reference means that the action he is undertaking is as rationally laid down as a theorem of Euclidean geometry, the conclusion following inevitably from the premise with the signal Q.E.D., abbreviating the Latin quod erat demonstrandum, "that which is to be demonstrated."

the Church Fathers are the medieval theologians such as saints Clement, Origen, Augustine, and Aquinas who systematized and defined orthodox Christian doctrine. Saint-Germain's undertaking therefore has intellectual sanction from church authorities.

the Fathers in the Indies. Roman Catholic missionaries, Jesuits prominent among them, ran risk of death when they went to the East and West Indies. The reference is also a reminder of Zinzendorf's zealous Moravian missionaries who went to the Indies.

it was damnable. This sentence-ending repudiates the rationalizations just given.

What Saint-Germain is about to do would set the Inquisition on him as a heretic, just as it had attacked and exterminated the Cathars for failing to obey the Pope.

But he had paid his debt. The count is not regretting his past actions because he now sees them as steps on his spiritual path. He has fulfilled his moral obligation to de Rohan, his surrogate father, by infiltrating the Freemasons. He has paid his debt to Cagliostro by refusing to betray him and by letting him escape. Now Saint-Germain is free of both as he follows his true spiritual path in which he will sacrifice his life for an unattainable ideal.

Chapter XV, pp. 66–69

"I do not know". Elizabeth is speaking as she sits at the bedside of the still somewhat feverish Louis. She is answering his prior question, which is something like "why did the Indians give special names to the Moravian leaders?"

Susquehanna is the name of a large river flowing south through eastern Pennsylvania but lying west of the Lehigh and Delaware rivers, at whose confluence Bethlehem is situated. On the Susquehanna river northwest of Bethlehem, the Moravian missionary David Zeisberger established Friedenshuetten (German: Friedenshütten = "habitations of peace" or "tents of peace"), a community of Iroquois converts (*HMC*, 103–4; *G*, 243).

Lenni-Lenape is the Delaware Indians' name for themselves; it means "Indian men" or "original people" (*HB*, 45, 48; ZN, 6 [20], 11 [27]). "Our Delawares, Lenape or Lenni-lenape were another branch" of the Algonquin (*G*, 245, 233, 281n61; *HB*, 45).

Z'higochgoharo is the Native American name given to Christian Henry Rauch, who went as missionary to Shekomeko, New York, in 1741. The Native Americans gave new names to the Moravians because, they said, the European names were too hard to pronounce (*HB*, 242). H.D. stresses the sounds of these names as if they were musical or magical incantations. The name Z'higochgoharo gave her the clue to the meaning of an important spirit message she received in séance in 1943 that connects this novel with *The Gift* and *Majic Ring* (see *G*, 17, 242; *MR*, chap. 3, last paragraph).

to lose them. Benigna was broken-hearted that war had caused division between the "Bethlehem Indians," who left the settlement, and the Moravians with whom they had been united for a time in "heart-religion."

They are not lost. This phrase contains the theme of Dowding's spiritualist lectures assuring the bereaved that their sons were not dead (*S*, 6). H.D. paraphrases him in her dedication of *The Sword Went Out to Sea:* "To Gareth." Here she is quoting Bryher's speech of reassurance to her after Dowding's rejection: "It's not lost. This will go on somewhere" (*S*, 132, 154).

Sister Elizabeth, in her white cap. Elizabeth wears the tight-fitting white cap of the eighteenth-century Moravian Sisters, tied under the chin with ribbons whose color indicated the owner's choir. See illustrations for portraits of Benigna, Theodora, and Anna Nitschmann. H.D.'s grandmother Elizabeth wore a white cap though it was a later, much smaller and re-designed version. See photographs in *The Gift* (143, 138). The Moravian women's custom of addressing one another as "Sister" misled the poet Henry Wadsworth Longfellow. In 1825 he wrote a poem, "Hymn of the Moravian Nuns of Bethlehem at the Consecration of Pulaski's Banner," before he learned that the Moravian Sisters are not nuns and that the banner was not a large, flowing flag, but a guidon, or pennant. Both H.D. and Longfellow were romantically touched by the story of Count Casimir Pulaski's visit to the wounded La Fayette at Bethlehem in 1778. Pulaski was then presented with the banner designed and embroidered by Moravian women. H.D. tells the story in *The Gift*, p. 230, but in "Zinzendorf Notes" merely states "Pulaski Count Casimir" ([12]; *G*, 228). Levering supposes that the women wanted to honor Pulaski as a relative of Polish royalty because the haven of the episcopacy of the Bohemian Brethren had been in Poland (*HB*, 485, 488). Zinzendorf's stepfather, General von Nazmer, had been a friend of the King of Poland (*AGS*, 234). Pulaski carried the banner into battle at Savannah where he was killed in 1779. The banner is now in the Maryland Historical Society. The Moravian Historical Society in Bethlehem has a reproduction that was made to be "used as decoration in Baltimore on Pulaski Day, October 11, 1929," on the 150th anniversary of his death (Susan Dreydoppel, personal communication July 26, 2007).

Tganniatarechev is the Native American name (*G*, 264) given to John Christopher Pyrlaeus (d. 1785), who was a Leipzig University candidate in theology and thirty years old when he came to Bethlehem in October 1741. He was ordained bishop in 1742 (Thomas Minor, Moravian College head librarian, letter to the editor, December 21, 1987). Pyrlaeus is "chiefly noted as a student and teacher of Indian languages, particularly the Mohawk and Mohican dialects, and left some linguistic work of interest in manuscript, which is preserved in the Moravian archives at Bethlehem" (*HB*, 70; *G*, 155–65, 168, 170, 260, 275).

my grandfather's poems. The bibliography of Zinzendorf's work shows that he wrote around three thousand hymns. His followers also took down his sermons, for he often preached extemporaneously. John de Watteville, who taught Christian Renatus and later married Benigna, used shorthand to record Zinzendorf's sermons at Berlin in December 1738 (*AGS*, 239–40). These notes evidently form the nucleus of the *Sixteen Discourses on the Redemption of Man by the Death of Christ. Preached at Berlin . . .* , published in English translation in London in 1740.

one of the greatest extempore poets. Zinzendorf's poetry is praised in La Trobe's introduction to Samuel Jackson's 1838 translation of *AGS*, xxvi–xxxi.

Pyrlaeus. . . explained the Indian language. Pyrlaeus and his wife stayed at Tulpehocken in 1743 while he learned Mohawk from Conrad Weiser. In September 1745 as "master of the school of Indian languages at Bethlehem," he translated the first verses from the German hymnal into the Mohican language and put them with the tune *In Dulce Jubilo* for a missionary love-feast at which each person sang in his or her native language. "Thirteen languages figured in the polyglot harmony," noted Levering (*HB*, 204–5). At this time "the desire was increased to cultivate the musical talent of Bethlehem to a higher degree of excellence and serviceableness," a desire that did not die. J. Fred Wolle (1863–1933), H.D.'s uncle, who studied music in Munich, founded the famous Bach choir of Bethlehem (Guest, 12–13). Music is constantly present in Moravian life. Formerly, deaths and other kinds of news were announced by trombone motifs played from the church balcony (*G*, 57, 230). The *Singstunde* or "singing-hour," when people come together simply to sing, is still a favorite feature of Moravian life, and one in which non-Moravians may join (cf. *G*, 277). Since the end of the eighteenth century, Moravian hymnals have incorporated popular hymns from many other denominations (cf. *Offices of Worship*; H. Williams, personal communication, October 12, 1987).

the early settlement. When Pyrlaeus arrived in Bethlehem in 1741 with Gottlob Buettner and John William Zander, no Moravians had come since December 1740. These three men increased to thirty-four the number of Moravians who were connected with the European churches (*HB*, 70).

not quite fifty years. Since the date of this novel is 1788, the first pioneers arrived forty-eight years before, in May 1740, on a 5000–acre site in eastern Pennsylvania deeded by William Allen to George Whitefield on which he planned a school for Negroes at a place he named Nazareth. The Moravians, through purchase by Zinzendorf's wife, took over this site the following year and established the Nazareth and Bethlehem communities. The group of original settlers consisted of John Boehner, Martin Mack, Anton Seiffert, David and Rosina Zeisberger and their son David, Joanna Hummel, and two indentured boys from Savannah, Benjamin Sommers and James, whose last name is not recorded, he having soon run away (*HB*, 40–45).

My uncle Frederick. The historical Elisabeth von Watteville, like H.D., had an Uncle Frederick, Frederick von Watteville, the brother of John von Watteville. Their father, Baron Frederick von Watteville, was a student with Zinzendorf at the royal school at Halle and joined him when he formed the "Order of the Mustard Seed." Zinzendorf was inspired by Jesus' parable of the mustard seed in Matthew 13.31. It is "the least of all seeds. but when it is grown, it is the greatest among herbs" (AGS, 9). The "Spartans" in this passage are the Iroquois who have a confederation of tribes. The Delaware and others who have not formed a league are the "Athenians" (*G*, 246).

Iroquois . . . Tuscaroras. ZN, p. 4 [15, 16] on the left-hand page reads "Hist. 48" and on the right-hand page

Six Nations or Iroquois—"the five Nations," Mohawks, Oneidas, Onodagas, Cayugas + Senecas. In 1715 the Tuscaroras joined them—"the Six Nations."

H.D. found these phrases in the footnote on p. 48 of Levering. A similar list, but with slightly different spellings, appears in ZN, p. 11 [27] without a source cited.
the separate tribes are in the Algonquin nation.
began his record. Pyrlaeus began writing down the Native American languages around 1744 (cf. *HB*, 94; *G*, 260).
I was not considered gifted. This remark shows how much Elizabeth is a personal reflection of H.D. In *The Gift*, H.D. says of herself and her brothers:

> They had so much to give us, Papa and Papalie . . . but . . . we were none of us "gifted," they would say. . . . They didn't think any of us were marked with that strange thing they called a Gift, the thing Uncle Fred had had from the beginning. (*G*, 42–43, 231)

She wrote *The Gift* to show that, no matter what the elders thought, she has the "Gift of Vision . . . the Gift of Wisdom, the Gift of the Holy Spirit" (*G*, 214). In this passage H.D. is using the word "choir" in its modern English sense of "singers in church," not in the Zinzendorfian sense of *Chor* or group.

darkness—Manito? *He was God and Devil.* In the Algoquin or Algonkin language, *Manito, or Manitou,* means "he is a god" and is understood as "a spirit or force underlying the world and life, . . . a nature spirit of both good and evil influence" (WDUD, 1096). Translated as the "Great Spirit," it is equivalent of "God" in Christian thinking (*G*, 163, 247, 282nn86–89). Pound, in addressing H.D. as "Lynx" in his Canto LXXIX, makes an association to her American Moravian background in a prayer: "Manitou, god of lynxes, remember our corn" (*C*, 488).

He, *is the reply,* who walketh with a serpent. Zinzendorf's encounter with the puff adders links him with the Great Spirit. H.D. tells two versions of this story in *The Gift* (*G*, 245, 247). See notes to chapter 8.

all-heal implicit in the names. "Heal-all" or "self-heal" is the popular name given to several plants with healing properties. H.D.'s intent is both literal and symbolic.

powdered bark and dried berries. Hutton lists Indian remedies. "for head-ache and tooth-ache, white walnut bark; . . . for stomach disorders, the red berries of the wintergreen" (*HMM*, 84).

Our Lady. Elizabeth as a Visitor becomes "Our Lady," the Virgin Mary and feminine Divine, the dream-Lady mother goddess in *Tribute to the Angels*. In section 32, after images of the Virgin Mary, beginning in section 29, "We have seen her / the world over, / Our Lady of the Goldfinch, Our Lady of the Candelabra" come lines that link to Elizabeth's white lace scarf:

> For I can say truthfully,
> her veils were white as snow,
>
> as no fuller on earth
> can white them; (Mk. 9.2–3)

H.D.'s theology shifts the transfiguration of Jesus, the male god, to his Mother, a move that accords with Zinzendorf's view of the female Holy Spirit as well as with expression of the intense devotion to the Holy Mother that marks the Marian tradition.

a Protestant Jesuit. Zinzendorf might well be considered a Jesuit, if judged by his extensive use of military metaphors. Hutton quotes one example:

> Christ is the conquering Prince, with a voice like the blast of a trumpet, and His royal chariot rolls behind; His preachers, His warriors, His noble prisoners of war are "comrades of the Noble Order of Mockery"; and His Blood is their guide and their staff. (*HMM*, 185)

These military metaphors also remind H.D. of the medieval Knights Templar and the Moravian Agnus Dei banner with its motto "Our Lamb hath conquered; him let us follow" (*G*, 157, 265–66; 285n173).

Schekomeko, which has the English name Pine Plains, is in Dutchess County, New York State. There Christian Henry Rauch had begun a mission, an unwelcome presence to the provincial governors. Zinzendorf and Benigna encountered hostility there on their visit in July 1742. They were arrested for breaking the sabbath—she was observed copying a poem of her father's for him—and were brought before a justice of the peace, who made them pay a fine (Reichel, *Memorials*, 59–61). In 1744 in New York City, a hearing took place concerning the activities of Gottlob Buettner, Joachim Sensemann, and Joseph Shaw, "three Moravian priests" who lived with "many Indians at Schocomico." Since Moravians, like Quakers, do not take oaths on principle, they would not swear allegiance to the crown and were therefore thought to be pro-French, that is, secret Catholics. The Moravians' willingness to talk with anyone of any denomination fed this false rumor and caused the animosity that led Governor Clinton to order them out of New York State. The missionaries then returned with their Indian converts to Bethlehem (*Doc.Hist.*, 613–21; *HB*, 192).

It was the fur-traders. The logic of this speech is jumbled. The idea is that the fur-traders caused trouble for the Moravians, although Hutton says it was the whisky-merchants. "Their" does not refer to its nearest noun, "fur-traders," but to the Indians who had a farm community. The broken-off sentence after "need" should end with "they gave it away," that is, gave their excess corn to Indians not in their community, a practice which also raised suspicion in the authorities (*Doc.Hist.*, 615).

the crime of a whole nation refers to the slaughter and displacement of the Native American Indians by European settlers, particularly by getting them drunk in order to cheat them of their land, the settlers having discovered and exploited the Native Americans' susceptibility to alcoholism.

the same problem, after the conquistadores. In Mexico and South America the Spanish conquistadors also murdered the natives, a policy directly counter to the Jesuits' desire to convert them. The reference to "the white man's other contribution" has an ironic ring but is unclear. If the "first" contribution is war and slaughter, possibly the "other" is racism, although it may also be disease.

Jesuits in disguise, they called them. An official document of August 11, 1744, records "Further Orders Relating to the Moravians." It was issued by Governor Clinton of New York State, directing sheriffs of Albany, Ulster, and Dutchess counties "to give notice to the several Moravian & vagrant Teachers among the Indians . . . to desist . . . and to depart." Zinzendorf wrote a letter of protest (December 31, 1744), saying that they had come "to the colonies hoping to enjoy an unrestrained Freedom of Religion," but he failed to convince the Board of Trade, which advised Clinton (June 28, 1745) to enforce the "Act for securing of his Majesty's Government of New York" in order to "guard against . . . all wicked Practices of Designing Persons & Papists in Disguise" (*Doc.Hist.*, 617–21; *HMM*, 94).

Menakessi river is a variant of the name for the Monocacy river. H.D. noted: "Note 46. *Monocacy Creek*. *Menagassi* or *Menakessi* (*Monakasy*, Monocasy or Monocacy) i.e. *creek with bends*" (ZN, 5 [17–18]; cf. *HB*, 46). This creek flows into the Lehigh, in Delaware "Lechaweeki," that is *where there are forks*, just above Bethlehem. *Wunden Eiland*, the "Isle of Wounds," which figures in *The Gift* and where occasional meetings with Native Americans had taken place, was located in Monocacy Creek, but it had washed away long before H.D.'s childhood.

Friedenshuetten. In September 1745 the increasing number of Native American refugees led to the building of "the group of Indian houses at Bethlehem. . . . [T]he cluster of log cabins . . . received the name *Friedenshuetten—Habitations of Peace*" (*HB*, 192; *G*, 243, 262).

driven, remorselessly through the snow. In telling this story to Saint-Germain, Elizabeth/H.D. conflates two evacuations of Native American Moravians. The mention of "snow" shows that she is putting together the 1745 evacuation from Shekomeko with the final exodus, in 1765, of Indians who had lived at Wechquetank, near Bethlehem. This story begins in 1763 during "Pontiac's War" when white militiamen shot Indians on sight. Moravian Indians, settled in organized communities, suffered double enmity and danger, since non-Christian Indians hated their affluence and white people thought they were simply Pontiac's savages. In October 1763 the missionary Bernhard Grube evacuated 150 Moravian Indians to Nazareth from Wechquetank, after which the village was torched. At nearly the same time, a Moravian Indian named Renatus, of the community at Nain, near Wechquetank, was accused of killing John Stenton, who kept a tavern about nine miles from Bethlehem. Renatus was jailed, tried in May 1764, and acquitted, but as anti-Indian and anti-Moravian feeling was running high, the colonial government at Philadelphia ordered the 143 Wechquetank Indians into protective custody at Philadelphia. They were released on March 22, 1765, into a heavy snowstorm through which they were forced to walk to Bethlehem. Sixty of them died on the way, leaving eighty-three in the group, whose "arrival awakened much sympathetic interest at Bethlehem." On April 3, they departed for the Wyoming valley to the west, accompanied by government guard and the missionaries Zeisberger and Schmick, reaching Machwihilusing (Wyalusing) on May 9. "There a village was laid out, with gardens and fields . . . which received the name *Friedenshuetten—Habitations of Peace*—like the temporary Indian village of twenty years before, at Bethlehem" (*HB*, 393–407). Levering adds: "Thus, with the departure of those Indians from Bethlehem on April 3, 1765, Moravian Indian missions in the Lehigh Valley came to an end."

Small-pox. A smallpox epidemic broke out among the Indians in the summer of 1746 and spread to Bethlehem and Nazareth (*HB*, 193).

the lost tribes. Zinzendorf believed that the Indians of the Six Nations were, in his own words, "partly mixed Scythians, and partly Jews of the 10 lost Tribes." He cites as evidence certain prophecies in Deuteronomy and gives additional reasons why the Indians are Jews. "They have Jewish customs" and "*Achsa, onas,* and innumerable other words are pure Ebrew." William Penn also thought the Indians were "of the stock of the *Ten Tribes*," and said, "I find them of like countenance" (Reichel, *Memorials*, 18–19; *HMM*, 90–91).

Chingachgook is the Native American hero in Fenimore Cooper's novel, *The Last of the Mohicans*.

John Wasamapah. The smallpox epidemic of 1746 carried off "that most valuable Indian assistant to the missionaries, John Wasamapah ('Tschoop')." Tschoop is a corruption of Job, his baptismal name. H.D. noted. "Johannes, Joe, John Wasamapah. 596.—buried [in Bethlehem cemetery]" (ZN, 5 [18]). Tschoop is said to be the original of Cooper's Chingachgook (*HB*, 596). Tschoop was a drunkard; the story of his conversion by Rauch's genuineness and nonpuritanical approach inspired other missionaries (*HMM*, 86–87; cited in ZN, 5 [17–18]). H.D. fictionalizes the encounter in her notes to *The Gift*; it is in effect a short story (*G*, 238–42).

Johannites were an eastern Christian sect contemporary with the Templars. According to Lévi, they claimed that they alone were initiated into the Savior's religion. They claimed also to know the true history of Jesus Christ. They regarded the facts in the Gospels as allegories to which Saint John held the key. They gave as proof the last line (21.25), which says that if all things done by Jesus were recorded, "I suppose that even the world itself could not contain the books that should be written." They claimed that such a statement would be ridiculous exaggeration unless it referred to allegory and legend (*HM*, 208).

his favourite Disciple is Saint John, the one "whom Jesus loved" who was "leaning on Jesus' bosom" at the Last Supper (Jn. 13.23). The "heresy" is a Gnostic story that Jesus, "instead of being buried in the new tomb of Joseph of Arimathaea, having been swathed and perfumed, was brought back to life in the house of Saint John" (*HM*, 298). The legend that Jesus did not die on the cross, which has many variants, gave rise to H.D.'s 1929 novel, *Pilate's Wife*; there she constructs a variant of her own.

known as the Disciple. *Der Junger*, "the Disciple," is one of the many titles used for Zinzendorf. Martin Mack refers to him as "the sainted Disciple," *der selige Junger* (Reichel, *Memorials*, 100).

the Paraclete is the Holy Spirit as advocate or intercessor with God, as in John 14.16: "I will pray the Father, and he shall give you another Comforter." John 14.26 says: "But the Comforter, which is the Holy Ghost, whom the Father will send in my name, he shall teach you all things" (KJV).

I can read your rubrica. Saint-Germain seems to be saying that Elizabeth is to him what Beatrice was to Dante, that spiritually they had met in past lives, as H.D. believed she and Lord Dowding had met. He "reads" Elizabeth as the beginning of his "new life," as Dante "read" Primavera and Beatrice in his own "Book of Memory," *La Vita Nuova*.

Chapter XVI, pp. 70–73

"I cannot tell you," he said. The pronoun "he" refers to Henry Dohna, a reference that is not clear until the word "Goethe" appears as a reminder of Dohna's comments in chapter 3. Dohna is speaking to Saint-Germain, who is still lying ill in bed in his quarters but is alert enough to ask questions about Moravian history—the "exact channel of tradition" that brought Elizabeth to him in a "visitation." His broken-off sentence—"it was inevitable"—indicates his belief in a preordained connection in a previous life.

the Little Strength. This ship, bought by the Unitas Fratrum and captained by Nicholas Garrison, set sail from Rotterdam on September 16, 1743, with thirty-three young couples recruited from Herrnhaag and Marienborn to go to Nazareth, Pennsylvania, and another sixteen people from Herrnhut. The ship reached Cowes, England, by September 25 and took on fourteen English colonists, making the full complement of the Second Sea Congregation. (The First Sea Congregation had left in March of 1742 on the *Catherine*, arriving in America in May.) In the Sea Congregations [Seegemeine] passengers were organized in their choirs, as in their home communities, with separate quarters and duties. Garrison was both the captain of the *Little Strength* and the congregation's elder, its chief adviser. He was also a talented painter and took up painting as a career after he retired from the sea and settled in Bethlehem. The Moravian Archives there hold some of his work (*HB,* 108–1, 166–69; Moravian Archives newsletter, June 2007).

"*The ensign you say she carried*". Levering says that the ensign, the ship's flag, on the *Little Strength*

> is described as "a lamb passant [walking] with a flag on a blood covered field"—the device that has always figured . . . on the episcopal seal of the Church, and as its general official emblem. (*HB,* 166).

This ancient seal of the Unitas Fratrum he also describes as "a shield with the figure of a lamb carrying a cross from which is suspended a banner of victory, and around the shield is the motto *Vicit Agnus noster, Eum sequamur,* i.e., Our Lamb hath conquered, Him let us follow" (*HB,* 5). This symbol is called the Agnus Dei, Latin for "Lamb of God," in Roman Catholic and Anglican traditions.

Ehrenhold. H.D. wrote in ZN 5 [3]: "11 c. Z. family among 12 chief noble Austrian houses. Founder. Ehrenhold. to Z. 22 generations" (AGS, v).

the Templars' or the Crusaders' emblem. In *The Gift,* H.D.'s persona as the child Hilda remembers her grandmother having told her that the Unitas Fratrum has a "sign which is a lamb . . . a flag the crusaders used or a banner" (*G,* 156, 170, 229, 264–65).

In hoc signo vinces. "[I]n this sign thou shalt conquer" was a message seen in a dream by Constantine the Great (288?–337) along with a flaming cross, as he was about to lay siege to Rome in 312. This vision converted him to Christianity, and he succeded in conquering Rome that year, which greatly strengthened his faith. Upon becoming emperor, he secured toleration for Christians, hitherto persecuted, and paved the way for the Christianizing of the west (*Co.Enc.,* 633).

Lindsay House. This residence, "situate near the Thames at Chelsea," was bought by the Moravians in 1750. It had formerly belonged to the duke of Ancaster. In 1753 Zinzendorf moved there from Westminster and, while he always considered himself a pilgrim without permanent residence, used it as a convenient headquarters halfway between the American and European communities (AGS, 399, 428).

those last days. Christian Renatus had tuberculosis, a condition worsened by his strenuous efforts to make up for his misdemeanors at Herrnhaag. During the last stages of his illness, he was staying at Lindsay House, where he died on May 28, 1752, at the age of twenty-five.

I saw three ships a-sailing *is the first line of the carol.* This traditional English carol, sung at Christmas, is printed in *The Oxford Book of Carols,* but it is not attributed to Christian Renatus, although various sources for its tune are given. It is not a Moravian hymn—their hymns expressed theological doctrine—but is associated with the legend of the bringing of the Holy Grail to England by Joseph of Arimathaea. H. D. makes a parallel with the ships that brought the Moravians to the new world.

He did not wish to speak that word. The word is "revolution." A continuing subtext in this novel is H.D.'s wish to dissociate Christianity from the violence of war.

the match that would light the tinder. Historians generally believe that the success of the American revolt against the King of England gave impetus to the French Revolution. Thomas Carlyle wrote in *The French Revolution* of the period in which Louis XV lay dying in 1774:

> Borne over the Atlantic, to the closing ear of Louis, King by the Grace of God, what sounds are these; muffled—ominous, new in our centuries? Boston Harbour is black with unexpected Tea behold a Pennsylvania Congress gather; and ere long, on Bunker Hill, DEMOCRACY announcing, in rifle-volleys death-winged, under her Star Banner, to the tune of Yankee-doodle-doo, that she is born, and, whirlwind-like, will envelop the whole world! (7)

The lié *between your grandfather and the Premonstrants.* The French "lié" means "bond"—that which binds—or "connection," which came to Zinzendorf through his sense of "heart-religion" as more important than formal church affiliation. In Paris in 1720 as a student, he was attracted to Father de la Tour's unworldliness and opened a conversation with him. From it came an introduction to Cardinal de Noailles, who "acknowledged the grace that dwelt in the Count . . . spoke with him on Christian experience, and dismissed all disputes about religion." They agreed that each should "be faithful in the circumstances in which he was placed. . . . They were, therefore, united in heart, although each retained his peculiar creed." Nevertheless, the two prelates "endeavored to bring him over to the Romish church" (AGS, 20–21). Zinzendorf never intended to convert but wanted to foster an ecumenical spirit that could heal the rift between Protestants and Catholics, ending sectarian warfare.

secret records or of Arcana. Historically, it appears that there were no secret records to destroy. The "disgraceful Twelfth Appendix" to the Hymnal, whose hymns H.D. copied from Rimius, was withdrawn from use in 1750 as part of recovery after the Sifting Time (*HMC*, 281; H. Williams, personal communication, November 1987).

Christian Renatus' return . . . grace. The efforts of Zinzendorf's young son to compensate for his errors led to overexertion and undermined his health, a fact his father did not immediately observe, according to Spangenberg. He says of Christian Renatus:

> His former cheerfulness and vivacity was changed into an unwonted seriousness. His greatest pleasure consisted in composing hymns and poems, by means of which, he hoped to impart his altered sentiments and ardent love to the Saviour. . . . Having little time for this during the day, he often spent whole

nights in these labours. He was, at the same time, indefatigable in waiting upon his father, and did not let him know how often he had passed the night without sleep. . . . This . . . extraordinary state of heart and mind . . . excited in some of his most intimate friends, though least of all in his father, the idea that the Lord was hastening with him towards his dissolution. (AGS, 419)

the extravagances. Spangenberg's exact words are "[T]he young Count had been entangled in the extravagances which prevailed in some of the Moravian stations" (AGS, 418).

my grandfather's script. H.D. is here describing, with only slight modifications, the letter handwritten by Zinzendorf that she owned. It shows small, quite neat, German script in ink now aged to a brownish color, written in close lines on both sides of a small cream-colored sheet. Written to Count Reuss XXVIII (see chap. 2), it is dated February 6, 1757, and signed simply "Ludwig" (mss. box *Moravian Church*, Beinecke).

"My youth's dear book". Saint-Germain's quoting Dante to Elizabeth mirrors the early love of the young Ezra Pound for the young Hilda Doolittle. She is the subject of Pound's "youth's dear book," called "Hilda's Book," unpublished until printed in 1979 as an appendix to H.D.'s memoir of Pound, *End to Torment* (1958). "Hilda's Book" contains twenty-five love poems written to her between 1905 and 1907, highly influenced by Dante and the medieval and Provençal poetry that influenced the *Vita Nuova*. Pound deliberately evoked the parallel to Dante and Beatrice. One poem, "Shadow," reads. "I saw her yesterday. / And lo, there is no time / each second being eternity. . . . But trouble me not / I saw HER yesterday." Pound also called her "Is-hilda" and "Ysolt" (*ET*, 67–69; 76). In H.D.'s reconstructions of Arthurian legend in *The Sword Went Out to Sea* (242–66), she names herself, or selves, Iseult and Blanchefleur, "white flower." The emphasis on "HER" is a reminder of H.D.'s original title for her roman à clef about her youthful relationships with Pound and Frances Gregg, which New Directions printed under the compromise title *HER(mione)*.

the Plan of the Commedia. Saint-Germain's word choice overtly links Zinzendorf, Dante, and Goethe and covertly links them with Ezra Pound through his *Cantos*, as well as with the Moravian women who are manifestations of the Lady, the object of the troubadour's love, loyalty, and song. Poetry and the Lady are thus linked into Zinzendorf's Plan.

Chapter XVII, pp. 74–78

more than a week left. This novel's end coming near Christmas suggests the endings of the middle and last two books of *Trilogy*, in which the transcendent comes down to earth and becomes incarnate, symbolic parallels to the birth of Jesus that unites the human with the divine. In the final section 43 of *Tribute to the Angels*, "the jewel melts in the crucible" and leaves "not ashes, not ash-of-rose / . . . not *vas spirituale*, / not *rosa mystica* even / but a cluster of garden-pinks / or a face like a Christmas-rose." *The Flowering of the Rod*'s final section 43 ends with the three magi bringing gifts to the stable and to Mary, who is not the iconographic goddess but a new mother, "shy and simple and young." The Moravian Christmas at Bethlehem epitomized this spiritual unity for H.D. She describes the service in the voice of the child Hilda:

> for there is the church and we all belong together in some very special way, because of our candle service on Christmas Eve which is not like what anyone else has anywhere. (*TF*, 33; G, 88, 115)

Later she told Freud more about the candles, which are slender and small, specially made of beeswax and mounted in a red paper ruffle. One is given to each member of the congregation by attendants circulating with traysful of them, lighted, providing the only light in the darkened church. Hymns are sung throughout the distribution. His response makes clear how she arrived at the central symbolism of candles in this novel:

> I went on to tell him of our Christmas candles. . . . He said, "There is no more significant symbol than a lighted candle. You say you remember your grandfather's Christmas Eve service? The girls as well as the boys had candles?" . . . He said, "If every child had a lighted candle given, as you say . . . by the grace of God, we would have no more problems. . . . That is the true heart of all religion." (*TF*, 123–24)

the tempest is the Prague snowstorm, now associated with the Pennsylvania storm that killed the Wechquetank Indians, but the word choice also suggests Shakespeare's *The Tempest*, on which H.D. based *By Avon River*, a meditation on Elizabethan poetry but finally on the love of a father for a lost daughter. It was finished just as *The Mystery* was begun in 1949.

another dimension. Saint-Germain was not surprised to see de Rohan because they had shared "another dimension" of consciousness in the Masonic ceremonies. H.D. described her idea of this dimension in connection with her psychoanalysis, referring to Freud as "the Professor":

> Past, present, future, these three—but there is another time-element, popularly called the fourth-dimensional. . . . This fourth dimension, though it appears variously disguised . . . in the Professor's volumes . . . is yet very simple. . . . as simple and inevitable in the building of time-sequence as the fourth wall to a room.

She then numbers the walls of Freud's consulting room, and the fourth wall, opposite the couch and one the analysand looks into, is, she says,

> largely unwalled, as the space there is left vacant by the wide-open double doors. The room beyond may appear very dark or there may be broken light and shadow. Or even bodily, one may walk into that room. (*TF,* 23)

Friedman points out that H.D.'s language matches that of Evangeline Adams's description of "the vibrations of Uranus" in *Astrology: Your Place Among the Stars,* an essential reference for H.D. in the 1930s ("Myth," 322). "Vibrations" and bodily entrance into another dimension are integral concepts in theosophy and reincarnational theory generally (cf. Besant, 92ff., 119ff).

those who have wronged us. This version of a line from the Lord's Prayer is stronger than the standard version in the Moravian *Offices of Worship and Hymns* (1891) and which H.D. would have recited in school chapel and church services, if not at home: *forgive us our trespasses as we forgive them that trespass against us.*

the heart-shaped ruby. Before Saint-Germain received his "visitation" from the spirit of Elizabeth in Saint Wenceslas's chapel, he saw the gem "Charles" as an "uneven dark stone. . . . an uncut ruby" (chap. 6). Now, as he sees it in his mind's eye, it has the shape of a heart, the symbol of love indicating his heightened visionary sensibility. It seems also associated with the Sacred Heart, the flaming, pierced heart of Jesus in Christian art. The Virgin Mary and other saints are also often painted with red hearts revealed as a symbol of their love and compassion (*Ency.Sym.,* 139).

master of the black arts in Sicily. Goethe went to Italy in September 1786 in search of closer contact with classical art. In April 1787 he visited the Balsamo family in Sicily, evidently hoping to meet the magician there. But he did not meet him. Cagliostro was in England and in disgrace at the time. Goethe was impressed by the Balsamos' piety and sincerity. He promised to carry a letter to London from Cagliostro's sister, so possibly he met him there (Carlyle, *Essays,* 4: 289–92). In 1788 Goethe returned to Weimar and resumed work on Faust (Lange, vii). It is said that Goethe in his youth performed alchemical experiments similar to those in the Invocation scene of Faust (*F.Crit.,* 489). His own experience plays a large role in his characterization of Faust. Goethe's family had surrounded him with an interest in magic from childhood. See *Hemispheres* 4 (1945). In *Poetry and Truth* he reports that when he was involved with Susannah von Klettenberg and the Moravians, a Pietist physician recommended that he read "certain mystic, chemical or alchemical works" in support of a search for a "universal remedy." Goethe read Welling's "Opus Major Cabalisticum" and works by Paracelsus, Basil Valentine (a Gnostic), Helmont, Starkey, and others. He later alludes to "that interest with which super-sensuous things inspired me," and says that he formed his own religion, based on Neo-Platonism, to which "the hermetical, mystical and cabalistic also made their contribution" (*DW,* 304–5).

a small group about him. Candace *souls, he called them.* Because the Jews as a nation had not accepted the coming of Christ, Zinzendorf concluded that "no heathen nation, as such, could or would accept the Christian religion." He therefore did not try to enlarge established missions in the West Indies and North America, but sent messengers everywhere in search of "*Candace*-souls. . . . Each nation," he declared, "possessed a few chosen spirits in search of the truth. . . . The chief business of the Church of Christ was to find them and gratify their aspirations." The term "*Candace*-souls" alludes to the story in Acts 8.26–40 in which the apostle Philip baptizes a servant of Queen Candace of Ethiopia, a eunuch whom Philip encountered reading Isaiah, a sign of prior readiness to hear the gospel of Christ. Zinzendorf's concept of "*Candace*-souls" is linked to "First Fruits," since those early converts died before later ones and achieved salvation through their faith. A painting by the eighteenth-century Moravian John Valentine Haidt shows twenty-five of these in native costume standing before the throne of Christ in heaven (Rev.7.9). It bears the text, "These were redeemed from among men, being the first fruits."—Rev. 14. 4. (*HMM*, 155, 183; cf. *G*, 143). John Wasamapah, "Tschoop," is kneeling at Christ's immediate left. See illustrations. H.D. in ZN 9 [23] wrote under heading "CANDACE souls":

> Hutton—148—'55—'61—'83—'93. "a few chosen spirits in search of the truth . . . Candace-souls." "his First Fruits Idea." 1764 synod resolves "not merely to seek for Candace-souls, but to preach the Gospel to all."

Calixthenes. After Jan Hus (John Huss) was burned at the stake for heresy in 1415, the Hussites split into two factions, Taborites and Utraquists. The Taborites, political radicals from the lower classes, refused compromise with Rome. The more moderate Utraquists, also known as Calixthenes (Calixtenes or Calixtines) "embodied the university party, and most of the titled classes," and were more willing to compromise according to circumstances but nevertheless insisted on an essential church reform: communion with both bread and wine, administered from the chalice or cup, in Latin *calix* (*HB*, 9; *G*, 176). H.D. links the cup-shaped lily, the name Lilie and the Tarot cups or hearts with the communion chalice of the Holy Grail legend and the Arthurian tales of knightly chivalry.

Cromwellians or Puritans. The Puritans in England, like the Taborites in Bohemia, were interested in both democratic political reform and in freedom from an established church. H.D. is connecting the European and American religio-political patterns. She associated the Puritans with her father, the astronomer Charles Doolittle, who was of New England and English Puritan descent (*G*, 250–52, 277–78).

Royalists in art. The Royalist artists H.D. has in mind are Robert Herrick (1591–1674)—"For his Royalist sympathies he is ejected from his parish"—and other Cavalier poets whom she meditates upon in "The Guest," the second section of *By Avon River* (59). These did not take part in political action to restore a Catholic monarch, as did the "actual Catholic faction," but only had aristocratic sympathies, as H.D. had in her romantic identification with royalty, temporal and spiritual.

he had bartered his soul. "He" is Louis; a parallel is being drawn between Count Louis Saint-Germain and Count Nicolas Louis von Zinzendorf. H.D. uses the language of her valorized application of the Faust story to Zinzendorf that she used in chapter 8. In this context, "God" or "the Saviour" is Beatrice, "she who bears blessing," who appears in the form of Elizabeth, and the Devil is Cagliostro, who is now gone. Elizabeth's name, de Watteville, reminds him that she, the Lady who is Divine Love, is the real object of his knights-templar's and troubadour's quest.

the hieroglyphs, like light and shadow. Saint-Germain is re-enacting H.D.'s vision of the "writing on the wall." In *Tribute to Freud*, H.D. said of what she had seen that

> the pictures on the wall were like colorless transfers . . . the figure was dim light on shadow, not shadow on light . . . a silhouette cut of light, not shadow, and so impersonal it might have been anyone. (45)

The wording echoes chapter 5, in which Saint-Germain says that the Visitor "could manifest as anybody."

the slats of the Venetian blinds. Saint-Germain sees the fourth image of the hieroglyphs "written" on the wall. H.D. described it as a series of lines of light which draw themselves until

> at last, there it is, . . . a ladder of light. . . . There are seven rungs to this ladder, maybe five . . . it is Jacob's ladder, if you will; it is a symbol common to all religious myth or lore. (*TF,* 53–54)

the inner reading. Saint-Germain has been asked to read the letters, which he thinks are the *Arcana* about which Goethe has questioned Dohna. This "reading" is mystical and symbolical, like the reading of Tarot or a horoscope. Within "spiritual alchemy," the metaphor is that the world is a text which the adept reads. H.D., however, is linking the actual human content—they are love letters—to the cosmic and transcendent, a link established in Christian theology by the Incarnation: "the Word was God. . . . And the Word was made flesh and dwelt among us" (Jn. 1.1, 1.14).

It was already written. In "H.D. by *Delia Alton*," H.D. in the voice of her mediumistic alter ego "Delia Alton" says that *The Mystery* is "my last romance, which I know is written though I have not yet transcribed it." She sketches in plot and theme, then comments: "We [Delia Alton and H.D.] have not finished *The Mystery.* That is, we have not yet written it down" ("H.D.," 188). She thinks of what she writes not as a human invention but as the revelation of an eternal "text" related to the Logos, the creative "Word" that made the world in the beginning (Jn. 1.1).

only Saint-Germain would solve the Mystery and that, long afterwards. It seems that the spiritual progress of the recovering magician lets him understand his deathlessness as eternal life. According to nineteenth-century theosophists, Count Saint-Germain was one of the Twelve Ascended Masters, therefore eternal. From the point of view of eternity, there is no Mystery. An Ascended Master, having become pure spirit, would have the powers of "visitation" and "bi-location"—the capacity to "be where one is not" that is a variant of reincarnation.

find a place for you among them. Cagliostro's offer to Saint-Germain of an escape with the stable grooms suggests a diabolic parallel to Zinzendorf's meeting with Christian David at the house of the "Master of the Horse," that is, the stable-master's house at Schweinitz. Zinzendorf chose to follow up on this meeting, that is, to "act out the legend for himself" and take in the Moravian refugees, not refusing his role in history. Saint-Germain also has refused escape for the same reason. See notes to chapter 10.

that first circle is the original small group of Knights Templar under Hugh de Payens and Geoffrey Saint-Omer. See notes to chapter 9.

Theoclet, the Eastern Adept. "The inmost thought of Hugh de Payens," says Lévi, "in establishing his order was not precisely to serve the ambitions of the patriarchs of Constantinople." It was to join the secret church of the Johannites, founded, they said, by Saint John. The head of the Johannites

> at the epoch of the foundation of the Temple was named Theoclet. He was acquainted with Hugh de Payens, whom he initiated into the mysteries and hopes of his suppositious church; he seduced him by ideas of sovereign priesthood and supreme royalty; in fine, he designated him his successor. Thus was the order of Knights of the Temple tainted from the beginning with schism and conspiracy against kings. (*HM*, 210)

from Saint John. The Johannites' secret doctrine, according to Lévi, includes an alternative version of the life of Jesus. In it Miriam of Nazareth, who was betrothed to Jochanan, was raped by Pandira (or Panther). Jochanan left her "without compromising her." When the child Joshua or Jesus was born, he was adopted by a rabbi named Joseph who took him to Egypt where the boy was "initiated into the secret sciences" and "the priests of Osiris, recognizing that he was the true incarnation of Horus, consecrated him sovereign pontiff of the universal religion." Joseph and Joshua return to Judaea and discover the crime of Pandira and Miriam's sufferings. Joshua's first impulse is to deny his mother: "Woman, what is there in common between you and me?" but later he repents and says, "My mother has in nowise sinned . . . she is virgin and yet mother—let twofold honour be paid to her. As for me, I have no father on earth; I am the son of God and humanity" (*HM*, 208–9).

had punished the apostates. The Church Fathers, notably Irenaeus (fl. 170–90 AD) and Origen (185?–254? AD), opposed Gnosticism as heresy, and so did the

Council of Nicaea (325 AD), which formulated the doctrine of the Trinity, God in Three Persons—Father, Son, and Holy Spirit—that is central to Christian orthodox belief. Gnosticism proclaimed a profound dualism between good and evil, between the divine and the material worlds, and stressed mystical revelation as the key to salvation. In 1209, the Cathars or Albigenses of southern France, descendents of the Gnostics, and, like them, ascetic and Manichean, were burned as heretics in collective pyres during the Albigensian Crusade instigated by Saint Dominic and Pope Innocent III. A sect similar to the Cathars and the Waldenses, similarly ascetic and Manichean, made its way to Thrace around 970, where its members were called Bogomili, or Bogomils, who had connections with the early Bohemian church. For an understanding of the attacks on the Gnostics, see Elaine Pagels, *The Gnostic Gospels*.

their purpose. "Their" refers to Saint-Germain and de Rohan and a few companions who parallel the original Templars and who represent the "undefiled transmission" of true Christianity from the time of Jesus himself.

Dante . . . was Gnostic and Johannite because he wrote a vast allegory that can be read the way the Johannites (and the Christian theosophists) read Scripture, and because his vision is centered on Divine Love as female. For instance, in the Gnostic *Secret Gospel of John*, the female divine Wisdom, Sophia, is superior to the lower god; similarly, the God of the Israelites deludes himself that he is the ultimate and only god. Gnostic imagery emphasizes Light, as does Dante's.

acrobatic (was that acroamatique?). This virtual pun embodies H.D.'s belief that similar-sounding words, by the fact of their sound alone, establish a connection between their referents. This theory of language underlines sections 40, 41, and 43 in *The Walls Do Not Fall* with its wordplay on "Osiris" and "haven,/heaven." Sections 8, 11, 12, and 15 of *Tribute to the Angels* contain the "spiritual etymology" of "*marah-mar* / . . . mer, mere, mère, Maia, Mary / . . . Mother." Similar wordplays pervade *Majic Ring* as well. See notes to chapter 11.

by standing on his head Saint-Germain has "reversed dogma" and is psychologically escaping from Hell as Dante had done in Canto 34 of *Inferno*, when Virgil, the wise man who knows the escape route from evil, reversed direction while crawling along Satan's body and carried the poet up into the light at Mount Purgatory. Under Elizabeth's healing hands he is "seeing the light" at the end of his spiritual trial or initiation. In *The Sword Went Out to Sea*, H.D. refers to her 1946 breakdown as a descent into "Hell" (*S*, 95).

the dark magian power is corrupt since it comes from Simon Magus, a magician who offered to pay to learn Jesus' secrets. But it *is* power. Lévi explains: "The seal of a Cagliostro is as significant as that of Solomon and attests his initiation into the highest secrets of science" (*HM*, 301).

Was the Doctrine degraded. Lévi sheds light on this question. He writes:

The Templars had two doctrines; one was concealed and reserved to the leaders, being that of Johannism; the other was public, being Roman Catholic doctrine. . . . The Johannism of the adepts was the Kabalah of the Gnostics, but it degenerated speedily into a mystic pantheism, carried even to idolatry of Nature and hatred of all revealed dogma. . . . they went so far as to recognise the pantheistic symbolism of the grand masters of Black Magic. . . . With the seeds of death sown in its very principle, and anarchic because it was heretical, the Order of the Knights of the Temple had conceived a great work which it was incapable of executing. . . . The Templars were Jesuits who failed. (*HM*, 211)

A note on a back page of the fourth blue book of H.D.'s handwritten manuscript reads: "The Templars were Jesuits who failed. E.L."

Candace. . . . lilium candidum. Another "spiritual etymology" occurs as the sound-link ("can-")leads to a sense-link. *Lilium candidum* is the scientific or botanical name for the Madonna or Annunciation lily, with pure white waxy flowers, that appears as a fixed icon in paintings of the Virgin Mary. *Candidum* is Latin for "pure" or "white," from *candere*, to burn, to be white, to shine, which is the linguistic root of "candle" as well.

Ave coeleste Lilium. The translation of this Latin phrase is "Hail, celestial Lily," referring to a mystic vision of Saint Francis in which he saw the Virgin Mary.

holy frenzy had inflamed his followers. The word "inflamed" plays on the associations of "*candidum*" and "candle," drawing together two attributes of Our Lady and referring back to both the "extravagances" at Marienborn and the Moravian candlelight service.

like seeds burst from a weighted seed-pod. The imagery of the seed-pod follows from both Zinzendorf's "Order of the Mustard Seed" and from the term "hidden seed" for the Old Church of Bohemia, whose members continued, even after imperial edicts in 1627 "made every non-Romanist practically an outlaw," to meet in secret groups in Poland, Hungary, Silesia, and particularly in Moravia, where there was more opportunity to meet without incurring the death penalty (*HB*, 17–18).

Tibetan dictionary, even before the Jesuits got there. H.D.'s statement is both anachronistic and untrue; Jesuits were in Tibet in the seventeenth century, the first missionary to Lhasa being the Jesuit John Grueber, who arrived in 1661 (*EB* [1957], 13: 12; Bernstein, *New Yorker*, Dec. 14, 1987, 67). The Moravians did much linguistic work in Tibet, however. In 1866 "A Romanized Phonetic Tibetan and English Dictionary," compiled by the "most distinguished linguist of the Moravian Church," Henry Augustus Jäschke, was published. He also translated multitudinous sermons, tracts, and biblical materials into Tibetan. After leaving Tibet in poor health, he compiled a huge English-Tibetan dictionary, published in 1871 (*HMM*, 360).

Saint John inseparable companion of Our Lady. Saint John, the "beloved disciple," is said to have carried the wine-cup at the Last Supper and to have witnessed the Crucifixion. Jesus, on the cross, asked John to care for his mother Mary. The gospel passage reads:

> Now there stood by the cross of Jesus his mother, and his mother's sister. . . . When Jesus therefore saw his mother, and the disciple standing by, whom he loved, he saith unto his mother, Woman, behold thy son! Then saith he to the disciple, Behold thy mother! And from that hour that disciple took her unto his own home (Jn. 19.25–27, KJV).

they called me Lilie. H.D. had an experience in childhood that she recounts in *The Gift* and told to Freud. The story is that an old man living on Church Street invited her from among her brothers and boy cousins to come into his garden and choose whatever flower she wanted. She chose a lily "so the gardener, or whoever he was, the Young Man . . . cut off a white-lily" and gave it to her (*G*, 101–2). It was "an Easter Lily or Madonna lily," which she then put on her grandfather's new grave in Nisky Hill cemetery. She said to Freud, "I do not know if the white lily was a fantasy, dream or reality," although a day or so after she planted the lily, the season was winter. She is then sent a sleigh by the old man, who has said that if the girl asks for it, he will send it.

> It is a beautiful sleigh with sleigh-bells. The gardener is the coachman. There is a thick fur rug. We drive across the untrodden snow. . . . "When will he come again?" I ask my mother. . . . But no one had sent us a sleigh, my mother told me (*TF*, 121–22).

She thought it was odd that the lily was flowering but there was snow. "It could not be worked out. But it happened. I had the lily, in my hand" (*G*, 102).

Freud said that "the old man was obviously . . . God." H.D.'s wording, "the gardener, or whoever he was," suggests the passage in John 20.15, in which Mary Magdalene, after the crucifixion, goes again to look for the body of Jesus in the sepulcher in the garden. She finds it empty and sees a man who asks her:

> whom seekest thou? She, supposing him to be the gardener, saith unto him, Sir, if thou have borne him hence, tell me where thou hast laid him . . .

He speaks her name, and then she recognizes the risen Christ.

suppression of the Order. The first two pages of H.D.'s notes in ZN are taken from *Crusader Castles* by Robin Fedden. Page two reads: "22 Grand Masters of Temple (before 1312), 5 died in battle, 5 of wounds, + one [?] starved to death in Saracen prison" (Fedden, 1950 ed., 71).

names of those fortresses. In ZN 3 [2] H.D. lists, after the heading *Jerusalem*: "Montgizard / Ibelin / Blanche Garde / Beth Gibelin / Ascalon [p.44] / Darum / Kerak / Montreal / Ile de Graye" (Fedden, 26, 60). It seems she simply relished the romantic evocative sound of these names, although they also establish connections between the Middle East and Europe, and between Judaism, Islam, and Christianity.

true Crusaders or the inheritors of the lost Grail. In H.D.'s mind, the Moravians, descended from the Calixtenes who have the communion cup or chalice as their symbol, are the "true inheritors" of pure and unified Christianity represented by the Holy Grail, the cup used by Christ at the Last Supper. The Grail therefore symbolizes an eternal connection between God and the human world, a connection reaffirmed for H.D. wherever the cuplike shape is found. It also connects the Arthurian cycle of romances to medieval European Christianity through the legend that Joseph of Arimathaea brought the Holy Grail to England. Its miraculous powers could provide food and healing, but it would only be revealed to a pure knight. Its syncretism of Christianity, Celtic myth, and fertility cults makes it a universal symbol of spiritual quest (*USE*, 4965; *Co.Enc.*, 1118).

Castell has the same sound as *Kastell*, the German word meaning small fort or castle, cognate with the English word for castle. The "castle" of the new Crusaders, the Moravians under Zinzendorf, is not a building, however, but a human being. Theodora, in this allegorical construction. Since Theodora is an avatar of Elizabeth, it is re-affirmed that the Moravians also belong to "the Eternal Order."

Chapter XVIII, pp. 79–82

her father . . . exiled Huguenot. John de Watteville was born in Walschleben, Thuringia, but his adoptive father, Frederick de Watteville [von Wattewille], as a youth lived at Basle, Switzerland, where Zinzendorf visited in 1720 (AGS, 24). H.D. appears to be reiterating the sound-link of *Schweiz* (Switzerland) and de Schweinitz mentioned in chapter 2.

revealing bastardy. Historical evidence is lacking to substantiate the claim made by Saint-Germain to Prince Karl of Hesse that he was "the son of Prince Ragozki of Transylvania and his first wife, a Tekely" (*LCSG*, 85, trans. ed.). Conflicting stories exist concerning his parentage and he was often believed to be the bastard son of a king. To this extent the legend touches reality.

Prince Karl. One fact reported in several historical accounts is that Prince Karl of Hesse sheltered Saint-Germain for the last years of the magician's life, out of respect for his skill at alchemy.

Dauphin of France. "Dauphin" is the title given to the eldest son of the reigning king, the French equivalent of the Prince of Wales in England. The line of succession to the French throne is quite tangled. After the French Revolution and the Napoleonic era, there were over forty pretenders by the time the monarchy was restored in

1814. The Louis referred to here is likely to be Louis-Stanislaus-Xavier, grandson of Louis XV, who would become king after Louis XVI if the dauphin died and had no younger brothers. Louis-Stanislaus was not an imbecile but quite clever and came to the throne as Louis XVIII in 1814.

Was this symbolism . . . ?. If Saint-Germain "reads" the story of his birth and upbringing as symbolic rather than literal, then he would be undergoing initiation and would have understood his life story as an allegory of spiritual progress by an adept.

where have the cushions come from?. Both the replenished wine-decanter and new pillows suggest Faustian powers at work, reconstructed not as dark but as light in the reversal of Faust's bargain and in the spirit of Albertus Magnus, the scholastic philosopher to whom were attributed the powers of a "white" magician because he had vast chemical and mechanical knowledge. The scene is a parallel to Saint-Germain's meeting with de Rohan in chapter 9.

the then Dauphin was also a Louis, the oldest son among the seven children of Louis XV and his queen, Maria Leszczynska of Poland. The dauphin married Marie Joseph of Saxony; Louis XVI (b. 1754) was their son.

Saint-Germain, as they called him. One story describing how Saint-Germain got his name says that his two half-brothers, sons of Prince Ragozki by the Princess of Hesse-Rheinfeld, paid homage to the Holy Roman Emperor Charles VI and received the names Saint-Charles and Sainte-Elisabeth, after the Emperor and Empress. As the son of the Prince's first wife, Saint-Germain said to himself, *"Eh bien! je me nommerai Sanctus Germanus, le saint-Frère!"* (Oh, well, I'll call myself Saint-Germain, the saint-brother!) (*LCSG*, 85; tr. editor). This story makes etymological sense but does not comport with H.D.'s construction of him as the "second son" of Louis XV, a relationship which, upon the Dauphin's death, would make him King of France. The linguistic links in Latin and French, as H.D. was aware, parallel those in English: *germanus* means "brother" and *germain* "first cousin."

whose very substance he was. Elizabeth had come in wearing her furs, thus causing Saint-Germain to "live back" into a buried memory of his mother, who had left him when he was seven. He wanted to throw himself into her arms as into the arms of his mother, his "very substance," as he would have done if his mother had ever come back.

this other said, before. Saint-Germain's "living back" in memory continues. "This other" is a servant from his childhood, "not Stephanus," who has just said to the child Louis that his mother has "gone off," that is, she has gone away and left him.

San Souci was the mansion and favorite residence of Frederick the Great (1712–86), who became King of Prussia in 1740. I have been unable to find historical evidence for the meeting of Agnes and Moritz Graf zu Dohna there, although it would not be unlikely. Dohna was a captain in the Prussian army for a time, and his father was commanding general during the Seven Years' War in East Prussia, so inevitably the father would have been close to King Frederick.

a little France, within his empire. Frederick the Great strongly advocated French culture and literature, which were far more advanced than their German equivalents when Frederick was being educated. His friends who joined him in evenings at San Souci were mainly Frenchmen; he was at one time close to Voltaire (*EB* [1957], 9: 716–18). H.D. conflates, accidentally or deliberately, the figures of Frederick the Great, King of Prussia, and his father, Frederick William, whom Zinzendorf visited in October 1736 in order to clear up charges against him. They held a three-day conversation, after which Frederick William wrote that he found Zinzendorf "to be an honest and intelligent man, whose only intentions are to promote true and real religion." H.D. noted: "1736—The King, Frederick William, + Z.—1737 . . . King Fr.W. agrees to ordination of Z. as '"bishop of his Moravian brethren'" (ZN, 12 [9]; AGS, 219–22). Frederick the Great succeeded his father in 1740, but Spangenberg does not record any visits to him by Zinzendorf.

The Order of the Temple. This order of Knights Templar, called in French *Ordre du Temple,* had little connection with the similar military order of the Teutonic Knights of Saint Mary's Hospital at Jerusalem, founded in the Holy Land in 1190–91 as a charitable organization. This order soon became military, enrolling only German noblemen, and returned by 1228 to make its permanent home in Germany, acquiring much land and wealth as a kind of chartered company in the fourteenth century. Its power declined into extinction by the time of the French Revolution (*EB* [1957], 21: 983–84).

heroic Daughters of Saint Genevieve (in French *Les Filles de Ste. Geneviève*) functioned in Paris early in the French Revolution. Known also as the Miramionnes after their founder, Mme. de Miramion, they were a secular order whose activities—running of schools, a dispensary, and a retreat center—continued until the Convention decree of November 6, 1794. The Revolution abolished religious orders but made an exception for nuns who did socially useful work, such as managing hospitals. One order, the Augustines of the Hotel-Dieu, were able to stay in Paris throughout the Revolution (Boussoulade, 71).

the left-hand path is a specific theosophical term. Annie Besant says:

> The Right-hand Path is that which leads to divine manhood, to Adeptship used in the service of the world. The Left-hand Path is that which also leads to Adeptship, but to Adeptship that is used to frustrate the progress of evolution and is turned to selfish individual ends. They are sometimes called the White and Black Paths respectively (145–46).

This dual concept of adeptship helps H.D. to account for her periods of breakdown and put them to use, seeing them not as "dangerous symptoms," as Freud had indicated, but as evolutionary stages in her spiritual progress.

to bring the two together. "The two" are the Left-hand and Right-hand Paths. Saint-Germain wants to bridge the dichotomy between the true mysticism of Zinzendorf and the false magic of Cagliostro, between God and Devil, and between Love and Death.

They were Candace *souls*. Louis, who is now a spiritual Moravian, and Elizabeth are "first fruits," the first converts to this new religion that is the revived "lost" church of Provence, the Church of Love. His understanding of feminine-masculine equality within the godhead is foreshadowed.

There was another of their company. The impersonal construction indicates that Saint-Germain now recognizes Elizabeth as a member of the Eternal Order, those working for "a world unity without war." Her visitation led him to revise his conception of the spiritual path so that it is larger and truer than what de Rohan, erstwhile "father," had laid out for him. The daughter's view surpassing the father's view subtly mirrors the way H.D.'s religious thought both respected and expanded from "Papa" Freud's masculinist assumptions, here mirrored by the wholly male organizations, the Jesuits and the Knights Templar. "Their company" also suggests "companions of the flame" in sec. 13 of *The Walls Do Not Fall*: "We know our Name, / we nameless initiates / born of one mother, / companions of the flame."

Our Lady of the Snow translates *Maria von dem Schnee*, the name of a church in Vienna that appears in *Tribute to the Angels* (sec. 31). Through the power of naming the place, a manifestation of the Virgin Mary appears. The naming of the church of Santa Maria dei Miracoli in Venice—"Saint Mary of the Miracles"—functions similarly. Both are linked to H.D.'s vision of the "Cathedral as Dream" expressed in "H.D. by *Delia Alton*" (204). By similar synecdoches, Venice stands for magic and mysticism, and Vienna for psychoanalysis that heals and clarifies the mind, paving the way for entry into higher states of being.

Chapter XIX, pp. 83–86

"So, you married the nun Charity?". Since Zinzendorf's second wife was Sister Anna Charity Nitschmann, this remark makes clear that Saint-Germain is addressing a third Visitor, in fairy-tale style, after Elizabeth and Henry. It is Count Zinzendorf himself as a Presence. He apparently sits where Henry Dohna had sat at the sick man's bedside. Now that Saint-Germain has recovered and is on the right path, his heightened sensitivity permits him to "see" the great religious leader. The wording here echoes Saint Francis's declaration that he had wed the Lady Poverty.

whose goblet he re-filled when his own was empty. The scene parallels Saint-Germain's earlier interview with de Rohan when the wine supply was magically inexhaustible. The suggestion is that the two goblets are one. The projected presence is really there, as were the dead airmen in H.D.'s séances, and it is not relevant whether he is a projection from the unconscious or not. H.D. could not say where the "writing on the wall" had come from:

> Whether that hand or person is myself, projecting the images as a sign, a warning or a guiding sign-post from my own sub-conscious mind, or whether they are projected from outside—they are at least clear enough. (*TF,* 46)

the King's cousins. Saint-Germain re-tells the "legend" of how he came to France, but it remains one story of many that loosely link the historical figure to French royalty (*LCSG*, 91).

Saint-Étienne appears to name an invented character, someone close to the court at Versailles who originally told the story, parallel to Mme. de Gergy's, which the embassy valet repeated to Stephanus. See notes to chapter 5.

the fatuous Elixir. Saint-Germain's famous "elixir of life," much sought after by French aristocracy, was accompanied by a sensible regimen of light eating and non-drinking, which perhaps accounts for the healings, rejuvenations, and reincarnational powers attributed to him (Lang, 27).

Giovanni. This Italian name, John, makes another name-link in the chain of associations to Saint John, the "beloved disciple," and the Johannites, and in its feminine form Giovanna to Joanna, Monna Vanna, and the Primavera figure of Saint-Germain's fevered dreams in chapter 14.

What was I wearing?. If Saint-Germain knew what he was wearing when he met Casanova, he would have a clue to the date. He would know more about his transformation into "Visitor," or how a higher power had taken on his appearance, and thus understand the seeming "miracle" of his bi-location.

a Shadow of God . . . Who was again a Reflection. The "Shadow of God" is Christian David, who was a "Visitor," or incarnation of the Divine, guiding Zinzendorf's spiritual path when he met the Count in Schweinitz. Elizabeth is also a Shadow of God, a feminine incarnation of the Divine, as was Jesus in Zinzendorf's view of a female Holy Spirit. They join as one "Reflection" of God. Elizabeth appeared to the school-porter as a shadow that fell across the door to Saint Wenceslas's Chapel and extinguished the candles, that is, she can control the elements. The powerful mirror in the film *The Student of Prague* feeds into H.D.'s redemptive revision of the Faust legend. The endlessly flowing wine symbolizes ecstatic elevation in contrast to Mephistopheles' destructive power displayed in Auerbach's cellar when he turned men into swine. H.D., feeling the transformative power of psychoanalysis as if it were magic, said of Freud: "He is Faust, surely" (*TF,* 145).

indicated to Saint John. H.D.'s references to Saint John in this novel suggest that she thought one person alone wrote all the writings with the name St. John on them, but the canonical Gospel, the Epistles, the Book of Revelation, and the Gnostic *Apocryphon* or *Secret Gospel of John* all have different authors. The Gnostic John tells a dualistic creation myth that makes Jahweh a deluded ruler who creates human bodies as "duplicates" of the spiritual bodies of light in which souls should properly reside. This notion seems to fit with the capacity of members of an "eternal elite" to manifest in more than one human body. In the East Indian and theosophical view, an individual may reincarnate in more than one body and in either sex.

suppose . . . be written. The Johannites' view of Scripture expresses H.D.'s spiritual views as well as her allegiance to writing as a prophetic and religious vocation.

sur la berge . . . papillon. "On the bank a rose-tree flowers, with a single blooming rose which an immense butterfly is pillaging" (trans. ed.) The sense of "pillaging" or "plundering" suggests a bee's gathering honey. It is an erotic but elevated image, suggesting both Dante's celestial Rose shown to him by Beatrice, and the woman erotically loved in the allegorical *Roman de la Rose* and in hundreds of other poems. The butterfly is Psyche, the soul after death arisen from the cocoon of the human body, resurrected in a new body. The image is an expansion of the worm, cocoon, and butterfly imagery in *The Walls Do Not Fall*, sections 6, 7, and 39. (I have been unable to find the exact source of the French line; H.D. may have composed it herself.)

twelve children. Zinzendorf and his wife, Erdmuth, had twelve children, but only four lived to adulthood. Saint-Germain had not thought to ask himself if "she," Elizabeth, had children until he began to commune with Zinzendorf's spirit and was drawn into recognizing affinities between them.

She told over their names. "Told" refers to "telling the rosary," a Roman Catholic practice of saying a prayer while holding each bead of the rosary. "She" is Erdmuth, the mother who is mourning her dead children; H.D. identifies with her. The subtext is the poet's mourning for her own child stillborn during World War I as well as for all the dead in World War II.

Christian Frederick . . . Salome. These are the names of Zinzendorf's children who died in infancy or early childhood. H.D. in ZN records each of the deaths by name and date, as given in Spangenberg:

> 24 Nov. 1724—first infant now "departed this life" . . . 1729. Sept. 18, Christian Frederick. [died] Oct. 30. . . . March 19, 1732. John Ernest—[died] May 16, 1732./ 2nd Dec. Theodora Caritas "who went to her eternal home." (11 [7]) . . . Anna Theresa, 5 years old, "the Saviour took to himself" . . . 1736 " decease of his son, Christian Louis" (13, 12 [9]) 1741 "daughter Salome" (14 [10]).

They were all important to me. The pronoun "me" shows that Saint-Germain in his visionary intoxicated state is fully identified with Zinzendorf, "living back" into the Moravian leader's life, or perhaps reincarnating him. The "out-of-time" visionary experience comports with "deathlessness." A subdued suggestion exists here of Lord Dowding's cars for all of his "boys" and mourning those very young R.A.F. airmen who were killed under his command.

that La France rose seems to refer to the French royal lineage imagined as a rose-tree on which the "rose" is Queen Marie Antoinette, but it also accords with Saint-Germain's having been "grafted" onto the royal family. It alludes to the story of his birth as the illegitimate son of Louis XV and therefore heir to the French throne, a topic about which "we must not speak." In this passage there is also a hint of his repudiation of the orgies of Versailles and past love-affairs.

stars around her head. In seeing the Zinzendorfs' twelve children as stars around the head of the Virgin, H.D. is remembering Revelation 12.1: "And there appeared a great wonder in heaven; a woman clothed with the sun, and the moon under her feet, and upon her head a crown of twelve stars." Gustave Doré illustrated this passage in the German Doré Bible published in Stuttgart and other German cities circa 1875, calling it "The Crowned Virgin. A Vision of John." It does not appear, however, in the English Doré Bible of 1866 that made so great an impression on H.D. in childhood (Rose, intro. Doré; *G*, 89, 109, 126, 190; see illustrations). H.D. identified with Saint John the Divine, repeating his words in sec. 3 of *Tribute to the Angels*: "*I John saw; I testify*" (Rev. 22.8, 18) as a verification of her own "gift" of "seeing." The association of Erdmuth to Our Lady and Holy Mother recalls the "mer, mere, mère, mater, Maia, Mary / Star of the Sea, / Mother" passage in sec. 8 of *Tribute to the Angels*. Stars around the Virgin's head in medieval and Renaissance art signify iconographically her aspect as Mary Queen of Heaven, a Marian doctrine taken from the passage in Revelation cited above. This passage also suggests Beatrice in Paradise as Dante saw her: "I lifted up my eyes and saw her where she made for herself a crown, reflecting from her the eternal beams" (*Par.* 31. 70–73).

that it is experienced . . . once in a lifetime. "It" appears to refer to a "visitation," that is, the ability to be in two places at once, as H.D. had believed herself to have been when she met the "Man on the Boat," Pieter Rodeck, on the deck of the *Borodino*. He said later that he was not "consciously" aware of being there but believed she had been. He confirmed her "gift," or spiritual elevation, by telling her that such a supernormal experience was "a unique privilege that is granted to certain people from time to time, but very rarely" (*MR*, ts., 146).

you talked to the chairs. In childhood, Zinzendorf was "as fond of speaking as of hearing of his dear Saviour; and when he was alone, or left to himself, he even spoke of him to the chairs, which in his playfulness he had collected together" (AGS, 5). H.D. recorded in ZN: "wrote notes to Saviour . . . he even spoke of him to the chairs—" (8 [5]).

she told me—another child in Our Lady's rosary. Elizabeth, by speaking to him in his illness as if he were a child, has treated him as one of those she prays for by reciting a "rosary" of names. "Rosary" also means the prayers—traditionally paternosters and Aves—that Roman Catholics recite to ask for the Virgin Mary's blessing on those in need, or for her intercession on behalf of sinners.

your father died. In ZN, H.D. wrote, quoting Spangenberg: "father dies 6 weeks after birth of *Nicholas*—mother re-marries Prussian field-marshal after 4 yrs" (AGS, 2).

accused of gross and scandalous mysticism. The accusation comes from Rimius, who, after citing passages from Zinzendorf's sermons that offended him, says: "I question, whether Examples are to be found of a *Fanaticism* more extravagant, and a *Mysticism* more gross and scandalous" (*CN*, 70). H.D., in her notes to *The Gift*, quotes this phrase and adds that, while she personally found Rimius's words "highly stimulating and exciting," in her childhood there was no hint of this exoticism:

> We were a small community, respected and highly respectable . . . a body of what you might call, musical Quakers or Friends. . . . Our grandmother would be one of the last, I imagine, to have heard even distant, dim hints that there ever was or had been any suggestion of "gross and scandalous . . . Mysticism." (*G*, 259, 268)

so to tempt me. The temptation to Saint-Germain is to save his life by not returning to France to die a painful death, which will be for him an equivalent of Jesus' crucifixion. He could decide not to adhere to his code of honor. The language echoes the earlier scene with de Rohan in which Saint-Germain underwent a similar crisis of moral decision.

sacrifice the Guard for a dream, a legend. He is debating within himself a question that comes from the Presence, Zinzendorf, his alter ego also named Louis: why are you going to sacrifice yourself and the entire Swiss Guard in a hopeless attempt to preserve the monarchy and its medieval ideals when these are now only a dream and a legend?

the lilies can not be—disbanded. The lily is the fleur-de-lys, symbol of French royalty as well as of the purity associated with the Virgin Mary and the Calixtines' communion cup. A double metonymy makes the lily stand for France and for the Queen who stands for France but who is also the "Queen of Heaven." The lily extends the Grail quest theme that H.D. has entwined with Moravian and Zinzendorfian history.

can not dismiss the lilies. In another metonymy, the Swiss Guard are called "lilies" because, although they are not Frenchmen, they are completely loyal to and protectors of the French monarchy. If dismissed, they would of course go home to Switzerland.

play into our hands. The temptation to stay becomes very strong as Saint-Germain realizes that Stephanus, a loyal servant, will go back with him and be killed along with the Guard.

I feel a giant. The wine has gone to Saint-Germain's head so that he feels that he is a giant, enormously powerful. He is in Dionysiac ecstasy.

my trappings. . . . that little rumor has blown over. Saint-Germain is saying that he will don his full-dress knight's regalia—sword, decorations, and plumed helmet—to go to Elizabeth and Henry and make a formal farewell. He will lie to them, saying that the Revolution will not take place. He will act as if the King, at his Palace, Versailles or the Tuileries, has summoned him to return to Paris to engage in the ritual re-dedication of the Swiss Guard on New Year's Eve, the last day of 1788.

Joseph of Arimathaea's ships . . . took the Grail to England. Joseph of Arimathaea buried Jesus after the Crucifixion, according to all four Gospels. A "poetic" invention that now resembles established legend, at least among the British, says that afterwards he sailed to England "and constructed the first Christian Church in the land in Somerset, afterwards Glastonbury" (*EB* [1957], 13: 52). The story that he brought the Grail to England is invented as well, first appearing in Robert de Borron's *Joseph of Arimathaea*, a romance composed late in the twelfth century (*EB* [1957], 10: 604).

to you, Nicholas Louis . . . below the Ems. This list of titles, word for word, is taken from the introduction to Spangenberg. "Chase" is spelled "Chace" in AGS; "Ems" is H.D.'s typographical error for "Ens." Spangenberg's introduction adds: "and at one time Aulic and Justicial Counsellor to the Elector of Saxony" (v).

Also the Dresden Socrates. Spangenberg says that in 1725, while Zinzendorf was still serving as counselor in Dresden, he

> appeared before the public as the "Dresden Socrates," under which title he published a weekly periodical, without its being known, however, at first, that he was the author of it.

In this publication he speaks very freely. . . . Some were enraged at it. . . . The Count's object . . . was (to use his own words) "to bring, like Socrates, his fellow-citizens to reflect upon themselves, and by his example to show them the way to the attainment of real and lasting contentment." (62–63)

H.D.'s notes read: "1725—'Dresden Socrates,' republished later 'German Socrates.' Z. anon.—periodical confiscated, weekly, till 34th Number" (ZN, 11 [7]).

above the Mother. To Rimius and other detractors, one of the most offensive aspects of Zinzendorf's theology was his declared view that the Holy Spirit is female, the "mother of the Church." Rimius scornfully summarizes:

> The Holy Ghost is called by the Herrnhutters, the eternal wife of God, the mother of Christ, the Mother of the Faithful, the Mother of the Church. . . .

They make his [Jesus'] Name of the feminine Gender, calling him their Mother, their Mamma Jesua.

He quotes from Zinzendorf:

> The children of Grace . . . have a careful Mother amongst the holy Trinity, and also a dear Father and faithful Bridegroom of their souls.

It follows that the soul is the Bride of God. Everyone's soul, Rimius continues, is

> of the feminine Sex. There are only animae, no animi, says the Moravian bishop with great Elegance. To think that there are Male-Souls, would be . . . the greatest Folly. . . . All that is of the Male Quality, and was adapted to our Body, is detach'd from it as soon as it is interred. It belongs not to its natural and primitive State. 'Tis an Addition, made to it afterwards. (*CN*, 40–42, 59; Fogleman, 85; cf. *G*, 26, 276)

A principal purpose of H.D.'s writing in this novel, as well as in *The Gift* and *Trilogy*, is to assert women's spiritual power and set it as a force against male power that makes war. That Zinzendorf saw the Holy Spirit as female was the most important aspect of his character for H.D. In *The Gift* she calls him "a dreamer, a reformer, a man-of-the-world, a mystic, a great gentleman and an intimate friend of carpenters, wood-cutters, farmers, itinerant preachers and all women" (*G*, 276). These aspects are reflected in her protrayal of Saint-Germain.

Your poem to that effect—that the Holy Spirit is female—is cited by H.D. in ZN, quoting from Rimius:

> 41. 1896th Hymn to Holy Ghost. (Z.) Gott, du Mutter der Kirchen all, Gott Vaters ewiges Gemahl, which translates "God, thou mother of the whole church, eternal wife of God the Father." (8 [39])

The idea is Gnostic, as Lavington emphasizes (14, 16, 36), and was therefore viewed as heretical, sufficient cause for burning at the stake.

whom they bound, outside here by the Cathedral. Jan Hus was actually burned at the stake in Constance, in Baden, Germany, on the Swiss border, not in Prague.

the rosa mystica, the "mystic rose" unites sexual love, as expressed in the *Roman de la Rose*, with spiritual divine love, as represented by Beatrice/Our Lady and the Rose of Dante's *Paradiso*. The Sifting Time language of the worship of Christ's sidewound presents an extreme of sexual imagery that might only be excused by the felt passion of the devotee. H.D. notes: "44. . . . great Devotion for the *Five red Wounds*" (8 [39]). In ZN she copied in German and English a hymn of Zinzendorf's that illustrates the style:

Hymn 1883 [from the 12th Appendix, later suppressed]
What Pleasure doth a Heart perceive,
that rests in the precious Hole,
lives there, loves & sports, works & praises
the little Lamb. . . .
My heart dwells in Jesus' Side,
I kiss with the greatest Tenderness
the Scars on his Hands & Feet, I kiss
the Spear; how would I, O Soldier,
run over to kiss thee for this
Piercing. (ZN, 10 [41]; *CN*, 45)

    H.D. copied a number of hymns with similar extremely literal and erotic language, but used none of them, not surprisingly. Her own symbolism of the *Rosa mystica* expresses far more delicately and exactly the sense she shared with Zinzendorf, that sexuality is to be sanctified, like every other activity, by being united with love, especially in its religious aspect, with the love of God.
    to her with the Star five-pointed. Saint-Germain will offer the letters to the Virgin Mary, Queen of Heaven, the Blessed Mother, whose crown contains five-pointed stars, each symbolizing the Star that announced Jesus' birth. The wording intimates that she is the Star herself, the light that guided the wise men out of the east. The five points also represent the Five Wounds of Christ, a sign that she and Christ are one in the Holy Spirit. The emphasis on Christ's Wounds found resonance with H.D.'s traumatic childhood experience of seeing her father with a head-wound, dripping blood. She tells the story in *The Gift*, chapter 6, "What It Was" (*G*, 185–206), but in chapter 7 ends the book with transformation. The thundering war guns become the ritual chanting of "wound, wound, wound," re-invoking Zinzendorf's ecstatic celebration of Jesus' crucifixion that brings deliverance from death.
    à bientôt, Nicolas. Saint-Germain uses the name "Nicholas," not their name in common, Louis, as he is separating from the "presence" who is the essential "founder of a new religion" (*TF*, 37, 108) and with whom Elizabeth and Henry Dohna, initials H.D., are identified. Saint-Germain, the courtly lover and chevalier, is also going to sacrifice his life out of devotion to his Lady. Thus H.D. symbolically achieves spiritual union with the Dowding surrogate and lets him go. *À bientôt* does not mean "goodbye," which signifies final parting, but "I'll see you soon." Saint-Germain is, after all, in H.D.'s eyes, deathless. The suggestion is that he and Zinzendorf will meet in the afterlife as redeemed souls to be guided higher by the feminine Holy Spirit, much as the poet Dante is guided by Beatrice, Divine Love, through Purgatory into Paradise. Resurrection and eternal life have the last word, the triumph of love over death as the ultimate truth.

Works Cited and Consulted

Works by H.D.

"Autobiographical Notes." (1949). Typescript hand-annotated by either Susan Pearson or Louis Silverstein. Beinecke Rare Book and Manuscript Library, Yale University.

By Avon River. New York: Macmillan, 1949.

Collected Poems, 1912–1944. Edited by Louis L. Martz. New York: New Directions, 1983.

"Conrad Veidt: The Student of Prague." In *Close Up: 1927–33*, edited by J. Donald, A. Friedberg, and L. Marcus, 120–24. Princeton: Princeton University Press, 1998.

End to Torment: A Memoir of Ezra Pound. Edited by Norman Holmes Pearson and Michael King, with the poems from "Hilda's Book" by Ezra Pound. New York: New Directions, 1979.

The Gift by H.D.: The Complete Text. Edited with an introduction by Jane Augustine. Gainesville: University Press of Florida, 1998.

The Gift. Introduction by Perdita Schaffner. New York: New Directions, 1982. [Abridgement by Griselda Ohanessian not acknowledged on title page except in the British Virago edition.]

"H.D. by *Delia Alton*." [Notes on Recent Writing]. Edited by Adalaide Morris. *Iowa Review* 16, no. 3 (1986).

Helen in Egypt. New York: Grove Press, 1961; New Directions, 1974.

Hermetic Definition. New York: New Directions, 1972.

Majic Ring. Edited with an introduction by Demetres Tryphonopoulos. Gainesville: University Press of Florida, 2009.

Notes on Thought and Vision and The Wise Sappho. Edited with an introduction by Albert Gelpi. San Francisco: City Lights Books, 1982.

"Séance Notes." Typewritten copy 1946 of notes H.D. took by hand Sept.-Dec. 1943. Beinecke Rare Book and Manuscript Library, Yale University.

The Sword Went Out to Sea: Synthesis of a Dream by Delia Alton. Edited by Cynthia Hogue and Julie Vandivere. Gainesville: University Press of Florida, 2007.

Tribute to Freud. Foreword by Norman Holmes Pearson. New York: New Directions, 1984.

Trilogy. Introduction and readers' notes by Aliki Barnstone. New York: New Directions reissue, 1998.

Trilogy. Introduction by Norman Holmes Pearson. New York: New Directions, 1973. [Also included in *CP.*]

White Rose and the Red. Edited with an introduction by Alison Halsall. Gainesville: University Press of Florida, 2009.

"Zinzendorf Notes." (c. 1949) Manuscript at Beinecke Rare Book and Manuscript Library, Yale University. [Page numbers bracketed in text refer to the photocopy page of unnumbered notebook pages.]

Works by Others

A single asterisk indicates books in H.D.'s personal library, now dispersed among libraries at Yale. Double asterisks indicate books in the private Bryher Library in East Hampton, New York, owned by the Schaffner family, H.D.'s grandchildren.

Alighieri, Dante. *Dante's Vita Nuova.* A Translation and essay by Mark Musa. Bloomington and London: Indiana University Press, 1973.

———. *The Divine Comedy I: Hell.* Translation and notes by Dorothy L. Sayers. Middlesex, U.K.: Penguin Books, 1949.

———. *The Divine Comedy.* Translation and notes by John D. Sinclair. New York: Oxford University Press, 1961.

*———. *The New Life.* Translation by D. G. Rossetti. In *The Portable Dante*, edited with an introduction by Paolo Milano. New York: Viking, 1947.

Allen, Walser H. *Who are the Moravians?* Bethlehem, Pa.: Department of Publications, Moravian Church, 1981.

*Ambelain, Robert. *Adam, dieu rouge: L'ésotérisme judeo-chrétien, la gnose et les opites, lucifériens et rose + croix.* Paris: Editions Niclaus, 1941.

*———. *Dans l'ombre des cathédrales: Étude sur l'ésotérisme architectural et decoratif de Nôtre-Dame de Paris dans ses rapports avec le symbolisme hermétique, les doctrines secrètes, l'astrologie, la magie, et l'alchimie.* Paris: Editions Adyar, 1939.

*———. *La Martinisme, histoire et doctrine: La franc-maçonnerie occultiste et mystique (1643–1943).* Paris: Editions Niclaus, 1946.

Augustine, Jane. "Logos and Etymologies in H.D.'s *Trilogy.*" *Ninth Decade* 9 (1985): 38–45.

———. "Modernist Moravianism: H.D.'s Unpublished Novel *The Mystery.*" *Sagetrieb* 9.1 and 2 (1990): 65–78.

———. "*The Mystery* Unveiled: The Significance of H.D.'s 'Moravian' Novel." *The H.D. Newsletter* 4.1 (Spring 1991): 9–17.

———. "Powerful Modernist Re-examined." Review of *Signets: Reading H.D.*, edited by Friedman and DuPlessis, *Penelope's Web* by Susan Stanford Friedman, and *The Pink Guitar* by Rachel Blau DuPlessis. *New Directions for Women*, 21.1 (Jan.-Feb. 1992): 10.

———. "Preliminary Comments on the Meaning of H.D.'s *The Sword Went Out to Sea*." *Sagetrieb* 15.1 and 2 (Spring and Fall 1996): 121–32.

Baker, Gretchen Wolle. Letters to H.D. Beinecke Rare Book and Manuscript Library, Yale University.

Bangert, William, S.J. *A History of the Society of Jesus*. St. Louis: Institute of Jesuit Sources, 1972.

Barthel, Manfred. *The Jesuits: History and Legend of the Society of Jesus*. Translated by Mark Howson. New York: William Morrow, 1984.

*Benet, William Rose. *The Reader's Encyclopedia; An Encyclopedia of World Literature and the Arts*. New York: Crowell, 1948. [H.D.'s copy much used by her; page references in back.]

Benet, William Rose, and Norman Holmes Pearson, eds. "H.D.," *Oxford Anthology of American Literature*, vol. 2: 1288. New York: Oxford University Press, 1938..

*Berry, André, ed. *Florilège des Troubadours*. Paris: Librairie Fermin-Dedot, 1930. [Much read by H.D.]

Besant, Annie. *The Ancient Wisdom: An Outline of Theosophical Teachings*. Madras: Theosophical Publishing House, 1959.

The Bethlehem Diary. Vol. 1: 1742–44. Translated and edited by Kenneth G. Hamilton. Bethlehem: Archives of the Moravian Church, 1971.

Bolitho, William. *Twelve Against the Gods*. New York: Garden City Publishing Co., 1930. [Read by H.D. in 1934.]

Boussoulade, Jean de. *Moniales et hospitaliéres dans la tourmente révolutionnaire: Les communautés religieuses de l'ancien diocèse de Paris de 1789 à 1801*. Paris: Letouzy and Ané, 1962.

Brief Memoir of Count Henry the LV Reuss-Köstritz. London: Moravian Archives, 1846.

Brown, Raymond E. *The Community of the Beloved Disciple*. New York: Paulist Press, 1979.

**Bryher (Winifred Ellerman). *Beowulf: A Novel*. New York: Pantheon, 1956.

**———. *The Days of Mars, A Memoir, 1940–1946*. New York: Harcourt Brace Jovanovich, 1972.

**———. *The Heart to Artemis: A Writer's Memoirs*. New York: Harcourt Brace and World, 1962.

Burian, Jirí. *Katedrala Sv. Vita*. Fotographie Karel a Jana Neubertovi. Prague: Odeon, 1978.

Butler, Eliza M. *The Fortunes of Faust*. Cambridge, U.K.: Cambridge University Press, 1952.

———. Letters to H.D. Beinecke Rare Book and Manuscript Library, Yale University.

———. *The Myth of the Magus*. Cambridge, U.K., and New York: Cambridge University Press: Macmillan, 1952.

Carlyle, Thomas. "The Diamond Necklace." In *Critical and Miscellaneous Essays*, vol. 5: 131–200. London: Chapman and Hall, 1857.

———. *The French Revolution*. New York: Modern Library, 1934.

Cavalcanti, Guido. "Cavalcanti Poems." In *Translations*, edited with an introduction by Ezra Pound, 7–141. New York: New Directions, 1963. [Contains Cavalcanti's Italian.]

Chamier, J. Daniel. *The Dubious Tale of The Diamond Necklace*. London: Edward Arnold, 1939.

Collecott, Diana. "Images at the Crossroads: The H.D. Scrapbook." In *H.D.: Woman and Poet*, 319–67. Orono, Maine: National Poetry Foundation, 1986.

*Collins, Mabel. *Light on the Path and Karma*. 1885. Reprint London: Theosophical Publishing House, 1920.

Columbia Encyclopedia, 5th edition. New York: Columbia University Press, 1975; revised 1993.

The Continuum Encyclopedia of Symbols. Edited by Udo Becker. Translation by Lance W. Garmer. German edition, *Lexikon der Symbole*, 1992. New York: Continuum, 1994.

Cunliffe, J. W., J.F.A. Pyre, and K. Young. *Century Readings for a Course in English Literature*. New York: Century Co., 1913.

**Curtiss, Harriette Augusta, and F. Homer Curtiss, M.D. *The Inner Radiance*. Washington D.C.: Curtiss Philosophic Book Co., 1935.

**———. *The Key to Destiny*. San Francisco: Curtiss Philosophic Book Co., 1923.

**———. *The Key to the Universe*. Washington D.C.: Curtiss Philosophic Book Co., 1938.

**———. *The Message of Aquaria*. Washington D.C.: Curtiss Philosophic Book Co., 1932.

**———. *Realms of the Living Dead*. Washington D.C.: Curtiss Philosophic Book Co., 1929.

**———. *The Voice of Isis*. Washington D.C.: Curtiss Philosophic Book Co., 1931.

Davies, Andrew A. *The Moravian Revival of 1727 and Some of its Consequences*. London: Evangelical Library, 1977.

Delaney, John J. *Dictionary of Saints*. Garden City, N.Y.: Doubleday, 1980.

*Delarue-Mardrus, Lucie. *La Petite Thérèse de Lisieux*. Paris: Fasquelle, circa 1934.

Delorme, Marie-Raymonde. *Le comte de Saint-Germain: Ses témoins et sa légende.* Paris: Grasset, 1973.
Dembo, L. S., ed. Introduction to *H.D.: A Reconsideration.* Special issue, *Contemporary Literature* 10.4 (autumn 1969): 433.
DeShazer, Mary K. "'Write, Write or Die': The Goddess Muse of H.D." In *Inspiring Women: Reimagining the Muse,* 67–110. Elmsford, N.Y.: Pergamon Press, 1986.
DiPrima, Diane. "Notes on H.D." (May 1987). Unpublished typescript.
Dobson, Silvia. "'Shock Knit Within Terror': Living Through World War II." *Iowa Review* 16.3 (fall 1986): 232–45.
———. "Woof and Heave and Surge and Wave and Flow." In *H.D.: Woman and Poet,* 37–48. Orono, Maine: National Poetry Foundation, 1986.
Donoghue, Denis. Review of Janice S. Robinson's biography *H.D.: The Life and Work of an American Poet. New York Times Book Review,* February 14, 1982.
The Doré Bible Illustrations. (241 plates). Edited with an introduction by Millicent Rose. New York: Dover Publications, Inc., 1974.
Duncan, Robert. "H.D.'s Challenge." *Poesis: A Journal of Criticism,* 6.3 and 4: 21–34. [This double issue presents papers delivered March 29–30, 1985 at joint centennial for H.D. and Marianne Moore at Bryn Mawr College, Bryn Mawr, Pa.]
———. "In the Sight of a Lyre, a Little Spear, a Chair." *Poetry* 91 (January 1958): 256–60.
———. "The Truth and Life of Myth in Poetry." In *Parable, Myth and Language,* edited by Tony Stoneburner, 37–44. Cambridge, Mass.: Episcopal Church Society for College Work, 1968.
DuPlessis, Rachel Blau. "Family, Sexes, Psyche: An Essay on H.D. and the Muse of the Woman Writer." *Montemora* 6 (1979): 37–56. Reprinted in *H.D.: Woman and Poet,* 69–90.
———. *H.D.: The Career of That Struggle.* Bloomington: Indiana University Press, 1986.
———. "A Note on the State of H.D.'s *The Gift.*" *Sulfur 9,* 3.3 (fall 1984): 178–81.
———. "Romantic Thralldom in H.D." *Contemporary Literature* 20.2 (1979): 178–203.
———. *Writing Beyond the Ending: Narrative Strategies of Twentieth-Century Women Writers.* Bloomington: Indiana University Press, 1985: 66–83; 116–21.
Edwards, John Hamilton, and William W. Vasse, editors. *Annotated Index to the Cantos of Ezra Pound: Cantos I–LXXXIV.* Berkeley: University of California Press, 1957. Reprint 1971.
Encyclopedia Britannica, 10th edition [1902] and 14th edition [1957; 1971].
Encyclopedia of Occultism. Edited by Lewis Spence. New York: Strathmore Press, 1959.
Encyclopedia of Religion and Ethics. Edited by James Hastings, 1908–24. New York: Scribners, 1924–26.

Eschenburg, J. J. *Manual of Classical Literature*. London: Wiley and Putnam, 1857.
Fedden, Robin, and John Thomson. *Crusader Castles*. London: John Murray, 1957.
Flammarion, Camille. *Lumen*. Paris: E. Flammarion, 1896.
———. *Omega: The Last Days of the World*. New York: Cosmopolitan, 1894.
———. *Uranie*. New York: Cosmopolitan, 1896.
Fogleman, Aaron Spencer. *Jesus is Female: Moravians and Radical Religion in Early America*. Philadelphia: University of Pennsylvania Press, 2007.
Freud, Sigmund. Letters to H.D. (selection). In Appendix to *Tribute to Freud*, 189–94.
*Frey, Andrew. *A True and Authentic Account of Andrew Frey*; containing the Occasion of his coming among the HERRNHUTERS or MORAVIANS, his Observations on *their Conferences, Casting Lots, Marriages, Festivals, Merriments, Celebrations of Birth-Days, Impious Doctrines*, and *Fantastical Practices; Abuse of Charitable Contributions, Linnen Images, Ostentatious Profuseness*, and *Rancour* against any who in the least differ from them; together with the Motive for publishing this Account. London: printed for J. Robinson [et al.], 1754.
Friedman, Susan Stanford. "Mythology, Psychoanalysis and the Occult in the Late Poetry of H.D." Unpublished dissertation. Madison: University of Wisconsin, 1973.
———. *Penelope's Web: Gender, Modernity, H.D.'s Fiction*. Cambridge, U.K., and New York: Cambridge University Press, 1990.
———. *Psyche Reborn: The Emergence of H.D.* Bloomington: Indiana University Press, 1981.
———. "Psyche Reborn: Tradition, Re-vision and the Goddess as Mother-Symbol in H.D.'s Epic Poetry." *Women's Studies* 6.2 (1979): 149–60.
Friedman, Susan Stanford, editor. *Analyzing Freud: the Letters of H.D., Bryher and Their Circle*. New York: New Directions, 2002.
Friedman, Susan Stanford, and Rachel Blau DuPlessis, eds. *Signets: Reading H.D.* Madison: University of Wisconsin Press, 1990.
Fries, Adelaide L. *Customs and Practices of the Moravian Church*. Bethlehem, Pa.: Board of Christian Education and Evangelism, 1962.
*———. *The Road to Salem*. Winston-Salem: University of North Carolina Press, 1944.
Gelpi, Albert. Introduction to H.D.'s *Notes on Thought and Vision and The Wise Sappho*, 7–14. San Francisco: City Lights Books, 1982.
———. "Re-membering the Mother: A Reading of H.D.'s *Trilogy*." *Poesis* 6.3 and 4 (1985): 40–55. Reprinted in *H.D.: Woman and Poet*, 173–90. Orono, Maine: National Poetry Foundation, 1986.
Gervaso, Roberto. *Cagliostro*. London: Gollancz, 1974.
Godwin, Joscelyn. *The Theosophical Enlightenment*. Albany: State University Press of New York, 1994.

Goethe, Johann Wolfgang von. *Dichtung und Wahrheit*. Translated by R. O. Moon under the title *Autobiography*. Washington D.C.: Public Affairs Press, 1949.

———. *Faust: A Tragedy*. A Norton Critical Edition. Edited by C. Hamlin. New York: Norton, 1976.

———. *Faust: Part One*. Bilingual edition with translation and notes by Peter Salm. New York: Bantam, 1985.

———. *Faust: Part Two*. Translation by Philip Wayne. New York: Penguin Books, 1962.

Gollin, Gillian Lindt. *Moravians in Two Worlds: A Study of Changing Communities*. New York: Columbia University Press, 1967.

Guest, Barbara. *Herself Defined: The Poet H.D. and Her World*. New York: Doubleday and Co., 1984.

———. "The Intimacy of Biography." *Poesis* 6.3 and 4 (1985): 74–83.

Hamilton, John Taylor. *The History of the Moravian Church during the Eighteenth and Nineteenth Centuries*. New York: Christian Literature Co., 1895.

Hamilton, J. Taylor, and Kenneth G. Hamilton. *History of the Moravian Church: The Renewed Unitas Fratrum 1722–1957*. Bethlehem, Pa.: Board of Christian Education, 1967.

Hamilton, Kenneth G. *Church Street in Old Bethlehem*. "An historical pamphlet, published in the interest of the bi-centennial celebration of the founding of the Moravian Congregation of Bethlehem, Pennsylvania." Bethlehem, Pa.: Moravian Congregation of Bethlehem, 1942. Reprint 1988.

*Hare, William Loftus. *Mysticism of East and West*. London: Jonathan Cape, 1923.

Hasse, E. R. "Moravians" in Hastings' *Encyclopedia of Religion and Ethics*, vol. 8.

Heckewelder, John Gottlieb Ernestus. *A narrative of the mission of the United Brethren among the Delaware and Monhegan Indians 1740–1808*. Philadelphia: McCarty and Davis, 1820.

Henry, James. *Sketches of Moravian Life and Character*. Philadelphia, Pa.: J. B. Lippincott, 1859.

Hollenberg, Donna Krolik, ed. *Between History and Poetry: The Letters of H.D. and Norman Holmes Pearson*. Iowa City: University of Iowa Press, 1997.

The Holy Bible. King James Version.

Hutton, Joseph Edmund. *History of the Moravian Church*. London: Moravian Publication Office, 1909.

———. *History of the Moravian Missions*. London: Moravian Publication Office, 1923.

Ignatius of Loyola, Saint. *Spiritual Exercises of St. Ignatius*. Translated with commentary by Lewis Delmage, S.J. An American translation from the final version of the Exercises, the Latin Vulgate, into contemporary English. New York: Wagner, 1968.

———. *The Spiritual Exercises of Saint Ignatius*. Introduction by John Morris, S.J. Westminster, Md.: Newman Bookshop, 1943.

———. *The Spiritual Exercises of Saint Ignatius of Loyola*. Translated from the Spanish with commentary by W. H. Longridge. London: Scott, 1922.

Ivory, Michael, ed. *Fodor's Exploring Prague*. New York: Fodor's Travel Publications, 1995.

Lang, Andrew. *Historical Mysteries*. London: Smith, Elder and Co., 1905.

Lange, Victor. Introduction to *Faust* by Johann von Goethe. Translation by Bayard Taylor. New York: Modern Library, 1950.

Langton, Edward. *The History of the Moravian Church*. London: Allen and Unwin, 1956.

*Laveille, Auguste Pierre. *St. Thérèse de l'Enfant Jesu, 1873–97, According to the Official Documents of the Carmel of Lisieux*. London: Burns, Oates and Washbourne Ltd., 1928.

*[Lavington, George, Bishop of Exeter.] *Moravians Compared and Detected by the Author of the Enthusiasm of Methodists and Papists Compared*. London: printed for J. and P. Knapton, 1755.

*Levering, Joseph Mortimer. *A History of Bethlehem, Pennsylvania, 1741–1892*. Bethlehem, Pa.: Times Publishing Co., 1903. [Contains many hand-written notes by H.D.]

**Lévi, Éliphas. *The History of Magic*. London: Rider, 1913.

Mackay, Charles. *Extraordinary Popular Delusions and the Madness of Crowds*. London: Richard Bentley, 1841. Reprint New York: L. C. Page, 1932.

McAlmon, Robert. "Forewarned as Regards H.D.'s Prose." Introduction to *Palimpsest*, 1926. Reprint Carbondale and Edwardsville, Ill.: Southern Illinois University Press, 1968.

Meyer, Dietrich, ed. *Bibliographisches Handbuch zur Zinzendorf-Forschung*. Dusseldorf, 1987.

Meyer, Marvin W., trans. Introduction to *The Secret Teachings of Jesus: Four Gnostic Gospels*. New York: Random House Vintage Books, 1986.

Michalitschke, Anton. *Prag und Umgebung: Praktischer Reiseführer* (in series Griebens-Reiseführer). Berlin: A. Goldschmidt, 1923.

Morris, Adalaide. "Autobiography and Prophecy: H.D.'s *The Gift*." In *H.D.: Woman and Poet*, 227–36. Orono, Maine: National Poetry Foundation, 1986.

———. "A Relay of Power and of Peace: H.D. and the Spirit of the Gift." *Contemporary Literature* 27.4 (winter 1986): 493–524. [Also in *Signets* (1990), 52–82.]

———. Editor's introduction and commentary to *Iowa Review: H.D. Centennial Issue* 16.3 (fall 1986): 1–6; 174–78.

Myers, Elizabeth. *A Century of Moravian Sisters*. New York: Fleming Revell, 1918.

The New Larousse Encyclopedia of Mythology. Translation by Richard Aldington and

Delano Ames of *Larousse Mythologie Générale*. Edited by Felix Guirand. London: Hamlyn, 1959.

*Offices of Worship and Hymns of the Unitas Fratrum or the Moravian Church. Bethlehem, Pa.: Moravian Publication Office, 1891.

O'Callaghan, E. B., ed. *The Documentary History of the State of New York*. Vol. 3: 613–23. Albany: Weed, Parsons and Company, 1850.

O'Haire, Hugh. "H.D. Biography Spurs Interest in Imagist Poet." Review of Guest's biography. *New York Times*, Long Island section, Sunday, September 23, 1984.

Ostriker, Alicia Suskin. *Feminist Revision and the Bible*. Cambridge, Mass., and Oxford, U.K: Blackwell, 1993.

———. "The Poet As Heroine: Learning to Read H.D." In *Writing Like a Woman*, 7–41. Ann Arbor: University of Michigan, 1983.

———. "What do Women (Poets) Want?: Marianne Moore and H.D. as Poetic Ancestresses." *Poesis* 6.3 and 4 (1985): 1–9. Revised version in *Contemporary Literature* 27.4 (winter 1986): 475–92.

Pagels, Elaine. *The Gnostic Gospels*. New York: Random House Vintage Books, 1981.

Pearson, Norman Holmes. Foreword to *Hermetic Definition* by H.D. New York: New Directions, 1972.

———. Foreword to *Tribute to Freud*. New York: New Directions, 1984, v–xiv.

———. Foreword to *Trilogy* by H.D. New York: New Directions, 1973, v–xii.

———. Letters to H.D. Yale Collection of American Literature, Beinecke Rare Book and Manuscript Library, Yale University.

———. "Norman Holmes Pearson on H.D.: An Interview." *Contemporary Literature* 10.4 (autumn 1969): 436–46.

Photiades, Constantin. *Cagliostro: An Authentic Story of a Mysterious Life*. London: W.H.R. Trowbridge, 1932.

The Portable Dante. Edited with an introduction by Paolo Milano. New York: Viking, 1947. [Contains Rossetti's translation of the *Vita Nuova*.]

Pound, Ezra. *The Cantos of Ezra Pound*. New York: New Directions, 1970. [First printing of Cantos I–CXVII in one volume.]

———. *Poems and Translations*. Selected with a chronology and notes by Richard Sieburth. New York: Library of America, 2003.

———. *The Spirit of Romance*. Introduction by Richard Sieburth. New York: New Directions, 2005.

Pound, Ezra, editor and translator. *Translations*. Introduction by Hugh Kenner. New York: New Directions, 1963.

Prague. A Time Out guide. London: Ebury Publishing (div. Random House), 2006.

Praha: A Guidebook. Prague: Sportovnie a turisticke nakladatelstvi, 1958.

Rechcigl, Miroslav, Jr. "Moravian Brethren from the Czechlands: Renewal of Unitas

Fratrum as Moravian Church." Essay online at http://hometown.aol.com/rechcigl/myhomepage/faith.html (2008).

Reichel, William C. *Bethlehem Souvenir: A History of the Rise, Progress and Present Condition of the Bethlehem Female Seminary with a Catalogue of its Pupils 1785–1858.* Philadelphia: J. B. Lippincott, 1858.

———. *Memorials of the Renewed Church* Vol. 1. Philadelphia: J. B. Lippincott, 1870.

Rimius, Henry. *A Candid Narrative of the Rise & Progress of the Herrnhueters, Commonly Call'd Moravians or Unitas Fratrum, With a Short Account of Their Doctrines, Drawn From Their Own Writings, To Which Are Added Observations on Their Politics in General, and Particularly on Their Conduct While in the Country of Budingen in the Circle of the Upper-Rhine in Germany.* London: A. Linde, 1752.

*Rougemont, Denis de. *Love in the Western World.* Translation by Montgomery Belgion. Revised and augmented edition including new postscript. Princeton: Princeton University Press, 1983. [H.D. owned the 1939 French original, *L'Amour et L'Occident*, and the 1940 Belgion translation titled *Passion and Society*.]

Schaffner, Perdita. "Unless a Bomb Falls--." Introduction to H.D.'s *The Gift*, ix–xv. Abridged version. New York: New Directions, 1982.

Scholem, Gershom. *Kabbalah.* New York: New American Library, 1978.

Schweinitz, Edmund de. *The History of the Church Known as the Unitas Fratrum.* Bethlehem, Pa.: Moravian Publication Co., 1885.

Sessler, Jacob John. *Communal Pietism Among Early American Moravians.* New York: Holt, 1933.

"A Short History of Martinism." http://www.orderofthegrail.org/ a_short_history_of_martinism.htm. Unsigned, 1985, p.4; website updated February 2008.

Sigourney, Lydia. "Zinzendorff." In *Poems, Religious and Elegiac*, 325–26. London: R. Tyas, 1841.

Silverstein, Louis. "H.D. Chronology." Part 6 (May 1949–86, Misc. Info. http://www.imagists.org/hd/hdchron6.html. Online courtesy of Monty L. Montee.

Spangenberg, August Gottlieb. *Life of Nicholas Lewis Count Zinzendorf.* Translation and abridgement by Samuel Jackson. Introduction by the Rev. P.[Peter] La Trobe. London: Holdsworth, 1838.

Spiegelberg, Frederic. *Alchemy as a Way of Salvation.* Palo Alto, Calif.: Stanford University and James Ladd Delkin, 1945.

Stoeffler, F. Ernest. *German Pietism during the Eighteenth Century.* Leiden: E. J. Brill, 1973.

Svoboda, Alois. *Prague: A Guidebook.* Prague: Sportoini a Turisticke Nakladatelstvi, 1965; Olympia Press, 1968.

Thurston, H., S.S., and Donald Attwater. *Butler's Lives of the Saints.* Vol. 3: 570–71; 663–64. New York: P. J. Kennedy, 1965.

Toynbee, Paget, ed. and trans. *Dantis Alagherii Epistolae*. Oxford: Oxford University Press, 1920.

The Universal Standard Encyclopedia. An abridgment of The New Funk and Wagnalls Encyclopedia. Edited by Joseph Lappan Morse, editor in chief. New York: Unicorn Publishers, 1955.

Urzidil, Johannes. "De la magie et de la science psychique chez Goethe." Translated by Martin Jones. *Hemispheres: French-American Quarterly of Poetry* 2.5 (spring 1945).

Waite, A. E. *The Holy Kabbalah*. New Hyde Park, N.Y.: University Books, n.d.

Wallace, Paul A. W. *Conrad Weiser: Friend of Colonist and Mohawk*. Philadelphia: University of Pennsylvania, 1945.

Webster's Deluxe Unabridged Dictionary. 2nd Edition. New York: Simon and Schuster, 1979.

Wechsberg, Joseph. *Prague: The Mystical City*. New York: Macmillan, 1971.

Weinlick, John R. *Count Zinzendorf*. Nashville, Tenn.: Abingdon Press, 1956.

White, Eric W., and H.D. *Images of H.D. / From* The Mystery. London: Enitharmon Press, 1976.

Williams, the Reverend Henry. [Moravian clergyman, librarian and hymnologist]. Letters to the editor, fall 1987.

———. "H.D.'s Moravian Heritage." *H.D. Newsletter*, 4.1 (spring 1991): 4–8.

**Wolle, Francis. "A Moravian Heritage." Boulder: Empire Reproduction and Printing Company, 1972.

Zinzendorf, Nicholas Lewis, Count von. *Sixteen Discourses on Jesus Christ our Lord*. Translated from the German. "Being an exposition of the second part of the creed preached in Berlin." London: Bowyer, 1750.

Index

Abbot, 18, 20, 24, 25, 37, 41, 43, 51, 53, 54, 72, 148, 155
Acharat, 39, 42, 82, 152, 155
Acroamatique, 46, 49, 76, 77, 81, 158, 159, 161–63, 203, 204
Adept, 45, 76, 133, 157, 158, 162, 203, 208–10
d'Adhémar, Mme., 152, 153
Advent, 24, 132
Africans, 98
Agnus Dei (Lamb of God), 146, 173, 174, 192, 196. *See also* God; Lamb
Airmen, 186, 211, 213
À la lanterne, 51, 161, 164. *See also* Lanterns
Albertus Magnus, 8, 114, 154, 208
Alchemists 8, 12, 25, 102, 108, 114–15, 133; Street of the Alchemists, 1, 7, 12, 17, 25, 32, 37, 40, 46, 47, 59, 63,102, 120, 122, 124, 133, 144, 171. *See also* Golden Lane
Algonquin, 67, 191
Allen, William, 190
Althotas, 39, 49, 51, 82, 152, 153, 160, 164
Ambassador (from France), 12, 40, 41, 43, 44, 47–49, 52, 53, 155
America, 72, 85
American Indians, 193
American Revolution, 32, 131, 144, 197
Ancienne Chevalerie, 65
Ancien Évêque des Frères, 29
Angels, 186
Anthony's Bread, 27, 135
Antonius, Brother (disguise identity). *See* Saint-Germain, Louis, Count
Aquinas, Saint Thomas (Church Father), 187
Arcana, 8, 9, 28, 29, 72, 76, 116, 197, 202
Ash Wednesday, 186

Assumption, Feast of the, 62, 64, 75, 178
Astrology, 147, 185
Athenians, 67, 190
Au fil de l'epée, 37, 43, 149
Augustine, Saint (Church Father), 187
Augustines of the Hotel-Dieu (religious order), 209
Augustus Caesar, 2, 105
Austria, 45
Aves (prayers), 28, 60, 86, 136, 173, 214

Baden (Germany), 216
Badie, Jean de la, 113
Balsamo, Giuseppe. *See* Cagliostro, Count Alessandro
Bar-sur-Aube, 168
Barry, Mme. du, 168
Bavaria, 157
Bead-belt (fathom of wampum), 30, 139, 142, 171. *See also* Tulpehocken
Beatrice, 62, 63, 69, 73, 178–80, 182–84, 187, 195, 198, 202, 212, 213, 216, 217. *See also* Lady (beloved); Primavera; Watteville, Elizabeth de. *See also* Dante
Bells, 60, 174. *See also* Cups
Berthelsdorf, 9, 33, 115, 117, 119, 140, 146
Bethlehem (Pennsylvania), 9, 29, 32, 34, 58, 59, 61, 67–69, 85, 103, 110, 116, 118, 137, 142, 144–46, 169, 172, 176, 188–90, 192–94, 199
Bhaduri, Arthur, 182
Blessed Sacrament, 134
Blood (of Christ), 192
Blood and Wounds theology, 119, 147, 173, 174. *See also* Sifting Time
Boaz (pillar in Temple), 90, 156

Boeckel, George Frederick, 145
Boehler, Peter, 116, 118, 142
Boehner, John, 190
Bogomili, 204
Bohemia, 5, 9, 33, 34, 37, 101, 106, 110, 115, 181
Bohemia (wine), 39, 40, 152, 154
Bohemian Brethren, 28, 125, 139, 189. *See also* Unitas Fratrum
Boots, 16, 18, 20, 127, 129
Borivoy (duke of Bohemia), 106
Boxes, 21, 26, 29, 60, 73, 143
Brethren of Asia, 55
Bride of God, 216
Bridges, 49, 62, 69, 82, 83, 124, 178, 187
Brotherhood, 49, 51, 59, 184
Bryher (Annie Winifred Ellerman), 134, 137, 138, 141, 146, 182, 184, 188
Buddhism, 158
Buettner, Gottlob, 190, 192
Busenbaum, Herman, 151

Cagliostro, Count Alessandro (assumed identity of Giuseppe Balsamo), 13, 23, 39, 41, 42, 44, 47, 49, 51, 53, 54, 56, 57, 64, 65, 74–76, 79, 80, 82, 84, 89, 121, 123, 124, 131, 151–53, 155, 156, 159–62, 164, 165, 168, 185, 188, 200, 202–4, 210
Calixthenes, 75, 77, 145, 201, 207, 214
Campagnia (Italy), 39, 152
Campion, Edmund, 105
Candace souls, 75, 77, 82, 98, 201, 205, 210
Candelabra, 4, 22, 191
Candid Narrative of the Rise, A. See under Rimius, Henry
Candlemas, 22, 130
Candles, 4, 18, 19, 21–27, 32, 33, 51, 60, 68, 74, 79, 80, 82, 85, 118, 127, 129, 130, 132–35, 164, 173–75, 187, 199, 205, 211
Cantos of Ezra Pound, The, 179, 191
Cap (Moravian), 66, 189
Carnival 64, 186. *See also* Mardi Gras
Casanova (de Seingalt), 64, 75, 83, 185–87, 211
Cassandra, 153
Castell, Countess of (Theodora's mother), 10, 119
Castell, Sophie Theodora von, 6, 7, 9, 10, 33, 34, 59, 60, 72, 73, 78, 80, 84, 93, 112, 119, 138, 172, 189, 207
Castle (Prague), 12, 14, 18, 26, 28, 30, 43, 47, 50, 51, 53, 85, 101, 106, 121, 122. See also Prague Castle

Castle of Ruel, 50, 55, 63, 163, 165, 167, 177
Cathars, 188, 204
Cathedral. *See* Saint Vitus, Cathedral of
Cathedral of Saint Stephen, 177
Catholic Church, 2, 8, 38, 40, 44, 45, 53, 71, 76, 79, 105, 111, 113, 166, 196, 201
Cavalcanti, 62, 63, 76, 178–80, 182–84
Cayugas, 67, 142
Chair (papacy), 37, 149
Chairs, 79, 84, 213
Chandeliers, 9, 85, 117, 185
Charlemagne (Holy Roman Emperor), 22, 130, 150
Charles (jewel), 22, 74, 130
Charles Bridge, 124
Charles VI (Holy Roman Emperor), 208
Charles IX (king of France), 106
Chastel, Jean, 105, 106
Christmas, 22, 24, 71, 118, 198
Christmas Eve, 9, 118, 132, 148, 199
Christ's Passion, 102
Church Fathers, 65, 203
Church of Bohemia, 5, 8, 45, 56, 75, 95, 135, 139, 146, 157, 205. See also *Jednota*; Moravians; Unitas Fratrum
Church of Saint Mark, 186
Château Saint-Germain, 11, 39, 53, 71, 81, 83, 120, 122, 166
Clement, Saint (Church Father), 187
Clement V (pope), 40, 153
Clement XIV (pope), 2, 14, 40, 105, 153, 154
Cloister, 12, 16
Coffee, 4, 5, 56, 58, 109, 168, 172
Comenius, Johann Amos, 32–34, 145, 146, 181
Comes Cabalicus, 63, 184
Commedia, 73, 178, 184, 198
Communion, 134, 146
Confraternity, 12, 121
Conquistadores, 68
Constantine the Great (emperor of Rome), 2, 105, 196
Convent, 68
Corn, 68
Council of Nicaea, 204
Covenant (with God), 68
Crevasse, 63
Cross, 70
Crown: of Beatrice, 213; of the Holy Roman Empire, 22, 130; of stars, 100

Crucifixion, 206, 214, 215, 217
Crusaders, 70, 78, 196, 207; Crusaders' Emblem (*see under* Lamb)
Cups, 173; and bells, 60, 174; for coffee, 4, 56–58, 60, 168; for communion, 75, 145, 201, 207, 214; at the Last Supper, 77, 206; and lilies, 170, 201
Curtain, 1, 6, 7, 26, 41, 44, 59, 60, 113, 135, 176
Cyril, Saint, 70, 77, 110. *See also* Methodius, Saint

D'Albizi, Father Anthony Dionysius Simon, 45, 58, 72, 81, 113, 156, 157
Damnitz, Antoinette Sophie Emilia (painter), 93
Dante, 63, 69, 73, 76, 177–84, 195, 198, 204, 212, 213, 216, 217; *Commedia*, 73, 178, 184, 198; *Paradiso*, 64, 185; *Vita Nuova, La*, 73, 177, 179, 183, 184, 195, 198
Daughters of Saint Genevieve (religious order), 81, 209
David, Christian, 6, 8, 9, 30, 33, 75, 76, 83, 95, 103, 112, 115, 117, 138, 139, 147, 203, 211
Death, 210
Dee, John, 8, 114
De Lafayette, Marquis, 32, 145, 189
De la Tour, Father, 45, 72, 156, 197
Delaware (Indian tribe), 190
"Delia Alton" (H.D.'s psychic pseudonym). *See under* H.D.
Devil, 51, 68, 75, 114, 141, 191, 202, 210
De Watteville, Elizabeth. *See* Watteville, Elizabeth de
Diamond Necklace, affair of, 23, 56, 88, 123, 125, 165, 168
Diderot, Denis, 124, 164
Dionysus, 179
Divine Love, 184, 185, 202, 204, 217
Divine Philosophy, 63
Doctrine, 77, 204, 205
Dohna, Christoph, 4, 31, 108, 143
Dohna, Henry, 41, 43, 114, 122; with Elizabeth de Watteville, 4–7, 28–34, 108, 112–13, 135–48; with Goethe, 8–10, 116, 117; with Saint-Germain, 70–73, 195, 202; with Stephanus, 56–61, 167–69, 172
Dohna, Moritz Graf zu, 4, 31, 81, 109, 208, 209
Dominic, Saint, 126, 204
Dominicans, 45, 72, 81, 86, 157
Doolittle, Charles (H.D.'s father), 185, 201, 217
Doolittle, Helen Wolle (H.D.'s mother), 148

Doolittle, Hilda. *See* H.D.
Door, 12, 16, 17, 19, 47–50, 56, 57, 61, 80, 81, 120, 126–28, 130, 133, 144, 152, 159, 160, 163, 171, 176, 183, 200; to Chapel of Saint Wenceslas, 1, 6, 11, 14, 21, 25, 27, 32, 39, 59, 101, 112, 211
Doré, Gustave, 100
Dowding, Lord, 138, 163, 173, 182–84, 186, 188, 195, 213, 217
Drahomira, 106
Dream, 38, 64, 154, 177, 191, 206, 210, 214
Dresden, 28, 30, 45, 76, 85, 86, 91, 120, 135, 140, 215
"Dresden Socrates, the." *See under* Zinzendorf, Nicholas Louis, Count von
D'Urfé, Marquise, 87

Ecclesiolae in ecclesia. See Little Churches within the Church
Edward III (king of England), 121
Égalité, 53, 55, 56, 124, 165, 167, 170
Egypt, 203
Egyptian Rite (Freemasonry), 124, 131, 151, 152, 155, 187
Ehrenhold, 70, 196
Elixir of Life, 8, 13, 83, 108, 115, 123, 211
Elizabeth I (queen of England), 2, 105, 106, 114, 124
Elizabeth of Bohemia (abbess of Herford), 7, 33, 113
Elizabeth of Bohemia ("Winter Queen"), 7, 33, 112, 113
Élus-Cohen, 158
Embassy, 12, 37, 52, 55, 57, 64, 121, 122, 149
En chevalier, 72
England, 2, 44, 49, 53, 64, 70, 71, 75–77, 85, 104, 105, 109, 124, 143, 144, 185, 196, 207, 215
Epistles, Book of, 212
Épreuve, 64, 184
Eternal Lover, 122, 170, 176, 182
Eternal Order, 207, 210
Eucharist, 134
Euclid, 65, 187
Exercitia, 2, 11, 15, 17, 19, 40, 41, 43, 49, 85, 103, 104, 124, 133, 162

Fates (mythology), 64
Fathom of wampum. *See* Bead-belt; Tulpehocken
Father, 10, 54, 62, 79, 85, 148, 199, 204, 207, 210
Faust (Faustus) 8, 30, 58, 73, 75, 102, 114, 140, 154, 160, 200, 202, 208, 211

Ferdinand II (Holy Roman Emperor), 112
First Fruits, 99, 201, 210
First House, 9, 117
Florence, 62, 180, 182
Flowers, 39, 198, 212
Forest, 44, 49, 79, 156, 162
Foundation, 2, 34, 116, 131, 148
Franc-maçons, 2, 14, 39, 105, 149, 151
France, 2, 37, 40, 71, 80–82, 84, 104, 105, 110, 127, 144, 153, 182, 209, 213, 214
Franciscans, 16, 20, 81, 106, 125, 131, 155, 159, 164
Francis I (Holy Roman Emperor), 123
Francis of Assisi, Saint, 20, 77, 125, 129, 205, 210
Francis Xavier, Saint, 105, 163
Francke, August Hermann, 116
Frater et praeceptor, 38, 150
Fraternité, 124
Fraternity, 38, 41, 49, 151, 170
Frederick V ("Winter King"), 112, 113, 115, 147
Freemasons, 13, 52, 53, 89, 90, 104, 105, 124, 125, 153–56, 158–61, 164–66, 170, 182, 184, 187, 188
French and Indian War, 113
French Revolution, 39, 40, 49, 72, 88, 101, 103, 110, 122, 123, 131, 144, 145, 150–52, 154, 160, 165, 167, 197, 207, 209, 215
Freud, Sigmund, 102, 127, 152, 177, 199, 206, 210, 211
Frey, Andrew (Andreas), 8, 10, 111, 116, 120, 136; *True and Authentic Account*, 111, 116, 120
Friedenshuetten, 68, 79, 85, 188, 193, 194
Friend, 28, 30, 141
Frohlich, Christian, 118

Garrison, Nicholas (captain), 70, 141, 195
George Street, 126
Gergy, Mme. de, 123, 128, 211
Germany, 45, 66, 81
Gersdorf, Henriette Catherine, Countess von, 30, 119, 140
Ghibellines (Italian faction), 62, 63, 179–81
Gift, 67, 124, 132, 148, 162, 164, 170, 171, 175, 180, 182, 191, 206, 213
Gift, The, 108, 109, 111, 113, 116, 124, 130, 136, 138, 139, 143, 146, 148, 170–73, 181, 188–94, 196, 201, 206, 213, 216, 217
Gillray, James (artist), 89
Gladman, Thomas (captain), 116
Gnadenhuetten, 144, 170
Gnosis, 63, 162

Gnosticism, 77, 111, 128, 156, 195, 203–5, 216
God, 51, 62, 68, 75, 83, 99, 129, 191, 210; as Christ, 77, 99, 143, 206; as Jesus, 137, 192, 198, 203, 204; as Lamb of God (Agnus Dei), 146, 173, 174, 192, 196; as Our Lord, 20, 69, 86, 128
Goethe, Wolfgang von, 9, 28–30, 70, 72, 73, 75, 114, 116, 140, 152, 195, 198, 200, 202
Gold (product of alchemy), 108, 114
Golden Fleece, 11
Golden Lane, 102, 108, 126. See also Alchemists, Street of the
Grace, 2, 216
Grand arcanum, 115
Grand Copt, 164
Grand Masters of the Temple, 78, 206
Grape Cluster (inn), 1, 5, 37, 44, 57, 58, 111
Great Spirit, 67, 142, 191. See also *Manito*
Greek Orthodox Church, 38, 70, 76, 110, 147
Gregor, Christian, 9, 118
Gregory, Archbishop, 33, 148
Grey Friars, 16, 125
Grube, Bernhard, 193
Guard, 53, 64
Guelphs (Italian faction), 63, 179–81
Guillotine, 48, 161
Gypsies, 171, 175

H.D. (pen name of Hilda Doolittle), 102–13, 115–22, 124–28, 130–39, 141–50, 152, 154, 156–58, 161–64, 166, 167, 170, 171, 173–202, 204–17; as "Delia Alton," 113, 138, 173, 177, 202; and Bethlehem, 146, 148, 199; and Charles Doolittle (father), 185, 201, 217; and Freud, 102, 127, 152, 163, 177, 199–200, 206, 210; *The Gift* (see *Gift, The*); "H.D. by Delia Alton," 113, 138, 173, 177, 202; *Helen in Egypt*, 67, 159, 179, 184; *HER(mione)*, 198; and Lord Dowding, 138, 163, 173, 182–84, 186, 188, 195, 217; *Majic Ring*, 122, 127, 173, 186, 188; and mother theme, 108, 110, 124, 130, 132, 148, 170–71, 177, 191–92, 196, 204, 206, 214; and Pearson, 102, 103, 113–14, 121, 126, 135, 137, 138, 146; reflected in Elizabeth de Watteville, 110, 135, 137, 144, 170–71, 173, 176, 182, 190, 195, 206, 212, 217; *Tribute to Freud* (see *Tribute to Freud*), *Trilogy*, 186, 198; *The Walls Do Not Fall*, 186, 204, 210–11; "Zinzendorf Notes" (see "Zinzendorf Notes")
"H.D. by Delia Alton," 113, 138, 173, 177, 202

Haidt, John Valentine (painter), 94, 96–99, 201
Hat (worn by cardinals), 37, 149
Hausman, Elias Gottlob (painter), 91
Hausset, Mme. du, 123
Heart, 180, 199, 200, 217
Heart-religion, 98, 112, 157, 174, 188, 197
Heitz, John, 117, 140
Helen in Egypt, 67, 159, 179, 184
Hell, 204
Henry II (king of France), 168
Henry IV (king of France), 105, 106
Henry VIII (king of England), 2, 105
HER(mione), 198
Herrnhaag, 9, 59–61, 70, 73, 79, 108, 109, 111, 116–19, 144, 171, 173, 174, 195, 196
Herrnhut, 7–9, 31, 32, 45, 66–68, 70, 72, 79, 96, 109, 113, 115–19, 135, 138, 139, 143, 145, 147, 157, 170, 172, 195
Heydt, Erich, 122
Hierarchy, 5, 45, 157
High Altar (in the Cathedral), 17, 18, 21
Holy Grail, 78, 85, 135, 196, 201, 207, 214, 215
Holy Roman Empire, 109, 112
Holy See, 2, 51, 105, 182
Holy Spirit, 69, 119, 132, 143, 144, 158, 191, 192, 195, 204, 211, 215–17
Holy Water, 1
Horoscope, 185, 202
Horus (Egyptian god), 203
House of Köstriz, 3, 5, 8, 13, 14, 42–44, 55, 80, 107, 112
Hubertus, Saint, 29, 138
Huguenots, 79, 106
Hummel, Joanna, 190
Hungarian crusader uprising, 181
Hungary, 205
Hus, Jan, 75, 85, 109, 115, 145, 148, 201, 216

Ignatius of Loyola, Saint, 2, 3, 38, 39, 41, 42, 103–5, 107, 154, 163
Illuminism, 149, 158
Indians (Native Americans), 59, 99, 142, 176, 188
In hoc signo vinces. See Lamb
Innocent III (pope), 204
Inquisition, 13, 40, 65, 124, 149, 151, 153–55, 159, 164, 165, 168, 185, 188
Irenaeus, Saint (Church Father), 203
Iroquois (Indian tribe), 67, 142, 190

Islam, 207
Isle of Wounds, 193

Jablonsky, Daniel Ernst, 33, 34, 115, 146, 147
Jachin (pillar in Temple), 90, 156
Jacob (servant), 5, 6, 15, 28, 30, 56, 80, 111, 112, 151, 168
Jacob's ladder, 202
James I (king of England), 112
Jednota, 32–34, 68, 70, 75, 115, 144, 148. *See also* Church of Bohemia; Moravians; Unitas Fratrum
Jesuits. *See* Society of Jesus
Jerusalem, 9, 78, 118, 153, 206, 207, 209
Jewels, 21, 26, 74, 102, 130, 134, 199
Jews, 194, 201, 207
Jochanan (Miriam's fiancé), 203
Johannites, 69, 75, 77, 183, 194, 203–5, 211, 212; Legend of Jesus' birth, 203
John, Saint (author of the gospel), 171
John, Saint (amalgamation of all saints named John), 76, 77, 83, 100, 183, 194, 195, 203, 206, 211, 212
John, Saint (disciple), 171
John, Saint the Forerunner (Saint John the Baptist), 179, 180
John the Divine, Saint, 171, 213
Joseph (Jesus' father), 203
Joseph II (Holy Roman Emperor), 123, 165
Joseph of Arimathea, 85, 195–97, 207, 215
Judas, 82
Jäschke, Henry Augustus, 205

Karl (prince of Hesse), 64, 65, 79, 184, 207
Kelly, Edward, 102, 114
King of Bohemia. *See* Podiebrad, George
Klettenberg, Susannah von, 116, 200
Knights of Asia, 38, 151. *See also* Freemasons
Knights of St. John of Jerusalem, 171
Knights of the East or Sword, 38, 51, 151, 164. *See also* Freemasons
Knights Templar, 65, 70, 76, 77, 121, 146, 150, 151, 155, 156, 164, 171, 185, 187, 192, 194, 196, 202–5, 209, 210

Lace, 6, 7, 60, 112. *See also* Scarf; Veil
Lady (beloved), 183, 198, 217. *See also* Beatrice; Primavera; Watteville, Elizabeth de

Lady Poverty, 210
Lamb, 99, 138, 217; with the banner, 146; passant, 70, 85, 196. *See also under* God
Lamotte, Jeanne de, 56, 84, 85, 123, 125, 167, 168
Lanterns, 22, 49, 64, 75, 163, 185, 186. See also *À la lanterne*
Last Supper, 195, 207
La Trobe (Rev. P[eter]), 120, 136
Lavington, George, 111, 115, 136, 137, 216
Lent, 186
Lentmeritz (Bohemia), 37, 149
Leo III (pope), 130
Leszczynska, Maria, 208
Levering, Joseph Mortimer, 118, 145, 148, 172–74, 176
Liberté, 124
Lié, 45, 72, 197
Life of Nicholas Lewis Count Zinzendorf, 7, 72, 108, 113, 115
Lilies, 77, 84, 170, 201, 206, 214
Lilium candidum, 77, 205
Lindsay House, 71, 85, 196
Lischy, Jacob, 176
Little Churches within the Church (*Ecclesiolae in ecclesia*), 33, 45, 147
Little Strength (ship), 70, 71, 85, 195, 196
Living back, 19, 33, 50, 144, 148, 158, 162, 163, 170, 171, 175, 177, 178, 208, 212
Logos, 202
London, 29, 71, 72, 85, 115, 124, 136, 138, 171, 200
Longfellow, Henry Wadsworth, 189
Lord's Prayer, 17, 20, 126, 134, 200, 214
Lost Tribes, 194
Lots, 31, 59, 120, 143, 172
Louis, Dauphin of France (Louix XVI's father), 80, 208
Louis-Joseph-Xavier-François (dauphin of France under Louis XVI), 37, 149
Louis-Stanislaus-Xavier (dauphin, later Louis XVIII of France), 79, 207, 208
Louis XIV (king of France), 181
Louis XV (king of France), 37, 123, 149, 150, 183, 184, 197, 208, 213
Louis XVI (king of France), 38, 103, 123, 149, 150, 152, 208
Love, 33, 63, 77, 146, 154, 164, 168, 178–80, 182–84, 198–200, 202, 210, 213, 217
Love feasts, 109, 110, 146, 172, 190

Lucia (maid), 64, 185
Ludmilla, Saint, 2, 3, 11, 19, 25, 106
Lutheran Church, 110, 135, 139, 140, 147
Lynx, 179, 191

Mack, John Martin, 9, 118, 139, 190, 195
Majic Ring, 122, 127, 173, 186, 188
Mandetta of Toulouse, 62, 63, 180, 182
Manichaeism, 204
Manito, 67, 68, 191
Mantilla, 64, 186
Mardi Gras, 187. *See also* Carnival
Maria (servant), 5, 31, 56, 111, 168
Maria Theresa (consort of Holy Roman Emperor, archduchess of Austria), 110, 168
Maria von dem Schnee (church), 210
Marie Antoinette (Maria Theresa's daughter, later queen of France), 2, 14, 23, 38, 56, 84, 85, 103, 110, 123–25, 149, 150, 152, 168, 213, 214
Marienborn (Germany), 70, 79, 111, 115–17, 119, 171, 173, 174, 195, 205
Martin, Frederick, 142
Martinist, 158
Mary: as Blessed Virgin, 100, 130, 170, 177, 178, 180, 200, 205, 206, 213, 217; as Miriam of Nazareth, 203; as Our Lady, 18, 22, 24, 51, 52, 68, 77, 80, 82, 84, 86, 130, 132, 135, 164, 191, 205, 206, 216
Mary of Miracles (church). *See* Santa Maria dei Miracoli (Venice)
Master of the Horse in Schweinitz, House of, 1, 5, 6, 8, 30, 75, 76, 83, 95, 103, 203
Media, 38, 150
Medina, 39, 48, 51, 152, 160, 164
Melusine, 64, 84, 186
Memory, 52, 80, 104, 130, 180, 208
Messenger (divine), 64, 186
Methodius, Saint, 70, 77, 106, 110
Miracle, 51, 59, 65, 135, 164, 180, 187, 211
Miriam. *See under* Mary
Mirrors, 82, 83, 141
Missionaries, 28, 65, 187, 188, 194, 201, 205
Mohawk (Indian tribe), 66, 67, 142, 189, 190
Mohican (Indian tribe), 66, 68, 189
Molther, Johanna, 118
Monna Vanna, 62, 63, 69, 178, 179, 211
Montesquieu, 164
Moon, 100, 185

Moravia, 30, 205
Moravians, 68, 91, 97, 109, 111, 113, 115–18, 120, 125, 135, 136, 139, 143–46, 148, 170–75, 181, 187, 188, 190, 192, 193, 196, 197, 200, 205, 207. *See also* Church of Bohemia; *Jednota;* Unitas Fratrum
Morris, William, 182, 183
Morte, 63
Mother, 62, 85, 132, 171, 191, 192, 199, 203, 204, 213, 215, 216; of Saint-Germain, 49, 79–81, 162, 208. *See also* Mary
Mystery, 13, 14, 18, 19, 24, 27, 31, 59–61, 72–74, 76, 85, 128, 132, 138, 144, 155, 176, 202, 203

Naples (Italy), 2, 104
Nazareth (Pennsylvania), 110, 172, 190, 193–95
Nazmer, General von (Zinzendorf's stepfather), 189
New Year, 74, 85
Nieder Leuba, 103
Nitschmann, Anna Caritas (Bishop Nitschmann's daughter) 29, 32, 34, 83, 96, 97, 118, 138, 139, 148, 172, 189, 210
Nitschmann, David (first bishop of renewed Moravian Church; father of Anna), 33, 111, 138, 146–48
Nitschmann, David (called "Father," Bishop David Nitschmann's uncle), 111, 138, 148
Noailles, Cardinal de, 113, 197
Norbert, Saint, 156

Odysseus, 186
Office (of Saint-Germain), 19, 54, 128
Oneida (Indian tribe), 67, 142
Onondaga (Indian tribe), 67, 142
Ordered (as if by divine will), 22, 23, 74, 149
Order of Saint-Jakin, 44, 55, 156, 158, 159, 161, 164, 167
Order of the Garter, 11, 121
Order of the Golden Fleece, 121
Order of the Mustard Seed, 190, 205
Order of the Templars, 40, 153
Order of the Temple, 81, 209
Ordinarius Fratrum, 29, 30. *See also* Zinzendorf, Nicholas Louis, Count von
Origen, Saint (Church Father), 187, 203
Osiris (Egyptian god), 203, 204
Otto, John Matthew, 169

Pahlen, Anna von (Anna Maria von der Pahlen), 148
Palestine, 123
Pamplona (Spain), 2, 105
Pandira, 203
Paraclete, 69, 195
Paradise, 77, 213
Paradiso, 64, 185
Paris (France), 14, 38, 40–43, 47, 48, 52, 53, 57, 62, 65, 72, 75, 81, 85, 88, 106, 113, 119, 123, 124, 144, 148, 151, 154, 161, 162, 164, 166, 169, 178
Patriarchs of Constantinople, 150
Paul III (pope), 2, 38, 105, 150
Payens, Hugh de, 38, 76, 77, 150, 203
Peace, 142, 193, 194
Pearson, Norman Holmes, 102, 103, 113–14, 121, 126, 135, 137, 138, 146
Pedagogy, 11
Pennsylvania, 96
Perruque, 11, 15, 50, 72, 120, 126, 149
Petty Place, 12, 16, 52, 57, 122, 126, 133, 165
Philadelphia (Pennsylvania), 29, 137, 142
Philip (Apostle), 201
Philip the Fair, 40, 153
Philip the Good, 121
Philosoph inconnu, 45, 158
Philosopher's Stone, 8, 102, 114, 133
Piazza San Marco, 64, 75, 186
Pius VI (pope), 105, 150, 154
Pius VII (pope), 154
Plan, 8, 24, 33, 68, 73, 74, 116, 117, 132, 147, 176, 198
Podiebrad, George, 4, 33, 58, 107, 109, 148, 170
Poetry, 73, 85, 181, 197–99, 216, 217
Poland, 63, 145, 147, 181, 189, 205
Pompadour, Mme. de, 123
Poor Brothers. *See* Franciscans
Pound, Ezra, 131, 138, 179, 191, 198; *The Cantos of Ezra Pound*, 179, 191
Praetorian Guard, 2, 40, 105
Prague, 2–5, 8, 23, 30, 41, 44, 51, 61, 79, 101, 102, 105, 108, 110, 113–15, 122, 126, 135, 140, 147, 148, 155, 165, 169, 176, 181, 199, 211, 216
Prague Castle, 102, 132, 135. *See also* Castle (Prague)
Premonstrants, 45, 72, 113, 156, 157, 197
Priam, 153
Primavera, 62, 63, 68, 82, 178–80, 182, 187, 211. *See also* Beatrice; Lady (beloved); Watteville, Elizabeth de

Psyche, 212
Psychoanalysis, 102, 122, 132, 162, 199, 210, 211
Puff adders, 67, 139, 142, 191
Pulaski, Casimir, Count, 189
Puritans, 75, 201
Pyrlaeus, John Christopher, 66, 189–91

Quakers, 192, 214

Ragoczy, Leopold (H.D.'s spelling). *See* Rakoczi, Francis Leopold II
Rakoczi, Francis Leopold I (prince of Transylvania), 181
Rakoczi, Francis Leopold II (prince of Transylvania), 54, 63, 64, 76, 80, 84, 167, 171, 181, 183, 207, 208
Rauch, Christian Henry, 68, 188, 192, 194
Reflection, 74, 80, 83, 211
Reformation, 136
Relique, 26, 106, 133, 134
Reuss, Dorothea von, 5, 110
Reuss, Henry, Count von (Zinzendorf's friend), 9, 10, 72, 93, 119
Reuss, Henry LV, Count von, 4, 5, 107, 109, 110
Reuss, Henry XXVIII (Ignatius), Count von, 4, 109, 198
Reuss, Nicholas von, 72, 112
Revelation, Book of, 147, 175, 212, 213
Revolution, 64, 105, 124, 197
Ribbons, 29, 189
Richard the Lion-Hearted (king of England), 123
Rimius, Henry, 111, 115–17, 136, 137, 143, 147, 173, 197, 214–16; *A Candid Narrative of the Rise*, 111, 115, 147, 216
Rohan, Louis René Édouard, Cardinal de, 2, 13, 14, 23, 88, 123; with Saint-Germain, 37–46, 148–59; with Stephanus, 53–55, 166–67
Romanesque Rotunda, 131
Rosa mystica, 86, 199, 217
Rose, 41, 77, 83, 84, 154, 168, 173, 199, 212, 213, 216
Rosicrucians, 156, 158, 163, 184
Rossetti, Dante Gabriel, 177
Rotari, Pietro Antonio, 87
Rothe, John Andrew, 30, 112, 140, 146
Row (block of cottages), 12, 54, 57, 61, 122, 149, 166
Royal Priests, 38, 151
Rubrica, 63, 69, 184, 195

Rudolf II (Holy Roman Emperor), 108, 115
Rupert (prince, -Frederick V's son), 7, 113
Russia, 30, 142

Sachs, Hanns, 102
Sackcloth, 14, 38
Sacred Heart, 200
Sail, 63, 71, 183
Saint Bartholomew's Day Massacre, 2, 106
Saint Benedict on the Walls, 16, 17, 21, 26, 37, 81, 126, 134
Saint-Étienne, 211
Saint George's Basilica, 106, 126
Saint-Germain, Louis, Count, 87; as Brother Antonius, 1–3, 32, 101, 106, 125; with Cagliostro, 47–50, 159–63; with Cardinal de Rohan, 37–46, 148–59; as Chevalier, 44, 48, 121; encountering the Mystery, 16–26, 126–35; with Henry Dohna, 70–73, 195, 202; meditating, 74–82; origins of the name, 122, 208; with Stephanus, 11–15, 51–53, 120, 122–25, 163, 165, 166; thinking of Dante and Rakoczy, 62–65, 177–84; with Elizabeth de Watteville, 66–69, 188–89; with Zinzendorf, 83–86, 210, 213
Saint John, Gospel of, 159, 212
Saint Ludmilla, Chapel of, 21, 22
Saint-Martin, Louis-Claude de, 158
Saint Mary's Hospital, 209
Saint-Omer, Geoffrey de, 38, 150, 203
Saint Vitus, Cathedral of, 6, 7, 11, 13, 17, 18, 21, 22, 30, 33, 34, 37, 47, 57, 59–61, 65, 74, 81, 101, 102, 106, 108, 120, 124, 126–29, 133, 144, 149, 158, 159, 171, 175–77, 183, 210, 216
Saint Wenceslas, Chapel of, 1, 2, 10, 18, 22–25, 27, 31, 38, 44, 65, 69, 74, 102, 127, 130, 133, 149, 187, 200, 211
Sanctum (of the Freemasons), 39
Sandals (footwear), 16, 20, 26, 127
San Souci, 208, 209
Santa Maria dei Miracoli (Venice), 65, 83, 187, 210
Satan, 111
Saviour, 9, 28, 30, 132, 136, 137, 142, 143, 197, 202, 213
Saxony, 9, 10, 45, 73, 92, 95, 108, 112, 115, 119, 125, 135, 143, 157, 182, 208
Scarf, 1, 6, 7, 33, 60, 80, 82, 183, 186, 191. *See also* Screen; Veil
Schekomeko, 68, 188, 192, 193

Schleswig-Holstein, 184
Schweinitz (disguise identity of Henry Dohna), 1, 5–6, 14, 44, 57–58. *See also* Dohna, Henry
Schweinitz, Hans Christian Alexander von (Elizabeth's late husband), 4, 103, 108, 145
Screen, 69, 183. *See also* Scarf; Veil
Scripture, 212
Sea Congregation, First, 116, 195
Sea Congregation, Second, 195
Séances, 154, 163, 182, 186, 211
Secret Gospel of John, 171, 204, 212
Seidel, Christian, 108
Seiffert, Anton, 190
Seingalt, de. *See* Casanova.
Seneca (Indian tribe), 67, 142
Sensemann, Joachim, 192
Seven, 33, 124, 147, 185, 202; as an age, 3, 49, 79, 80, 106, 208; stars, 60, 175
Seventeen, 33, 124, 147
Seven Years' War, 108, 144, 209
Sèvres, 4, 6, 58, 113, 168
Shadow, 30, 75, 83, 135, 141, 198, 200, 202, 211
Shaw, Joseph, 192
Ships, 85
Sicily, 76
Sifting Time, 111, 115, 116, 119, 120, 125, 137, 171–74, 187, 197, 216. *See also* Blood and Wounds theology
Sigismund (Holy Roman Emperor), 107, 115
Silesia, 205
Simon Magus, 204
Sister Charity, 59, 60. *See also* Nitschmann, Anna Caritas
Sitkovius, Bishop Christian, 147
Six Nations, 30, 59, 61, 67, 139, 142, 170, 171, 176, 191, 194
Sixteen Discourses, 5, 110, 189
Snow, 1, 6, 12, 16, 17, 26, 38, 39, 44, 47, 50, 60, 63, 68, 81, 82, 126, 128, 129, 154, 159, 165, 192–94, 199, 206, 210
Society of Jesus, 3, 45, 68, 103, 104, 107, 116, 131, 134, 149, 151, 154, 158, 185, 193; and the Knights Templar, 38, 76, 150, 155, 164, 205, 210; reinstatement, 39, 52, 125; suppression, 2, 14, 40, 42, 65, 78, 105, 153, 187, 206
Solomon's Temple, 156
Soul, 30, 75

Spain, 2, 104
Spangenberg, August Gottlieb, 8, 29, 72, 103, 107–9, 111, 115, 136, 137, 142, 143, 148, 157, 197, 198, 209, 214, 215; *Life of Nicholas Lewis Count Zinzendorf*, 7, 72, 108, 113, 115
Spartans, 67, 190
Spener, Philipp Jakob, 140, 147
Spiriti, 63, 182
Star, 11, 60, 84, 86, 100, 121, 175, 197, 213, 217; of Bethlehem, 121
Stephanus, 101; with Cardinal de Rohan, 53–55, 166–67; with Saint-Germain, 11–15, 51–53, 120, 122–25, 163, 165, 166; in Tower, 56–61, 167–69, 172
Street of the Alchemists. *See under* Alchemists
Sun, 100, 185
Svatovit (Slavic god), 101
Swiss Guard, 1, 2, 48, 84, 85, 103, 160, 166, 178, 185, 214, 215
Switzerland, 79
Sword, 41, 141, 215
Sword-hilt (imagined by Saint-Germain), 18, 47, 82, 127, 159

Table, 4, 43, 60, 79, 141, 183
Tapestry, 29, 32, 34, 138, 178, 186. *See also* Threads
Tarot, 60, 201, 202
Tavolàto, 63, 182, 183
Temple of Solomon, 90, 151, 153
Theoclet, 76, 77, 203
Theocracy, 5
Thirty Years' Year, 33, 120, 147
Thomas, Saint (island), 138
Threads, 4, 10, 31–34, 62, 64, 84, 138, 178, 186. *See also* Tapestry
Thurnstein, 10, 85, 119. *See also* Zinzendorf, Nicholas Louis, titles of.
Thérèse of Lisieux, Saint, 173
Tower (Prague Castle), 3, 5, 8, 14, 28, 42, 43, 55, 85, 108, 111, 114, 135, 167, 169
Trance, 15, 104, 108, 125, 130, 133, 134, 154, 166, 178
Transylvania, 85
Tribute to Freud, 127, 152, 162, 177, 186, 199, 200, 202, 206, 211, 217
Trilogy, 186, 198
Trinity, 85, 204, 216
True and Authentic Account, 111, 116, 120. *See also* Frey, Andrew

Tulpehocken (Pennsylvania), 139, 142, 170, 171, 176, 189, 190
Tuscany (Italy), 39, 152
Tuscarora (Indian tribe), 67, 142
Twelve, 70, 196; Ascended Masters, 203; children of Zinzendorf, 83, 84, 92, 115, 212, 213; elders, 143; stars, 100

Unitas Fratrum, 8, 32, 58, 59, 61, 68, 96, 103, 109–11, 115, 135, 136, 140, 144–47, 160, 170, 176, 195, 196. *See also* Church of Bohemia; *Jednota*; Moravians
United States of America, 32, 145
Upper Lusatia (Saxony), 103

Veil, 65, 69, 80, 82, 183, 186, 192. See also *Velo* (veil)
Vela. *See* Sail
Velo (veil), 63, 183. *See also* Veil
Venice (Italy), 2, 13, 18, 19, 39, 53, 55, 62, 64, 65, 69, 83, 104, 123, 128, 166, 178, 180, 185, 187, 202, 210
Verona (Italy), 62, 180
Versailles (France), 13, 19, 23, 37, 39, 44, 48–50, 52, 56, 64, 65, 82, 83, 85, 124, 128, 131, 149, 152, 160, 162, 165, 211, 213, 215
Vicit Agnus noster, 70
Viduae et Virgines, 3, 43, 107
Vienna (Austria), 5, 13, 43, 44, 72, 102, 110, 112, 123, 144, 165, 177, 181, 210
Virgil, 204
Visitor, 19, 23, 75, 202; as Elizabeth, 191; as Saint-Germain, 65, 128, 185, 211; as school-porter, 18, 20, 127, 129; as Count Zinzendorf, 76, 210
Vita Nuova, 73, 177, 179, 183, 184, 195, 198
Vitus, Saint, 101, 102
Voltaire (François-Marie Arouet), 124, 164, 209

Wachovia, Vale of, 10, 85, 119
Waldenses, 146, 147
Walls Do Not Fall, The, 186, 204, 210–11
War, 2, 32, 132, 135, 144, 181, 182, 188, 192, 197, 217
Wasamapah, John, 194, 201
Washington, George, 32, 145
Watteville, Elizabeth de (historically Elisabeth), 24, 27, 84, 94, 101, 103, 107, 145; encountering Saint-Germain in cathedral, 6, 7; with Henri Dohna, 4–7, 28–34, 108, 112–13, 135–48; as the Lady, 44, 125, 127, 128; as Lilie, 58–61, 77, 170, 174, 177, 201, 206; as Love, 62, 178, 183, 195; with Saint-Germain, 66–69, 188–89; with Stephanus, 56–61, 167–69, 172; as Theodora von Castell, 33–34, 60, 175. *See also* Beatrice; Lady (beloved); Primavera
Watteville, Frederick Rudolph von, 31, 67, 108, 190
Watteville, Frederick von (Elizabeth's grandfather), 4, 108, 190, 207
Watteville, John de, 81, 94, 101, 108, 118, 143, 145, 189, 207
Watteville, Marie Justine von, 4–6, 60, 107–9, 174
Weiser, Conrad, 142
Wenceslas, Saint, 2, 18, 21, 24, 25, 51, 60, 68, 101, 102, 106, 130, 131, 133, 173
West Indies, 201
White and Black Friars, 16, 126
Whitefield, George, 190
White Mountain, 112, 115, 147
William, Frederick (king of Prussia), 209
Williams, Henry, 143
Wind, 1, 6, 7, 18, 21–23, 25, 26, 32, 33, 46, 59, 63, 81, 126, 141, 143, 144, 158, 171, 183
Wisdom, 191, 204
Wolle, Elizabeth Weiss Seidel (H.D.'s grandmother), 108, 170
Wolle, Francis, 110, 118, 137
Wolle, J. Fred, 190
Wolle, Peter, 181
World-unity without war, 33, 74, 81, 132, 147, 176, 181, 183, 210
World War I, 212
World War II, 124, 138, 144, 173, 181, 182, 212
Wounds, 84, 86, 104, 216, 217
Writing on the wall (H.D. vision), 152, 163, 186, 202

Zander, John William, 176, 190
Zeisberger, David, 188, 190
Zeisberger, Rosina, 190
Zeist (Netherlands), 9, 85, 117, 118, 185
Zinzendorf, Benigna, 4, 9, 28, 29, 58, 59, 61, 68, 84, 94, 101, 108, 118, 137, 142, 145, 148, 170, 176, 188, 189, 192
Zinzendorf, Christian Renatus von, 8, 29, 72, 77, 84, 85, 111, 115, 116, 137, 174, 189, 196, 197
Zinzendorf, Elizabeth von (Elizabeth de Watteville's aunt, Zinzendorf's daughter), 4, 58, 108

Zinzendorf, Erdmuth Dorothea von, 4, 9, 10, 29, 66, 67, 84, 92–94, 107, 109, 119, 138, 212, 213

Zinzendorf, George Louis von, 119

Zinzendorf, Maria Agnes von, 4, 81, 84, 108, 109, 208

Zinzendorf, Nicholas Louis, Count von, 4–6, 8, 10, 28, 31, 34, 45, 55, 68, 74, 81, 91–95, 97, 98, 101, 104, 107, 108, 116, 119, 131, 132, 135–38, 140, 143, 148, 157, 171, 183, 189, 192, 196–98, 202, 203, 209, 210, 212, 214, 216, 217; as Aulic Councillor, 91, 140, 215; as "Dresden Socrates," 85–86, 215; legends of, 4, 28, 58, 75–76, 85, 113; as pilgrim 196; as seen by Saint-Germain, 83–86, 210, 213; and the Sifting Time, 111, 115, 137, 173–74, 216; *Sixteen Discourses*, 5, 110, 189; titles of, 85; as Visitor, 76, 210

"Zinzendorf Notes," 109, 111, 113, 115–18, 138, 142, 147, 150, 156, 194, 196, 201, 206, 212–13, 215–17

Zrinyi, Helen, 181